The Devil in Winter

Lisa Kleypas

W F HOWES LTD

This large print edition published in 2013 by
W F Howes Ltd
Unit 4, Rearsby Business Park, Gaddesby Lane,
Rearsby, Leicester LE7 4YH

1 3 5 7 9 10 8 6 4 2

First published in the United Kingdom in 2010
by Piatkus

ISBN 978 1 47122 230 6

Typeset by Palimpsest Book Production Limited,
Falkirk, Stirlingshire
Printed and bound in Great Britain
by MPG Books Ltd, Bodmin, Cornwall

MIX
Paper from
responsible sources
FSC® C018575
FSC
www.fsc.org

To Christina, Connie, Liz, Mary and Terri,
for friendship that makes my heart sing.

Love always,
L.K.

CHAPTER 1

London, 1843

As Sebastian, Lord St Vincent, stared at the young woman who had just barged her way into his London residence, it occurred to him that he might have tried to abduct the wrong heiress last week at Stony Cross Park.

Although kidnapping had not, until recently, been on Sebastian's long list of villainous acts, he really should have been more clever about it.

In retrospect Lillian Bowman had been a foolish choice, though at the time she had seemed the perfect solution to Sebastian's dilemma. Her family was wealthy, whereas Sebastian was titled and in financial straits. And Lillian herself had promised to be an entertaining bed partner, with her dark-haired beauty and her fiery temperament. He should have chosen far less spirited prey. Lillian Bowman, a lively American heiress, had put up fierce resistance to his plan until she had been rescued by her fiancé, Lord Westcliff.

Miss Evangeline Jenner, the lamblike creature who now stood before him, was as unlike Lillian

Bowman as it was possible to be. Sebastian regarded her with veiled contempt, pondering what he knew of her. Evangeline was the only child of Ivo Jenner, the notorious London gambling club owner, and a mother who had run off with him – only to quickly realize her mistake. Though Evangeline's mother had come from decent lineage, her father was little better than gutter scum. Despite the inglorious pedigree, Evangeline might have made a decent enough match if not for her crippling shyness, which resulted in a torturous stammer.

Sebastian had heard men say grimly that they would wear a hair shirt until their skin was bloody rather than attempt a conversation with her. Naturally Sebastian had done his utmost to avoid her whenever possible. That had not been difficult. The timid Miss Jenner was wont to hide in corners. They had never actually spoken directly – a circumstance that had appeared to suit both of them quite well.

But there was no avoiding her now. For some reason Miss Jenner had seen fit to come uninvited to Sebastian's home at a scandalously late hour. To make the situation even more compromising, she was unaccompanied – and spending more than a half minute alone with Sebastian was sufficient to ruin any girl. He was debauched, amoral, and perversely proud of it. He excelled at his chosen occupation – that of degenerate seducer – and he had set a standard few rakes could aspire to.

Relaxing in his chair, Sebastian watched with deceptive idleness as Evangeline Jenner approached. The library room was dark except for a small fire in the hearth, its flickering light playing gently over the young woman's face. She didn't look to be more than twenty, her complexion fresh, her eyes filled with the kind of innocence that never failed to arouse his disdain. Sebastian had never valued or admired innocence.

Though the gentlemanly thing would have been for him to rise from his chair, there seemed little point in making polite gestures under the circumstances. Instead, he motioned to the other chair beside the hearth with a negligent wave of his hand.

'Have a seat if you like,' he said. 'Though I shouldn't plan to stay long if I were you. I'm easily bored, and your reputation is hardly that of a scintillating conversationalist.'

Evangeline didn't flinch at his rudeness. Sebastian couldn't help but wonder what kind of upbringing had inured her so thoroughly to insult, when any other girl would have flushed or burst into tears. Either she was a pea wit, or she had remarkable nerve.

Removing her cloak, Evangeline draped it over one arm of the velvet-upholstered chair, and sat without grace or artifice. *Wallflower*, Sebastian thought, recalling that she was friends not only with Lillian Bowman, but also with Lillian's younger sister, Daisy, and with Annabelle Hunt.

The group of four young women had sat at the side of numerous balls and soirees all last season, a band of perpetual wallflowers. However, it seemed that their bad luck had changed, for Annabelle had finally managed to catch a husband, and Lillian had just brought Lord Westcliff up to scratch. Sebastian doubted that their good fortune would extend to this bumbling creature.

Though he was tempted to demand her purpose in visiting him, Sebastian feared that might set off a round of prolonged stammering that would torment them both. He waited with forced patience, while Evangeline appeared to consider what she was about to say. As the silence drew out, Sebastian watched her in the gamboling firelight, and realized with some surprise that she was attractive. He had never really looked at her directly, had only received the impression of a frowsy red-haired girl with bad posture. But she was lovely.

As Sebastian stared at her, he became aware of a slight tension building in his muscles, tiny hairs rising on the back of his neck. He remained relaxed in his chair, though the tips of his fingers made slight depressions in the soft-napped velvet uphol-stery. He found it odd that he had never noticed her, when there was a great deal worth noticing. Her hair, the brightest shade of red he had ever seen, seemed to feed on the firelight, glowing with incandescent heat. The slender wings of her brows and the heavy fringe of her lashes were a darker shade of auburn, while her skin was that of a true redhead, fair and a bit freckled on the nose and cheeks. Sebastian was amused by the festive scattering of little gold flecks, sprinkled as if by the whim of a friendly fairy. She had unfashionably full lips that were colored a natural rose, and large, round blue eyes . . . pretty but emotionless eyes, like those of a wax doll.

'I r-received word that my friend Miss Bowman is now Lady Westcliff,' Evangeline remarked in a careful manner. 'She and the earl went on to Gr-Gretna Green after he . . . dispatched you.'

'"Beat me to a pulp" would be a more accurate choice of words,' Sebastian said pleasantly, knowing that she couldn't help but notice the shadowy bruises on his jaw from Westcliff's righteous pummeling. 'He didn't seem to take it well, my borrowing of his betrothed.'

'You k-kidnapped her,' Evangeline countered calmly. '"Borrowing" implies that you intended to give her back.'

Sebastian felt his lips curve with his first real smile in a long time. She wasn't a simpleton, apparently. 'Kidnapped, then, if you're going to be precise. Is that why you've come to visit, Miss Jenner? To deliver a report on the happy couple? I'm weary of the subject. You had better say something interesting soon, or I'm afraid you'll have to leave.'

'You w-wanted Miss Bowman because she is an heiress,' Evangeline said. 'And you need to marry someone with money.'

'True,' Sebastian acknowledged easily. 'My father, the duke, has failed in his one responsibility in life: to keep the family fortune intact so that he can pass it on to me. My responsibility, on the other hand, is to pass my time in profligate idleness and wait for him to die. I've been doing my job splendidly. The duke, however, has not. He's made a botch of managing the family finances, and at present he is unforgivably poor, and even worse, healthy.'

'My father is rich,' Evangeline said without emotion. 'And dying.'

'Congratulations.' Sebastian studied her intently. He did not doubt that Ivo Jenner had a considerable fortune from the gambling club. Jenner's was a place where London gentlemen went for gaming, good food, strong drink, and inexpensive whores. The atmosphere was one of extravagance tinged with a comfortable degree of shabbiness. Nearly twenty years earlier, Jenner's had been a second-rate alternative to the legendary Craven's, the grandest and most successful gaming club that England had ever known.

However, when Craven's had burned to the ground and its owner had declined to rebuild, Jenner's club had inherited a flood of wealthy patrons by default, and it had risen to its own position of prominence. Not that it could ever be compared to Craven's. A club was largely a reflection of its owner's character and style, both of which Jenner was sorely lacking. Derek Craven had been, indisputably, a showman. Ivo Jenner, by contrast, was a ham-fisted brute, an ex-boxer who had never excelled at anything, but by some miraculous whim of fate had become a successful businessman.

And here was Jenner's daughter, his only child. If she was about to make the offer that Sebastian suspected she might, he could not afford to refuse it.

'I don't want your c-congratulations,' Evangeline said in response to his earlier remark.

'What *do* you want, child?' Sebastian asked softly. 'Get to the point, if you please. This is becoming tedious.'

'I want to be with my father for the last few days of his l-life. My mother's family won't allow me to see him. I've tried to run away to his club, but they always catch me, and then I'm punished. I w-will not go back to them this time. They have plans that I intend to avoid – at the cost of my own life, if necessary.'

'And those plans are?' Sebastian prodded idly.

'They are trying to force me to marry one of my cousins. Mr Eustace Stubbins. He cares n-nothing for me, nor I for him . . . but he is a willing pawn in the family's scheme.'

'Which is to gain control of your father's fortune when he dies?'

'Yes. At first I considered the idea, because I thought that Mr Stubbins and I could have our own house . . . and I thought . . . life might be

7

bearable if I could live away from the rest of them. But Mr Stubbins told me that he has no intention of moving anywhere. He wants to stay under the family's roof . . . and I don't think I can survive there much longer.' Faced with his seemingly incurious silence, she added quietly, 'I believe they mean to k-kill me after they've gotten my father's money.'

Sebastian's gaze did not move from her face, though he kept his tone light. 'How inconsiderate of them. Why should I care?'

Evangeline did not rise to his baiting, only gave him a steady stare that was evidence of an innate toughness Sebastian had never encountered in a woman before. 'I'm offering to marry you,' she said. 'I want your protection. My father is too ill and weak to help me, and I will not be a burden to my friends. I believe they would offer to harbor me, but even then I would always have to be on guard, fearing that my relations would manage to steal me away and force me to do their will. An unmarried woman has little recourse, socially or legally. It isn't f-fair . . . but I can't afford to go tilting at windmills. I need a h-husband. You need a rich wife. And we are both equally desperate, which leads me to believe that you will agree to my pr-proposition. If so, then I should like to leave for Gretna Green tonight. Now. I'm certain that my relations are already looking for me.'

The silence was charged and heavy as Sebastian contemplated her with an unfriendly gaze. He didn't trust her. And after the debacle of last week's thwarted abduction, he had no wish to repeat the experience.

Still, she was right about something. Sebastian was indeed desperate. As a multitude of creditors would attest, he was a man who liked to dress well, eat well, live well. The stingy monthly allotment he received from the duke was soon to be cut off, and he hadn't enough funds in his account to last the month. To a man who had no objection to taking the easy way out, this offer was a godsend. If she was truly willing to see it through.

'Not to look a gift horse in the mouth,' Sebastian said casually, 'but how close is your father to dying? Some people linger for years on their deathbeds. Very bad form, I've always thought, to keep people waiting.'

'You won't have to wait for long,' came her brittle reply. 'I've been told he'll die in a fortnight, perhaps.'

'What guarantee do I have that you won't change your mind before we reach Gretna Green? You know what kind of man I am, Miss Jenner. Need I remind you that I tried to abduct and ravish one of your friends last week?'

Evangeline's gaze shot to his. Unlike his own eyes, which were a pale shade of blue, hers were dark sapphire. 'Did you try to rape Lillian?' she asked tautly.

'I threatened to.'

'Would you have carried out your threat?'

'I don't know. I never have before, but as you said, I am desperate. And while we're on the subject . . . are you proposing a marriage of convenience, or are we to sleep together on occasion?'

Evangeline ignored the question, persisting, 'Would you have f-forced yourself on her, or not?'

Sebastian stared at her with patent mockery. 'If I say no, Miss Jenner, how would you know if I were lying or not? No. I would not have raped her. Is that the answer you want? Believe it, then, if it makes you feel safer. Now as for my question . . .'

'I will sl-sleep with you once,' she said, 'to make the marriage legal. Never again after that.'

'Lovely,' he murmured. 'I rarely like to bed a woman more than once. A crashing bore, after the novelty is gone. Besides, I would never be so bourgeois as to lust after my own wife. It implies that one hasn't the means to keep a mistress. Of course, there is the issue of providing me with an heir . . . but as long as you're discreet, I don't expect I'll give a damn whose child it is.'

She didn't even blink. 'I will want a p-portion of the inheritance to be set aside for me in a trust. A generous one. The interest will be mine alone, and I will spend it as I see fit – without answering to you for my actions.'

Sebastian comprehended that she was not dullwitted by any means, though the stammer would cause many to assume otherwise. She was accustomed to being underestimated, ignored, overlooked . . . and he sensed that she would turn it to her advantage whenever possible. That interested him.

'I'd be a fool to trust you,' he said. 'You could back out of our agreement at any moment. And you'd be an even greater one to trust me. Because once we're married, I could play far greater hell with you than your mother's family ever dreamed of doing.'

'I would r-rather have it be from someone *I* chose,' she returned grimly. 'Better you than Eustace.'

Sebastian grinned at that. 'That doesn't say much for Eustace.'

She did not return his smile, only slumped a little in her chair, as if a great tension had left her, and stared at him with dogged resignation. Their gazes held, and Sebastian experienced a strange shock of awareness that went from his head to his toes.

It was nothing new for him to be easily aroused by a woman. He had long ago realized that he was a more physical man than most, and that some women set off sparks in him, ignited his sensuality, to an unusual degree. For some reason this awkward, stammering girl was one of them. He wanted to bed her.

Visions darted from his seething imagination, of her body, the limbs and curves and skin he had not yet seen, the swell of her bottom as he cupped it in his hands. He wanted the scent of her in his nostrils, and on his own skin . . . the drag of her

11

long hair over his throat and chest . . . He wanted to do unspeakable things with her mouth, and with his own.

'It's decided, then,' he murmured. 'I accept your proposition. There's much more to discuss, of course, but we'll have two days until we reach Gretna Green.' He rose from the chair and stretched, his smile lingering as he noticed the way her gaze slid quickly over his body. 'I'll have the carriage readied and have the valet pack my clothes. We'll leave within the hour. Incidentally, if you decide to back out of our agreement at any time during our journey, I will strangle you.'

She shot him a sardonic glance. 'You w-wouldn't be so nervous about that if you hadn't tried this with an unwilling victim l-last week.'

'Touché. Then we may describe you as a willing victim?'

'An *eager* one,' Evangeline said shortly, looking as though she wanted to be off at once.

'My favorite kind,' he remarked, and bowed politely before he strode from the library.

CHAPTER 2

As Lord St Vincent left the room, Evie let out a shaky sigh and closed her eyes. St Vincent needn't worry that she might change her mind. Now that the agreement had been made, she was a hundred times more impatient than he to start on their journey. The knowledge that Uncle Brook and Uncle Peregrine were most likely searching for her this very moment filled her with fear.

When she had escaped the house near the end of summer, she had been caught at the entrance to her father's club. By the time Uncle Peregrine had brought her home, he had knocked her about in the carriage until her lip was split, one eye was blackened, and her back and arms were covered with bruises. Two weeks of being locked in her room had followed, with little more than bread and water being thrust past her door.

No one, not even her friends Annabelle, Lillian, and Daisy, knew the full extent of what she had undergone. Life in the Maybrick household had been a nightmare. The Maybricks, her mother's family, and the Stubbinses – her mother's sister

Florence and her husband, Peregrine – had joined in a collective effort to break Evie's will. They were angered and puzzled as to why it had been so difficult . . . and Evie was no less puzzled than they. She wouldn't have ever thought that she could endure harsh punishment, indifference, and even hatred, without crumbling. Perhaps she had more of her father in her than anyone had guessed. Ivo Jenner had been a bare-knuckle bruiser, and the secret to his success, within the rope ring and outside it, was not talent but tenacity. She had inherited the same stubbornness.

Evie wanted to see her father. She wanted it so badly that the longing was a physical ache. She believed he was the only person in the world who cared for her. His love was negligent, but it was more than she had ever gotten from anyone else. She understood why he had abandoned her to the Maybricks long ago, directly after her mother had died in childbirth. A gaming club was no place to raise an infant. And while the Maybricks were not of the peerage, they were of good blood. Evie could not help but wonder, though . . . if her father had known how she was to be treated, would he have made the same choice? If he'd had any inkling that the family's anger at their youngest daughter's rebellion would become focused on a helpless child . . . but there was no use in wondering now.

Her mother was dead, and her father very nearly so, and there were things that Evie needed to ask him before he passed away. Her best chance of escaping the Maybricks' clutches was the insufferable aristocrat whom she had just agreed to marry.

She was amazed that she had managed to communicate so well with St Vincent, who was more than a little intimidating, with his golden beauty and wintry ice-blue eyes, and a mouth made for kisses and lies. He looked like a fallen angel, replete with all the dangerous male beauty that Lucifer could devise. He was also selfish and unscrupulous, which had been proved by his attempt to kidnap his best friend's fiancée. But it had occurred to Evie that such a man would be a fitting adversary for the Maybricks.

St Vincent would be a terrible husband, of course. But as long as Evie harbored no illusions about him, she would be all right. Since she cared nothing about him, she could easily turn a blind eye to his indiscretions and a deaf ear to his insults.

How different her marriage would be from those of her friends. At the thought of the wallflowers, she felt a sudden urge to cry. There was no possibility that Annabelle, Daisy, or Lillian – particularly Lillian – would remain friends with Evie after she married St Vincent. Blinking back the sting of incipient tears, she swallowed against the sharp pain in her throat. There was no use crying. Although this was hardly a perfect solution to her dilemma, it was the best one she could think of.

Imagining the fury of her aunts and uncles upon learning that she – and her fortune – were forever out of their reach, Evie felt her misery ease a little.

It was worth anything not to have to live under their domination for the rest of her life. Worth anything, too, not to be forced into marriage with poor, cowardly Eustace, who took refuge in eating and drinking to excess, until he was nearly too corpulent to fit through the doorway of his own room. Though he hated his parents almost as much as Evie did, Eustace would never dare to defy them.

It had been Eustace, ironically, who had finally driven Evie to escape this evening. He had come to her earlier in the day with a betrothal ring, a gold band with a jade stone. 'Here,' he had said, a bit sheepishly. 'Mother said I was to give this to you – and you won't be allowed to have any meals unless you wear it to the dining table. The banns will be announced next week, she said.'

It had not been unexpected. After trying for three failed seasons to find an aristocratic husband for Evie, the family had finally come to the conclusion that they would get no advantageous social affiliation through her. And in light of the fact that she would be coming into her fortune soon, they had hatched a plan to keep her inheritance for themselves by marrying her to one of her cousins.

Upon hearing Eustace's words, Evie had felt a surge of astonished fury that brought a violent tide of scarlet to her face. Eustace had actually laughed at the sight, and said, 'Lud, you're a sight when you blush. It makes your hair look positively orange.'

Biting back a caustic reply, Evie had fought to calm herself, and concentrated on the words that swooped and dashed inside her like leaves in a wind squall. She had collected them painstakingly, and managed to ask without stammering, 'Cousin Eustace . . . if I agree to marry you . . . would you ever take my part against your parents? Would you allow me to go see my father, and take care of him?'

The smile had died on Eustace's face, the plump pouches of his cheeks drooping as he stared into her grave blue eyes. His gaze dropped away and he said evasively, 'They wouldn't be so harsh with you, cuz, if you weren't such a stubborn little rodent.'

Losing her patience, Evie had felt the stammer getting the better of her. 'Y-you would take my f-fortune, a-a-and do nothing for me in return—'

'What do you need a fortune for?' he had asked scornfully. 'You're a timid creature who scurries from corner to corner . . . you have no need of fancy clothes or jewels . . . you're no good for conversation, you're too plain to bed, and you have no accomplishments. You should be grateful that I'm willing to marry you, but you're too stupid to realize it!'

'I-I-I—' Frustration had made her impotent. She couldn't summon the words to defend herself, could only struggle and glare and gasp with the effort to speak.

'What a blithering idiot you are,' Eustace said

impatiently. He threw the ring to the floor in a fit of temper, his arm jiggling heavily with the motion. The ring bounced and rolled out of sight beneath the settee. 'There, it's lost now. And it's your fault for vexing me. You'd better find it, or you'll starve. I'll go tell Mother that I've done my part by giving it to you.'

Evie had foregone supper, and instead of searching for the lost ring, she had feverishly packed a small valise. Escaping through the second-floor window and sliding down a rain gutter, Evie had then bolted through the yard. By a stroke of luck an available hackney had stopped for her as soon as she ran out the gate.

That was probably the last she would ever see of Eustace, Evie thought with morose satisfaction. One did not often see him in society. As his girth expanded, he confined himself more and more to Maybrick House. No matter how things turned out, she would never regret having escaped the fate of becoming his wife. It was doubtful that Eustace would ever have tried to bed her . . . he did not seem to possess a sufficient quantity of what was genteelly referred to as 'animal spirits.' His passion was reserved exclusively for food and wine.

Lord St Vincent, on the other hand, had seduced and compromised too many women to count. While many women seemed to find that appealing, Evie was not one of them. However, there would be no doubt in anyone's mind that their marriage had been thoroughly consummated.

Her stomach gave a nervous leap at the thought. In her dreams she had envisioned marrying a kind and sensitive man, who might be just a little boyish. He would never mock her for her stammering. He would be loving and gentle with her.

Sebastian, Lord St Vincent, was the complete opposite of her dream lover. There was nothing kind, sensitive, or remotely boyish about him. He was a predator who undoubtedly liked to toy with his prey before killing it. Staring at the empty chair where he had sat, Evie thought of how St Vincent had looked in the firelight. He was tall and lean, his body a perfect frame for elegantly simple clothes that provided a minimum of distraction from his tawny handsomeness. His hair, the antique gold of a medieval icon, was thick and slightly curly, with streaks of pale amber caught in the rich locks. His pale blue eyes glittered like rare diamonds from the necklace of an ancient empress. Beautiful eyes that showed no emotion when he smiled. The smile itself was enough to steal the breath from one's body . . . the sensuous, cynical mouth, the flash of white teeth . . . Oh, St Vincent was a dazzling man. And well he knew it.

Oddly, however, Evie was not afraid of him. St Vincent was far too clever to rely on physical violence when a few well-chosen words would skewer someone with a minimum of fuss. What Evie feared far more was the simpleminded brutishness of Uncle Peregrine, not to mention the

19

vicious hands of Aunt Florence, who was fond of delivering stinging slaps and nasty pinches.

Never again, Evie vowed, brushing absently at the smudges on her gown where accumulated grime from the drainpipe had left black streaks. She was tempted to change into the clean gown that she had packed in her valise, which she had left in the entrance hall. However, the rigors of traveling would soon make anything she wore so dusty and rumpled that there was hardly any point in changing clothes.

A sound from the doorway caught her attention. She looked up to see a plump housemaid, who asked rather diffidently if she wanted to freshen up in one of the guest rooms. Thinking ruefully that the girl seemed entirely too accustomed to the presence of an unaccompanied woman in the house, Evie allowed the maid to show her to a small upstairs room. The room, like the other parts of the house she had so far seen, was handsomely furnished and well kept. Its walls were covered in a light-colored paper adorned with hand-painted Chinese birds and pagodas. To Evie's pleasure, an adjoining antechamber contained a sink with spigots of running water, the handles cleverly shaped like dolphin fish, and nearby a cabinet that opened into a water closet.

After seeing to her private needs, Evie went to the sink to wash her hands and face, and drank thirstily from a silver cup. She went to the bedroom to search for a comb or brush. Finding none, she smoothed her hands over the pinned-up mass of her hair.

There was no sound, nothing to warn her of anyone's presence, but Evie felt a sudden ripple of awareness. She turned with a start. St Vincent was standing just inside the room, his posture relaxed, his head slightly tilted as he watched her. A peculiar sensation passed through her, a gentle heat like light passing through water, and suddenly she felt weak all over. She was very tired, she realized. And the thought of all that awaited her . . . the journey to Scotland, the hasty wedding, the consummation afterward . . . was exhausting. She squared her shoulders and began to move forward, but as she did so, a rain of blinding sparks fell over her vision, and she paused and swayed heavily.

Shaking her head to clear her eyes, Evie slowly became aware that St Vincent was standing with her, his hands gripping her elbows. She had never been this close to him before . . . her senses were swiftly imprinted with the smell and feel of him . . . the subtle touch of expensive cologne, and clean skin covered with layers of fine linen and wool-blended broadcloth. He radiated health and virility. Sharply unnerved, Evie blinked up into his face, which was much farther above hers than she would have expected. She was surprised by the realization of how large he was – his size wasn't appreciable until one stood very close.

'When was the last time you ate?' he asked.

'Yesterday m-morning . . . I think—'

One of his tawny brows lifted. 'Don't say the family was starving you?' He glanced heavenward as she nodded. 'This becomes more maudlin by the moment. I'll have the cook pack a basket of sandwiches. Take my arm, and I'll help you downstairs.'

'I don't need help, th-thank you—'

'Take my arm,' he repeated in a pleasant voice that was underlaid with iron. 'I won't let you fall and break your neck before we even reach the carriage. Available heiresses are difficult to come by. I'd have a devil of a time replacing you.'

Evie must have been more unsteady than she had thought, for as they walked together to the staircase, she was glad of his support. Sometime during their descent St Vincent slid his arm behind her back and took her free hand, guiding her carefully down the rest of the steps. There were a few light bruises on his knuckles – remnants of the fight with Lord Westcliff. Thinking of how this pampered aristocrat would fare in a physical confrontation with her hulking uncle Peregrine, Evie shivered a little, and wished that they were already at Gretna Green.

Feeling the tremor, St Vincent tightened his arm around her as they reached the last step. 'Are you cold?' he asked, 'or is it nerves?'

'I w-want to be away from London,' she replied, 'before my relations find me.'

'Is there any reason for them to suspect that you've come to me?'

'Oh n-no,' she said. 'No one would ever believe I could be so demented.'

Had she not already been somewhat light-headed, his brilliant grin would have made her so. 'It's a good thing my vanity is so well developed. Otherwise you'd have demolished it by now.'

'I'm certain you already have many women to f-fortify your vanity. You don't need one more.'

'I always need one more, darling. That's my problem.'

He took her back to the library, where she sat before the fire for a few more minutes. Just as she began to doze in the chair, St Vincent returned to take her outside. Groggily she went with him to a gleaming black-lacquered carriage in front of the house, and St Vincent handed her inside the vehicle deftly. The plush cream-colored velvet upholstery inside was supremely impractical but magnificent, glowing in the soft light of a tiny carriage lamp. Evie experienced an unfamiliar sense of well-being as she settled back against a silk-fringed cushion. Her mother's family lived according to a narrow set of rules governing good taste, and they distrusted anything that smacked of excess. For St Vincent, however, she suspected that excess was common-place, especially when it came to matters of bodily comfort.

A basket made of thin woven strips of leather had been set on the floor. Searching it tentatively, Evie found several napkin-wrapped sandwiches made of thick slices of buttermilk bread and filled

23

with thin-sliced meats and cheeses. The scent of the smoked meat aroused a sudden overwhelming hunger, and she ate two of the sandwiches in rapid succession, nearly choking with ravenous eagerness.

Entering the carriage, St Vincent folded his long, lean body into the opposite seat. He smiled slightly at the sight of Evie finishing the last few crumbs of a sandwich. 'Feeling better?'

'Yes, thank you.'

St. Vincent opened the door of a compartment that had been cleverly built into the inner wall of the carriage and extracted a small crystal glass and a bottle of white wine that had been placed there by a servant. He filled the glass and gave it to her. After a cautious sip of the sweet, ice-cold vintage, Evie drank thirstily. Young women were seldom allowed to have full-strength wine . . . it was usually heavily watered. Finishing the glass, she barely had time to wish for another before it was replenished. The carriage started with a gentle lurch, and the edge of Evie's teeth clicked lightly against the rim of the glass as the vehicle jostled along the street. Fearing that she might spill the wine on the cream velvet uphol-stery, she took a deep swallow, and heard St Vincent's quiet laugh.

'Drink slowly, pet. We've a long journey ahead of us.' Relaxing back against the cushions, he looked like an idle pasha in one of the torrid novels that Daisy Bowman adored. 'Tell me, what would

24

you have done had I not agreed to your proposition? Where would you have gone?'

'I suppose I would have gone to st-st-stay with Annabelle and Mr Hunt.' Fleeing to Lillian and Lord Westcliff had not been an option, as they were on their month-long honeymoon. And it would have been futile to approach the Bowmans . . . although Daisy would have argued passionately in her favor, her parents would have wanted nothing to do with the situation.

'Why wasn't that your first choice?'

Evie frowned. 'It would have been difficult, if not impossible, for the Hunts to keep my uncles from taking me back. I am far s-safer as your wife than as someone else's house guest.' The wine made her pleasantly dizzy, and she sank lower in her seat.

Regarding her thoughtfully, St Vincent leaned down to remove her shoes. 'You'll be more comfortable without these,' he said. 'For God's sake, don't shy away. I'm not going to molest you in the carriage.' Untying the laces, he continued in a silken tone, 'And if I were so inclined it's of little consequence, since we're going to be married soon.' He grinned as she jerked her stocking-clad foot away from him, and he reached for the other.

Allowing him to remove her remaining shoe, Evie forced herself to relax, though the brush of his fingers against her ankle sent a strange hot ripple through her.

'You might loosen your corset strings,' he advised. 'It will make your journey more pleasant.'

'I'm not wearing a c-corset,' she said without looking at him.

'You aren't? My God.' His gaze slid over her with expert assessment. 'What a happily proportioned wench you are.'

'I don't like that word.'

'Wench? Forgive me . . . a force of habit. I always treat ladies like wenches, and wenches like ladies.'

'And that approach is successful for you?' Evie asked skeptically.

'Oh yes,' he replied with such cheerful arrogance that she couldn't help smiling.

'You're a dr-dreadful man.'

'True. But it's a fact of life that dreadful people usually end up getting far better than they deserve. Whereas nice ones, such as you . . .' He gestured to Evie and her surroundings, as if her current situation was a perfect case in point.

'Perhaps I'm not as n-n-nice as you might think.'

'One can only hope.' His light, glittering eyes narrowed thoughtfully. Evie noticed that his lashes, indecently long for a man, were several shades darker than his hair. Despite his size and broad-shouldered build, there was a feline quality about him . . . he was like a lazy but potentially deadly tiger. 'What is the nature of your father's illness?' he asked. 'I've heard rumors, but nothing of a certainty.'

'He has consumption,' Evie murmured. 'He was diagnosed with it six months ago – I haven't seen him since. It's the l-longest period I've ever gone without visiting him. The Maybricks used to allow me to go to the club to see him, as they saw no harm in it. But last year Aunt Florence decided that my chances of finding a husband were being harmed by my association with my father, and therefore I should distance myself from him. They want me to pretend he doesn't exist.'

'How surprising,' he murmured sardonically, and crossed his legs. 'Why the sudden passion to hover over his deathbed? Want to ensure your place in his will, do you?'

Ignoring the hint of malice that was embedded in his question, Evie thought over her reply, and spoke coolly. 'When I was a little girl, I was allowed to see him often. We were close. He was – and is – the only man who has ever cared for me. I love him. And I don't want him to die alone. You may m-mock me for it, if it amuses you. I don't care. Your opinion means nothing to me.'

'Easy, pet.' His voice was laced with soft amusement. 'I detect evidence of a temper, which I've no doubt you inherited from the old man. I've seen his eyes flash just that way when his dander is up over some trifle.'

'You know my father?' she asked with surprise.

'Of course. All men of pleasure have been to Jenner's for one kind of stimulation or another. Your father is a decent fellow, for all that he's as

27

stable as a tinderbox. I can't help but ask – how in God's name did a Maybrick marry a cockney?'

'I think that, among other things, my mother must have regarded him as a means of escaping her family.'

'Just as in our situation,' St Vincent commented blandly. 'There's a certain symmetry in that, isn't there?'

'I h-hope the symmetry ends there,' Evie replied. 'Because I was conceived not long after they were married, and then my mother died in childbirth.'

'I won't make you belly-full, if you don't wish it,' he said agreeably. 'It's easy enough to avoid pregnancy . . . sheaths, sponges, douches, not to mention the most clever little silver charms that one can—' He stopped at her expression, and laughed suddenly. 'My God, your eyes are like saucers. Have I alarmed you? Don't tell me that you've never heard of such things from your married friends.'

Evie shook her head slowly. Although Annabelle Hunt was, on occasion, willing to explain some of the mysteries of the marital relationship, she had certainly never mentioned any devices to prevent pregnancy. 'I doubt they've ever heard of them either,' she said, and he laughed again.

'I'll be more than willing to enlighten you when we finally reach Scotland.' His lips curved in the smile that the Bowman sisters had once found so utterly charming . . . but they must have missed

28

the calculating gleam in his eyes. 'My love, have you considered the possibility that you might enjoy our consummation sufficiently to want it more than once?'

How easily endearments seem to trip from his tongue. 'No,' Evie said firmly. 'I won't.'

'Mmm . . .' A sound almost like a cat's purr left his throat. 'I like a challenge.'

'I m-might enjoy going to bed with you,' Evie told him, staring at him steadily, refusing to look away even though the prolonged shared gaze made her flush with discomfort. 'I rather hope I will. But that won't change my decision. Because I know you for what you are – and I know what you're capable of.'

'My dear . . .' he said almost tenderly, 'you haven't begun to learn the worst of me.'

CHAPTER 3

For Evie, who had been uncomfortable during the previous week's twelve-hour drive from Westcliff's Hampshire estate, the forty-eight-hour journey to Scotland was nothing short of torture. Had their pace been more moderate, it would have been much easier. However, at Evie's own insistence they went straight through to Gretna Green, stopping only to change drivers and horse teams at three-hour intervals. Evie feared that if her relations had managed to discover what she was doing, they would be in close pursuit. And considering the outcome of St Vincent's battle with Lord Westcliff, Evie had little hope that he could win in a physical standoff against her uncle Peregrine.

Well-sprung and equipped though the carriage was, traveling at such relentless speed caused the vehicle to jolt and sway until Evie began to feel nauseated. She was exhausted and could find no comfortable position in which to sleep. Her head bumped constantly against the wall. It seemed that whenever she did manage to nod off, only a few minutes passed before she was awakened.

St Vincent was less obviously miserable than Evie, though he too had acquired a rumpled, travel-worn appearance. Any attempts at conversation had long since dwindled, and they rode together in stoic silence. Surprisingly, St Vincent did not utter a word of protest about this grim exercise in endurance. Evie realized that he felt the same urgency that she did to reach Scotland. It was in his best interests, even more than hers, to see that they were legally married as soon as possible.

On and on and on . . . the carriage bounced on rough patches of road, at times nearly pitching Evie from the seat to the floor. The pattern of fitful dozing and forced awakenings continued. Every time the carriage door opened, with St Vincent leaping down to check on a new team, a blast of freezing air came into the vehicle. Cold and aching and stiff, Evie huddled in the corner.

Night was followed by a day of biting temperatures and drizzling rain that soaked through Evie's cloak as St Vincent shepherded her across an inn yard. He took Evie to a private room, where she ate a lukewarm bowl of soup and made use of the chamber pot while he went to oversee yet another change of horses and driver. The sight of the bed nearly made Evie ill with longing. But sleep could come later, after she had gone to Gretna Green and permanently removed herself from her family's reach.

All totaled, the duration of the stay was less than

a half hour. Returning to the carriage, Evie tried to remove her wet shoes without smearing mud onto the velvet upholstery. St Vincent climbed in after her and bent to help. While he untied her shoes and drew them from her cramped feet, Evie wordlessly removed the rain-soaked hat from his head and tossed it to the opposite seat. His hair looked thick and soft, the locks containing every shade between amber and champagne.

Moving to sit beside her, St Vincent contemplated her pinched-looking face and reached out to touch the chilled curve of her cheek. 'I'll say this for you,' he murmured. 'Any other woman would be howling with complaints by now.'

'I c–c–can hardly complain,' Evie said, shivering violently, 'when I'm the one who asked to go straight thr–through to Scotland.'

'We're halfway there. One more night, and a day, and we'll be married by tomorrow evening.' His lips quirked with the wry suggestion of a smile. 'No doubt there's never been a bride more eager for the marital bed.'

Evie's trembling lips curved in an answering smile as she understood his implicit meaning – that she was eager for sleep, not for love play. As she stared into his face, so close to hers, she wondered absently how the signs of weariness on his face and the shadows beneath his eyes could make him look so appealing. Perhaps it was because he seemed human now, rather than like some heartless and beautiful Roman god. Much of his aristocratic hauteur had melted away, no doubt to reappear later when he was fully rested. For now, however, he was relaxed and approachable. It seemed as if some frail bond had been established between them during this hellish journey.

The moment was interrupted by a knock on the carriage door. St Vincent opened it to reveal a bedraggled chambermaid standing in the rain. ''Ere you are, milor',' she said, peering from beneath the hood of her dripping cloak as she handed two objects to him. 'An 'ot pot an' a brick, just as you asked.'

St. Vincent fished a coin from his waistcoat and gave it to her, and she beamed at him before dashing back to the shelter of the inn. Evie blinked in surprise as St Vincent handed her a tin-glazed earthenware cup filled with steaming liquid. 'What is this?'

'Something to warm your insides.' He hefted a brick wrapped in layers of gray flannel. 'And this is for your feet. Lift your legs onto the seat.'

Under any other circumstances Evie might have objected to his casual handling of her legs. However, she made no demur as he arranged her skirts and tucked the hot brick at her feet. 'Ohhhhh . . .' She shuddered with comfort as the delicious heat wafted around her frozen toes. 'Oh . . . n-nothing has ever felt so good . . .'

'Women say that to me all the time,' he said with a smile in his voice. 'Here, lean back against me.'

Evie obeyed, half lying on him with his arms

curved around her. His chest was solid and very hard, but it cushioned the back of her head perfectly. Bringing the earthenware cup to her lips, she took a tentative sip of the hot drink. It was spirits of some kind, mixed with water and flavored with sugar and lemon. As she drank slowly, it filled her body with warmth. A long, contented sigh escaped her. The carriage lurched forward, but St Vincent immediately adjusted his hold, keeping her tucked comfortably against his chest. Evie could scarcely conceive how hell could have turned so abruptly into heaven.

She had never experienced this physical closeness with a man before. It seemed terribly wrong to enjoy it. On the other hand, she would have to be unconscious not to. Nature had squandered an unreasonable quantity of male beauty on this undeserving creature. Better yet, he was incredibly warm. She fought the urge to squirm deeper against him. His clothes were made of exquisite fabrics; a coat of fine wool, a waistcoat of heavy silk, a shirt of butter-soft linen. The hints of starch and expensive cologne mingled with the salty-clean scent of his skin.

Fearing that he might want to set her apart from him after the hot pot was finished, Evie tried to make it last as long as possible. To her regret, she finally drained the last sweet drops at the bottom of the cup. Taking the earthenware vessel from her, St Vincent set it on the floor. Evie was profoundly relieved as she felt him settle back with her in his arms once more. She heard him yawn over her head. 'Go to sleep,' he murmured. 'You have three hours before the next team change.'

Wedging her toes more tightly against the hot brick, Evie half turned and nestled deeper against him, and let herself drift into the inviting depths of slumber.

The rest of the journey became a great blur of movement and weariness and rude awakenings. As Evie's exhaustion deepened, she became increasingly dependent on St Vincent. With each new relay, he managed to bring her a mug of tea or broth, and he reheated the brick in every available hearth. He even found a quilted blanket from somewhere, dryly advising Evie not to question how he had acquired it. Convinced that she would have been frozen solid by now without him, Evie quickly lost all reservations about attaching herself to him whenever he was in the carriage. 'I-I'm not making advances,' she told him as she flattened herself against his chest. 'You're just an available s-source of heat.'

'So you say,' St Vincent replied lazily, tucking the quilt more tightly around them both. 'However, during the past quarter hour you've been fondling parts of my anatomy that no one's ever dared to touch before.'

'I v-very much doubt that.' She burrowed even further into the depths of his coat, and added in a muffled voice, 'You've probably been h-handled more than a hamper at Fortnum and Mason.'

'And I can be had at a far more reasonable price.' He winced suddenly, and moved to arrange her on his lap. 'Don't put your knee there, darling, or your plans of consummating the marriage may be thrown very much into doubt.'

She dozed until their next stop, and just as she found herself relaxing into a deep sleep, St Vincent gently shook her awake. 'Evangeline,' he murmured, smoothing back her straggling hair. 'Open your eyes. We're at the next coaching stop. Time to go inside for a few minutes.'

'Don't want to,' she mumbled, pushing at him irritably.

'You must,' he insisted gently. 'We're coming to a long stretch after this. You'll have to use the convenience now, as it will be your last opportunity for a while.'

Evie was about to protest that she had no need of a convenience, when suddenly she realized that she did. The thought of getting up and walking out into the freezing gray rain again nearly brought tears to her eyes. Bending over, she tugged on her clammy, filthy shoes and fumbled miserably with the laces. St Vincent brushed her hands away and tied them himself. He helped her from the carriage, and Evie gritted her teeth as a bitter gust of wind struck her. It was perishing cold outside. After tugging the hood of her cloak farther over her face, St Vincent clamped a supportive arm around her shoulders and helped her across the inn yard. 'Believe me,' he said, 'you'd rather spend a few minutes here than have to stop by the side of the road later. Knowing what I do about women and their plumbing—'

'I know about my own plumbing,' Evie said testily. 'There's no need to explain it to me.'

'Of course. Forgive me if I'm talking excessively – I'm trying to keep myself awake. And you too, for that matter.'

Holding on to his lean waist, Evie trudged through the icy mud and distracted herself by thinking about cousin Eustace, and how glad she was not to have to marry him. She would never again have to live under the Maybricks' roof. The thought gave her strength. Once she married, they would have no more power over her. Good Lord, it could not happen soon enough.

After arranging for the temporary use of a room, St Vincent took Evie by the shoulders and evaluated her with a thorough glance. 'You look ready to faint,' he said frankly. 'Sweet, there's time enough for you to rest here an hour or two. Why don't you—'

'No,' she interrupted stonily. 'I want to keep going.'

St Vincent regarded her with obvious annoyance, but asked without rancor, 'Are you always so stubborn?' Taking her up to the room, he reminded her to lock the door when he left. 'Try not to fall asleep on the chamber pot,' he advised helpfully.

When they returned to the carriage, Evie followed their by-now familiar pattern, removing her shoes and allowing St Vincent to tuck the hot brick at her feet. He settled her between his spread legs, resting one of his own stockinged feet near the brick, while his other foot remained on the floor to secure their balance. Evie's heartbeat quickened, her veins dilated with a rush of tingling blood as St Vincent took one of her hands in his and began to toy with her cold fingers. His hand was so warm, his fingertips velvety, the nails short and smoothly filed. A strong hand, but one that unquestionably belonged to a man of leisure.

St Vincent laced their fingers together lightly, drew a small circle in her palm with his thumb, then slid his fingers up to match them against hers. Although his complexion was fair, his skin was warm-toned, the kind that absorbed the sun easily. Eventually St Vincent ceased his playing and kept her fingers folded in his.

Surely this couldn't be she . . . the wallflower Evangeline Jenner . . . alone in a carriage with a dangerous rake, racing madly to Gretna Green. *Look what I've started,* she thought dizzily. Turning her head on his chest, she rested her cheek against the fine linen of his shirt and asked drowsily, 'What is your family like? Do you have brothers and sisters?'

His lips played among her curls for a moment, and then he lifted his mouth to reply. 'There's no one left, save for my father and myself. I have no memories of my mother – she died of cholera when I was still an infant. I had four older sisters.

Being the youngest, and the only boy, I was spoiled beyond reason. But when I was a child, I lost three of my sisters to scarlet fever . . . I remember being sent to our country estate when they fell ill, and when I was brought back, they were gone. The one that was left – my eldest sister – married, but like your mother, she died in labor. The babe didn't survive.'

Evie was very still during the matter-of-fact recitation, forcing herself to remain relaxed against him. But inside she felt a stirring of pity for the little boy he had been. A mother and four doting sisters, all vanishing from his life. It would have been difficult for any adult to comprehend such loss, much less a child. 'Do you ever wonder what your life might have been like,' she found herself asking, 'if you'd had a mother?'

'No.'

'I do. I often wonder what advice she'd have given me.'

'Since your mother ended up married to a ruffian like Ivo Jenner,' St Vincent replied sardonically, 'I wouldn't have put too much stock in her advice.' A quizzical pause. 'However did they meet? It isn't often that a gently bred girl encounters Jenner's sort.'

'That's true. My mother was riding in a carriage with my aunt – it was one of those winter days when the London fog is so thick at noon that one can scarcely see a few yards ahead. The carriage swerved to avoid a street vendor's cart, and threw down my father, who happened to be standing on the nearby pavement. At my mother's insistence, the carriage driver stopped to ask after his condition. He was just a bit bruised, nothing more. And I suppose . . . I suppose my father must have interested her, because she sent a letter to him the following day, inquiring once more after his health. They began a correspondence – my father had someone else write his letters for him, as he wasn't literate. I know of no other details, save that they eventually eloped.' A smile of satisfaction curved her lips as she imagined the fury of the Maybricks upon discovering that her mother had run away with Ivo Jenner. 'She was nineteen when she died,' she said reflectively. 'And I'm twenty-three. It seems odd to have lived longer than she did.' Twisting in Sebastian's arms, she glanced up at his face. 'How old are you, my lord? Thirty-four? Thirty-five?'

'Thirty-two. Although at the moment I feel no less than a hundred and two.' He was staring at her curiously. 'What happened to your stammer, child? It disappeared somewhere between here and Teesdale.'

'Did it?' Evie asked with mild surprise. 'I suppose . . . I must feel comfortable with you. I tend to stammer less with certain people.' How odd – her stammer never completely vanished like this unless she was talking to children.

His chest moved beneath her ear in a huff of amusement. 'No one's ever told me that I'm a comfortable sort. I'm sure I don't like it. I'll have to do something diabolical soon to correct your impression.'

'No doubt you will.' She closed her eyes and slumped more heavily against him. 'I think I'm too tired to stammer.'

His hand came up to her head, lightly stroking her hair and the side of her face, his fingertips massaging her temple. 'Sleep,' he whispered. 'We're almost there. If you're going to hell in a handcart, my love, you should be warmer soon.'

She wasn't, however. The farther north they traveled, the colder it became, until Evie reflected dourly that a portion of devil's brimstone or hell broth would have been quite welcome. The village of Gretna Green lay in the county of Dumfriesshire, just north of the border between England and Scotland. In defiance of the strict marriage laws of England, hundreds of couples had traveled the coaching road from London, through Carlisle, to Gretna Green. They came on foot, by carriage or horseback, seeking an asylum, where they could say their marriage vows and return to England as man and wife.

After a couple crossed the bridge over the Sark River and entered Scotland, they could be married anywhere in the country. A declaration before witnesses was all that was necessary. A flourishing marriage trade had developed in Gretna Green, with the residents competing to perform wedding services in private homes, hostelries, or even out-of-doors. The most famous – and infamous – location for a Gretna wedding, however, was the blacksmith's shop, where so many hasty services had been performed that a marriage *anywhere* in Gretna Green was referred to as an 'anvil wedding.' The tradition had started in the seventeen hundreds when a blacksmith had set himself up as the first of a long line of blacksmith priests.

At last, St Vincent's carriage reached its destination, an inn located next to the blacksmith's shop. Seeming to suspect that Evie might collapse from weariness, St Vincent kept a firm arm around her as they stood before the innkeeper's battered desk. The innkeeper, a Mr Findley, beamed with delight upon learning that they were an eloping couple, and assured them with broad winks that he always kept a room at the ready for situations such as this.

"'Tisn't legal till ye consummate the weddin', ye know,' he informed them in a nearly incomprehensible accent. 'We've 'ad tae sneak a puir gruim an' 'is bride ou' the back duir o' yon smithy, whilst their pursuers were 'ammering aweey a' th' front. When they came tae the inn an' found baith lovers together abed, the bridegruim was still weering 'is boots! But there was no doubt the bonnie deed 'ad been doon.' He laughed uproariously at the memory.

'What did he say?' Evie mumbled against St Vincent's shoulder.

'I have no idea,' he said in her ear. 'And I'd

rather not speculate.' Raising his head, he said to the innkeeper, 'I want a hot bath in the room when we return from the blacksmith's cottage.'

'Aye, milord.' Eagerly the innkeeper received the coins that St Vincent handed to him in exchange for a old-fashioned looking key. 'Wad ye 'ave a supper tray as weel, milord?'

St Vincent gave Evie a questioning glance, and she shook her head. 'No,' St Vincent replied, 'but I expect we'll want a large breakfast on the morrow.'

'Aye, milord. Ye're goin' tae wed a' the smithy, aren't ye? Ah, guid. There's nae better priest in Gretna than Paisley MacPhee. A literate man, 'e is . . .'e'll serve as a clark tae the weddin', an make oot a fine certificate for ye.'

'Thank you.' St Vincent kept his arm around Evie as they walked out of the inn and headed to the blacksmith's cottage next door. A quick glance down the street revealed rows of tidy cottages and shops, with lamps being lit to relieve the gathering darkness of early evening. As they approached the front of the whitewashed building, St Vincent murmured, 'Bear up just a bit longer, sweetheart. It's almost done.'

Leaning heavily against him with her face half hidden in his coat, Evie waited as he rapped on the door. It opened soon thereafter to reveal a bulky, ruddy-faced man with a handsome mustache that connected to his profuse side whiskers. Fortunately his Scottish burr was not nearly as

43

thick as the innkeeper's, and Evie was able to follow what he said.

'Are you MacPhee?' St Vincent asked curtly.

'Aye.'

Rapidly St Vincent made introductions and explained their purpose. The blacksmith smiled broadly. 'Sae ye wish tae marry, do ye? Come inside.' He summoned his two daughters, a pair of chubby, dark-haired girls whom he introduced as Florag and Gavenia, and he led them to the shop that was attached to the residence. The MacPhees exhibited the same relentless cheer as the innkeeper Findley, which disproved much of what Evie had always heard about the reputedly dour nature of the Scots.

'Will ye have my two lasses stand as witnesses?' MacPhee suggested.

'Yes,' St Vincent said, glancing around the shop, which was filled with horseshoes, carriage equipment, and farming implements. The lamplight struck tiny glints in the golden bristle on the lower half of his face. 'As you can no doubt see, my . . .' He paused as if debating how to refer to Evie. '. . . bride . . . and I are quite weary. We've traveled from London at a bruising pace, and therefore I would like to hasten the proceedings.'

'From London?' the blacksmith inquired with obvious enjoyment, beaming at Evie. 'Why have ye come tae Gretna, lass? Have yer parents nae gi'en ye leave tae wed?'

Evie smiled back at him wanly. 'I'm afraid it's not qu-quite that simple, sir.'

''Tis seldom simple,' MacPhee agreed, nodding sagely. 'But I maun warn ye, lass . . . if ye wad fain to marry rashly . . . the Scottish marriage vow is an irrevocable bond that ne'er can be broken. Be certain that yer love is true, and then—'

Interrupting what promised to be a long spate of fatherly advice, St Vincent said in a clipped voice, 'It's not a love match. It's a marriage of convenience, and there's not enough warmth between us to light a birthday candle. Get on with it, if you please. Neither of us has had a proper sleep in two days.'

Silence fell over the scene, with MacPhee and his two daughters appearing shocked by the brusque remarks. Then the blacksmith's heavy brows lowered over his eyes in a scowl. 'I don't like ye,' he announced.

St. Vincent regarded him with exasperation. 'Neither does my bride-to-be. But since that's not going to stop her from marrying me, it shouldn't stop you either. Go on.'

MacPhee turned a now-pitying gaze on Evie. 'The lass has nae flowers,' he exclaimed, now determined to lend a romantic atmosphere to the proceedings. 'Florag, run tae fetch sae white heather.'

'She doesn't need flowers,' St Vincent snapped, but the girl scampered away nonetheless.

''Tis an auld Scottish custom for a bride tae carry white heather,' MacPhee explained to Evie. 'Shall I tell ye why?'

Evie nodded and fought to suppress a helpless titter of amusement. In spite of her fatigue – or perhaps because of it – she was beginning to take a perverse enjoyment in the sight of St Vincent struggling to control his annoyance. At the moment, the unshaven, ill-tempered man who stood beside her bore no resemblance to the smug aristocrat who had attended Lord Westcliff's house party in Hampshire.

'A lang, lang time ago . . .' MacPhee began, ignoring St Vincent's low groan, 'there was a bonnie maid called Malvina. She was the betrothed of Oscar, the braw warrior who won her heart. Oscar bade his beloved tae wait for him while he went tae seek his fortune. But one black day Malvina received word that her lover had been killed in battle. He would lie forever in eternal rest in the faraway hills . . . lost in endless slumber . . .'

'God, I envy him,' St Vincent said feelingly, rubbing his own dark-circled eyes.

'As Malvina's tears o' grief wet the grass like dew,' MacPhee continued, 'the purple heather at her feet turned white. An' that's why every Scottish bride carries white heather on her weddin' day.'

'*That's* the story?' St Vincent asked with an incredulous scowl. 'The heather comes from the tears of a girl over her dead lover?'

'Aye.'

'Then how in God's name can it be a token of good luck?'

MacPhee opened his mouth to reply, but at that

moment Florag returned to give Evie a sprig of dried white heather Murmuring her thanks, Evie allowed the blacksmith to lead her to the anvil in the center of the shop. 'Do ye have a ring for the lass?' MacPhee asked St Vincent, who shook his head. 'Sae I thought,' the blacksmith said smugly. 'Gavenia, fetch the ring box.' Leaning closer to Evie, he explained, 'I join precious metals as well as iron. 'Tis fine workmanship, an' all in Scottish gold.'

'She doesn't need—' St Vincent stopped with a scowl as Evie raised her gaze to his. He let out a taut sigh. 'All right. Choose something quickly.'

Withdrawing a square of wool from the ring box, MacPhee spread it on the anvil and tenderly placed a selection of a half-dozen rings on the fabric. Evie leaned closer to view them. The rings, all gold bands of varying sizes and patterns, were so exquisite and delicate that it seemed impossible for them to have been created by the blacksmith's burly, broad-fingered hands. 'This one is thistles an' knotwork,' MacPhee said, holding one up for her inspection. 'This is a key pattern, an' this, a Shetland rose.'

Evie picked up the smallest of the rings and tried it on the fourth finger of her left hand. It fit perfectly. Raising it closer to her face, she examined the design. It was the simplest of all the rings, a polished gold band engraved with the words *Tha Gad Agam Ort*. 'What does this mean?' she asked MacPhee.

'It says, "My love is upon ye."'

There was no sound or movement from St Vincent. Evie flushed in the awkward silence that followed, and slipped the ring off, now regretting having taken any interest in the rings. The sentiment of the phrase was so out of place in this hasty ceremony that it emphasized what a hollow mockery of a wedding it was. 'I don't think I want one after all,' she mumbled, placing the little ring gently onto the cloth.

'We'll take it,' St Vincent stunned her by saying. He picked up the gold circlet. As Evie glanced up at him with wide eyes, he added curtly, 'They're just words. It means nothing.'

Evie nodded and bent her head, her violent blush remaining.

MacPhee regarded the two of them with a frown and pulled on the side whiskers of his right cheek. 'Lasses,' he said to his daughters with determined cheer, 'we'll have a song from ye now.'

'A song—' St Vincent protested, and Evie tugged at his arm.

'Let them,' she murmured. 'The more you argue, the longer it will take.'

Swearing beneath his breath, St Vincent stared at the anvil with a narrowed gaze, while the sisters crooned in practiced harmony.

> *Oh, my love is like a red, red rose*
> *That's newly sprung in June*
> *Oh, my love is like a melody*
> *That's sweetly played in tune*

48

As fair art thou, my bonnie lass,
so deep in love am I
And I will love thee still, my dear
Till all the seas gang dry . . .

Listening to his daughters with glowing pride, the blacksmith waited until the last drawn-out note was finished, and then he praised them lavishly. He turned to the couple by the anvil and said importantly, 'Now I maun ask ye this: Are ye both unmarried persons?'

'Yes,' St Vincent replied shortly.

'An' have ye a ring for the lass?'

'You just—' St Vincent stopped with a muttered imprecation as MacPhee's bushy brows raised expectantly. Clearly if they wanted the ceremony to be done with, they would have to follow the blacksmith's lead. 'Yes,' he growled. 'I have one right here.'

'Then place it on the lass's finger, an' match yer hand to hers.'

Evie felt queer and light-headed as she stood facing St Vincent. The moment he slid the ring onto her finger, her heart began beating much too fast, setting off reckless currents of something that was neither eagerness nor fear, but a new emotion that heightened her senses unbearably. There was no word for it, this feeling. Tension gripped her while the pounding of her pulse refused to abate. Their hands flattened together, his fingers much longer than hers, his palm smooth and hot.

His head inclined slightly, his face covering hers. Although he was expressionless, a hint of color had glazed the high planes of his cheekbones and crossed the bridge of his nose. And his breath was faster than usual. Surprised by the realization that she had already come to know something as intimate as the normal rhythm of his breathing, Evie averted her gaze. She saw the blacksmith taking a length of white ribbon from one of his daughters, and she flinched a little as he looped it firmly around their joined wrists.

A wordless murmur tickled her ear, and she felt St Vincent's free hand come up to the side of her neck, stroking her as if she were a nervous animal. She relaxed at his touch, while his fingertips moved over her skin with sensitive lightness.

MacPhee busily wrapped the ribbon around their wrists. 'Now we tie the knot,' he said, doing so with a flourish. 'Repeat after me, lass . . . "I do take thee to my husband."'

'I do take thee to my husband,' Evie whispered.

'Milord?' the blacksmith prompted.

St Vincent looked down at her, his eyes cool and diamond-bright, revealing nothing. And yet she sensed somehow that he too felt the queer, eager tension that was building between them, a charge as strong as lightning.

His voice was low and quiet. 'I do take thee to my wife.'

Satisfaction rang in MacPhee's voice. 'Before

God an' these witnesses I declare ye to be married persons. Whom God hath joined let no man put asunder. That will be eighty-two pounds, three crowns, an' one shilling.'

St. Vincent tore his gaze from Evie with difficulty and glanced at the blacksmith with a raised eyebrow.

'"Tis fifty pounds for the ring,' MacPhee said in answer to the wordless question.

'Fifty pounds for a ring with no stones?' St Vincent inquired acidly.

'That's *Scottish gold*,' MacPhee said, looking indignant that his price should be called into question. 'Frae the burns o' the Lowther hills it came—'

'And the rest of it?'

'Thirty pounds for the rites, one pound for the use o' my shop, one guinea for the marriage certificate, which I will have ready at the morrow, one crown apiece for the witnesses' – the blacksmith paused to gesture to his daughters, who giggled and bobbed in curtsies – 'another crown for the flowers—'

'A crown for a handful of dried weeds?' St Vincent asked in outrage.

'I'll gi' ye the song at no charge,' MacPhee conceded graciously. 'Oh, an' a shilling for the ribbon . . . which ye maun *not* untie till the marriage is consummated . . . or ill luck will follow ye from Gretna.'

St. Vincent opened his mouth to argue, but after one glance at Evie's exhausted face, he reached into his coat for the money. His movements were awkward, for he was right-handed and his left was the only one available for use. Pulling out a wad of banknotes and a few coins, he tossed them onto the anvil. 'There,' he said gruffly. 'No, don't return the change. Give it to your daughters' – a sardonic note entered his voice – 'along with my gratitude for the song.'

A chorus of thanks erupted from MacPhee and the girls, who were inspired to follow them to the door of the building, singing an extra verse of the wedding song.

> *And I will love thee still, my dear*
> *Till all the seas gang dry . . .*

CHAPTER 4

The rain had worsened by the time they left the blacksmith's cottage, coming down in stinging sheets of silver and black. Evie quickened her pace, summoning the last of her strength to return to the shelter of the inn. She felt as if she were walking through a dream. Everything seemed out of proportion – it was difficult to focus her eyes, and the muddy ground seemed to shift capriciously beneath her feet. To her disgruntlement, St Vincent stopped her by the side of the building under the shelter of a dripping eave.

'What is it?' she asked numbly.

He reached for their bound wrists and began to tug at the knotted ribbon. 'I'm getting rid of this.'

'No. Wait.' The hood of her cloak fell back as she fumbled to stop him. Her hand covered his, temporarily stilling the motion of his fingers.

'Why?' St Vincent asked impatiently. Water trickled from the edge of his hat as he looked down at her. Evening had fallen, and the only illumination was the feeble glow shed by the sputtering street lamps. Dim though the light was, it seemed to catch in his pale blue eyes, causing them to gleam as if with their own inner illumination.

'You heard what Mr MacPhee said – it's bad luck if we untie the ribbon.'

'You're superstitious,' St Vincent said in a disbelieving tone. Evie nodded apologetically.

It was not difficult to see that his temper was being held in check by a thread far more tenuous than the ribbon that connected their wrists. As they stood together in the dark and cold, their tethered arms held upward at an awkward angle, Evie felt the fingers of his imprisoned hand cupping over her fist. It was the only warm part of her body, the place where his hand covered hers.

St Vincent spoke with an exaggerated patience that, had Evie been in full possession of her wits, would have warned her to withdraw her objections immediately. 'Do you really want to go into the tavern like this?'

It was irrational, but Evie was too exhausted to make sense of her feelings. All she knew was that she'd had enough ill fortune to last a lifetime and she did not want to invite any more. 'This is Gretna Green. No one will think anything of it. And I thought you didn't care about appearances.'

'I've never had any objection to appearing depraved or villainous. But I draw the line at looking like a prize idiot.'

'No, *don't*,' Evie said urgently as St Vincent reached for the ties once more. She grappled with him, her fingers tangling with his. And then suddenly his mouth had caught hers, and he pushed her against the side of the building, anchoring her with his own body. His free hand caught the nape of her neck, beneath the weight of her damp hair. The lush pressure of his mouth caused a shock of response in every part of her body, all at once. She didn't know how to kiss, what to do with her mouth. Bewildered and shaking, she urged her closed lips back against his, while her heart thumped wildly and her limbs went weak.

He wanted things that she didn't know how to give. Sensing her confusion, he drew back and possessed her mouth with small, persistent kisses, the bristle on his face scraping gently against hers. His fingers came to the fragile structure of her jaw, tilting her chin, his thumb coaxing her lower lip apart from the upper. The instant he gained an opening, he sealed his mouth over hers. She could taste him, a subtle and alluring essence that affected her like some exotic drug. His tongue pushed inside her, exploring in caressing strokes . . . sliding deeper as she offered no resistance.

After a luxuriously probing kiss, he eased back until their mouths were barely touching, their breath mingling in steamy puffs that were visible in the chilled night air. He brushed a half-open kiss against her lips, and another, his soft exhalations filling her mouth. The light kisses strayed across her cheek to the intricate hollow of her ear, and she gasped shakily as she felt his tongue trace the fragile rim, just before his teeth caught softly at the tiny lobe. She writhed in response, sensation streaking down to her breasts and farther, gathering low in intimate places.

Straining against him, she searched blindly for his hot, teasing mouth, the silken stroke of his tongue. He gave it to her, his kiss gentle but sure. She curled her free arm around his neck to keep from falling, while he kept the other wrist pressed against the wall, their pulses throbbing hard together beneath the wrapping of white ribbon. Another deep kiss, somehow raw and soothing at the same time . . . he ate at her mouth, tasted and licked inside her . . . the pleasure of it threatened to blot out her consciousness. *No wonder* . . . she thought dizzily. No wonder so many women had succumbed to this man, had thrown away their reputations and their honor for him . . . had even, if rumor could be believed, threatened to kill themselves when he left them. He was sensuality incarnate.

As St Vincent lifted his body away from hers, Evie was surprised that she didn't crumple bonelessly to the ground. He was breathing as hard as she, harder, his chest rising and falling steadily. They were both silent as he reached to untie the ribbon, his ice-blue gaze focused completely on the task. His hands were shaking. He couldn't bring himself to look at her face, though she could not fathom whether it was to keep from seeing her expression, or to prevent her from seeing his. After the length of white silk had fallen away, Evie felt as if they were still bound, her wrist retaining the sensation of being fastened against him.

Finally daring to glance at her, St Vincent silently challenged her to protest. She held her tongue and took hold of his arm, and they walked the short distance to the inn. Her mind was spinning, and she barely heard Mr Findley's jovial congratulations as they entered the little building. Her legs felt heavy as she ascended a flight of dark, narrow steps.

Finally it had come to this, a teeth-gritting effort to put one foot in front of the other in the hopes that she wouldn't drop in her tracks. They came to a small door in the upstairs hallway. Resting her dropping shoulders against the wall, Evie watched St Vincent fumble with the lock. The key turned with a scraping sound, and she staggered toward the open doorway.

'Wait.' St Vincent bent to lift her.

She inhaled quickly. 'You don't have to—'

'In deference to your superstitious nature,' he said, picking her up as easily as if she were a child, 'I think we had better adhere to one last tradition.' Turning sideways, he carried her through the doorway. 'It's bad luck if the bride trips over the threshold. And I've seen men after a three-day bacchanal who were steadier on their feet than you are.'

'Thank you,' Evie murmured as he set her down.

'That will be a half crown,' St Vincent replied. The sardonic reminder of the blacksmith's fees brought a sudden smile to her face.

The smile faded, however, as she glanced around the tidy little room. The bed, large enough for two, looked soft and clean, the coverlet worn from countless launderings. The bedstead was made of brass and iron with ball-shaped finials. A rosy glow emanated from an oil lamp made of ruby glass that had been set on the bedside table. Muddy, cold, and numb, Evie stared mutely at the ancient wood-rimmed tin tub that had been placed before the small, flickering hearth.

St Vincent latched the door and came to her, reaching for the fastening of her cloak. Something like pity flickered across his features as he saw that she was shaking with weariness. 'Let me help you,' he said quietly, taking the cloak from her shoulders. He laid it over a chair near the hearth.

Evie swallowed hard and tried to stiffen her knees, which seemed inclined to buckle. Cold dread weighted her stomach as she glanced at the bed. 'Are we going to . . .' she started to ask, her voice turning scratchy.

St Vincent began on the front fastenings of her gown. 'Are we going to . . .' he repeated, and followed her gaze to the bed. 'Good God, no.' His fingers moved rapidly along her bodice, freeing the row of buttons. 'Delectable as you are, my love, I'm too tired. I've never said this in my entire life – but at the moment I would much rather sleep than fuck.'

Overwhelmed with relief, Evie let out an unsteady sigh. She was forced to clutch at him for balance as he pushed the loosened gown down over her hips. 'I don't like that word,' she said in a muffled voice.

'Well, you had better get used to it,' came his caustic reply. 'That word is said frequently at your father's club. God knows how you managed to escape hearing it before.'

'I did,' she said indignantly, stepping out of the discarded gown. 'I just didn't know what it meant until now.'

St. Vincent bent to untie her shoes, his broad shoulders quivering. A curious gasping, choking noise came from him. At first Evie wondered anxiously if he had suddenly been taken ill, and then she realized that he was laughing. It was the first genuine laughter she had ever heard from him, and she had no idea what he found so funny. Standing over him in her chemise and drawers, she crossed her arms over her front and frowned.

Still snorting with quiet amusement, St Vincent removed her shoes one at a time, tossing them aside. Her stockings were rolled down her legs with swift efficiency. 'Take your bath, pet,' he finally managed to say. 'You're safe from me tonight. I may look, but I won't touch. Go on.'

Having never undressed before a man in her life, Evie felt a prickling blush cover her body as she eased down the straps of her chemise. Tactfully St Vincent turned his back and went to the washstand with a ewer of hot water that had been set by the hearth. While he proceeded to gather his shaving implements from his trunk, Evie clumsily stripped away her underclothes and climbed into the bath. The water was hot, wonderfully so, and as she sank into the tub her cold legs tingled as if they were being pricked with a thousand needles.

A jar of gelatinous brown soap had been set on a stool beside the tub. Scooping some of it in her fingers, Evie spread the acrid-smelling stuff over her chest and arms. Her hands felt clumsy . . . she couldn't quite seem to make her fingers work properly. After dunking her head in the water, she reached for more of the soap, nearly dropping the jar in the process. She washed her hair, made a sound of discomfort as her eyes began to sting, and splashed handfuls of water on her face.

Quickly St Vincent approached the tub with the ewer. She heard his voice through the splashing. 'Tilt your head back.' He poured the remainder of the clear water over her soapy hair. Deftly he blotted her face with a length of clean but scratchy toweling and bade her to stand. Evie took his proffered hand and obeyed. She should have been mortified, standing naked in front of him, but she had finally reached an extremity of exhaustion that did not allow for modesty. Trembling and enervated, she let him help her from the tub. She even allowed him to dry her, as she was unable to do anything but stand listlessly, not caring or even noticing if he was looking at her.

St Vincent was more efficient than any lady's maid, dressing Evie swiftly in the white flannel nightgown he had found in her valise. He used the towel to wring the water from her hair, then guided her to the washstand. Evie registered incuriously that he had found her toothbrush in the valise and had sprinkled the bristles with tooth powder. Brushing and rinsing with jerky movements, she spit into the creamware washbowl. The toothbrush dropped from her nerveless fingers, clattering to the floor. 'Where's the bed?' she whispered, her eyes closed.

'Here, sweetheart. Take my hand.' St Vincent led her to the bed, and she crawled onto the mattress like a wounded animal. The bed was dry and warm, the mattress soft, the weight of the sheets and wool blankets exquisite on her aching limbs. Burying her head in the pillow, she let out a sighing groan. There was a slight tugging at her scalp, and she comprehended that St Vincent was combing the snarls from her damp hair. Passively accepting his ministrations, she let him turn her over to reach the other side. When the task was finished, St Vincent left the bedside to attend to his own bath. Evie managed to stay awake just long enough to crack her swollen lids open for a view of his lean, gold-tinted body in the firelight. Her eyes closed as he stepped into the tub . . . and by the time he had sat down, she was fast asleep.

No dreams leavened her slumber. There was nothing but sweet, heavy darkness, and the soft bed, and the quietness of a Scottish village on a cold autumn night. The only time she stirred was at daybreak, when noises from outside filtered into the room . . . the cheerful cries of the muffin seller, a rag man, the sounds of animals pulling carts through the street. Her eyes slitted open, and in the diluted light that shone through the rough-woven fawn-colored curtains, she registered the surprising sight of another person in bed with her.

St Vincent. Her husband. He was naked, or at least the upper half of him was. He slept on his stomach, his smoothly muscled arms curved around the pillow beneath his head. The broad lines of his shoulders and back were so perfect that they seemed to have been carved from pale Baltic amber and sanded to a glossy finish. His face was much softer in repose than it was in wakefulness . . . the calculating eyes were closed, and his mouth was relaxed into gentle, innocently sensuous lines.

Closing her own eyes, Evie dwelled on the thought that she was now a married woman, and would be able to see her father soon and stay with him for as long as she wished. And as it was likely that St Vincent would care little about what she did or where she went, she would have some freedom. Despite the worries that lurked in the back of her mind, a feeling that resembled happiness crept through her, and she sighed and drifted to sleep once more.

This time, she dreamed. She was walking along a sun-drenched lane lined with purple asters and swaying spikes of goldenrod. It was a path in Hampshire that she had traversed many times before, past wet fields filled with yellow meadow-sweet and tall late-summer grasses. She strolled alone in the sunken lane until she approached the wishing well where she and the other wallflowers had once tossed pins into the churning water and made wishes. Having learned of the local supersti-tion about the well spirit who lived deep in the ground, Evie had been nervous about standing too close to the edge. According to legend, the spirit was waiting to capture an innocent maiden and pull her down with him into the well, to live as his consort. In her dream, however, Evie was fear-less, even daring to remove her shoes and dip her toes into the sloshing water. To her surprise, it was not cool, but deliciously warm.

Lowering herself to the edge of the well, Evie dangled her bare legs in the soothing water and lifted her face to the sun. She felt a soft touch on her ankles. She held very still, feeling no fear even as she sensed something moving beneath the surface of the water. Another touch . . . a hand . . . long fingers smoothed over her feet and massaged tenderly, rubbing over the sore insteps until she sighed in pleasure. The big masculine hands slid higher, caressing her calves and knees, while a large, sleek body emerged from the depths of the well. The spirit had taken the form of a man to court her. His arms slipped around her, and the feel of him was strange but so lovely that she kept her eyes closed, fearing that if she tried to look at him, he might vanish. His skin was hot and silken, the muscles of his back rippling beneath her fingers.

Her dream lover whispered endearments as he embraced her, his mouth playing over her throat. Everywhere he touched, she felt a glow of sensation. 'Shall I take you?' he whispered, carefully drawing away her clothes, baring her skin to the light and air and water. 'Don't be afraid, little love, don't . . .' And as she shivered and held him blindly, he kissed her throat and breasts, and touched her nipples with his tongue. His hands coasted over her front, slipping down to cradle her breasts while his half-parted lips brushed over a budded peak. His tongue darted out to flick the sweetly aching flesh again and again, until a moan rose in her throat and she slid her fingers into his thick hair. Opening his mouth, he covered her nipple and drew on it with a gentle tug, then stroked with his tongue and pulled again . . . licking and suckling in a soft, clever rhythm. She arched and gasped, helplessly widening her thighs as he moved more tightly between them . . . and then . . .

Evie's eyes flew open. Her mind reeled as she awoke in a tangle of confusion and desire, her lungs laboring wildly. The dream faded, and she comprehended that she was not in Hampshire but in the rented room at the Gretna inn, and the sounds of water were not from a wishing well but from a heavy rain outside. There was no sunlight, but instead the blaze of a newly lit fire in the hearth. And the body over hers was not that of a well spirit, but of a warm, living man . . . his head over her stomach, his mouth wandering lazily over her skin. Evie stiffened and whimpered in surprise at the realization that she was naked . . . that St Vincent was making love to her and had been for some minutes.

St. Vincent glanced up at her. With the slight flush on the crests of his cheeks, his eyes seemed lighter and more startling than usual. The hint of a relaxed but devious smile touched the corners of his mouth. 'You're difficult to awaken,' he said huskily, and his head lowered again, while one of his hands coasted stealthily along her thigh. Shocked, she uttered a hoarse protest and shifted beneath him, but he soothed her with his hands, stroking her legs and hips, resettling her on the mattress. 'Lie still. You don't have to do anything, my love. Let me take care of you. Yes. You can touch me if you . . . mmm, yes . . .' He purred as he felt her trembling fingers touch his gleaming hair, the back of his neck, the hard slope of his shoulders.

He moved lower, his hair-roughened legs sliding along the insides of hers, and she realized that his face was just above the triangle of fiery red curls. Flooded with embarrassment, she automatically reached down to cover the private area with her hand.

St Vincent's erotic mouth lowered to her hip, and she felt him smile against her tender skin. 'You shouldn't do that,' he whispered. 'When you hide something from me, I want it all the more. I'm afraid you're filling my head with the most lascivious ideas . . . you'd better take your hand away, sweet, or I might do something really depraved.' As her shaking hand withdrew, he let one fingertip wander into the springy hair, delicately searching the cushiony softness. 'That's right . . . obey your husband,' he whispered wickedly, stroking farther, deeper, until he had separated the cluster of curls. 'Especially in bed. How beautiful you are. Open your legs, my love. I'm going to touch inside you. No, don't be afraid. Will it help if I kiss you here? Be still for me . . .'

Evie sobbed as his mouth searched through the triangle of brilliant red hair. His warm, ruthlessly patient tongue found the little peak half concealed beneath the vulnerable hood. His long, agile finger probed the entrance of her body, but he was momentarily dislodged as she jerked in surprise.

Whispering reassurances against her swollen flesh, St Vincent slid his finger inside her again, deeper this time. 'Innocent darling,' came his soft murmur, and his tongue tickled a place so excruciatingly sensitive that she quivered and moaned.

At the same time, his finger stroked her inner softness with a languid rhythm. She tried to keep quiet, gritting her teeth together, but little noises kept climbing in her throat. 'What do you think would happen,' she heard him ask lazily, 'if I kept doing this without stopping . . .'

Evie's vision blurred as their gazes met over the quivering plane of her stomach. She knew that her face was contorted and flushed . . . she felt heat blazing over every inch of her skin. He seemed to expect a reply, and she could hardly force the words from her constricted throat. 'I-I don't know,' she said faintly.

'Let's try it, shall we?'

She couldn't reply, could do nothing but watch in astonishment as he pressed his mouth into the patch of red curls. Her head fell back as she felt his tongue dance skillfully across her pulsing flesh. The pounding of her heart increased to hard thumps. She felt a slight burn as he slipped a second finger inside her, stretching tenderly, and then he suckled the taut bud of her sex, licking slowly at first, increasing the pace as she twisted beneath him. He stayed with her, his long fingers working in controlled thrusts, his mouth compelling and demanding, until pleasure washed over her in faster and faster rushes, and suddenly she couldn't move at all. Arched tightly against his mouth, she cried out and gasped, and cried out again. His tongue gentled but continued its artful play, nursing her through the lingering peaks of sensation, bathing her sex with warm strokes as she began to shudder violently.

A great weariness flooded her, and with it a physical euphoria that made her feel drunk. Unable to control her limbs, she squirmed tremulously beneath him, and offered no resistance as St Vincent turned her over to her stomach. His hand slipped between her thighs and his fingers entered her once more. The opening to her body was sore and, to her mortification, saturated with moisture. He seemed excited by the wetness, however, breathing against the sensitive nape of her neck in rapid pants. Keeping his fingers inside her, he kissed and nibbled his way down her back.

Evie felt the brush of his sex against her legs . . . it was hard and engorged, the skin burning hot. She was not surprised by the change in him . . . Annabelle had told her enough in the past to give her a fair understanding of what happened to a man's body during the act of love. But Annabelle had said nothing about the hundred other intimacies that made the experience not merely physical, but one to change the very alchemy of her soul.

Crouching over her, St Vincent teased and fondled until he felt her hips rising tentatively against his hand. 'I want to be inside you,' he whispered, kissing the side of her neck. 'I want to go deep into your body . . . I'll be so gentle, love . . . let me turn you over, and . . . God, you're so lovely . . .' He pressed her on her back and settled between her widespread thighs, his whisper

68

becoming frayed and unsteady. 'Touch me, sweet-heart . . . put your hand there . . .' He sucked in a quick breath as her fingers curved gently around the hard length of his sex. Evie stroked him hesitantly, understanding from the quickening of his breath that the caress gave him pleasure. His eyes closed, the thick lashes trembling slightly against his cheeks, his lips parting from the force of his sharp respirations.

Awkwardly she gripped the heavy shaft and guided it between her thighs. The head of it slipped against the wetness of her sex, and St Vincent groaned as if in pain. Trying again, Evie positioned him uncertainly. Once in place, he nudged strongly into the vulnerable cove. It burned far more than when he had put his fingers in her, and Evie tensed against the pain. Cradling her body in his arms, St Vincent moved in a powerful thrust, and another, and then he was all the way inside. She writhed with the impulse to escape the hurtful invasion, but it seemed that each movement only drew him deeper.

Filled and stretched and opened, Evie forced herself to lie still in his arms. She held on to his shoulders, her fingertips digging into the hard quilting of muscle and sinew, and she let him soothe her with his mouth and hands. His brilliant eyes were heavy-lidded as he bent to kiss her. Welcoming the warm sleekness of his tongue, she drew it into her mouth with eager, awkward suction. He made a low sound of surprise, shuddering, and his shaft jerked violently inside her in a series of rhythmic spasms. A groan vibrated in his chest as he spent himself inside her, his breath hissing between his clenched teeth.

Her hands slipped down to his chest, the firm surface covered with a light fleece of coarse golden hair. With his body still joined to hers, St Vincent held still beneath her inquisitive fingers. She touched his lean sides, exploring the hard vaulting of his ribs and the satiny plane of his back. His blue eyes widened, and then he dropped his head to the pillow beside hers, growling as his body worked inside hers with a deep thrust, as he was helplessly shaken with new tremors of rapture.

His mouth fastened on hers with a primal greed. She opened her legs wider, pulled at his back to urge more of his weight on her, trying in spite of the pain to tug him deeper, harder. Braced on his elbows to keep from crushing her, he rested his head on her chest, his breath hot and light as it fanned over her nipple. The bristle of his cheek stung her skin a little, the sensation causing the tips of her breasts to contract. His sex was still buried inside her, though it had softened. He was silent but awake, his eyelashes a silky tickle against her skin.

Evie remained quiet as well, her arms encircling his head, her fingers playing in his beautiful hair. She felt the weight of his head shift, the wet heat of his mouth seeking her nipple. His lips fastened over it, and his tongue slowly traced the outer edge of the gathered aureole, around and around until he felt her stirring restlessly beneath him. Keeping the tender bud inside his mouth, he licked steadily, sweetly, while desire ignited in her breasts and her stomach and loins, and the soreness dissolved in a fresh wave of need. Intently he moved to the other breast, nibbling, stroking, seeming to feed on her pleasure. He levered upward enough to allow his hand to slide between them, and his cunning fingers slid into the wet nest of hair, finding the tingling feminine crest and teasing skillfully. She felt herself sliding into another climax, her body clamping voluptuously on the hot flesh that was insinuated deep inside her.

Gasping, St Vincent lifted his head to stare at her as if she were a variety of creature he had never seen before. 'Good Lord,' he whispered, his expression not one of gratification, but of something close to alarm.

CHAPTER 5

Sebastian left the bed and went to the wash-stand on unsteady legs. He felt dazed, uncertain, as if he were the one who had just lost his virginity instead of Evangeline. He had long thought that there was nothing new for him to experience. He had been wrong. For a man whose lovemaking was a practiced blend of technique and choreography, it had been a shock to find himself at the spontaneous mercy of his own passions. He had meant to withdraw at the last moment, but he had been so mindless with desire that he'd been unable to control his body. Damn. That had never happened before.

Fumbling with the clean linen towel at the wash-stand, he made a project of dampening it with fresh water. By now his breathing had returned to normal, but he wasn't at all calm. After what had just happened, he should have been satiated for hours. But it hadn't been enough. He had experienced the longest, hardest, most wrenching climax of his life . . . and yet the need to have her again, open her, bury himself inside her, had not faded. It was madness. But why? Why with her?

She had the kind of amply feminine form that he'd always adored, voluptuous and firm, with plump thighs to cushion him. And her skin was as smooth as pressed velvet, with golden freckles scattered like festive sparks shed by rockets and Catherine wheels. The hair . . . as red and curly down below as it was on her head . . . yes, that was also irresistible. But all the physical riches of Evangeline Jenner could not account for her extraordinary effect on him.

Feeling, impossibly, the stirring of desire once more, Sebastian scrubbed himself roughly with the cold cloth and reached for a fresh one. He brought it to Evangeline, who lay half curled on her side. To his relief, it seemed there would be no virginal tears or complaints. She appeared contemplative rather than upset . . . she was staring at him intently, as if she were trying to solve a puzzle. Murmuring quietly, he coaxed her onto her back and washed the blood and fluid from between her thighs.

It wasn't easy for Evangeline to lie still and naked before him . . . Sebastian saw the rosy color that covered her in a swift tide. He had known very few women who blushed at nudity. He had always chosen women of experience, having little taste for innocents. Not for reasons of morality, of course, but because virgins were, as a rule, quite dull in bed.

Setting the cloth aside, Sebastian braced his hands on either side of Evangeline's shoulders, his palms making deep depressions in the mattress. They studied each other curiously. Evangeline was comfortable with silence, he realized – she didn't seek to fill it as most women did. A nice quality. He leaned over her, still staring into her eyes . . . but as his head lowered to hers, a little growling sound interrupted the silence. It was her stomach, protesting its emptiness. Turning a deeper shade of red, if that were possible, Evangeline clapped her hands over her midriff as if to silence the willful rumble.

A grin crossed Sebastian's face, and he bent swiftly to kiss her stomach. 'I'll send for breakfast, sweet.'

'Evie,' she murmured, reaching down to pull the covers up to her chest. 'That's what my father and my friends call me.'

'Are we finally ready for first names?' A teasing smile lurked in the corners of his lips. 'Sebastian,' he said softly.

Evie reached out slowly, as if he were a wild animal that might bolt if startled, and her fingers laced through his front locks with careful lightness. Brushing aside the swath of stray hair, she said in a low voice, 'We're truly married now.'

'Yes. God help you.' He inclined his head, enjoying the stroke of her fingers in his hair. 'Shall we depart for London today?'

Evie nodded. 'I want to see my father.'

'You'd better choose your words with care when you explain that I'm his son-in-law,' he said. 'Otherwise the news will finish him off.'

She drew her hand back. 'I want to hurry. If the weather improves, perhaps we can better our time. I want to go straight to my father's club and—'

'We'll get there soon,' Sebastian said evenly, 'but we won't be traveling at the full-bore speed we maintained all the way to Scotland. We'll spend at least one night at a coaching inn.' As she opened her mouth to object, he said in an inexorable manner, 'It will do your father no good for you to arrive at his club half dead with exhaustion.'

Now it began – the exercise of husbandly authority, and the obligation of the wife to obey him. It was clear that Evie longed to argue, but instead she stared at him with a frown notched between her eyes. Softening his voice, he murmured, 'You're in for a difficult time of it, Evie. Having me for a husband will be trial enough. But caring for a consumptive during the last stage of his illness . . . you'll need all your strength. No use in depleting it before you even get there.'

Evie stared at him with a renewed intensity that made him uncomfortable. What eyes she had, as if someone had collected layers of blue glass and shone the brightest sunlight through it. 'Are you concerned about my welfare?' she asked.

He made his voice mocking, his gaze cool. 'Of course, pet. It's in my best interest to keep you alive and healthy until I can collect your dowry.'

Evie soon discovered that St Vincent – Sebastian – was as comfortable naked as fully dressed. She tried

75

to react nonchalantly to the sight of a man moving about the room without a stitch of clothing. But she stole discreet glances whenever possible, until he extracted a suit of clothes from the trunk. He was long-limbed and lean, with sleek expanses of flesh that must have been toned by gentlemanly exercise like riding, pugilism, and fencing. His back and shoulders were well-developed, with muscles flexing beneath the taut skin. More fascinating still was his front view, including a chest that was not bare, as one usually saw with marble or bronze statues, but lightly covered with hair. The hair on his chest – and in other places – had surprised her. It was yet another of the many mysteries of the opposite gender that were now – literally – being revealed to her.

Unable to bring herself to stride across the room in a similarly exposed fashion, Evie tugged one of the bed linens around herself before going to her valise. She unearthed a clean gown made of heavy brown broadcloth and a fresh set of undergarments, and best of all a pair of clean shoes. Her other pair were so soiled and clammy that she shuddered at the thought of putting them on. In the midst of dressing, she felt Sebastian's gaze on her. Hastily she yanked her chemise down to conceal her pinkening torso.

'You're beautiful, Evie,' came his soft comment.

Having been raised by relations who had always lamented the garish color of her hair and the proliferation of freckles, Evie gave him a skeptical smile. 'Aunt Florence has always given me a bleaching lotion to make my freckles vanish. But there's no getting rid of them.'

Sebastian smiled lazily as he came to her. Taking her shoulders in his hands, he slid an appraising glance along her half-clad body. 'Don't remove a single freckle, sweet. I found some in the most enchanting places. I already have my favorites . . . shall I tell you where they are?'

Disarmed and discomfited, Evie shook her head and made a movement to twist away from him. He wouldn't let her, however. Pulling her closer, he bent his golden head and kissed the side of her neck. 'Little spoilsport,' he whispered, smiling. 'I'm going to tell you anyway.' His fingers closed around a handful of the chemise and eased the hem slowly upward. Her breath caught as she felt his fingers nuzzling tenderly between her bare legs. 'As I discovered earlier,' he said against her sensitive throat, 'there's a trail inside your right thigh that leads to—'

A knock at the door interrupted them, and Sebastian lifted his head with a grumble of annoyance. 'Breakfast,' he muttered. 'And I wouldn't care to make you choose between my lovemaking or a hot meal, as the answer would likely be unflattering. Put on your gown, while I go to the door.'

After Evie obeyed with fumbling haste, he opened the door to reveal a pair of chambermaids bearing trays of covered dishes. As soon as they got a glance at the handsome guest with the seraphic face and hair the color of ripe wheat, the two women gasped and giggled uncontrollably. It hardly improved their composure to see that he was only partially dressed, his feet bare beneath his trousers, his white shirt and collar left open at the throat, and a silk cravat hanging loose on either side of his neck. The infatuated maids nearly overturned the trays twice before they had managed to set the breakfast dishes on the table. Noticing the rumpled bed, they found it difficult to contain their squeals of delight as they speculated on what had taken place there during the night. Annoyed, Evie shooed the chambermaids from the room and closed the door firmly behind them.

She glanced at Sebastian to observe his reaction to the chambermaids' dazzled admiration, but he seemed oblivious. Clearly, their behavior was so commonplace as to go unnoticed. A man of his looks and position would always be sought after by women. Evie had no doubt that it would be devastating to a wife who loved him. However, she would never allow herself to suffer the bite of jealousy or the fear of betrayal.

Coming to seat Evie at the table, Sebastian served her first. There was porridge flavored with salt and butter, as the Scots considered it a sacrilege to sweeten it with treacle. There were also yeast rolls called bannocks, rashers of cold boiled bacon, smoked haddock, and a large bowl of smoked oysters, and broad slices of toasted bread heaped with marmalade. Evie devoured her food hungrily, washing it down with strong tea. The meal was a simple one, hardly comparable to the spectacular English breakfasts at Lord Westcliff's Hampshire estate, but it was hot and plentiful, and Evie was far too ravenous to find fault with anything.

She lingered over breakfast while Sebastian shaved and finished dressing. Dropping a leather roll of shaving implements into his trunk, he closed the lid and spoke casually to Evie. 'Pack your belongings, pet. I'm going downstairs to see that the carriage is made ready.'

'The marriage certificate from Mr MacPhee—'

'I'll take care of that as well. Lock the door behind me.'

In approximately an hour he returned to collect Evie, while a brawny lad carried the trunk and valise to the waiting carriage. A faint smile touched Sebastian's lips as he saw that Evie had used one of his silk cravats to tie her hair at the back of her neck. Evie had lost most of her hairpins during the journey from England, and she had not had the foresight to tuck an extra rack of them into her valise. 'With your hair like that, you look too young to marry,' he murmured. 'It adds a piquant note of debauchery to the situation. I like it.'

Becoming accustomed by now to his indecent remarks, Evie gave him a look of resigned forbearance and followed him from the room. They descended to the first floor and exchanged farewells with Mr Findley, the innkeeper. As Evie accompanied Sebastian to the entrance, Findley called out sunnily, 'I bid ye a safe juirney, Lady St Vincent!'

Startled to realize that she was now a viscountess, Evie managed to stammer out her thanks.

Sebastian helped her to the waiting carriage, while the horses stomped and shifted and blew white breath from their flared nostrils. 'Yes,' he commented sardonically, 'besmirched though it is, the title is now yours to share.' He helped her up the movable step and into the vehicle. 'Moreover,' he continued as he swung in to sit beside her, 'we will someday rise to even greater heights, as I'm first in line for the dukedom . . . though I advise you not to hold your breath until it happens. The men in my family are regrettably long-lived, which means you and I probably won't inherit until we're both too decrepit to enjoy it.'

'If you—' Evie began, and stopped in surprise as she saw a bulky object on the floor. It was a large pottery container of some sort, with a stoppered opening at one end. Its shape was round, but it was flat on one side to ensure its stability on the floor. She threw a glance of bewilderment at Sebastian, tentatively touched the sole of her shoe to the object and was rewarded with a strong waft of heat that went right up her skirts. 'A foot warmer,' she exclaimed. The heat from the boiling water that was contained in the pottery casing would last much longer than the hot brick she had used before. 'Where did you manage to find it?'

'I bought it from MacPhee when I saw it in his

cottage,' Sebastian replied, seeming amused by her giddy excitement. 'Naturally he was overjoyed at the prospect of charging me for something else.'

Impulsively Evie half rose from her seat to kiss his cheek, which was smooth and cool against her lips. 'Thank you. It was very kind of you.'

His hands came to her waist, preventing her retreat. He exerted just enough force to bring her onto his lap, until their faces were so close that their noses were nearly touching. His breath caressed her mouth as he murmured, 'Surely I deserve more thanks than that.'

'It's only a foot warmer,' she protested mildly.

He grinned. 'I should point out, darling, that the thing is going to cool eventually . . . and then, once again, I will be your only source of available warmth. And I don't share my body heat indiscriminately.'

'According to rumor you do.' Evie was discovering an unfamiliar delight in the exchange. She had never bantered with a man like this, nor had she ever experienced the fun of withholding something he wanted, teasing him with it. She saw from the glimmer in his eyes that he was enjoying it as well. He looked as if he wanted to pounce on her.

'I'll bide my time,' he said. 'The damned bottle can't last forever.'

He let her scramble off his lap, and watched as she settled the fall of the skirts over the foot warmer. Leaning back blissfully as the carriage began to roll forward, Evie felt gooseflesh rise on her thighs at the delicious drafts of heat that drifted through the legs of her drawers and sank into the weave of her stockings. 'My lord . . . that is . . . Sebastian . . .'

His eyes were as bright and reflective as a looking glass. 'Yes, sweet?'

'If your father is a duke, then why are you a viscount? Shouldn't you be a marquess, or at least an earl?'

'Not necessarily. It's a relatively modern practice to add a number of lesser titles when a new one is created. As a rule, the older the dukedom, the less likely that the eldest son is a marquess. My father chooses to make a virtue of it, of course. Don't ever start him on the subject, especially when he's in his cups, or you'll receive a mind-numbing discourse on how foreign and feminine-sounding the word "marquess" is, and how the rank itself is nothing but an embarrassing half step beneath a dukedom.'

'Is he an arrogant man, your father?'

The hint of a bitter smile curved his lips. 'I used to think it was arrogance. But I've come to realize that it's more an obliviousness to the world outside his own. To my knowledge, he's never put on his own stockings, or put powder on his own tooth-brush. I doubt he could survive a life without privilege. In fact, I believe he would starve in a room filled with food if there were no servants to bring it to the table where he sat. He thinks nothing of using a priceless vase as a target for shooting practice or putting out a fire in the hearth by throwing a fox-fur coat on it. He even keeps the forests around the estate perpetually lit with torches and lamps in case he should ever take it in his mind to go walking through them at night.'

'No wonder you're poor,' Evie said, appalled by such waste. 'I hope you're not a spendthrift as well.'

He shook his head. 'I have yet to be accused of unreasonable financial excess. I rarely gamble, and I don't keep a mistress. Even so, I have my share of creditors nipping at my heels.'

'Have you ever considered going into a profession?'

He gave her a blank look. 'What for?'

'To earn money.'

'Lord, no, child. Work would be an inconvenient distraction from my personal life. And I'm seldom disposed to rise before noon.'

'My father is not going to like you.'

'If my ambition in life were to earn other people's liking, I would be most distressed to hear that. Fortunately it's not.'

As the journey continued in a companionable vein, Evie was aware of a contradictory mixture of feelings toward her husband. Although he possessed a large measure of charm, she found little in him that was worthy of respect. It was obvious that he had a keen mind, but it was employed for no good purpose. Furthermore, the knowledge that he had kidnapped Lillian, and betrayed his own best friend in the bargain, made it clear that he was not to be trusted. However . . . he was capable of an occasional cavalier kindness that she appreciated.

With every stop between relays Sebastian saw to Evie's needs, and despite his threats about letting the foot warmer cool, he had it refilled with boiling water. When she grew tired he allowed her to nap against his chest, anchoring her as the carriage wheels bounced over broken stretches of road. As she drowsed in his arms, it occurred to her that he provided the illusion of something she had never had before. Sanctuary. His hand passed repeatedly over her hair in the gentlest of caresses, and she heard him murmur in his dark-angel voice, 'Rest, my love. I'm watching over you.'

CHAPTER 6

Although Sebastian was eager to reach London and take stock of his new circumstances, he did not regret his decision to travel more slowly on their return route. Evie had become pale and uncommunicative by nightfall, her reserves of strength depleted after the ardors of the past few days. She needed rest.

Finding a suitable coaching inn at which they could spend the night, Sebastian paid for the best room available and requested food and a hot bath to be sent up immediately. Evie bathed in a small slipper tub, while Sebastian made arrangements for a change of horses in the morning and saw to it that the driver received lodging. Returning to the room, which was small but clean, with somewhat threadbare blue curtain panels covering the windows, Sebastian discovered that his wife had finished her bath and was dressed in her nightgown.

He wandered to the table, lifted the napkin that covered his plate, and discovered a portion of roast chicken, a few wilted root vegetables, and a small pudding. Noting that Evie's plate was empty, he glanced at her with a wry smile. 'How was it?'

'Better than no supper at all.'

'I will confess to having a new appreciation for the talents of my London chef.' He sat at the rickety table and draped a fresh napkin over his lap. 'I think you will find his creations to your liking.'

'I don't expect that I will have many meals at your home,' Evie said guardedly.

Sebastian paused with his fork poised halfway to his mouth.

'I will be staying at my father's club,' Evie continued. 'As I told you before, I intend to take care of him.'

'During the day, yes. But you won't stay there at night. You'll return in the evenings to my . . . *our* . . . house.'

She regarded him with an unblinking stare. 'His illness won't go away at nightfall and resume at daybreak. He will need constant care.'

Sebastian shoved a bite of food into his mouth as he replied irritably. 'That's what servants are for. You may hire a woman to care for him.'

Evie shook her head with a stubborn firmness that further annoyed him. 'That isn't the same as being nursed by a loving relative.'

'Why should you give a damn about the quality of his care? Precious little he's done for you. You hardly know the bastard—'

'I don't like that word.'

'That's a pity. Because it's one of my favorites, and I intend to keep using it whenever it applies.'

'Then it is fortunate we will see each other so seldom after we return to London.'

Glaring at his wife, whose sweet face concealed an unexpectedly mulish disposition, Sebastian was reminded that she was willing to take drastic measures to get what she wanted. The devil knew what she would do if he pushed her too hard. Forcing his hands to relax on the handles of his knife and fork, he resumed eating. It didn't matter that the chicken was tasteless. Had it been swathed in the most delectable French sauce, he still wouldn't have noticed it. His crafty mind was busy sorting through strategies to deal with her.

Finally, adopting an expression of kind concern, he murmured, 'My love, I can't allow you to stay at a place filled with thieves, gamblers and drunkards. Surely you see the inherent dangers in such a situation.'

'I will make certain that you receive my dowry as quickly as possible. And then you won't have to worry about me.'

His self-control, always so solid, evaporated like hot water on a stove plate. 'I'm not worried about you, damn it! It's just – holy hell, it's *not done*, Evie. The Viscountess St Vincent can't live in a gaming club, even for a few days.'

'I didn't realize you were so conventional,' she said, and for some reason the sight of his ferocious scowl elicited a twitch of amusement at the corners of her lips. Subtle as the twitch was, Sebastian saw it, and he was instantly thrown from anger to bemusement. He would be damned if he would be put through a wringer by a twenty-three-year-old virgin . . . near-virgin . . . who was so naive as to believe that she was any kind of match for him.

His gaze of icy contempt should have withered her. 'In your fantasy of playing ministering angel, sweet, just who did you imagine would protect you in that place? Sleeping there alone at night is an invitation to be raped. And I'll be damned if I stay there with you – I have better things to do than sit in a second-rate gambling palace and wait for old Jenner to turn up his toes.'

'I haven't asked you to watch over me,' she replied in a level tone. 'I'll manage quite well without you.'

'Of course you will,' Sebastian muttered sarcastically, suddenly losing interest in the cold supper before him. Tossing his napkin over the half-finished plate, he stood from the table and removed his coat and waistcoat. He was dusty and travel-weary, and he intended to make use of the slipper bath. With any luck the water would still be warm.

As he undressed and threw each garment over the chair, he couldn't help but think of all the women who had wanted to marry him over the years – beautiful and well endowed, both physically and financially – they would have done anything short of murder to please him. He had been far too busy with his rakish pursuits to consider offering for any of them. And now, through a combination of circumstances and bad timing, he had ended up wedded to a socially awkward creature with an unsavory bloodline and an obstinate temperament.

Noticing the way Evie had averted her gaze from the sight of his naked body, Sebastian felt a sneer twist his lips. He went to the tiny folding tub and lowered himself into the lukewarm water, his long legs straddled on either side of it. Washing himself idly, sluicing his soapy chest and arms with great handfuls of water, he watched his wife with narrowed eyes. He was pleased to observe that some of her composure had vanished as he bathed. Her color heightened as she took an undue interest in the pattern of the quilted counterpane on the bed.

As she traced a pattern of stitches with her fore-finger, the gleam of the Scottish-gold ring caught Sebastian's eye. He experienced a strange reaction to the sight, a nearly overwhelming urge to go over to her, shove her back on the bed, and take her without preliminaries. To dominate her, and force her to admit his ownership. The rush of primal lust was more than a bit alarming to a man who had always considered himself civilized. Troubled and inflamed, he finished washing, snatched up the damp length of toweling that she had used, and dried himself efficiently. The sight of his arousal did not escape Evie's notice – he heard her quick intake of breath from across the room. Casually he wrapped the toweling around his waist and tucked in the loose end as he went to his trunk.

He rummaged for a comb, took it to the washstand, and ruthlessly tugged the comb through his wet locks. The corner of the looking glass atop the washstand revealed a partial view of the bed, and he saw that Evie was watching him.

Without turning, he murmured, 'Am I to be a butcher's dog tonight?'

'Butcher's dog?' Evie repeated in confusion.

'The dog who lies in the corner of the shop and is not allowed to have any meat.'

'That comparison is hardly a c-compliment to either of us.'

There was a nearly imperceptible pause in his combing as Sebastian registered the return of the stammer. Good, he thought callously. She was not nearly as composed as she pretended to be. 'Are you going to answer my question?'

'I . . . I'm sorry, but I would pr-prefer not to have intimate relations with you again.'

Stunned and offended, Sebastian set down his comb and turned to face her. Women never refused him. And the fact that Evie could do so after the pleasures of this morning was difficult to comprehend.

'You told me that you didn't like to bed a woman more than once,' Evie reminded him half apologetically. 'You said it would be a crashing bore.'

'Do I look bored to you?' he demanded, the towel doing little to conceal the outline of a roaring erection.

'I suppose that depends on which part of you one is looking at,' Evie mumbled, dropping her gaze to the counterpane. 'I needn't remind you, my lord, that w-w-we had an agreement.'

'You're allowed to change your mind.'

'I won't, however.'

'Your refusal smacks of hypocrisy, pet. I've already had you once. Does it really make any difference to your virtue if we do it again?'

'I am not refusing you for the sake of virtue.' Her stammer disappeared as she regained her composure. 'I have an entirely different reason.'

'I'm all agog to hear it.'

'Self-protection.' With obvious effort, Evie brought her gaze to his. 'I have no objection if you choose to have paramours. It's just that I don't want to be one of them. The sexual act means nothing to you, but it does mean something to me. I have no desire to be hurt by you, and I think that would be inevitable if I agreed to keep sleeping with you.'

As he struggled to maintain his surface calm, Sebastian's insides stewed with a mixture of desire and resentment. 'I won't apologize for my past. A man is *supposed* to have experience.'

'From all indications, you've acquired enough for ten men.'

'Why should that matter to you?'

'Because your . . . your romantic history, to put it politely, is like that of a dog who goes to every back door on the street, collecting scraps at every threshold. And I won't be one more door. You can't be faithful to one woman – you've proven that.'

'Just because I've never tried doesn't mean that I can't, you judgmental bitch! It simply means that I haven't wanted to.'

The word 'bitch' caused Evie to stiffen. 'I wish you wouldn't use such foul language.'

'It seemed appropriate, given the proliferation of dog analogies,' Sebastian snapped. 'Which, by the way, is an inaccurate characterization in my case, because women beg *me* for it, and not the other way around.'

'Then you should go to one of them.'

'Oh, I will,' he said savagely. 'When we return to London, I'm going to embark on a spree of orgiastic debauchery that won't end until someone is arrested for it. But in the meanwhile . . . do you truly expect that the two of us are going to share a bed tonight – and tomorrow night – as chastely as a pair of nuns on holiday?'

'That will pose no difficulty for me,' Evie said gingerly, conscious that she was delivering an insult of the highest order.

His incredulous glare should have burned a hole in the bed linens. Muttering a string of words that extended her forbidden-profanity list to a considerable degree, Sebastian dropped the towel and went to turn down the lamp. Aware of her uneasy gaze straying to his rampant arousal, Sebastian shot her a scornful glance. 'Pay it no mind,' he said, climbing into bed with her. 'From now on, I have every expectation that proximity to you will affect my private parts like a prolonged swim in a Siberian lake.'

CHAPTER 7

The weather improved substantially during their journey back to London, with the rain finally disappearing. However, the warming temperatures outside the coach were offset by the degree of frostiness that had developed between the newly-weds inside. Although Sebastian grudgingly kept the foot warmer filled, there were no more invitations for Evie to snuggle in his arms or sleep against his chest. She knew it was for the best. The more she became acquainted with him, the more convinced Evie was that any closeness between them would result in disaster. He was dangerous to her in ways that even he wasn't aware of.

She reassured herself with the knowledge that as soon as they arrived in town, they would more or less part company. She would stay at the club, and he would go to his house and continue his usual pursuits until he received word of her father's death. At that time, it was likely that he would want to sell the club and use the proceeds, along with the rest of her inheritance, to replenish his family's empty coffers.

The thought of selling Jenner's, which had been the center of her father's life, gave Evie a feeling of melancholy. However, it would be the most sensible course of action. Few men possessed the ability to run a gaming club successfully. Its owner had to possess the magnetism to lure people into the club, and the artful shrewdness to find ways to make them stay and spend great quantities of money. Not to mention the business sense to invest the profits wisely.

Ivo Jenner had possessed the first two qualities in moderation, but the third not at all. In the recent past he had lost a fortune at Newmarket, having become susceptible in his old age to the glib-tongued rogues who populated the racing world. Fortunately the club was such a powerful financial engine that it was able to absorb the heavy losses.

Sebastian's unkind taunt that Jenner's was a second-rate gambling palace was only partially correct. Evie knew from past conversations with her father, who had never bothered to mince words, that although his club was successful by anyone's standards, it had never reached the heights to which he had aspired. He had wanted it to equal Craven's, the rival club that had burned down so long ago. But Ivo Jenner had never been able to match the flair and devilish guile of Derek Craven. It was said that Craven had won the money of an entire generation of Englishmen. That Craven's had disappeared at its zenith had solidified its legendary status in the collective memory of British society.

And while Jenner's had not come close to the glory of Craven's, it had not been for a lack of trying. Ivo Jenner had moved his own club from Covent Garden to King Street, which had once been a mere passageway into the fashionable shopping and residential area of St James, but was now a regular roadway. After purchasing a large portion of the street and razing four buildings, Jenner had built a large and handsome club and advertised it as having the largest hazard bank in London. When gentlemen wished to play deep, they went to Jenner's.

Evie remembered the club from her childhood, on the occasions when she had been allowed to visit her father for the day. It had been a well-appointed, if somewhat over-elaborate place, and she had delighted in standing with him on the second-floor interior balcony and watching the action on the main floor. Grinning indulgently, Jenner would walk his daughter to St James Street, where they would go to any shop she cared to visit. They went to the perfumer, the hatter's, the book and print seller, and the bread and biscuit baker, who gave Evie a hot cross bun so fresh that the white piping of icing was half melting from the surface of the warm bread.

As the years passed, Evie's visits to King Street had been curtailed. Although she had always blamed the Maybricks for it, she now realized that her father had also been partly responsible. It had been much easier for Jenner to love her as a child, when he could make her squeal by tossing her in the air and catching her in his burly arms. He could rumple her red hair, the same shade as his own, and soothe her tears upon leaving him by pressing a sweet or a shilling into her palm. But when she became a young woman, and he could no longer treat her like a little girl, their relationship had become awkward and distant. 'This club's no place for you, tibby,' he had told her with gruff fondness. 'You has to stay away from a milling cove like me, and find some rum cull to marry.'

'Papa,' she had begged, stammering desperately, 'd-don't send me back there. Pl-please, please let me stay with you.'

'Little tangle-tongue, you belong with the Maybricks. And no use to hop the twig and run back here. I'll only send you off again.'

Her tears had failed to sway him. During the ensuing years, Evie's visits to her father's club had dwindled to once every six months, or longer. Whether or not it was for her own good, the sense of being unwanted had sunk deep into her marrow. She had become so uneasy around men, so certain that they would be bored by her, that it had become a self-fulfilling prophecy. Her stammer worsened – the harder she fought to get the words out, the more incoherent she had become, until it was easiest to remain silent and fade into the woodwork. She had become an expert at being a wallflower. She had never been asked to dance, never been kissed, never been teased or courted. The only proposal she had ever received had been cousin Eustace's reluctant offer.

Marveling at her change in fortune, Evie glanced at her husband, who had brooded silently during the past two hours. His eyes narrowed as he looked back at her. With his cold expression and cynical mouth, he seemed completely unlike the seductive scoundrel who had shared a bed with her two days earlier.

She turned her attention to the window as the scenery of London passed by her. Soon they would be at the club, and she would see her father. It had been six months since they had been together, and Evie had braced herself for a great change in him. Consumption was a common disease, and everyone was aware of its ravages.

It was a slow death of lung tissue, accompanied by fever, coughing, weight loss, and drenching sweats at night. When death arrived, it was usually welcomed by the victim, and all those who cared for him, as an end to the terrible suffering. Evie could not imagine her robust father being reduced to such a condition. She feared seeing him equally as much as she yearned to care for him. However, she kept this all to herself, suspecting that Sebastian would only mock her if she told him of her fears.

Her pulse quickened as the carriage rolled along St James and turned onto King Street. The long brick and marble front of Jenner's became visible, silhouetted against the yellows and reds of a ripening sunset that glowed through the ever-present haze that hung over London. Staring through the carriage window, Evie let out a tense sigh as the vehicle passed through one of the many alleys that led from the main thoroughfare to the mews and yards behind the row of buildings.

The carriage came to a halt at the back entrance, which was far preferable to entering through the front of the building. Jenner's was not a place that nice women frequented. A gentleman might bring his mistress, or even a prostitute who had captured his passing interest, but he would never think of escorting a respectable lady into the club. Evie became aware that Sebastian was watching her with the dispassionate interest of an entomologist observing a new species of beetle. Her sudden paleness and her visible trembling could not have escaped his notice, but he offered no word or gesture of comfort.

Preceding her from the carriage, Sebastian fitted his hands around Evie's waist and helped her down to the ground. The smell of the back alley was the same as it had been since Evie's childhood – manure, garbage, liquor, and the crisp overlay of coal smoke. No doubt she was the only young woman of privileged upbringing in London to think that it smelled rather like home. At least it struck her nostrils more agreeably than the atmosphere at the Maybrick house, which was redolent of rotting carpets and bad cologne.

Wincing at the ache of muscles that had been cramped in the carriage for far too long, Evie went to the doorway. Entrances to the kitchen and other service rooms were located farther along the building, but this one opened to a staircase that went up to her father's apartments. The driver had already summoned a club employee with a few decisive pounds of his fist at the door, and stepped back perfunctorily.

A young man appeared, and Evie was relieved to see a face that she recognized. It was Joss Bullard, a long-familiar figure at the club, who had worked there as a debt collector and an usher. He was large, stocky, and dark-haired, with a bullet-shaped head and a heavy jaw. Possessing a natural inclination toward surliness, Bullard had treated Evie with a bare minimum of courtesy whenever she had visited the club. However, she had heard her father praise him for his loyalty, and for that she was appreciative.

'Mr Bullard,' she said, 'I've c-come to see my father. Please allow me i-i-inside.'

The burly young man did not move. ''E 'asn't asked for you,' he said gruffly. He switched his gaze to Sebastian, taking note of his expensive garments. 'Go to the front, sir, if you're a member.'

'Idiot,' Evie heard Sebastian mutter, and before he could continue, Evie interrupted hastily.

'Is Mr Egan available at pr-present?' she asked, naming the club's factotum, who had worked for her father for the past ten years. She had no great liking for Egan, who was a boastful, blustering sort, but he wouldn't dare refuse her entrance to her own father's club.

'Nay.'

'Then Mr Rohan,' Evie said desperately. 'Please tell him that M-Miss Jenner is here.'

'I told ye—'

'Get Rohan,' Sebastian snapped at the young man, and wedged his boot against the door to prevent it from being closed. 'We'll wait inside. My wife isn't going to be kept standing out on the street.'

Looking startled by the cold gleam in the taller man's eyes, the employee muttered his assent and disappeared swiftly.

Sebastian guided Evie over the threshold and glanced at the nearby staircase. 'Shall we go upstairs?'

She shook her head. 'I would rather speak to Mr Rohan first, actually. I'm sure he'll be able to tell me something about my father's c-condition.'

At the sound of her slight stammer, Sebastian lifted his hand to the nape of her neck, slid it beneath her untidy hair, and squeezed gently. Though his face was still cold, his hand was warm and soothing, and she felt herself relax involuntarily. 'Who is Rohan?'

'He's one of the croupiers . . . he has been employed here since he was a boy. My father started him as a listmaker's runner. You would

101

remember Mr Rohan, if you've seen him before. He is rather difficult to overlook.'

Sebastian pondered the remark and murmured, 'He's the Gypsy, isn't he?'

'Half Gypsy, I believe, on his mother's side.'

'What is the other half?'

'No one knows.' She threw him a guarded glance as she said quietly, 'I've always wondered if he might be my half brother.'

Interest flickered in his pale eyes. 'Did you ever ask your father?'

'Yes. He denied it.' However, Evie had never been quite convinced. Her father had always demonstrated a vaguely paternal manner with Cam. And she was not so naive as to believe that he hadn't sired a few illegitimate children. He was a man of renowned physical appetites, and moreover he had never been one to worry over the consequences of his actions. Wondering if the same could be said of her husband, she asked cautiously, 'Sebastian, have you ever . . .'

'Not that I'm aware of,' he said, understanding immediately. 'I've always been inclined to use French letters – not only to prevent conception, but also to avoid the more exotic ailments that afflict the unwary.'

Bewildered by the statement, Evie murmured. 'French letters? What are those? And what do you mean, ailments? Do you mean that doing . . . *that* . . . could make one ill? But how—'

'Good God,' Sebastian muttered, his fingers

touching her mouth to still the questions. 'I'll explain later. It's not the kind of thing one likes to discuss on the doorstep.'

Evie was prevented from asking further questions by the appearance of Cam Rohan. As Cam saw Evie, a faint smile came to his face, and he bowed gracefully. Even when Cam's manner and movements were restrained, there seemed to be an invisible flourish, a suggestion of physical charisma. He was by far the best croupier at Jenner's, though his appearance – that of a boy pirate – would hardly lead one to think so at first. He was about twenty-five, his body imbued with the slimness of young adulthood. The swarthy hue of his skin and the inky blackness of his hair betrayed his heritage, not to mention his first name, which was common for a Romany. Evie had always liked the soft-spoken young man, whose fierce loyalty to her father had been demonstrated numerous times over the years.

Cam was well-dressed in dark clothes and polished shoes, but as usual his hair wanted cutting, the thick black locks curling over the crisp white edge of his collar. And his long, lean fingers were adorned with a few gold rings. As his head lifted, Evie saw the glitter of a diamond stud in one ear – an exotic touch that suited him. Cam regarded her with the remarkable golden-hazel eyes that often lulled people into forgetting about the nimble mind behind them. At times his gaze was so penetrating that he seemed to be looking right through you . . . as if he were watching something behind you.

'*Gadji*,' Cam said softly, a friendly use of the Romany name for a non-Gypsy woman. He had an unusual accent, cultured, but tainted with hints of cockney and a sort of foreign rhythm, all blended in a unique mixture. 'Welcome,' he said with a brief but dazzling smile. 'Your father will be pleased to see you.'

'Thank you, Cam. I . . . I was afraid he might already h-have—'

'No,' Cam murmured, his smile dimming. 'He is still alive.' He hesitated before adding, 'Most of the time he sleeps. He won't eat. I don't think it will be long. He's asked for you. I tried to send for you, but—'

'The Maybricks wouldn't allow it,' Evie half whispered, her mouth tightening with anger. They had not bothered to tell her that her father had asked for her. And Joss Bullard had just lied to her. 'Well, I'm away fr-from them for good, Cam. I've married. And I will remain here until my father . . . no longer n-n-needs me.'

Cam's gaze swerved to Sebastian's implacable countenance. Recognition kindled, and he murmured, 'Lord St Vincent.' If he had an opinion about Evie's union with such a man, he did not reveal it.

Evie touched the surface of Cam's coat sleeve. 'Is my father awake now?' she asked anxiously. 'May I go up to see him?'

'Of course.' The Gypsy took both her hands in a light grip, the gold rings warmed by the liberal heat of his fingers. 'I will see to it that no one interferes.'

'Thank you.'

Suddenly Sebastian reached between them and plucked one of Evie's hands away, pulling it decisively to his own arm. Though his manner was casual, the firm pressure of his fingers ensured that she would not try to pull away.

Puzzled by the display of possessiveness, Evie frowned. 'I have known Cam since childhood,' she said pointedly. 'He has always been quite kind to me.'

'A husband always likes to hear of kindnesses done for his wife,' Sebastian replied coolly. 'Within limits, of course.'

'Of course,' Cam said softly. His attention returned to Evie. 'Shall I show you upstairs, milady?'

She shook her head. 'No, I know the way. Please r-return to what you were doing.'

Cam bowed again and exchanged a swift glance with Evie, both of them acknowledging tacitly that they would find an opportunity to talk later.

'Do you dislike him because he's a Rom?' Evie asked her husband as they went to the stairs.

'I rarely dislike people for things they can't change,' Sebastian replied sardonically. 'They usually give me sufficient cause to dislike them for other reasons.'

Her hand fell away from his arm as she picked up her skirts.

'Where is the factotum, I wonder?' Sebastian continued, setting a palm at the small of her back as they ascended the stairs. 'It's early evening. The hazard room and the dining room are open – he should be busy.'

'He drinks,' Evie commented.

'That explains a great deal about the way this club is run.'

Sensitive to any insult about her father's club, and uncomfortably aware of the gentle pressure of his hand on her back, Evie had to bite her tongue to hold back a stinging reply. How easy it was for a pampered nobleman to criticize the way professional men did things. If he had to run a place like this himself – perish the thought – he might have a great deal more respect for what her father had accomplished.

They climbed to the second level and proceeded along a second-floor gallery that wrapped completely around the upper part of the room. One had only to look over the balcony railings to view all the action of the main floor. This, the largest area of the club, was devoted entirely to hazard. Three oval tables covered with green baize cloth and yellow markings were surrounded by dozens of men. The sounds that floated upward – the constant rattle of dice, the quiet but intense exclamations of the casters and the croupiers, the soft drag of the little wooden rakes as they pulled money from the table into the croupier's hands – they were among some of Evie's earliest childhood recollections. She glanced at the magnificent carved desk in the corner of the room where her father had sat, approving credit, granting temporary memberships, and raising the hazard bank if the play had been too deep. At the moment the desk was occupied by a man of rather seedy appearance whom she did not know. Her gaze moved to the opposite corner of the room, where another stranger acted as general supervisor, regulating payments and overseeing the pace of the play.

Pausing at the railing, Sebastian looked down at the main floor with an oddly intent expression. Wanting to go to her father at once, Evie gave an impatient tug at his arm. However, Sebastian did not budge. In fact, he barely seemed to notice her, so absorbed was he in the activities taking place downstairs. 'What is it?' Evie asked. 'Do you see something unusual? Something wrong?'

Sebastian shook his head slightly and dragged his attention from the main floor. His gaze moved around them, taking in the faded painted panels on the walls, the chipped molding, the threadbare piling of the carpeting. Jenner's had once been splendidly decorated, but as the years had passed, it had lost much of its luster. 'How many members of the club are there?' he asked. 'Excluding temporary memberships.'

'There used to be something like two thousand,'

Evie replied. 'I don't know what the current figures are.' She tugged at his arm again. 'I want to see my father. If I must go unaccompanied—'

'You're not to go *anywhere* unaccompanied,' Sebastian said, focusing on her with an bright immediacy that startled her. His eyes were like polished moon-stones. 'You could be pulled into one of the bawdy rooms by some top-heavy drunkard – or an employee, for that matter – and raped before anyone realizes you're missing.'

'I'm perfectly safe here,' she countered with annoyance. 'I am still acquainted with many of the employees, and I know my way around the club better than you do.'

'Not for long,' Sebastian murmured, and his gaze returned almost compulsively to the main floor. 'I'm going to go over every inch of this place. I'm going to know all its secrets.'

Taken aback by the statement, Evie gave him a perplexed glance. She realized that subtle changes had taken place in him from the moment they had entered the club . . . she was at a loss to account for his strange reaction. His customary languid manner had been replaced by a new alertness, as if he were absorbing the restless energy of the club's atmosphere.

'You are staring at the club as if you'd never seen it before,' she murmured.

Sebastian ran his hand along the balcony railing experimentally, regarded the smudge of dust on his palm, and brushed it off. His expression was contemplative rather than critical as he replied, 'It looks different now that it's mine.'

'It's not yours yet,' Evie replied darkly, realizing that he must be assessing the value of the place for its future sale. How like him to think of money while her father lay on his deathbed. 'Do you ever think of anyone other than yourself?'

The question seemed to pull him out of his absorption, and his face became inscrutable. 'Rarely, my love.'

They stared at each other, Evie's eyes accusing, Sebastian's opaque, and she understood that to expect any decency from him was to invite recurring disappointment. His ruined soul could not be repaired by her kindness and understanding. He would never become one of the reformed rakes that were featured in Daisy Bowman's trove of scandalous novels.

'I expect that you'll get everything you want quite soon,' she said coldly. 'In the meantime, I'm going to my father's room.' She started off along the gallery without him, and in a few long strides he fell into step beside her.

By the time they reached the private apartments that Ivo Jenner occupied, Evie's blood was rustling madly in her ears. Equal parts of fear and longing caused her palms to dampen and her stomach to turn hollow. As she reached for the doorknob to the suite of rooms, her palm slipped on the tarnished brass.

'Allow me,' Sebastian said brusquely, brushing

her hand aside. He opened the door and held it for her, and followed her into the dark receiving room. The only light came from the open doorway of the bedroom, where a small lamp gave off an indifferent glow. Evie went through the next threshold and paused, blinking until her eyes adjusted to the shadowy atmosphere. Barely aware of the presence of the man beside her, she approached the bed.

Her father was sleeping, mouth slightly open, his skin pale and glowing with a peculiar delicacy, as if he were a wax figure. Deep lines crossed his face, giving his cheeks the appearance of window shutters. He was half the size he had once been, his arms astonishingly thin, his form shrunken. Evie struggled to reconcile the unfamiliar, slight form on the bed with the big, burly father she had always known. Grief-stricken tenderness flooded her as she saw his red hair, now heavily mixed with silver, standing up in places on his head as if it were a baby bird's ruffled feathers.

The room smelled of burned candle wicks, medicine, and unwashed skin. It smelled of sickness and approaching death. She saw a pile of dirty bedclothes in the corner, and a litter of crumpled bloodstained handkerchiefs on the floor. The night table was covered with a collection of dirty spoons and colored glass medicine bottles. Evie bent to pick up some of the soiled articles on the floor, but Sebastian caught her by the arm. 'You don't have to do that,' he muttered. 'One of the house-maids can see to it.'

'Yes,' Evie whispered bitterly. 'I see what a fine job they've been doing.' Jerking her arm away from his, she snatched up the dirty handkerchiefs and went to drop them into the pile of discarded bed linens.

Sebastian wandered to the bedside and glanced down at Jenner's wasted form. He picked up one of the medicine bottles, passed it beneath his nose, and murmured, 'Morphine.'

For some reason it provoked Evie to see him standing near her helpless father and examining his medicine. 'I have things in hand,' she said in a low voice. 'I wish you would leave now.'

'What do you intend to do?'

'I'm going to straighten the room and change the bed linens. And then I'm going to sit by him.'

The pale blue eyes narrowed. 'Let the poor devil sleep. You need to eat, and change from your traveling clothes. What good do you think it will do him, for you to sit in the dark and—' He broke off with a muttered curse as he saw her obstinate expression. 'Very well. I'll give you one hour, and then you will share a meal with me.'

'I intend to stay with my father,' she said flatly.

'Evie.' His voice was soft, but it contained an inflexible note that caused her nerves to prickle in warning. Approaching her, he turned her rigid body to face him, and gave her the slightest hint of a shake, forcing her to look up at him. 'When I send for you, you'll come. Is that understood?'

Evie felt herself quiver with outrage. He issued the command as if he owned her. Good God, she had spent her entire life so far having to obey the edicts of her aunts and uncles, and now she would have to submit to her husband.

However . . . to give him his due, Sebastian still had a long way to go before he could equal the combined efforts of the Maybricks and Stubbinses to make Evie's life miserable. And he was hardly being unreasonable or cruel in demanding that she take a meal with him. Swallowing back her anger, Evie managed a nod. As his gaze moved over her strained features, there was an odd gleam in his eyes, like the sparks struck from a black-smith's hammer as it met a sheet of molten metal.

'Good girl,' he murmured with a mocking smile, and left the room.

CHAPTER 8

Sebastian was briefly tempted to leave Evie at the club and go to his own household, which was walking distance of St James. The lure of his quiet home, with its modern plumbing and well-stocked pantry and larder, was difficult to resist. He wanted to eat at his own table, and relax before the hearth dressed in one of the velvet-lined silk robes that hung in his bedroom armoire. To hell with his stubborn wife – she could make her own decisions and learn to live with the consequences.

However, as he wandered discreetly around the second-floor gallery, taking care to avoid being seen by those on the busy main floor, Sebastian was aware of a nagging curiosity that would not be denied. With his hands tucked negligently in his coat pockets, he leaned against a column. He watched the croupiers at work and noticed the indifferent efforts of the general supervisor to oversee the play and keep everything moving at a satisfactory pace. Activity at all three hazard tables seemed a bit sluggish. Someone needed to stir things up and create an atmosphere that would urge the guests into deeper, faster play.

Slovenly house wenches sauntered lazily through the room, pausing to interact with the male guests. Like the meals at the dining hall sideboard and the coffee room downstairs, the women were a free benefit of membership. Whether a man needed a wench for consolation or for celebration, the prostitutes would accompany him to one of several upstairs rooms reserved for this purpose.

Wandering down to the ground-floor card rooms and coffee room, Sebastian surveyed his surroundings. There were small but prolific signs that it was a business in decay. Sebastian guessed that when Jenner had fallen ill, he had failed to appoint a reliable replacement for himself. His factotum, Clive Egan, was either inept or dishonest, or both. Sebastian wanted to see the account books, the records of expense and profit, the private financial records of the members, rent rolls, mortgages, debts, loans, credit – everything that would contribute to a complete portrait of the club's health. Or lack thereof.

As he turned back to the staircase, he saw the Gypsy, Rohan, waiting in the shadowy corner, his posture relaxed. Sebastian remained strategically silent, forcing the boy to speak first.

Rohan held his stare as he said with meticulous politeness, 'May I help you, milord?'

'You can start by telling me where Egan is.'

'He's in his room, milord.'

'In what condition?'

'Indisposed.'

'Ah,' Sebastian said softly. 'Is he often indisposed, Rohan?'

The Gypsy remained silent, but his steady, sloe-eyed gaze was filled with speculation.

'I want the key to his office,' Sebastian said. 'I want to have a look at the account ledgers.'

'There is only one key, milord,' Rohan replied, studying him. 'And Mr Egan always keeps it with him.'

'Then get it for me.'

The boy's heavy dark brows lifted a fraction. 'You want me to rob a man when he is drunk?'

'It's a hell of a lot easier than waiting until he's sober,' Sebastian pointed out sardonically. 'And it's not robbery when the key is, for all intents and purposes, mine.'

Rohan's young face hardened. 'My loyalty is to Mr Jenner. And his daughter.'

'So is mine.' That wasn't true, of course. The majority of Sebastian's loyalty was reserved for himself. Evie and her father were, respectively, a distant second and third on the list. 'Get me the key, or prepare to follow in Egan's footsteps when he departs on the morrow.'

The air was charged with masculine challenge. However, after a moment, Rohan gave him a look of distaste mingled with reluctant curiosity. When he acceded, and moved toward the staircase with long, fluid strides, it was not out of fearful obedience, but rather out of the desire to observe what Sebastian would do next.

By the time Sebastian had dispatched Cam Rohan to bring Evie downstairs, she had straightened her father's room and enlisted the grudging help of a housemaid to change the bed linens. The sheets were damp from night sweats. Though her father stirred and muttered as they carefully rolled him to one side and then the other, he did not awaken from his morphine-induced stupor. His rawboned body, swamped in the folds of his nightshirt, startled Evie with its lightness. Anguished pity and protectiveness filled her as she drew the new linens and blankets up to his chest. Dampening a cool cloth, she laid it over his forehead. A sigh escaped him, and at last his eyes opened into dark, shiny slits amid the furrows of his face. He regarded her without comprehension for a long moment, until a smile stretched his cracked lips, revealing the edges of tobacco-varnished teeth.

'Evie,' came his low croak.

Leaning over him, Evie smiled while the inside of her nose stung and her eyes ached with unshed tears. 'I'm here, Papa,' she whispered, saying the words she had longed to say for her entire life. 'I'm here, and I'm never going to leave you again.'

He made a sound of contentment and closed his eyes. Just as Evie thought he had fallen asleep, he murmured, 'Where shall we walk first today, lovey? The biscuit baker, I s'pose . . .'

Realizing that he imagined this was one of her long-ago childhood visits, Evie replied softly, 'Oh yes.' Hastily she knuckled away the excess moisture from her eyes. 'I want an iced bun . . . and a cone of broken biscuits . . . and then I want to come back here and play dice with you.'

A rusty chuckle came from his ravaged throat, and he coughed a little. 'Let Papa take forty winks before we leaves . . . there's a good girl . . .'

'Yes, sleep,' Evie murmured, turning the cloth over on his forehead. 'I can wait, Papa.'

As she watched him slip back into his drugged slumber, she swallowed against the sharp pain in her throat and relaxed in the bedside chair. There was no other place in the world that she wanted to be. She let herself slump a little, her sore shoulders lowering as if she were a marionette whose strings had been released. This was the first time that she had ever felt needed, that her presence had ever seemed to matter to someone. And though her father's condition grieved her, she was grateful that she could be with him for the last hours of his life. It wasn't nearly enough time to come to know him – they would always be strangers to each other – but it was more than she had ever hoped to have.

Her thoughts were interrupted by a tap on the doorjamb. She glanced up to see Cam at the threshold. His arms were loosely folded over his chest, his body arranged in a posture of deceptive leisure. Evie gave him a tired imitation of a smile. 'I s-suppose he has sent you to collect me?'

There was, of course, no need to define who 'he' was. 'He wants you to eat with him in one of the private dining rooms.'

Evie shook her head slightly, her smile turning wry. 'I hear and obey,' she muttered in a parody of an obedient wife. Standing, she paused to straighten the blankets over her sleeping father's shoulders.

Cam didn't move from the doorway as she approached him. He was taller than the average man, though not quite so much as Sebastian. 'How did you end up wedded to Lord St Vincent?' he asked. 'I know of his financial problems – we were nearly at the point of refusing him credit the last time he was here. Did he come to you with the idea of a marriage bargain?'

'How do you know it isn't a love match?' Evie parried.

He gave her a wry glance. 'The only love match is between St Vincent and himself.'

The pressure of a real smile worked up to Evie's lips, and she made a stern effort to hold it back. 'I w-went to him, actually. It was the only way I could think of to escape the Maybricks for good.' Her smile vanished at the thought of her relations. 'Did they come here after I went missing, Cam?'

He nodded. 'Both your uncles. We had to let them search the club themselves before they were satisfied that you weren't hiding here.'

'Drat,' Evie muttered, borrowing Daisy Bowman's favorite curse word. 'They'll have gone next to my fr-friends, I suspect. The Hunts, and the Bowmans. The news that I've gone missing will worry them.' However, learning the truth of what she had done would worry them far more. Distractedly she smoothed back the straggles of her hair and wrapped her arms around herself. She would have to send word to Annabelle and Daisy that she was all right. Since Lillian was traveling on the continent, she would not have heard the news of Evie's disappearance.

Tomorrow, she thought. Tomorrow she would deal with the repercussions of her soon-to-be-infamous elopement. She wondered if she dared send someone to the Maybrick home to fetch the rest of her clothes . . . or if there was any chance that they would let her have them. Probably not. More things for her ever-lengthening list of things to be done . . . she would have to have some day dresses and shoes made in short order.

'Once m-my relations discover that I'm here,' she said, 'they'll come to take me back. They may try to annul the marriage. I . . .' She paused to steady her voice. 'I very much fear what might happen to me if I am forced to go with them.'

'Won't St Vincent stop them?' Cam asked, reaching out to settle a calming hand on her shoulder. It was an innocuous point of contact, just the light weight of his palm resting on the fragile curve of her shoulder bone, but she took reassurance from it.

'If he is here at the time. If he's sober. If he's able.' She gave him a humorless smile. 'If and if . . .'

'I'll be here,' Cam murmured. 'I'll be sober, and able. Why don't you think St Vincent will be?'

'It's a marriage of convenience. I don't expect that we shall see very much of him once he collects my dowry. He told me that he has far better things to do than sit in a second-rate gambling club and wait for . . . for . . .' Hesitating, she glanced over her shoulder at her father's bed.

'He may have changed his mind about that,' Cam remarked sardonically. 'Once I let him have the key to the office, he pulled out every ledger and started poring over them page by page. By the time he's finished, he'll have gone through the entire club with a flea comb.'

Evie's eyes widened at the information. 'What could he be looking for?' she asked, more to herself than to him. Sebastian was behaving oddly. There was no reason for him to dive into the club's financial records with such urgency when they had just arrived from a long journey. Nothing would change between now and tomorrow. She thought of the compulsive quality of his gaze as they had watched the activity on the main floor, and his murmur . . . *I'm going to go over every inch of this place. I'm going to know all its secrets . . .* As if it were something more than a mere building filled with faded carpets and hazard tables.

Puzzled, Evie went with Cam through a series of back halls and passageways that provided the most direct route to the downstairs dining rooms. Like most gaming clubs, Jenner's had its share of secret places for hiding, for observing, for smuggling people and objects. Cam showed her to a small private room, held the door for her, and bowed as she turned to thank him.

Advancing farther into the room, Evie heard the door close quietly behind her. Sebastian was sprawled in a heavy armchair with the relaxed confidence of Lucifer on his throne, using a pencil lead to make notations in the margin of an account ledger. He sat at a table that was laden with plates from the sideboard in the main dining room.

Tearing his gaze from the ledger, Sebastian nudged it aside and stood, pulling the second chair away from the table. 'How is your father?'

Evie replied cautiously as she allowed him to seat her. 'He woke for just a moment. He seemed to think that I was a little girl again.' Seeing a platter piled with cuts of roast fowl, and another filled with hothouse peaches and grapes, she reached out to serve herself. Her overwhelming hunger, paired with weariness, caused her hands to tremble. Seeing her difficulty, Sebastian silently transferred choice tidbits onto her empty plate; tiny boiled quail eggs, a spoonful of creamed vegetable marrow, a slice of cheese, cold cuts and fish and soft bread.

'Thank you,' Evie said, nearly too tired to know what she was eating. She lifted her fork to her mouth, took a bite of something, and closed her eyes as she chewed and swallowed. When her lashes lifted, she found Sebastian's gaze on her.

He looked as weary as she felt, with faint smudges beneath his blue eyes. The skin over his cheekbones was taut, and he was pale beneath the sun-kissed tint of his complexion. His night beard, which was inclined to grow quickly, was a shadow of glittering golden stubble. Somehow the roughening of his looks made him even more handsome, lending a textured grace to what otherwise might have been the sterile perfection of a marble masterpiece.

'Are you still fixed on the notion of staying here?' he asked, deftly carving a peach and divesting it of the pit. He handed her a neat golden half.

'Oh yes.' Evie accepted the peach and took a bite, its tart juice trickling over her tongue.

'I was afraid you might say that,' he replied dryly. 'It's a mistake, you know. You have no idea of what you'll be exposed to . . . the obscenities and lewd comments, the lecherous gazes, the groping and pinching . . . and that's just at my house. Imagine what it would be like here.'

Uncertain whether to frown or smile, Evie regarded him curiously. 'I will manage,' she said.

'I'm sure you will, pet.'

Lifting a goblet of wine to her lips, Evie glanced at him over the rim as she drank. 'What is in that ledger?'

'A lesson in creative record keeping. I'm sure you won't be surprised to learn that Egan has been draining the club's accounts. He shaves away increments here and there, in small enough quantities that the thefts have gone unnoticed. But over time, it totals up to a considerable sum. God knows how many years he's been doing it. So far, every account book I've looked at contains deliberate inaccuracies.'

'How can you be certain that they're deliberate?'

'There is a clear pattern.' He flipped open a ledger and nudged it over to her. 'The club made a profit of approximately twenty thousand pounds last Tuesday. If you cross-check the numbers with the record of loans, bank deposits, and cash outlays, you'll see the discrepancies.'

Evie followed the trail of his finger as he ran it along the notes he had made in the margin. 'You see?' he murmured. 'These are what the proper amounts should be. He's padded the expenses liberally. The cost of ivory dice, for example. Even allowing for the fact that the dice are only used for one night and then never again, the annual charge should be no more than two thousand pounds, according to Rohan.' The practice of using fresh dice every night was standard for any gaming club, to ward off any question that they might be loaded.

'But here it says that almost three thousand pounds was spent on dice,' Evie murmured.

'Exactly.' Sebastian leaned back in his chair and smiled lazily. 'I deceived my father the same way in my depraved youth, when he paid my monthly upkeep and I had need of more ready coin than he was willing to provide.'

'What did you need it for?' Evie could not resist asking.

The smile tarried on his lips. 'I'm afraid the explanation would require a host of words to which you would take strong exception.'

Spearing a quail egg with her fork, Evie popped it into her mouth. 'What is to be done about Mr Egan?'

His shoulders lifted in a graceful shrug. 'As soon as he is sober enough to walk, he'll be dismissed.'

Evie brushed away a stray lock of hair that had fallen over her cheek. 'There is no one to replace him.'

'Yes, there is. Until a suitable manager can be found, I'll run the club.'

The quail egg seemed to stick in her throat, and Evie choked a little. Hastily she reached for her wine, washed it down, and regarded him with bulging eyes. How could he say something so preposterous? 'You can't.'

'I can hardly do worse than Egan. He hasn't managed a damned thing in months . . . before long, this place will be falling down around our ears.'

'You said you hated work!'

'So I did. But I feel that I should try it at least once, just to be certain.'

She began to stammer in her anxiety. 'You'll pl-play at this for a few days, and then you'll tire of it.'

'I can't afford to tire of it, my love. Although the club is still profitable, its value is in decline. Your father has a load of outstanding debt that must be settled. If the people who owe him can't muster the cash, we'll have to take property, jewelry, artwork . . . whatever they can manage. Having a good idea of the value of things, I can negotiate some acceptable settlements. And there are other problems I haven't yet mentioned . . . Jenner has a string of failing Thoroughbreds that have lost a fortune at Newmarket. And he's made some insane investments – ten thousand pounds he put into an alleged gold mine in Flintshire – a swindle that even a child should have seen through.'

'Oh God,' Evie murmured, rubbing her forehead. 'He's been ill – people have taken advantage—'

'Yes. And now, even if we wanted to sell the club, we couldn't without first putting it in order. If there were an alternative, believe me, I would find it. But this place is a sieve, with no one who is capable or willing to stop the holes. Except for me.'

'You know nothing about filling holes!' she cried, appalled by his arrogance.

Sebastian responded with a bland smile and the

slightest arch of one brow. Before he could open his mouth to reply, she clapped her hands over her ears. 'Oh, *don't* say it, don't!' When she saw that he was obligingly holding his silence – though a devilish gleam remained in his eyes – she lowered her hands cautiously. 'If you ran the club, where would you sleep?'

'Here, of course,' came his prosaic reply.

'I've taken the only available guest room,' she said. 'All the others are occupied. And I'm not going to share a bed with you.'

'There will be rooms aplenty tomorrow. I'm getting rid of the house wenches.'

The situation was changing too rapidly for her staggering brain to follow. Sebastian's assumption of authority over her father's business and all his employees was alarming in its speed. She had the unnerving feeling of having brought a tame cat into the club and seeing it transform into a rampaging tiger. And all she could do was watch helplessly as he proceeded to slaughter at will. Perhaps, she thought desperately, if she indulged him for a few days, he would tire of the novelty. In the meantime, she could only try to minimize the damage.

'You're just going to throw the h-house wenches out into the streets?' she asked with forced calm.

'They'll be dismissed with generous parting sums as a reward for their labors on the club's behalf.'

'Do you intend to hire new ones?'

Sebastian shook his head. 'While I have no moral aversion to the concept of prostitution – in fact, I'm all for it – I'm damned if I'll become known as a pimp.'

'A what?'

'A pimp. A cock bawd. A male procurer. For God's sake, did you have cotton wool stuffed in your ears as a child? Did you never hear anything, or wonder why badly dressed women were parading up and down the club staircase at all hours?'

'I always visited in the daytime,' Evie said with great dignity. 'I rarely saw them working. And later, when I was old enough to understand what they were doing, my father began to curtail my visits.'

'That was probably one of the few kind things he ever did for you.' Sebastian waved away the subject impatiently. 'Back to the subject at hand . . . not only do I *not* want the responsibility of maintaining mediocre whores, but we don't have the room to accommodate them. On any given night, when all the beds are occupied, the club members are forced to take their pleasures out in the stables.'

'They are? They do?'

'And it's damned scratchy and drafty in that stable. Take my word for it.'

'You—'

'However, there is an excellent brothel two streets over. I have every expectation that we can come to an arrangement with its proprietress, Madame Bradshaw. When one of our club members desires female companionship, he can walk to Bradshaw's, receive their services at a discounted price, and return here when he's refreshed.' He raised his brows significantly, as if he expected her to praise the idea. 'What do you think?'

'I think you would still be a cock bawd,' Evie said. 'Only by stealth.'

'Morality is only for the middle classes, sweet. The lower class can't afford it, and the upper classes have entirely too much leisure time to fill.'

Evie shook her head slowly, staring at him with huge eyes, not moving even when he leaned forward to press a grape between her slack lips. 'There's no need to say anything,' he murmured, smiling. 'Clearly you're speechless with gratitude at the prospect of having me here to keep an eye on you.'

Her ruddy brows lowered in a scowl, and he laughed softly. 'If your concern is that I may be overcome with manly ardor and ravish you in a moment of weakness . . . I may. If you ask nicely.'

Evie clamped her teeth on the sweet, pulpy grape and maneuvered the seeds out with her teeth and tongue. As he watched her mouth working on the fruit, Sebastian's smile faded slightly, and he leaned back. 'At the moment you're too much of a novice to be worth the bother,' he continued coolly. 'Perhaps I'll seduce you in the future, after some other men have taken the trouble to educate you.'

'I doubt it,' she said sullenly. 'I would never be so bourgeois as to sleep with my own husband.'

A catch of laughter escaped him. 'My God. You must have been waiting for days to use that one. Congratulations, child. We haven't yet been married a week, and you're already learning how to fight.'

CHAPTER 9

Evie never knew where her husband had slept that first night, but she suspected that it had been someplace uncomfortable. Her own sleep had been far from restful, as worry had awakened her with clocklike regularity. She had gone to check on her father several times, giving him sips of water, straightening the bedclothes, administering more medicine when the coughing worsened. Each time he awakened, Jenner regarded his daughter with renewed surprise. 'Am I dreaming you're 'ere, tibby?' he had asked her, and she had murmured softly and stroked his hair.

At the first sign of daylight, Evie washed and dressed, and pinned her damp hair into a braided coil at the back of her neck. Ringing for a chambermaid, she ordered mulled eggs, broth, tea, and any other sickroom food she could think of to tempt her father's failing appetite. Mornings at the club were quiet and still, as most of the employees were sleeping after having worked into the wee hours of the morning. However, there was always a skeleton staff, who were available for light tasks. A cook-maid stayed in the kitchen while the chef was gone, preparing simple fare for those who required it.

The sound of cruel hacking came from her father's room. Hurrying to the bedside, Evie found him coughing spasmodically into a handkerchief. It made her own lungs hurt as she heard the harrowing convulsions of his chest. Rummaging through the bottles on the night table, she found the morphine syrup and poured it into a spoon. She wedged an arm behind her father's damp, hot head and neck, lifting him into a half-sitting position. Once again shocked by how light he was, she felt his body tense as he tried to hold back another cough. The resulting shudders jolted the spoon in her hand, and the medicine dribbled onto the bedclothes.

'I'm sorry,' Evie murmured, quickly moving to blot the sticky syrup and refill the spoon. 'Let's try again, Papa.' He managed to take the medicine, his veined throat moving as he swallowed. Then, sputtering with a few residual coughs, he waited as she wedged supportive pillows behind him.

Evie eased him back and pressed a folded handkerchief into his hand. Staring into his gaunt face with its grizzled beard, she searched for any sign of her father in this unrecognizable stranger. He had always been full-faced, robust, ruddy . . . he had never been able to hold a conversation without the expressive use of his hands, making fists and punching the air in gesticulations that seemed particular to ex-boxers. Now he was a pale shadow of that man, the skin on his face gray and sagging from rapid weight loss. However, the blue eyes were the same . . . round and dark, the shade of the Irish sea. Finding reassurance in the familiarity of those eyes, Evie smiled.

'I've sent for breakfast,' she murmured. 'I expect it will be here soon.'

Jenner shook his head slightly, indicating that he did not want food.

'Oh yes,' Evie insisted, half sitting beside him on the bed. 'You'll have to eat *something*, Papa.' Taking a corner of a blotting cloth, she dabbed at a drop of blood at the bristly corner of his mouth.

A frown insinuated itself between his graying brows. 'The Maybricks,' he said raspily. 'Will they come for you, Evie?'

Her smile was infused with grim satisfaction. 'I've left them for good. A few days ago I ran off to Gretna Green and got m-married. They have no power over me now.'

Jenner's eyes widened. 'Who?' he asked succinctly.

'Lord St Vincent.'

A tap came at the door, and the housemaid entered, bearing a tray laden with dishes. Evie rose to help her, clearing some articles from the night table. She saw her father recoil from the smell of the food, bland though it was, and she winced sympathetically. 'I'm sorry, Papa. You must take a little broth, at least.' She draped a napkin over his chest and brought a cup of warm broth to his lips. He drank a few sips and leaned back, studying her as she blotted his mouth. Knowing that he was waiting for her to explain the situation, Evie smiled ruefully. Having given some previous thought to the matter, she had decided that there was no need to counterfeit a romance for his benefit. Her father was a practical man, and it had probably never occurred to him to hope that his daughter might marry for love. In his view, one took life as it came, doing whatever was necessary to survive. If one found a bit of enjoyment along the way, one should take advantage of it, and not complain afterward when the price had to be paid.

'Hardly anyone knows about the marriage yet,' she said. 'It's not a bad match, actually. We get on well enough, and I have no illusions about him.'

Jenner opened his mouth as she slipped a bite of mulled eggs inside. He contemplated the information, swallowed, and ventured, 'His father, the duke, is a paper skull what doesn't know 'is arse from an axe 'andle.'

'Lord St Vincent is quite intelligent, however.'

'A cold sort,' Jenner remarked.

'Yes. But not always. That is—' She stopped suddenly, her cheeks reddening as she remembered Sebastian rising over her in bed, his body hard and warm, his back muscles flexing beneath her fingers.

'A muff chaser, 'e is,' Jenner commented in a matter-of-fact tone.

'That doesn't matter to me,' Evie replied with equal frankness. 'I would never ask fidelity of him.

I've gotten what I wanted from the marriage. As for what he wants . . .'

'Aye, I'll post the cole,' her father said amicably, using the cockney term for paying money that was owed. 'Where is 'e now?'

She gave him another bite of mulled egg. 'No doubt he is still abed.'

The chambermaid, who had been leaving the room, paused at the doorway. 'Pardon, but 'e's not abed, miss . . . er, milady. Lord St Vincent woke Mr Rohan at first light, and is dragging him to an' fro, asking questions and giving 'im lists. Put Mr Rohan in the devil's own mood, 'e 'as.'

'Lord St Vincent has that effect on people,' Evie said dryly.

'Lists for what?' Jenner asked.

Evie did not dare admit that Sebastian had taken it upon himself to interfere with the running of the club. That would likely upset her father. News of his daughter's loveless marriage was something he could take in stride, but anything that affected his business would be a source of grave concern. 'Oh,' she said vaguely, 'I believe he saw a patch of carpeting that wanted replacing. And he thought of an improvement to the sideboard menu. That sort of thing.'

'Hmm.' Jenner scowled as she brought the cup of broth to his mouth once again. 'Tell 'im 'e's not to touch anyfing wivout Egan's leave.'

'Yes, Papa.'

Evie exchanged a covert glance with the

chambermaid, narrowing her eyes in warning to prevent the girl from volunteering further information. Understanding the silent command, the chambermaid nodded.

'You're not so tangled in the gob as you were,' Jenner remarked. 'Why is that, carrot pate?'

Evie considered the question thoughtfully, knowing that her stammer had indeed improved during the last week. 'I'm not certain. I think perhaps being away from the Maybricks has helped me to feel . . . calmer. I noticed it soon after we left London . . .' She gave him an expurgated version of their journey to Gretna Green and back, even provoking a few chuckles that caused him to cough into his handkerchief. As they conversed, she saw the relaxing of his face, betraying the pain-easing effect of the morphine. She ate a piece of his untouched toast, drank a cup of tea, and set the breakfast tray by the door.

'Papa,' she said evenly, 'before you go to sleep, I'll help you to wash and shave.'

'No need,' he replied, his eyes glazed from the effects of morphine.

'Let me take care of you,' she insisted, going to the washstand, where a ewer of hot water had been left by the housemaid. 'You'll sleep better afterward, I think.'

He seemed too listless to argue, only sighed and coughed, and watched as she brought a porcelain bowl and his shaving implements to the bedside. She tucked a length of toweling over his chest and around the base of his throat. Having never shaved a man before, Evie picked up the shaving brush, dipped it into the water, and dabbed it tentatively into the mug of soap.

'An 'ot towel first, tibby,' Jenner murmured. 'That softens the whiskers.'

Following his directions, Evie soaked and wrung out another towel, and laid it gently over his jaw and throat. After a minute, she lifted the towel and used the shaving brush to spread the soap over one side of his jaw. Deciding to shave his face one section at a time, she opened the razor, regarded it dubiously, and cautiously leaned over her father. Before the razor touched his face, a sardonic voice came from the doorway.

'Good God.' Glancing over her shoulder, Evie beheld Sebastian. He spoke not to her, but to her father. 'I don't know whether to commend your bravery or to ask if you've taken leave of your senses, allowing her near you with a blade.' He approached the bed in a few leisurely strides and extended his hand. 'Give me that, love. The next time your father coughs, you're going to cut his nose off.'

Evie surrendered the razor without a qualm. Regardless of her husband's lack of sleep, he seemed far more refreshed today. He was immaculately shaven, his hair washed and combed into gleaming clipped layers. His lean body was clad in a precisely tailored suit of clothes, the coat made of a dark charcoal fabric that set off his golden coloring beautifully. And as she had noticed last evening, a sense of vital energy clung to him, as if he were animated somehow merely by being in the club. The contrast between the two men, one so old and ill, the other so large and healthy, was startling. As Sebastian drew closer to her father, Evie experienced an instinctive urge to put herself between them. Her husband resembled nothing so much as a predator moving in to finish its helpless prey.

'Fetch the strop, pet,' Sebastian told her, his lips curved in a faint smile.

She went to obey, and when she returned from the washstand, he had taken her place at the bedside. 'Always sharpen the razor before and after a shave,' Sebastian murmured, running the open blade along the strop, back and forth.

'It looks sharp enough already,' Evie said doubtfully.

'It can never be too sharp, sweet. Lather his entire face before you begin. The soap will soften the beard.' He moved back while she applied soap to her father's face, then nudged her aside to half sit on the mattress. Razor in hand, he asked Jenner, 'May I?'

To Evie's amazement, her father nodded, seeming to have no qualms about letting Sebastian give him a shave. Evie went to the other side of the bed for a clearer view.

'Let the razor do the work,' Sebastian said, 'rather than use the pressure of your hand. Shave with the grain, in the direction the hair grows . . . like this. And take care never to draw the blade in a parallel stroke. Start with the sides of the face . . . then the cheeks . . . then the sides of the neck, like so . . .' As Sebastian spoke, he scraped the blade over the grizzled beard, removing it in neat strokes. 'And rinse the blade often.' His long-fingered hands were gentle on her father's face, varying the angle, stretching sections of skin taut as he shaved. The motions were light and clever, accomplished with skillful economy. Evie shook her head slightly, unable to believe that she was watching Sebastian, Lord St Vincent, shave her father with the expertise of a seasoned valet.

Finishing the masculine ritual, Sebastian wiped the residue of soap from Jenner's gleaming-smooth face. There was only one tiny nick on the edge of his jaw. Pressing the towel to it, Sebastian murmured, 'The soap needs more glycerin. My valet makes far better shaving soap than this . . . I'll have him bring some later today.'

'Thank you,' Evie replied, aware of a ticklish warmth inside her breast as she watched him.

Sebastian's gaze strayed to her face, and whatever he saw in her expression seemed to fascinate him. 'The bedsheets need changing,' he said. 'I'll help.'

Evie shook her head, recoiling from the idea of him seeing her father's wasted form. She knew that her father would feel very much at a disadvantage with him afterward. 'Thank you but no,' she said firmly. 'I will ring for the maid.'

'Very well.' He glanced at Jenner. 'With your permission, sir, I will visit later, after you've rested.'

'Yes,' her father agreed, his gaze unfocused. He closed his eyes and reclined with a sigh.

Evie straightened the room as Sebastian cleaned the razor, sharpened it once more on the strop, and closed it in its leather case. Walking with Sebastian to the threshold of the room, Evie stopped to face him, pressing her back against the doorjamb. Her worried gaze lifted to his face. 'Have you dismissed Mr Egan yet?'

Sebastian nodded, bracing one hand on the jamb above her head as he leaned over her. Although his posture was loose and easy, Evie still had a feeling of being subtly dominated. To her bemusement, it was not an altogether unpleasant sensation. 'He was hostile at first,' Sebastian replied, 'until I told him that I had looked through some of the account books. After that he was as docile as a lamb, knowing how bloody fortunate he is that we've decided not to bring charges against him. Rohan is helping him to pack, and ensuring that he will leave at once.'

'Why don't you wish to bring charges against Mr Egan?'

'It's bad publicity. Any hint of financial trouble makes people nervous about the club's stability. We're better off to absorb the losses and go on from here.' His gaze slid over her strained features, and he stunned her by saying softly, 'Turn around.'

Her eyes became huge. 'Wh-what? Why?'

'Turn around,' Sebastian repeated, waiting until she complied slowly. Her heart pounded painfully hard as he reached around her, took her wrists, and brought her hands up to the doorjamb. 'Take hold, sweet.'

Bewildered, she waited and wondered nervously what he was going to do. Her eyes closed, and she tensed as she felt his big hands settle on her shoulders. His fingers smoothed lightly over her upper back, as if he were searching for something . . . and then he began to knead her back with gentle, sure motions, easing the soreness of her tortured muscles. His artful fingertips probed places of aching tension, causing her to inhale sharply. The pressure of his hands intensified, his palms rolling over her back, his thumbs stroking deeply on either side of her spine. To Evie's mortification, she found herself arching like a cat. Slowly working his way upward, Sebastian found the knotted muscles at the junctures of her shoulders and neck and concentrated on them, kneading and pressing until she felt a soft moan rise in her throat.

A woman could become a slave to those experienced hands. He touched her with perfect sensuality, drawing acute pleasure from her sore flesh. Leaning most of her weight against the doorjamb, Evie felt her breathing turn slow and deep. Her back softened, lengthened beneath the coaxing manipulation, and it felt so wonderful that she dreaded the moment when he would stop.

When at last Sebastian's hands eased away from

her body, Evie was surprised that she didn't melt into a puddle on the floor. She turned around and glanced at his face, expecting a taunting smile or a sarcastic remark. Instead she saw that his color had heightened, and his expression was impassive. 'I have something to tell you,' he muttered. 'In private.' Taking her by the arm, Sebastian drew her out of her father's apartments and into the next available room, which happened to be the one that she had occupied the previous night. Sebastian closed the door and loomed over her. His face was impassive. 'Rohan was right,' he said bluntly. 'Your father doesn't have long. It will be a miracle if he lasts another day.'

'Yes. I . . . I think that is obvious to everyone.'

'This morning I talked with Rohan at length about your father's condition, and he showed me a leaflet that the doctor had left upon the diagnosis.' Reaching into his coat, Sebastian extracted a small folded piece of paper covered with minute printing, and gave it to her.

Evie read the words *A New Theory of Consumption* at the top of the leaflet. Since the only light in the room came from the small window, and her eyes were tired, she shook her head. 'May I read it later?'

'Yes. But I will tell you the gist of the theory – that consumption is caused by living organisms – so tiny that they are invisible to the naked eye. They abide in the afflicted lungs. And the disease is transferred when a healthy person draws in part of a breath that the ill person emits from his lungs.'

'Tiny creatures in the lungs?' Evie repeated blankly. 'That's absurd. Consumption is caused by a natural predisposition to the ailment . . . or by staying out too long in the cold and damp . . .'

'Since neither of us are doctors or scientists, a debate on the issue would be rather pointless. However, to be safe . . . I'm afraid I'm going to have to limit the amount of time you spend with your father.'

The paper fell from her hand. Shocked by the statement, Evie felt her pulse beating at a furious tempo. After all she had gone through to be with her father, Sebastian was trying to deny her the last few days she would ever have with him – all because of some unproven medical theory printed on a leaflet? *'No,'* she said violently. Her throat constricted, and her words tumbled out too quickly for her mouth to accommodate them. 'A-a-absolutely not. I will spend as long as I like with him. You d-don't give a . . . a *damn* about me, or him . . . you just want to be cruel to show me that you have the p-power to—'

'I saw the bedclothes,' Sebastian said curtly. 'He's coughing up blood, mucus, and the devil knows what else . . . and the more time you spend with him, the greater the chance that you'll inhale whatever the hell is killing him.'

'I don't believe your silly theory. I could find a

d-dozen doctors who would hold it up to ridicule—'

'I can't let you take the chance. Bloody hell, do you want to find yourself in that bed six months from now with your lungs rotting away?'

'If th-th-that happens, it's no concern of yours.'

As they confronted each other in the anger-snarled silence that followed, Evie had a fleeting sense that her bitter words had pierced deeper than she would have expected.

'You're right,' Sebastian said savagely. 'If you want to turn yourself into a consumptive, go right ahead. But don't be surprised when I decline to sit wringing my hands at your bedside. I won't do a thing to help you. And as you lie there coughing your lungs out, I'll take the devil's own delight in reminding you that it was your own damned fault for being such a stubborn idiot!' He concluded the speech with an irritated motion of his hands.

Unfortunately, Evie had been conditioned by too many encounters with Uncle Peregrine to discern between angry gestures and the beginnings of a physical attack. She flinched instinctively, her own arms flying up to shield her head. When the expected pain of a blow did not come, she let out a breath and tentatively lowered her arms to find Sebastian staring at her with blank astonishment.

Then his face went dark.

'Evie,' he said, his voice containing a bladelike ferocity that frightened her. 'Did you think I was about to . . . *Christ*. Someone hit you. Someone hit you in the past – who the hell was it?' He reached for her suddenly – too suddenly – and she stumbled backward, coming up hard against the wall. Sebastian went very still. 'Goddamn,' he whispered. Appearing to struggle with some powerful emotion, he stared at her intently. After a long moment, he spoke softly. 'I would never strike a woman. I would never harm you. You know that, don't you?'

Transfixed by the light, glittering eyes that held hers with such intensity, Evie couldn't move or make a sound. She started as he approached her slowly. 'It's all right,' he murmured. 'Let me come to you. It's all right. Easy.' One of his arms slid around her, while he used his free hand to smooth her hair, and then she was breathing, sighing, as relief flowed through her. Sebastian brought her closer against him, his mouth brushing her temple. 'Who was it?' he asked.

'M-my uncle,' she managed to say. The motion of his hand on her back paused as he heard her stammer.

'Maybrick?' he asked patiently.

'No, th-the other one.'

'Stubbins.'

'Yes.' Evie closed her eyes in pleasure as his other arm slid around her. Clasped against Sebastian's hard chest, with her cheek tucked against his shoulder, she inhaled the scent of clean male skin, and the subtle touch of sandalwood cologne.

'How often?' she heard him ask. 'More than once?'

'I . . . i-it's not important now.'

'How often, Evie?'

Realizing that he was going to persist until she answered, Evie muttered, 'Not t-terribly often, but . . . sometimes when I displeased him, or Aunt Fl-Florence, he would lose his temper. The l-last time I tr-tried to run away, he blackened my eye and spl-split my lip.'

'Did he?' Sebastian was silent for a long moment, and then he spoke with chilling softness. 'I'm going to tear him limb from limb.'

'I don't want that,' Evie said earnestly. 'I-I just want to be safe from him. From all of them.'

Sebastian drew his head back to look down into her flushed face. 'You are safe,' he said in a low voice. He lifted one of his hands to her face, caressing the plane of her cheekbone, letting his fingertip follow the trail of pale golden freckles across the bridge of her nose. As her lashes fluttered downward, he stroked the slender arcs of her brows, and cradled the side of her face in his palm. 'Evie,' he murmured. 'I swear on my life, you will never feel pain from my hands. I may prove a devil of a husband in every other regard . . . but I wouldn't hurt you that way. You must believe that.'

The delicate nerves of her skin drank in

sensations thirstily . . . his touch, the erotic waft of his breath against her lips. Evie was afraid to open her eyes, or to do anything that might interrupt the moment. 'Yes,' she managed to whisper. 'Yes . . . I—'

There was the sweet shock of a probing kiss against her lips . . . another . . . She opened to him with a slight gasp. His mouth was hot silk and tender fire, invading her with gently questing pressure. His fingertips traced over her face, tenderly adjusting the angle between them.

As Sebastian felt her sway, her equilibrium unraveling, he took one of her hands and drew it gently up to the back of his neck. She brought the other up as well, clinging to his hard nape as she responded to the sweetly nuzzling kisses. He was breathing fast, the movements of his chest a beguiling friction against her breasts. Suddenly his kisses were deeper, more forceful, bringing the passion to a burning urgency that made her twist against him, desperate for more closeness with his hard masculine form.

A sound of pained desire came from low in Sebastian's throat, and he lifted his mouth from hers. 'No,' he whispered raggedly. 'No, wait . . . love . . . I didn't mean to start this. I just . . . *hell.*'

Evie's fingers curled tightly into the fabric of his coat, and she buried her face against the slick gray silk of his necktie. Sebastian's hand cupped the back of her head, his body supporting her unsteady weight. 'I still mean what I said before,' he said into her hair. 'If you want to care for your father, you'll have to follow my rules. Keep the room ventilated – I want the door and window open at all times. And don't sit too close to him. Furthermore, whenever you're with him, I want you to tie a handkerchief over your mouth and nose.'

'What?' Evie squirmed away from him and gave him an incredulous glance. 'So that the tiny invisible creatures won't fly into my lungs?' she asked sarcastically.

His eyes narrowed. 'Don't try me, Evie. I'm close to forbidding you visit him at all.'

'I'll feel ridiculous, wearing a handkerchief on my face,' she protested. 'And it will hurt my father's feelings.'

'I don't give a damn. Bear in mind that if you disobey me, you won't see him.'

Evie jerked away from him as a surge of new anger filled her. 'You're no better than the Maybricks,' she said bitterly. 'I married you to gain my freedom. And instead I've exchanged one set of jailers for another.'

'None of us have complete freedom, child. Not even me.'

Closing her hands into fists, she glared at him. 'At least you have the right to make choices for yourself.'

'And for you,' he mocked, seeming to enjoy the

flare of temper he had provoked in her. 'Good Lord, what a display. All that tempestuous defiance . . . it makes me want to bed you.'

'Don't touch me again,' she snapped. 'Ever!'

Maddeningly, he began to laugh as he went to the door.

CHAPTER 10

When Evie went back to her father's room in the evening, she knew at once that it was his time. His color was waxen and skull white, his lips turning blue as his tortured lungs were no longer able to draw in sufficient oxygen. She wished that she could breathe for him. Taking his cool hand in hers, she chafed his fingers as if she could warm them, and she stared into his face with a fixed smile. 'Papa,' she murmured, smoothing his faded hair. 'Tell me what to do. Tell me what you want.'

He regarded her with a mild, affectionate gaze, while his lips, shrunken in his wrinkled face, tilted in an answering smile. 'Cam,' he whispered.

'Yes, I'll send for him.' Evie let her agitated fingers stroke over his hair. 'Papa,' she asked softly, 'is Cam my brother?'

'Ahhhh,' he sighed, his eyes crinkling. 'No, tibby. Would've liked that. Good lad . . .'

Evie leaned over and kissed one of his wasted hands, and left the bed. Hurrying to the bellpull, she yanked it several times, and a housemaid appeared with unusual alacrity. 'Yes, milady?'

'Get Mr Rohan,' Evie said, her voice shaking only a little. She paused and considered sending for Sebastian as well . . . but her father had not asked for him. And the thought of Sebastian's cool, cerebral presence providing such a jarring contrast to her own emotions . . . no. There were some ways in which she might lean on him, but this was not one of them. 'Go quickly,' she murmured to the housemaid, and went back to her father.

Some of her fear must have shone through her effort to maintain a reassuring facade, for her father took one of her hands and exerted a feeble tug to bring her closer to him. 'Evie,' came his faint whisper, 'I'm going to your mother, y'see . . . she's got 'em to leave a back door open . . . so I can steal into 'eaven.'

She laughed quietly even as a few hot tears spilled from her eyes.

Soon Cam entered the room. His jet-black hair was tousled and his clothes were uncharacteristically rumpled, as if he had dressed in haste. Although he was calm and self-possessed, his golden eyes held a soft liquid glitter as he beheld Evie. She stood and backed away, finding it necessary to swallow several times before she could speak. 'You have to bend low to hear him,' she said huskily.

Cam leaned over the bedside, clasping Jenner's hands in his just as Evie had done. 'Father of my heart,' the young Gypsy said softly, 'be at peace with every soul you leave behind. And know that God will open your way in the new life.'

As Jenner whispered to him, the boy inclined his head and rubbed the old man's hands soothingly. 'Yes,' Cam said readily, though Evie sensed from the tension of his broad shoulders that he had not liked whatever it was that her father had asked of him. 'I will see that it is done.'

After that, Jenner relaxed and closed his eyes. Cam eased away from the bedside and drew Evie forward. 'It's all right,' the boy murmured as he felt her trembling. 'My grandmother always told me, "Never try to turn back on a new road – you don't know what adventures await you."'

Evie tried to take comfort in the words, but her eyes blurred and her throat hurt. Sitting beside her father, she curled an arm around his head and laid a gentle hand on his chest. His rattling breath quieted, and he made a slight sound as if he welcomed her touch. As she felt the life gradually passing from him, she felt Cam's large hand slide around her upper arm in a gentle grip.

It was painfully quiet in the room. Evie's heart thudded almost audibly. She had never encountered death before, and to have to confront it now, and lose the one person who had ever loved her, filled her with the cold pressure of fear. Throwing a watery glance to the doorway, she found Sebastian's tall form standing there, his face unreadable, and she realized suddenly that she did need him to be there after all. As he stared at her with his bright moonstone eyes, something in his gaze helped to steady her.

The softest of exhalations left Ivo Jenner's lips . . . and then there was nothing more.

Realizing that it was finally over, Evie pressed her cheek to his head and closed her brimming eyes. 'Good-bye,' she whispered, tears slipping into the locks of his once-ruddy hair.

After a moment, Evie felt Cam's capable hands lifting her away from the bed.

'Evie,' the boy murmured, his face averted, 'I have to . . . have to arrange the body. Go with your husband.'

Evie nodded and tried to move, but her legs had locked. She felt Cam smooth her hair back, and then the dry brush of his mouth over her forehead in a sweet, chaste kiss. Blindly she turned away and stumbled toward her husband. Sebastian came to her in a few strides and pressed a handkerchief into her palm. She took it gratefully. Too distraught to notice or care where they were going, she wiped her eyes and blew her nose, while Sebastian led her from Ivo Jenner's apartments. His arm was strong behind her back, his hand anchored at her waist.

'He was in constant pain,' Sebastian said in a matter-of-fact tone. 'This is better.'

'Yes,' Evie managed to reply numbly. 'Yes, of course.'

'Did he say anything to you?'

'He mentioned . . . my mother.' The thought

152

brought a fresh burn to her eyes, but a crooked smile pulled at her lips. 'He said she was going to help him through the back door of heaven.'

Sebastian guided her into her bedroom. Sinking onto the bed, Evie clamped the handkerchief over her nose and curled on her side. She had never cried like this before, without sobs, misery oozing from her throat, while the pressure of grief in her chest refused to abate. She was dimly aware of the curtains being drawn and of Sebastian sending a housemaid for some wine and a jug of cold water.

Although Sebastian stayed in the room, he did not come near, only paced for a few minutes and eventually lowered himself into a bedside chair. It was obvious that he did not want to hold Evie while she cried, that he would shrink from such emotional intimacy. She could abandon herself to him in passion, but not in grief. And yet it was clear that he had no intentions of leaving her.

After the housemaid brought the wine, Sebastian propped Evie up on the pillows and gave her a liberally filled glass. As she drank, he took a cold wet cloth and pressed it gently to her swollen eyes. His manner was kind and oddly careful, as if he were taking care of a young child.

'The employees,' Evie mumbled after a while. 'The club. The funeral . . .'

'I'll take care of all of it,' Sebastian said calmly. 'We'll close the club. I'll make the funeral arrangements. Shall I send for one of your friends?'

Evie shook her head immediately. 'It would put

them in a difficult position. And I don't feel like talking to anyone.'

'I understand.'

Sebastian stayed with her until she had downed a second glass of wine. Realizing that he was waiting for some cue from her, Evie set the empty vessel on the night table. Her tongue felt thick as she spoke. 'I think I could rest now. There's no need for you to watch over me, when there is so much to be done.'

His assessing gaze swept over her, and he stood from the chair. 'Send for me when you awaken.'

Lying tipsy and drowsing and alone in the semi-darkness, Evie wondered why people always said that the death of a loved one was easier when one had time to prepare for it. This didn't seem easy. And those same people might have added that her grief should be lessened by the fact that she had never really known her father. That made it worse, however. There were so few memories with which she could comfort herself . . . so little time they had spent together. Along with the sadness came a gloomy sense of deprivation . . . and beneath that, even a touch of anger. Was she so unworthy of love, that she'd had so little of it in her life? Did she lack some essential gift for drawing others to herself?

Aware that her thoughts were drifting danger-ously toward self-pity, she closed her eyes and let out a shaking sigh.

★　　★　　★

Just as Cam left Ivo Jenner's apartments, St Vincent met him in the hall. There was a scowl on the blond man's face, and a vein of chilling arrogance in his tone. 'If my wife finds comfort in trite Gypsy homilies, I have no objection to your offering them. However, if you ever kiss her again, no matter how platonic the fashion, I'll make a eunuch of you.'

The fact that St Vincent could stoop to petty jealousy when Ivo Jenner was not yet cold in his bed might have outraged some men. Cam, however, regarded the autocratic viscount with speculative interest.

Deliberately calibrating his reply to test the other man, Cam said softly, 'Had I ever wanted her that way, I would have had her by now.'

There it was – a flash of warning in St Vincent's ice-blue eyes that revealed a depth of feeling he would not admit to. Cam had never seen anything like the mute longing that St Vincent felt for his own wife. No one could fail to observe that whenever Evie entered the room, St Vincent practically vibrated like a tuning fork.

'It is possible to care about a woman without wanting to bed her,' Cam pointed out. 'But it appears that you don't agree. Or are you so obsessed with her that you can't fathom how anyone else could fail to feel the same?'

'I'm not obsessed with her,' St Vincent snapped.

Leaning a shoulder against the wall, Cam stared

into the man's hard eyes, his usual reserve of patience nearly depleted. 'Of course you are. Anyone could see it.'

St Vincent gave him a warning glance. 'Another word,' he said thickly, 'and you'll go the way of Egan.'

Cam raised his hands in a mocking gesture of self-defense. 'Warning taken. By the way . . . Jenner's last words were about Bullard. There is a financial bequest for him in the will . . . Jenner wanted it to be honored.'

St Vincent's eyes narrowed. 'Why would he leave money to Bullard?'

Cam shrugged. 'I couldn't say. But if I were you, I wouldn't gainsay Jenner's last wish.'

'If I do, there isn't much that he or anyone else can do about it.'

'Then you'll take the risk of having his ghost haunt the club because of unfinished business.'

'Ghost?' St Vincent shot him an incredulous glance. 'Christ. You're not serious, are you?'

'I'm a Gypsy,' Cam replied matter-of-factly. 'Of course I believe in ghosts.'

'Only half Gypsy. Which led me to assume that the rest of you was at least marginally sane and rational.'

'The other half is Irish,' Cam said, a touch apologetically.

'*Christ,*' St Vincent said again, shaking his head as he strode away.

★   ★   ★

156

With the funeral to be arranged, and the club's business in disarray, and the building itself in dire need of restoration, Sebastian should have been far too busy to take notice of Evie and her condition. However, she soon realized that he was demanding frequent reports from the housemaids about how much she had slept, and whether she had eaten, and her activities in general. Upon learning that Evie had gone without breakfast or lunch, Sebastian had a supper tray sent upstairs, accompanied by a terse note.

My lady,

This tray will be returned for my inspection within the hour.
    If everything on it is not eaten, I will personally force-feed it to you.

Bon appetit,
S.

To Sebastian's satisfaction, Evie obeyed the edict. She wondered with annoyance if his orders were motivated by concern or by a desire to browbeat her. However, soon after that, Sebastian did something very considerate, by paying a dressmaker double her usual commission to have three mourning frocks run up for Evie at remarkable speed. Unfortunately, the fabric selection was entirely inappropriate.

Women in their first year of mourning were obliged to dress only in crepe, a dull, stiff, scratchy fabric made of gummed threads. No one considered this a pleasant choice, as crepe was dangerously flammable, and it tended to shrivel and nearly fall to pieces in the rain. Sebastian, however, had ordered one gown made of rich black velvet, one of soft cambric, and one of cashmere.

'I can't wear these,' Evie told him with a frown, smoothing her hands over the gowns. She had put them on the counterpane of her bed, where the garments lay heaped like midnight flowers.

Sebastian had brought the gowns upstairs himself, as soon as they had been delivered to the club. He stood at the corner of the bed, casually leaning back against the heavy carved post. With the exception of his snowy white shirt and collar, he was dressed in black from head to toe. As one would expect, he was astonishingly handsome in the severe clothes, their darkness providing an exotic contrast to his glowing golden skin and hair. Not for the first time, Evie wondered wryly if any man with such remarkable looks could possess a decent character – no doubt he had been spoiled since infancy.

'What is your objection to the clothes?' Sebastian asked, glancing at the gowns. 'They're black, aren't they?'

'Well, yes, but they're not made of crepe.'

'Do you *want* to wear crepe?'

'Of course not – no one does. But if people saw me wearing anything else, there would be terrible gossip.'

One of Sebastian's brows arched. 'Evie,' he said dryly, 'you eloped against your family's wishes, you married a notorious rake, and you're living in a gaming club. How much more damned gossip do you think you could cause?'

She cast an uncertain glance over the dress she was wearing, one of the three that she had taken with her the night that she had escaped the Maybricks. Although she and the maids had done their best to clean it, the brown wool was travel-stained, and shrunken in the places where it had gotten wet and muddy. And it was itchy. She wanted to wear something fresh and soft and clean. Reaching out to the folds of the black velvet, she stroked it gently, her fingertips leaving sleek trails in the soft nap.

'You must learn to ignore what people say,' Sebastian murmured, coming to her. Standing behind her, he rested his fingers lightly on her shoulders, causing her to start a little. 'You'll be much happier that way.' Suddenly his voice was tipped with amusement. 'I've learned that while gossip about others is often true, it's never true when it is about oneself.'

Evie stiffened nervously when she felt his hands moving along the line of fasteners on the back of her brown wool. 'What are you doing?'

'Helping you to change your gown.'

'I don't want to. Not now. I . . . oh, please don't!'

But he persisted, sliding one hand around her front to keep her in place, while his other continued to release the row of buttons. Rather than resort to an undignified struggle, Evie flushed and held still, goose bumps rising on her exposed skin. 'I w-wish you wouldn't handle me in such a cavalier manner!'

'The word "cavalier" implies indifference,' he replied, pushing the gown over her hips. It fell in a scratchy heap to the floor. 'And there is nothing indifferent about my reaction to you, love.'

'One could wish for a bit of respect,' Evie exclaimed, shivering before him in her underclothes. 'Especially after . . . after . . .'

'You don't need respect. You need comfort, and holding, and possibly a good long tumble in bed with me. But since you won't allow that, you'll get a shoulder rub and a few words of advice.' Sebastian settled his warm hands over her shoulders, which were bare except for the tapes of her chemise straps. He began to rub her stiff muscles, his thumbs fanning in strong arcs across her upper back. Evie made a little sound and tried to step away, but he hushed her and continued to massage her with infinite skill.

'You're not the same as you were a few days ago,' he murmured. 'You're no longer a wallflower, nor a virgin, nor the helpless child who had to endure life with the Maybricks. You're a viscountess with a sizable fortune, and a scoundrel of a husband. Whose rules will you adhere to now?'

Evie shook her head in weary confusion. She discovered that as Sebastian worked the tension out of her back, her control over her emotions seemed to dissolve at an equal rate. She was afraid that if she tried to speak, she might cry. Instead she remained silent, squeezing her eyes shut and fighting to keep her breathing even. 'So far you've spent your life striving to please others,' she heard him say. 'With a rather poor rate of success. Why don't you try pleasing yourself for a change? Why not live by your own rules? What has obeying the conventions ever gotten you?'

Evie pondered the questions, and her breath hissed in pleasure as he found a particularly sore spot. 'I like the conventions,' she said after a moment. 'There is nothing wrong with being an ordinary person, is there?'

'No. But you're not ordinary – or you never would have come to me instead of marrying cousin Eustace.'

'I was desperate.'

'That wasn't the entire reason.' His low voice sounded like a purr. 'You also had a taste for the devil.'

'I didn't! I don't!'

'You enjoyed cornering me, an infamous rake, in my own home with an offer I couldn't afford to refuse. Don't try to deny it – I know you well enough by now.'

Incredibly, despite her grief and worry, Evie felt a smile working up to her lips. 'Perhaps I did enjoy it, for a moment,' she admitted. 'And I certainly enjoyed thinking about how furious my family would be when they learned of it.' The trace of a smile vanished as she added morosely, 'How I hated living with them! If only my father had kept me with him. He could have paid someone to look after me . . .'

'Good Lord,' Sebastian said, not sounding at all sympathetic, 'why should he have wanted a young child in his sphere?'

'Because I was his family. Because I was all that he had!'

That earned a decisive shake of his head. 'Men don't think that way, sweet. Your father assumed – and rightly so – that you would be better off living away from him. He knew you would never marry well unless you were brought up in a respectable manner.'

'But if he had known how the Maybricks would treat me . . . the way I was abused—'

'What makes you assume that your father wouldn't have done the same?' Sebastian shocked her by asking. 'He was an ex-boxer, for God's sake. He was hardly known for his self-restraint. You may have become entirely familiar with the back of his hand, had you seen him more often.'

'I don't believe that!' Evie said hotly.

'Settle your feathers,' Sebastian murmured, reaching for the velvet gown on the bed. 'As I told you, I would never condone striking a woman for any reason. But the world is full of men who don't have that particular scruple, and it's likely your father was one of them. Argue if you like – but don't be so naive as to put Jenner on a pedestal, love. In the context of his world – the rookeries, the gaming hells, the rogues, criminals, and confidence tricksters – he was a decent enough man. I'm sure he would think that a fitting eulogy. Lift your arms.' Expertly he pulled the velvet over her head, tugged the skirts into a soft, heavy fall over her hips, and helped her to push her arms through the sleeves. 'This life isn't for you,' he said, not unkindly. 'You belong on some country estate, sitting on a blanket spread over green lawn, eating a dish of strawberries and cream. Going for carriage drives. Calling on your friends. Someday you should probably let me give you a baby. It would be something to occupy you. And it would give you something in common with your friends, who have doubtless have already begun breeding.'

Startled by the casualness with which the suggestion had been delivered, Evie stared into the handsome face so close to hers. One might have thought he had just proposed to buy her a puppy. Was he really as callous as he seemed?

'Would you take any interest in a baby?' Evie managed to ask after several hard swallows.

'No, pet. I'm no more meant for a wife and family than your father was. But I would see to it that you were handsomely provided for.' A wicked spark entered his eyes. 'And I would participate enthusiastically in the begetting of children, if not their rearing.' He moved behind her to fasten the gown. 'Think about what you want,' he advised. 'There's very little you can't have . . . so long as you dare to reach for it.'

CHAPTER 11

Any friendly feeling that Evie had for her husband promptly vanished the next morning when Sebastian left the club just before noon, ostensibly on an errand to Madame Bradshaw's. He had finished making arrangements for Ivo Jenner's funeral, which would be held the following day, and was now turning his attention to business matters involving the club. Jenner's would be closed for a fortnight, during which there would be a massive invasion of carpenters, masons, painters, all employed to refurbish the building.

Sebastian had also begun to make decisive changes in the club's procedures, including promoting Cam to the position of factotum. In light of the boy's mixed heritage, it was certain to be a controversial decision. Gypsies were universally believed to be a light-fingered and deceptive lot. For Cam to be responsible for collecting and paying large sums of money, and arbitrating whenever the legality of a play was in question, would be viewed by some as asking a cat to watch over a nest of baby chicks. The power of the position was such that no one, not even Sebastian, could

165

question his judgments on the games. However, Cam was a familiar and well-liked figure, and Sebastian was willing to gamble that his popularity would induce the club members to accept him in this new position. Besides, none of the other thirty club employees was remotely qualified to run the hazard room.

Now that the house wenches were gone it was imperative that something should be done so that when the club reopened, the members would have access to female companionship. To Evie's disgruntlement, Cam had agreed with Sebastian that an arrangement with Madame Bradshaw would be an excellent solution to the problem. And naturally, Sebastian had taken it upon himself to make a proposition to the notorious madam. Knowing of her husband's infamous sexual appetite, Evie was certain that his visit to Madame Bradshaw's would include far more than a mere business negotiation. Sebastian had not slept with anyone since their sojourn to Gretna Green. No doubt he was primed and eager to indulge himself with some willing female.

Evie told herself repeatedly that she didn't care. He could sleep with ten women . . . a hundred . . . a thousand . . . and she would not care. She would be an idiot if she did. Sebastian was no more capable of loyalty than a stray tom who wandered the alleys, mating with every she-cat he encountered.

Fuming beneath her stoic facade, Evie brushed

and pinned her hair in an intricate plaited coil. Turning away from the small looking glass that sat atop the dresser, Evie set down her brush. As the gleam of her gold wedding ring caught her eye, the engraved Gaelic words seemed to mock her. 'My love is upon you,' she whispered bitterly, and tugged it off. There was no point in wearing a wedding ring for a sham of a marriage.

She started to set it on the dresser, thought better of it, and slipped it into her pocket, deciding she would ask Cam to store it in the club's safe. Just as she made to leave the room, there was a rap at the door. It couldn't have been Sebastian, who never bothered to knock. Opening the door, Evie beheld Joss Bullard's heavy features.

While Bullard was not actively disliked by the other employees, it was obvious that his popularity did not begin to approach Cam's. It was unfortunate for Bullard that since he and Cam Rohan were of an age, they were often measured against each other. It would have been unfair to compare most men to the darkly beautiful Cam, whose sly charm and dry humor made him a favorite among employees and club patrons. To make matters worse, Bullard was a humorless man, dissatisfied with his lot in life and jealous of all those whom he perceived had been given more. Sensing that he found it difficult even to be civil to her, Evie treated him with guarded politeness.

Bullard's hard, flat eyes stared into hers. 'Visitor at the back entrance what's askin' for you, milady.'

167

'A visitor?' Evie frowned, feeling her stomach turn hollow at the suspicion that her uncles had finally learned of her whereabouts. The news of Jenner's death, the temporary closure of the club, and her own presence there must have traveled swiftly through London. 'Who? Wh-what name did he give?'

'I was bid to tell you it was Mrs 'Unt, milady.'

Annabelle. The sound of her dear friend's name caused Evie's heart to quicken with relief and eagerness, though she could scarcely credit that Annabelle would dare to come to a gaming club. 'That is good news,' she exclaimed. 'Please bring her upstairs to my father's receiving room.'

'I was bid to say that you mus' come down to the back step, milady.'

'Oh.' But that wouldn't do. A girl of Annabelle's sheltered background should not be allowed to wait at the back of the club. Filled with concern, Evie crossed the threshold and strode from the room, thinking only of reaching Annabelle as quickly as possible. With Bullard at her heels, she descended the two long flights in a rush, grasping the railing at measured intervals. By the time she reached the bottom, her heart was thumping with exertion. Struggling a little with the heavy door, she pushed it open—

—and reared back in startled surprise as she saw not Annabelle Hunt's trim figure, but the hulking form of her uncle Peregrine.

Evie's mind went blank. She gave him a shocked

stare that lasted for a mere fraction of a second, then reared back as terror suffused her. Peregrine had always been more than willing to use his fists to force her into compliance. It didn't matter that she was now Lady St Vincent, and therefore legally out of his reach. Her uncle would take his revenge in any manner possible, beginning with a harsh beating.

Blindly Evie turned to flee, but to her amazement, Bullard moved to block her way.

''E paid me a sovereign to fetch you,' Bullard muttered. 'That's as much as I make in a month.'

'No,' she gasped, shoving at his chest. 'Don't – I'll give you anything – don't let him take me!'

'Jenner made you stay wiv them, all those years,' the young man sneered. ''E didn't want you 'ere. No one does.'

As she screamed in protest, Bullard shoved her inexorably toward her uncle, whose broad features were mottled with furious triumph. 'There, I did as you asked,' Bullard said brusquely to the man just behind Peregrine, whom Evie recognized in a flash – her uncle Brook. 'Now post the cole.'

Looking uncomfortable and vaguely shamed by the transaction, Brook handed him the sovereign.

Peregrine seized Evie in a hard grip, rendering her as helpless as a rabbit caught by the scruff of the neck. His big, square face was florid with rage. 'You stupid, worthless girl!' he cried, shaking her hard. 'If you weren't still of some use, I would dispose of you like so much rubbish. How long did you think you could hide from us? There'll be hell to pay, I promise you!'

'Bullard, stop him, *please,*' Evie screamed, fighting and arching as Peregrine dragged her toward a waiting carriage. *'No!'*

But Bullard didn't move to help her, only watched from the doorway with hate-filled eyes. She didn't understand what she had done to make him despise her so. Why was there no one to help her? Why was no one answering her cries? Fighting for her life, Evie clawed and elbowed her uncle, her struggles hampered by her heavy skirts. She was hopelessly outmatched. Infuriated by her resistance, Peregrine growled, 'Submit, you damned little hellion!'

From the corner of her eye, Evie saw a boy coming from the stable yard, pausing uncertainly at the sight of the conflict in the alley. She screamed to him, 'Get Cam—' Her shout was stifled by Peregrine's crushing palm as it covered her mouth and nose. She bit into his dusty-tasting flesh, and he jerked his hand away with an enraged howl. 'Cam!' Evie shrieked again, before she was silenced by a hard cuff to the ear.

Peregrine shoved her at Uncle Brook, whose lean face swam in her blurring vision. 'Put her in the carriage,' Peregrine commanded, reaching inside his coat for a handkerchief to bind his bleeding hand.

Evie writhed in Brook's grip. As he pushed her

roughly toward the vehicle, Evie twisted and managed to deliver a glancing blow to the front of his throat. The impact caused Brook to choke for breath and release her.

Peregrine seized Evie with his plate-sized hands. He slammed her against the side of the carriage. Her head hit the hard lacquered paneling, and there was an explosion of sparks before her eyes, and a piercing pain in her skull. Dazed by the impact, Evie could only grapple feebly as she was thrust into the vehicle.

To Evie's astonishment, her cousin Eustace was waiting inside, pale and corpulent, appearing like a baby whale that had been loaded into the seat. He locked her against the massive, stale-smelling folds of his body, exhibiting surprising strength as he plumped a fleshy forearm over her throat. 'Got you,' he said, panting with effort. 'Troublesome bitch – you broke your promise to marry me. But my parents said that *I'm* to have your fortune, and they'll get it for me no matter what must be done.'

'Already married—' Evie wheezed, smothering in the mountain of human flesh that seemed to surround her, as if she were being swallowed whole by some exotic undersea creature.

'The marriage won't stand. We're going to have it annulled. So you see, your plan to ruin things for me hasn't worked.' Eustace sounded like a petulant boy as he continued. 'You had better not annoy me, cousin. My father has said I may do whatever I like with you after we're married.

How would you like to be locked in a closet for a week?'

Evie couldn't summon enough air to reply. His ponderous arms compressed her into the huge doughy mass of his chest and stomach. Tears of pain and despair prickled at the corners of her eyes as she pried frantically at the clench-hold around her neck.

Through the buzzing in her ears, she heard new sounds from outside, shouting and cursing. All of a sudden the carriage door was wrenched open and someone vaulted inside. Evie squirmed to see who it was. Her remaining breath was expelled in a faint sob as she saw a familiar glitter of dark golden hair.

It was Sebastian as she had never seen him before, no longer detached and self-possessed, but in the grip of bone-shaking rage. His eyes were pale and reptilian as his murderous gaze fastened on Eustace, whose breath began to rattle nervously behind the pudgy ladder of his chin.

'Give her to me,' Sebastian said, his voice hoarse with fury. '*Now,* you pile of gutter sludge, or I'll rip your throat out.'

Seeming to realize that Sebastian was eager to carry out the threat, Eustace released his choke-hold on Evie. She scrambled toward Sebastian and took in desperate pulls of air. He caught her with a low murmur, his hold gentle but secure. 'Easy, love. You're safe now.' She felt the tremors of rage that ran in continuous thrills through his body.

Sebastian sent a lethal glance to Eustace, who was trying to gather his jellylike mass into the far end of the seat. 'The next time I see you,' Sebastian said viciously, 'no matter what the circumstances, I'm going to kill you. No law, nor weapon, nor God Himself will be able to stop it from happening. So if you value your life, don't let your path cross mine again.'

Leaving Eustace in a quivering heap of speechless fear, Sebastian hauled Evie from the vehicle. She clung to him, still trying to regain her breath as she glanced apprehensively around the scene. It appeared that Cam had been alerted to the fracas, and was keeping her two uncles at bay. Brook was on the ground, while Peregrine was staggering backward from some kind of assault, his beefy countenance turning ruddy from enraged surprise.

Swaying as her feet touched the ground, Evie turned her face into her husband's shoulder. Sebastian was literally steaming, the chilly air striking off his flushed skin and turning his breath into puffs of white. He subjected her to a brief but thorough inspection, his hands running lightly over her, his gaze searching her pale face. His voice was astonishingly tender. 'Are you hurt, Evie? Look up at me, love. Yes. Sweetheart . . . did they do you any injury?'

'N-no.' Evie stared at him dazedly. 'My uncle Peregrine,' she whispered, 'he's very p-powerful—'

'I'll handle him,' he assured her, and called out to Cam. 'Rohan! Come fetch her.'

The young man obeyed instantly, approaching Evie with long, fluid strides. He spoke to her with a few foreign-sounding words, his voice soothing her overwrought nerves.

She hesitated before going with him, casting a worried glance at Sebastian.

'It's all right,' he said without looking at her, his icy gaze locked on Peregrine's bullish form. 'Go.'

Biting her lip, Evie took Cam's arm and allowed him to draw her aside.

'How kind of you to pay us a call, Uncle,' came the biting lash of Sebastian's voice. 'Come to offer us felicitations, have you?'

'I've come to collect my niece,' Peregrine snarled. 'She is promised to my son. Your illicit marriage will not stand!'

'She's *mine*,' Sebastian snapped. 'Surely you can't be so dimwitted as to think I would simply let her go without a protest.'

'I will have the marriage annulled,' Peregrine assured him.

'That would only be possible if the marriage hasn't been consummated. And I assure you, it has.'

'We have a physician who has promised to testify that her maidenhead is still intact.'

'Like hell,' Sebastian said with chilling pleasantness. 'Do you know what kind of reflection that would have on me? I've worked too hard to cultivate my reputation – I'll be damned if I'll allow any suggestion of impotence to mar it.' He shrugged out of his coat and tossed it to Cam, who caught it in one fist. Sebastian's lethal gaze never left Peregrine's livid features. 'Has it occurred to you that I may have made her pregnant by now?'

'If so, that will be remedied.'

Not fully comprehending what her uncle meant, Evie shrank back into Cam's protective hold. His arms tightened, even as he regarded Peregrine with a rare flash of hatred in his golden eyes. 'Don't worry, sweetheart,' he whispered to Evie.

Sebastian's color rose at Peregrine's words, making his eyes appear like splintered glass. 'Charming,' he said. 'I would kill her myself before I'd let you have her.'

Appearing to lose all vestige of self-control, Peregrine lunged for him with a roar. 'I'll go *through* you if need be, you preening son of a whore!'

Evie inhaled sharply as Sebastian sidestepped her charging uncle and waited for him to come around. 'Stupid,' she heard Cam mutter. 'He should have tripped him.' The boy fell silent as Sebastian barely managed to block the drive of Peregrine's massive fist, then delivered a swift right to the jaw. Forceful though the blow was, it appeared to have little effect on Evie's hulking uncle. Horrified, Evie watched the pair of them exchange a series of swift jabs and punches.

Although Sebastian was far more agile, Peregrine managed to land a few blows of bone-jarring might, causing Sebastian to reel backward from the impact.

Employees began to drift from the club, giving encouraging shouts to Sebastian, while passersby from the street hurried toward the source of the noise. A wide circle formed around the brawlers, the air filled with hoots and bellows.

Evie clung tightly to the arm around her middle. 'Cam, do something,' she begged.

'I can't.'

'You know how to fight. My father always said—'

'No,' Cam said grimly. 'It's his battle. If I were to jump in now, it would appear as if he couldn't handle your uncle on his own.'

'But he can't!' Evie flinched as Sebastian staggered back after another brutal combination from Peregrine.

'You're underestimating him,' Cam said, watching as Sebastian moved forward again. 'He – *there's* a fellow. Grand right hook. Good on his feet too. Men his size can't usually move that fast. Now if he would just – *damn*, there's a missed opportunity—' He suddenly whooped with approval as Sebastian felled Peregrine with a hard left to the jaw. 'There's some pile-driving force!' he exclaimed. 'He's got power and accuracy . . . all that's wanting is some decent instruction.'

Reduced to a groaning heap on the ground,

Peregrine seemed oblivious to the hard-faced man who stood over him.

Realizing that the fight was over, the club employees ventured forward with approving cries and slaps on Sebastian's back, assuring him that he was not quite the namby-pamby they had thought him to be. Sebastian received the dubious praise with a sardonic expression, and brusquely supervised the loading of his disabled opponent into the carriage.

Gently Cam turned Evie to face him. 'Tell me how it started,' he said urgently. 'Now, before your husband reaches us.'

Rapidly Evie explained how Bullard had deceived her into coming downstairs, and how he had literally handed her over to her relations in exchange for a sovereign. Her words came out in a jumbled stammer, but Cam managed to follow the disjointed explanation. 'All right,' he murmured, his honey-skinned face wiped clean of expression. 'I'll deal with Bullard. You go take care of St Vincent. He'll need you. Men are always full of sap after a good fight.'

Evie shook her head in confusion. 'Sap? What? I have no idea what you're talking about.'

Sudden amusement sparkled in his eyes. 'You will.'

Before she could question him, Sebastian reached them. It seemed that the sight of Evie in Cam's arms was not at all pleasing to him. His face took on a sullen cast. 'I want to know what the hell happened,' he said furiously, snatching Evie back with possessive hands. 'I leave for two hours on a peaceful Sunday morning, and I come back to find the damned place upside-down—'

'She'll explain,' Cam interrupted, staring beyond Sebastian as his attention was caught by someone in the stable yard. 'Pardon, I have to attend to something—' He vaulted lightly over the short railing and disappeared into the crowd.

CHAPTER 12

Cam found Joss Bullard near the stable yard, and confronted him warily. Bullard breathed with flared nostrils, the whites of his eyes showing. They had never been friends. Their relationship had been more like that of warring siblings who had lived under the same roof, with Jenner as a parental figure. As boys, they had played and fought together. As adults, they had worked side by side. After the many small acts of kindness Jenner had showed to Bullard, Cam would never have expected him to behave like this. Confusion and fury tangled inside him, and he shook his head slowly as he stared at Bullard.

'I don't know why you gave her over,' Cam began, 'or what you thought you had to gain from it—'

'I got a sovereign for it,' Bullard shot back. 'An' well worv it to be rid of that idiot tangle-tongue.'

'Are you mad?' Cam demanded in a flare of rage. 'What's the matter with you? We're talking about *Jenner's daughter*. You shouldn't have done it even if you'd been given a bloody fortune!'

'She's never done nofing for Jenner,' Bullard interrupted harshly, 'or nofing for the club. But she comes 'ere at the very last to watch 'im kick off, an' then she takes everything. Bugger the 'igh-kick bitch an' 'er sodding 'usband!'

Cam listened closely, but he failed to grasp the reason for Bullard's jealousy. A Gypsy rarely understood resentment of other's material possessions. Money was good only for the temporary pleasure of spending it. In the wandering tribe that Cam had belonged to until the age of twelve, no one had ever thought of wishing for more than he needed. A man could only wear one suit of clothes or ride one horse at a time.

'She was Jenner's only child,' Cam replied. 'What he gave to her has nothing to do with you or me. But nothing is worse than breaking the trust of someone who depends on your protection. To betray her . . . to help someone take her away against her will . . .'

'I'd do it again!' Bullard said, and spat on the ground between them.

Cam stared intently at the other man, realizing that he didn't look well at all. His complexion was pale and wormy, and his eyes were dull. 'Are you ill?' Cam asked softly. 'If so, tell me. I'll go to St Vincent on your behalf. Maybe I can get him to—'

'Pox on you! I'm well rid o' you, 'alf-bred Gypsy filth. Well rid o' all o' you.'

The violent hatred in Bullard's tone left no room for doubt. There would be no turning back for him. The only question now was whether Cam should collar him and drag him to the club, or let him flee. Recalling the vicious gleam in St Vincent's gaze, Cam reflected that if given a chance, the viscount might actually kill Bullard, which would lead to a great deal of unpleasantness for everyone, especially Evie. No . . . better to allow Bullard to disappear.

Staring at the hatchet-faced young man whom he had known for so many years, Cam shook his head in angry puzzlement. Soul loss, his people called it . . . the essence of a man becoming trapped in some dark otherworld realm. But how had it happened to Bullard? And when?

'You had better stay away from the club,' Cam murmured. 'If St Vincent catches you—'

'St Vincent can rot in 'ell,' Bullard grunted, taking a hasty swipe at him.

Evading the tight arc of his fist with a startled reflex, Cam drew to the side of the stable yard. His eyes narrowed as he watched the other man turn and flee.

His attention was caught by the nervous nicker of a horse tethered to a nearby post, and Cam reached out a gentle hand and stroked the bay's satiny neck. The gold rings on his fingers gleamed in the afternoon light. 'He was a foolish man,' Cam told the horse mildly, calming the animal with his voice and touch. A sigh escaped him as he thought of something else. 'Jenner left him a bequest . . . and I promised to make certain that he got it. *Now* what am I supposed to do?'

Sebastian pulled Evie inside the club, where the silence was startling after the tumult of the alley. She labored to keep pace with his ground-eating strides, her own breath coming fast by the time they reached the reading room on the main floor. The built-in mahogany shelves were filled with leather volumes. Against the walls, a multitude of papers and periodicals were draped over racks made with rows of clever movable dowels. Pushing Evie into the room, Sebastian closed them both inside with a decisive slam.

'Were you hurt?' he asked roughly.

'No.' Evie tried to hold back her next words, but they came out in a burst of resentment. 'Why were you gone for so long? I needed you, and you weren't here!'

'You had thirty employees to protect you. Why did you go downstairs in the first place? You should have stayed upstairs until you knew for certain who was outside.'

'Mr Bullard told me that Annabelle Hunt was waiting for me. And then when I saw that it was my uncle, Bullard wouldn't let me back inside the club. He pushed me right into my uncle's arms.'

'My God.' Sebastian's eyes widened. 'I'm going to disembowel him, the gutter scum—'

'And while all that was happening,' Evie continued wrathfully, 'you were in bed with a prostitute!' As the words left her lips, she realized that to her, this was the crux of the matter . . . even more important than Bullard's betrayal, or her uncles' assault, her emotions were roiling at the fact that Sebastian had betrayed her so soon with another woman.

Sebastian focused on her with an alert gaze. 'I wasn't.'

'Don't lie,' Evie said, while their mutual fury seethed in the air. 'I know you were.'

'Why are you so bloody certain?'

'Because you stayed at Madame Bradshaw's for more than two hours!'

'I was talking about business. *Talking*, Evie! If you don't believe that, then you can go to hell. Because if I *had* slept with someone, I guarantee you that I would be a lot more relaxed than I am now.'

Staring into Sebastian's eyes, which were as hard as a frozen pond, Evie felt her outrage begin to drain away. She had no choice but to believe him – his offended anger was obvious.

'Oh,' she muttered.

'*Oh?* That's all you have to say?'

'I suppose . . . I shouldn't have jumped to conclusions. But knowing what I do of your past . . . I assumed . . .'

Her lame attempt at an apology seemed to erode the remnants of Sebastian's self-control. 'Well, your assumption was wrong! If you haven't yet noticed, I'm busier than the devil in a high wind, every minute of the day. I don't have the damned *time* for a tumble. And if I did—' He stopped abruptly. All semblance of the elegant viscount Evie had once watched from afar in Lord Westcliff's drawing room had vanished. He was rumpled and bruised and furious. And he wasn't breathing at all well. 'If I did—' He broke off again, a flush crossing the crests of his cheeks and the bridge of his nose.

Evie saw the exact moment when his self-restraint snapped. Alarm jolted through her, and she lurched toward the closed door. Before she had even made a step, she found herself seized and pinned against the wall by his body and hands. The smell of sweat-dampened linen and healthy, aroused male filled her nostrils.

Once he had caught her, Sebastian pressed his parted lips against the thin skin of her temple. His breath snagged. Another moment of stillness. Evie felt the electrifying touch of his tongue at the very tip of her eyebrow. He breathed against the tiny wet spot, a waft of hellfire that sent chills through her entire body. Slowly he brought his mouth to her ear, and traced the intricate inner edges.

His whisper seemed to come from the darkest recesses of her own mind. 'If I did, Evie . . . then by now I would have shredded your clothes with my hands and teeth until you were naked. By now I would have pushed you down to the carpet, and put my hands beneath your breasts and lifted them up to my mouth. I would be kissing them . . .

licking them . . . until the tips were like hard little berries, and then I would bite them so gently . . .'

Evie felt herself drift into a slow half swoon as he continued in a ragged murmur. '. . . I would kiss my way down to your thighs . . . inch by inch . . . and when I reached those sweet red curls. I would lick through them, deeper and deeper, until I found the little pearl of your clitoris . . . and I would rest my tongue on it until I felt it throb. I would circle it, and stroke it . . . I'd lick until you started to beg. And then I would suck you. But not hard. I wouldn't be that kind. I would do it so lightly, so tenderly, that you would start screaming with the need to come . . . I would put my tongue inside you . . . taste you . . . eat you. I wouldn't stop until your entire body was wet and shaking. And when I had tortured you enough, I would open your legs and come inside you, and take you . . . take you . . .'

Sebastian stopped, anchoring her against the wall while they both remained frozen, aroused, panting.

At length, he spoke in a nearly inaudible voice. 'You're wet, aren't you?'

Had it been physically possible to blush any harder, Evie would have. Her skin burned with violated modesty as she understood what he was asking. She tipped her chin in the tiniest of nods.

'I want you more than I've ever wanted anything on this earth.' Sebastian took a shivering breath. 'Tell me what I have to do to get you. Tell me what it will take for you to let me into your bed.'

Evie pushed at him helplessly, unable to dislodge the stimulating weight of his body. 'Th-there is nothing you could do. Because I would want the one thing you couldn't give. I would want you to be faithful to me, and you could never do that.'

'I could.' But the assertion came too easily. It reeked of insincerity.

'I don't think so,' she whispered.

His long hands cupped her face, his thumbs running over the curves of her cheeks. His mouth was just above hers as he spoke. 'Evie . . . I can't hold to our agreement. I can't live with you, see you every day, and not have you. I can't . . .' Feeling the little tremors that ran through her body, he dipped his head and kissed the side of her throat. Her senses responded to the persuasive heat of his mouth, so erotic and tender . . . the searching fingers that slid over the curve of her breast.

Hearing her muffled whimper, he took her mouth in a consuming kiss. Feebly she turned her face away, her lips tingling from the exquisite friction. 'No, Sebastian.'

He rubbed his face against her hair and the top of her head. Something about the situation, or his own reaction to it, must have struck a chord of humor, for he let out a soft, sardonic laugh. 'You'll have to think of a way to solve this, Evie. Think of something fast . . . because otherwise . . .' He paused to nip hungrily at her ear, '. . . otherwise I'm about to screw you senseless.'

Her eyes flew open. 'That word—' she began indignantly, and he silenced her with a hard kiss.

Drawing back, Sebastian regarded her with amused exasperation, his color still high. 'Do you object to the word itself, or the sentiment behind it?'

Relieved to see that he had regained at least a modicum of sanity, Evie wriggled out from between his body and the wall. 'I object to the fact that you want me only because I'm unavailable, and therefore a novelty—'

'That's not the reason,' he interrupted swiftly.

Evie sent him a disbelieving glance. 'F-further-more, I will not be part of a stable of women whom you visit at random.'

Suddenly Sebastian was quiet, looking away from her. Evie waited, nearly choking on her impatience as she waited for him to admit that she was right. She waited until his gaze slowly lifted, and his winter-blue eyes stared into hers.

'All right,' Sebastian said huskily. 'I agree to your terms. I'll be . . . monogamous.' He seemed to have a bit of difficulty with the last word, as if he were trying to speak a foreign language.

'I don't believe you.'

'Good God, Evie! Do you know how many women have tried to obtain such a promise from me? And now, the first time I'm willing to take a stab at fidelity, you throw it back in my face. I admit that I've had a prolific history with women—'

'Promiscuous,' Evie corrected.

He gave an impatient snort. 'Promiscuous,

debauched – whatever you want to call it. I've had a hell of a good time, and I'll be damned if I say I'm sorry for it. I've never bedded an unwilling woman. Nor, to my knowledge, did I leave anyone unsatisfied.'

'That's not the point.' A frown creased her forehead. 'I don't blame you for your past . . . or, at least . . . I'm not trying to punish you for it.' Ignoring his skeptical snort, she continued, 'But it doesn't make you an especially good candidate for fidelity, does it?'

His tone was surly as he replied. 'What do you want of me? An apology for being a man? A vow of celibacy until you've decided that I'm worthy of your favors?'

Struck by the question, Evie stared at him.

Women had always come far too easily to Sebastian. If she made him wait for her, would he lose interest? Or was it just possible that they might come to know each other, understand each other, in an entirely new way? She longed to find out if he could come to value her in ways beyond the physical. She wanted the chance to be something more than a mere bed partner to him.

'Sebastian . . .' she asked carefully, 'have you ever made a sacrifice for a woman?'

He looked like a sullen angel as he turned to face her, leaning his broad shoulders against the wall, one knee slightly bent. 'What kind of sacrifice?'

That drew a wry glance from her. 'Any kind at all.'

'No.'

'What is the longest period of time you've ever gone without . . . without . . .' She floundered for an acceptable phrase. '. . . making love?'

'I never call it that,' he said. 'Love has nothing to do with it.'

'How long?' she persisted.

'A month, perhaps.'

She thought for a moment. 'Then . . . if you would forswear intercourse with all women for six months . . . I would sleep with you afterward.'

'*Six months?*' Sebastian's eyes widened, and then he threw her a scornful glance. 'Sweetheart, what gives you the idea that you're worth a half-year of celibacy?'

'I may not be,' Evie said. 'You're the only one who can answer that.'

It was obvious that Sebastian would have loved to have informed her that she wasn't worth waiting for. However, as his gaze traveled over her from head to toe, Evie saw the unmistakable glow of lust in his eyes. He wanted her badly.

'It's impossible,' he snapped.

'Why?'

'Because I'm Sebastian, Lord St Vincent. I can't be celibate. Everyone knows that.'

He was so arrogant, and so indignant, that Evie suddenly had to gnaw on the insides of her lips to keep from laughing. She struggled to master her amusement, and finally managed to say calmly, 'Surely it wouldn't harm you to try.'

'Oh, yes it would!' His jaw hardened as he labored to explain. 'You're too inexperienced to understand, but . . . some men are possessed of a far greater sexual drive than others. I happen to be one of them. I can't go for long periods of time without—' He broke off impatiently as he saw her expression. 'Damn it, Evie, it's unhealthy for a man not to release his seed regularly.'

'Three months,' she said, 'and that's my final offer.'

'No!'

'Then go find another woman,' she said flatly.

'I want *you*. Only you. The devil knows why.' Sebastian glared at her, his eyes narrowing into hot, brilliant slits. 'I should force you. You have no legal right to refuse me your bed.'

Suddenly Evie's heart stopped, and she felt herself blanch. But she would not shrink from him. Something inside demanded that she stand up to him as an equal. 'Go on, then,' she challenged coolly. 'Force me.' She saw the flicker of surprise in his eyes. His throat worked, but he remained silent. And then . . . she understood. 'You can't,' she said in wonder. 'You would never have raped Lillian. You were only bluffing. You could never force a woman.' A faint smile rose to her lips. 'She was never in a moment's danger, was she? You're not nearly the villain you pretend to be.'

'Yes, I am!' Sebastian seized her and kissed her angrily, stabbing his tongue inside her, assaulting her mouth with his own. Evie didn't resist him. She closed her eyes and let him do as he wished, and soon he was groaning and kissing her with a tender passion that wrung pleasure from every nerve. By the time he lifted his head, they were both shaking.

'Evie . . .' His voice was hoarse. 'Don't ask this of me.'

'Three months of celibacy,' she said. 'And if you succeed, I-I will go to bed with you willingly, as often as you wish.'

'For how long?'

'For as long as we both shall live. But if you fail . . .' Evie paused to think of the direst consequences possible . . . something that would revolt him to the very core. 'If you fail, then you will have to go to your former friend Lord Westcliff, and apologize for abducting Lillian Bowman.'

'Holy hell!'

'That is my price.'

'Your price is too damn high. I never apologize.'

'Then you had better not accept my challenge. Or if you do accept it . . . you had better not fail.'

'You'll have no way of knowing if I cheat.'

'I'll know.'

A long moment of silence passed.

'Where is your ring?' Sebastian asked suddenly.

Evie's smile disappeared instantly. Embarrassed to admit that she had removed it in a fit of pique, she mumbled, 'I took it off.'

191

'What did you do with it?'

Awkwardly she reached into her pocket. 'I . . . it's here. I'll put it back on if you wish—'

'Give it to me.'

Assuming that he intended to take it away from her for good, Evie closed her fingers tightly around the circlet. All of a sudden she discovered that she had become rather attached to the blasted thing. However, pride kept her from asking him to let her keep it. Reluctantly she withdrew the gold ring from her pocket, surreptitiously stroking the engraved surface with her fingertip one last time. *Tha Gad Agam Ort . . .*

Taking the ring from her, Sebastian slid it onto his own hand. His hands were so much larger that the circlet would only fit the tip of his smallest finger. Grasping her chin in an intractable hold, he glared into her eyes. 'I'll take your bet,' he said grimly. 'I'm going to win it. And in three months, I'm going to put this back on your finger, and take you to bed, and do things to you that are outlawed in the civilized world.'

Evie's resolve did not shield her from the heart-thumping alarm that any rational woman would feel upon hearing such an ominous statement. Nor did it prevent her knees from turning to jelly as he jerked her against his body and fitted his mouth to hers. Her hands, suspended in mid-air, went to his head in a trembling butterfly descent. The texture of his hair, the locks so cool and thick on the surface, so warm and damp at the roots, was too alluring to resist. She slid her fingers into the gleaming golden layers and pulled him even closer, helplessly reveling in the urgent pressure of his mouth.

Their tongues mated, slid, stroked, and with each slippery-sweet caress inside the joined cavern of their mouths, she felt a hot coiling deep in her belly . . . no, deeper than that . . . in the tightening, liquefying core where she had once taken his invading flesh. It shocked her to realize how much she wanted him there again.

She whimpered as he pulled away from her, while frustration washed over them both.

'You didn't say that I couldn't kiss you,' Sebastian said, his eyes bright with devil-fire. 'I'm going to kiss you as long and as often as I like, and you're not to utter a word of protest. That's the concession you'll give in return for my celibacy. Damn you.'

Giving her no time either to agree or to object, he released her and strode to the door. 'And now, if you'll excuse me . . . I'm going to go kill Joss Bullard.'

CHAPTER 13

Sebastian encountered Cam in the hallway outside the reading room. 'Where is he?' he demanded without preamble.

Stopping before him with an expressionless face, Cam said shortly, 'He's gone.'

'Why didn't you follow him?' White-hot fury blazed in Sebastian's eyes. This news, added to the frustration of his vow of celibacy, was the last straw.

Cam, who had been exposed to years of Ivo Jenner's volcanic temper, remained unruffled. 'It was unnecessary in my judgment,' he said. 'He won't return.'

'I don't pay you to act on your own damned judgment. I pay you to act on mine! You should have dragged him here by the throat and then let *me* decide what was to be done with the bastard.'

Cam remained silent, sliding a quick, subtle glance at Evie, who was inwardly relieved by the turn of events. They were both aware that had Cam brought Bullard back to the club, there was a distinct possibility that Sebastian might actually have killed him – and the last thing Evie wanted was a murder charge on her husband's head.

'I want him found,' Sebastian said vehemently, pacing back and forth across the reading room. 'I want at least two men hired to look for him day and night until he is brought to me. I swear he'll serve as an example to anyone who even thinks of lifting a finger against my wife.' He raised his arm and pointed to the doorway. 'Bring me a list of names within the hour. The best detectives available – *private* ones. I don't want some idiot from the New Police, who'll foul this up as they do everything else. *Go.*'

Though Cam undoubtedly had a few opinions to offer on the matter, he kept them to himself. 'Yes, my lord.' He left the room at once, while Sebastian glared after him.

Seeking to calm his seething temper, Evie ventured, 'There is no need to take your anger out on Cam. He—'

'Don't even try to excuse him,' Sebastian said darkly. 'You and I both know that he could have caught that damned gutter rat had he wanted to. And I'll be damned if I'll tolerate your calling him by his first name – he is not your brother, nor is he a friend. He's an employee, and you'll refer to him as "Mr Rohan" from now on.'

'He *is* my friend,' Evie replied in outrage. 'He has been for years!'

'Married women don't have friendships with young unmarried men.'

'Y-you dare to insult my honor with the implication that . . . that . . .' Evie could hardly speak for

195

the multitude of protests that jammed inside her. 'I've done nothing to merit such a lack of tr-tr-trust!'

'I trust you. It's everyone else that I hold in suspicion.'

Suspecting that he might be mocking her, Evie stared at him with a reproachful frown. 'You're carrying on as if I am being chased by hordes of men, when that is obviously not the case. At Stony Cross Park, men went out of their way to avoid my company – and you were one of them!'

The charge, though true, seemed to startle Sebastian. His face became taut, and he stared at her in stony silence. 'You hardly made it easy for anyone to approach you,' he said after a moment. 'A man's vanity is more fragile than you might think. It's easy for us to mistake shyness for cold-ness, and silence for indifference. You could have exerted yourself a bit, you know. One brief meeting between the two of us . . . one smile from you . . . was all the encouragement I would have needed to jump on you like a grouse on laurel.'

Evie stared at him with round eyes, having never considered things in that light before. Was it possible that she herself was partly responsible for her history as a perennial wallflower? 'I suppose . . .' she said reflectively, 'I could make more of an effort to overcome my shyness.'

'Do as you please. But when you're with Rohan or any other man, you had better keep in mind that you belong completely to me.'

Trying to interpret the comment, Evie stared at him with astonishment. 'Are you . . . is it possible . . . . you're jealous?'

Sudden bafflement flickered across his features. 'Yes,' he said gruffly. 'It would seem so.' And throwing Evie a glance of bewildered annoyance, he left the room.

The funeral was held the next morning. Sebastian had done a splendid job of arranging the event, somehow managing to achieve the perfect balance between total somber dignity and slightly theatrical pomp. It was the kind of procession that Ivo Jenner would have adored, so large that it took up the full breadth of St James.

There was a black and gilded hearse drawn by four horses, two mourning coaches similarly drawn by fours, with all the bridles adorned with tall dyed ostrich plumes. The handsome oak coffin, adorned with brass nails and a gleaming inscription plate, was lined with lead and welded shut to prevent the intrusion of grave robbers, a common problem in London churchyards. Before the lid had closed over her father's body, Evie had seen one of Cam's gold rings on his finger, a parting gift that had touched her. What had touched her equally, however, had been the glimpse she'd caught of Sebastian smoothing her father's faded red hair with a comb, when he'd thought no one was watching him.

It was bitterly cold. The biting wind penetrated

Evie's heavy wool cloak as she sat on horseback, with Sebastian walking beside her and holding the horse's reins. Two dozen men serving as pages, feathermen, and coachmen walked at the end of the procession, their breaths blowing white in the early winter air. They were followed by a great crowd of mourners, a curious mingling of well-to-do people, merchants, flash gentry, and outright criminals. Friends and enemies alike were there. No matter what someone's occupation or disposition, the tradition of mourning had to be observed.

It was expected that Evie would not attend the funeral, as ladies' natures were considered too delicate to tolerate such harsh reality. However, Evie had insisted on participating. She found comfort in the ritual, as if it helped her to bid farewell to her father. Sebastian had been inclined to argue, until Cam had intervened.

'Jenner must be released from the fetters of his daughter's grief,' the Gypsy had told Sebastian, just as the argument had become heated. 'The Rom believe that if someone grieves too much for a loved one who has died, the deceased one will be forced to come back through the veil, to try to comfort the sorrowing one. If attending the funeral will help her to let him go . . .' He had stopped and shrugged prosaically.

Sebastian had given him a withering glance. 'Ghosts again,' he said sourly. But he had let the matter drop and gave in to Evie's wishes.

Having cried until it seemed that she had no

more tears left, Evie managed to be stoic throughout the funeral, even when earth was shoveled over the coffin that had been lowered into the ground. A few salty drops did slip from the corners of her eyes, however, as the coffin was completely covered, and Cam stepped forward with a small silver flask. According to Romany tradition, he solemnly poured a drink of brandy onto the grave site.

Angered by the gesture, the elderly clergyman stepped forward, scolding, 'Stop that! We'll have none of your heathen practices! Soiling a sacred place with cheap spirits—'

'Sir,' Sebastian interrupted, stepping forward and resting a large hand on the clergyman's shoulder. 'I don't think our friend Jenner would have minded.' He let a conspiratorial smile touch his lips as he added, 'It's French brandy, and an excellent year. Perhaps you will allow me to send a few bottles to your residence, to sample at your leisure?'

Mollified by the viscount's abundant charm, the clergyman smiled back. 'That is very kind, my lord. Thank you.'

Once most of the mourners had departed, Evie let her gaze travel over the shop fronts, the houses, and the blacking factory that surrounded the square. Her attention was suddenly caught by the face of a man standing by a lamppost on the other side of the square. Dressed in a dark coat and a dirty gray cap, he was not recognizable until a slow smile split his face.

It was Joss Bullard, she realized with a start of

recognition. It seemed that he had wanted to pay his respects to Ivo Jenner, if only from a distance. However, he did not wear the expression of a man in mourning. He looked positively evil, his face twisted with a malice that sent a chill down her spine. Watching her steadily, he drew his finger across his throat in an unmistakable gesture that caused her to take an involuntary step backward.

Noticing the movement, Sebastian turned toward her, automatically taking her shoulders in his black-gloved hands. 'Evie,' he murmured, staring down at her pale face with a touch of concern. 'Are you all right?'

Evie nodded, letting her gaze flicker back to the lamppost. Bullard was gone. 'I'm just a bit c-cold,' she replied, her teeth chattering as a gust of bitter wind swept the hood of her cloak back from her face.

Immediately Sebastian pulled the hood back into place and snuggled the cloak more closely around her neck. 'I'm going to take you back to the club,' he said. 'I'll give a few coins to the feathermen and coachmen, and then we'll leave.' Reaching into his greatcoat, he pulled out a small leather bag and went to the group of men waiting respect-fully near the graveside.

Catching Evie's anxious stare, Cam approached her, the gleam of a smudged tear track on his lean cheek. She caught at his sleeve and said under her breath, 'I just saw Mr Bullard. Over there, at the lamppost.'

His eyes widened slightly, and he nodded.

There was no opportunity to say anything further. Sebastian returned and put his arm around Evie's shoulders. 'The carriage is waiting,' he said.

'There was no need to have arranged for a carriage,' she protested. 'I could have walked.'

'I had them fill the foot warmer,' he said, and a smile tugged at his lips as he saw the flicker of anticipation in her expression. He glanced at Cam. 'Come to the carriage with us.'

'Thank you,' came the boy's guarded reply, 'but I would prefer to walk.'

'We'll see you at the club, then.'

'Yes, my lord.'

As Evie accompanied Sebastian to the carriage, she steeled herself not to look back at Cam. She wondered if he would manage to find Bullard, and what might happen if he did. Stepping onto the movable stool, she climbed into the vehicle. She hurriedly arranged her skirts over the foot warmer and shuddered in pleasure as it sent wafts of heat up to her knees. Sebastian sat beside her, a faint smile on his lips.

Remembering their madcap journey to Gretna Green, which had not been all that long ago, Evie thought that it seemed as if an eternity had passed since then. She snuggled against Sebastian, gratified that he did not try to ease her away.

'You held up quite well, all things considered,' he said as the carriage began to move.

'It was the most elaborate funeral procession I've

ever seen,' she replied. 'My father would have adored it.'

Sebastian let out a huff of amusement. 'When in doubt, I chose to err on the side of excess, hoping it would have suited him.' He hesitated before continuing. 'Tomorrow I'm going to have your father's apartments completely emptied and stripped,' he said. 'We'll never be rid of the sick-room smell otherwise.'

'I think that is an excellent idea.'

'The club will reopen the week after next. I'll let you stay here until then, to have a little time to adjust to your father's death. But when Jenner's doors are open again, I want you to be comfortably settled in my town house.'

'What?' Startled by the statement, Evie drew away to look at him. 'The one in Mayfair?'

'It's well-appointed, and fully staffed. If it doesn't please you, we'll find something else. In the meantime, however, you'll have to stay there.'

'Are you planning to . . . to live there with me?'

'No. I will continue to live at the club. It's far more convenient to manage everything that way.'

Evie struggled to cope with his indifference. What was the reason for his sudden coolness? She had been no trouble to him . . . she had made few demands of him, even in her grief. Bewildered and angry, she stared down at her hands and made a knot of her gloved fingers.

'I want to stay,' she said in a low voice.

Sebastian shook his head. 'There is no reason

for you to remain there. You're not needed. It will be better for all concerned if you live in a proper home, where you can receive your friends, and not be awakened at all hours of the night by the commotion downstairs.'

'I am a sound sleeper. That doesn't bother me. And I can receive my friends at the club—'

'Not openly.'

It made no difference that he was right. Evie was silent, while the phrase *'you're not needed'* caused an ugly echo in her head.

'I want you to live in safe and respectable surroundings,' Sebastian continued. 'The club is no place for a lady.'

'I'm not a lady,' Evie countered, striving for a tone of light irony. 'I'm a gambler's daughter and a scoundrel's wife.'

'All the more reason to remove you from my influence.'

'I don't think I'll leave, just the same. Perhaps we can discuss it in the spring, but until then—'

'Evie,' he said quietly, 'I'm not giving you a choice.'

She stiffened and inched away from him. An entire room filled with foot warmers couldn't have banished the frost that lined her veins. Her mind searched frantically for arguments to dissuade him . . . but he was right . . . there was no reason for her to stay at the club.

Her throat became very tight and she thought with despair that by now she should be used to this . . . being unwanted, being alone . . . why in God's name did it still hurt? Oh, how she wished she could be like Sebastian, with a wall of protective ice around her heart. 'What about our bargain?' she asked dully. 'Do you intend to ignore it, or—'

'Oh no. I'm going to live as chastely as a monk until the time comes for me to collect my reward. But it will be easier for me to resist temptation with you out of reach.'

'Perhaps *I* won't resist temptation,' Evie heard herself murmur. 'I may find some accommodating gentleman to keep me company. You wouldn't mind, would you?'

Until the words had left her lips, she would never have believed herself capable of saying such a thing. However, the desperate need to wound him, anger him, break through to his emotions, was overpowering. Her attempt failed. After a short silence, she heard his silken reply.

'Not at all, pet. It would be selfish of me to deny you such amusement in your private hours. Do as you wish . . . just as long as you're available when I have need of you.'

Behind the fashionable streets and respectable squares of the affluent areas of London, there was a hidden world of dark alleys and decaying rookeries, where humanity lived in unspeakable squalor. Crime and prostitution were the only means of survival in these places. The air was thick with the odors of refuse and sewage, and the buildings were crammed so close together that in some places a man could only pass between them if he moved sideways.

Cam ventured into the intricate maze of streets with great care, mindful of the infinite traps and dangers that awaited an unwary visitor. He entered a courtyard through a dark archway, forty yards long, ten feet wide. It was lined with tall wooden structures, their overhead abutments shutting out the winter sky above. The buildings were padding kens, or common lodging houses, where the homeless slept in piles like so many corpses in a mass graveyard. Hangings of putrid matter, two and three feet in length, extended downward from the abutments. Rats wriggled and scuttled along sides of walls, and disappeared into the cracks of the buildings' foundations. The court was empty save for a pair of girls sitting together on a doorstep, and a few scrawny children who searched for refuse bones or stray rags. Throwing Cam suspicious glances, the children vanished at the far end of the court.

One of the fuzzy-haired young prostitutes grinned to reveal a few broken stumps of teeth and said, 'Whot's a big 'andsome cull like you come to 'Angman's Court for?'

'I'm looking for a man, about so tall' – Cam gestured to indicate a man of five feet and eight inches – 'with black hair. Has he come through the court in the past minute?'

The girls cackled as he spoke. 'Listen to 'im talk,' one of them exclaimed in delight.

'Lovely,' the other girl agreed. 'Come, dearie, you don't want a *man,* when you could lay atop Lushing Lou.' She tugged down her blouse to reveal a scrawny chest and meager, drooping breasts. ''Ave a little crack-the-crib wiv me. I'll bet you does it 'andsome-like, don't you?'

Cam withdrew a silver coin from his pocket, and her gaze followed it hungrily. 'Tell me where he went,' he said.

'I'll tell you for sixpence *an'* a tup,' she said. 'You 'as pretty eyes, you does. I newer 'ad a knock from a boy with such a lovely—'

A low, harsh laugh echoed across the court, and then came Joss Bullard's mocking voice. 'You won't find me, you filthy 'alf bred!'

Cam swung around, scanning the buildings, where scores of soot-smeared faces stared out of doorways and windows and peered over the tile-less rooftops. Not one of them was recognizable. 'Bullard,' he said cautiously, turning slowly as his glance swept the scene. 'What do you want with Jenner's daughter?'

Another ugly laugh, seeming to come from a different direction this time. Cam ventured farther into the court, unable to identify Bullard's location. 'I wants to snuff 'er!'

'Why?'

'Because she's a bloody leech what's taken eweryfing from me. I wants 'er dead. I wants to throw 'er to the rats until there's nofing but bones left.'

'Why?' Cam asked in bewilderment. 'She's asked me to help you, Joss, even after you betrayed her. She wants to honor her father's request, to leave you enough to—'

'Devil take the filthy bitch!'

Cam shook his head slightly, unable to understand where such hostility had come from, or why Bullard harbored such mad wrath toward Evie.

Hearing a scraping sound behind him, he ducked and turned, just as the whistling arc of a board swung through the air where his head had been. The attacker was not Bullard, but a tosher, a scavenger who had impulsively decided to try his luck at back-alley robbery. He had the peculiar young-old look of someone who had lived in the streets since birth. Cam dispatched him in a few efficient movements, sending him to the ground in a groaning heap. A few more toshers appeared at the other end of the court, apparently deciding it was best to attack in numbers. Realizing that he would soon be overrun, Cam retreated to the archway, while Bullard's voice followed him.

'I'll get 'er, I will.'

'You'll never touch her,' Cam retorted, filled with a flare of impotent anger as he cast a last glance into Hangman's Court. 'I'll send you to hell before you ever lay a finger on her!'

'I'll bring you with me, then,' came Bullard's gloating reply, and he laughed again as Cam strode away from the court.

★　★　★

Later in the day, Cam sought out Evie. Sebastian was occupied with a group of carpenters who were repairing the intricate parquet work of the wooden flooring in the main dining room. Finding Evie in the empty hazard room, sorting absently through baskets of gaming chips and separating them into neat stacks, Cam approached her with a noiseless tread.

She started a little at the light touch on her arm, and smiled with quick relief as she looked up into his face. It was rare for him to appear visibly troubled. A young man of his prosaic nature was not given to hand wringing or anxiety. Cam met each moment as it came, living as much as possible in the present. However, the events of the day had left their mark, imparting a stark tension that temporarily aged him.

'I couldn't reach him,' Cam said softly. 'He disappeared into a rookery, and spoke to me from the shadows. Nothing he said made sense. He harbors an evil feeling against you, *gadji*, though I don't understand why. He's never been what anyone would call a cheerful sort, but this is different. A kind of madness. I have to tell St Vincent.'

'No, don't,' came Evie's instant reply. 'It would only worry and anger him. He has enough to deal with at present.'

'But if Bullard tries to harm you—'

'I'm safe here, am I not? He wouldn't dare come

to the club with the price that my husband has put on his head.'

'There are hidden ways into the building.'

'Can you seal them? Lock them?'

Cam considered the questions with a frown. 'Most of them. But it's not a matter of traipsing back and forth with a set of keys—'

'I understand. Do what you can.' She drew her fingers through a pile of discarded chips and added morosely, 'It doesn't really matter, since I'll be gone soon. St Vincent wants me to leave after next week. He doesn't think I should live at the club, now that my father . . .' She trailed off into disconsolate silence.

'Perhaps he's right,' Cam offered, his tone deftly stripped of pity. 'This isn't the safest place for you.'

'He's not doing it for reasons of safety.' Her fingers curled around a black chip, and then she sent it spinning like a top on the surface of the hazard table. 'He's doing it to keep distance between us.' She was both frustrated and heartened by the faint smile that touched his lips.

'Patience,' Cam counseled in a soft murmur, and left her to watch the chip spinning until its momentum had dwindled to stillness.

CHAPTER 14

Evie was glad of the constant activity in the club during the next fortnight, as it helped to distract her from her grief. When she told Sebastian that she wished to be of use, she was promptly assigned to the office, where correspondence and account books lay in great disorganized piles. She was also called upon to direct painters, decorators, carpenters, and masons to their various tasks, a responsibility that would have terrified her long ago. Speaking to so many strangers was a nerve-wracking effort at first, and for the first few days she struggled with her stammer. However, the more often she did it, the easier it became. It helped that the workers all listened to her with a mixture of patience and respect that had never been accorded her before.

The first thing that Sebastian did after Ivo Jenner's funeral was to arrange a meeting with the commissioner of police regarding the recent tightening of gaming laws. With persuasive charm, Sebastian made the case that Jenner's was a social club, as opposed to being specifically a gaming club. Therefore, it was not the kind of place that should be subjected to police raids, as its members were, as Sebastian solemnly put it, 'men of the highest integrity.' Swayed by Sebastian's artful reasoning, the commissioner promised that there would be no raids on Jenner's, as long as it maintained an appearance of respectability.

Upon learning of Sebastian's success with the commissioner, Cam Rohan remarked admiringly, 'That was a spruce trick, my lord. I'm beginning to think you can persuade anyone to do nearly anything.'

Sebastian grinned and glanced at Evie, who was sitting nearby. 'I should think Lady St Vincent is proof of that,' he said.

It seemed that Sebastian and Cam had decided to form a tentative alliance for the purposes of getting the club back on its feet. Their interactions were not precisely friendly, but neither were they hostile. Cam had certainly taken note of Sebastian's leadership abilities, which were greatly needed in the days after Ivo Jenner's demise. Sebastian had discarded his air of upper-class indolence, and had taken over the running of the club with decisiveness and authority.

As one might have expected, Sebastian was the kind of man that the club employees had contempt for, at first regarding him as nothing more than one of the 'pigeons' or 'culls' who came to the club. A spoiled, self-indulgent aristocrat who had no conception of what it was like to be a workingman. It was likely they all assumed, as Evie had, that Sebastian would quickly tire of the responsibilities that running the club entailed. However, no one dared to challenge him when it was clear that he was entirely willing to fire anyone who failed to heed his commands. There could have been no more effective statement of authority than the way he had summarily dismissed Clive Egan.

Furthermore, Sebastian's sincere passion for the club could not be ignored. He had a keen interest in everything from the kitchen cuisine to the specific costs of running the hazard room. Recognizing that he had a great deal to learn about the operation of the games, Sebastian undertook to understand the mathematics of gambling. Evie ventured into the hazard room one evening to find Sebastian and Cam standing at the central table, while Cam explained his system of odds.

'. . . there are only thirty-six possible combinations of two dice, and of course each die has six sides. When you cast two dice simultaneously, whatever combination you end up with is called an 'accumulated chance' and the odds of achieving it are thirty-five to one.' Cam paused, giving Sebastian an assessing glance.

Sebastian nodded. 'Go on.'

'As anyone who plays hazard knows, the sum of the two face-up sides is called a point. Two ones added together are a point of two. Two sixes added together are a point of twelve. But the odds of throwing any particular number vary, since there is only one way to throw a two, but there are six ways to throw a point of seven.'

'Seven being a natural,' Sebastian murmured, frowning in concentration. 'And since the greatest number of combinations will result in a natural, the probability of throwing a seven with one cast is . . .'

'Sixteen percent,' Cam supplied, picking up the dice. The gold rings on his dark fingers caught the light as he sent the dice tumbling to the end of the table. Rebounded off the back edge of the table, the ivory cubes settled on the green baize. The faces were both sixes. 'Throwing a twelve, on the other hand, has a probability of only two point seven percent. And of course, the more you throw, the more the probability increases . . . so that by the time you've cast the dice one hundred and sixty-six times, the probability of having thrown a twelve point by then is ninety-nine percent. Of course, with other points, the probability is going to be different. I can show you on paper – it's easier to understand that way. You'll have a great advantage once you learn how to figure the odds. Few players ever do, and it's what separates the rooks from the pigeons. Hazard is a prejudiced game, even when played honestly, with the advantage going to the banker in most—' Cam paused respectfully as Evie came to the table. A smile glowed in his dark eyes. 'Good evening, milady.'

Sebastian frowned as he saw the air of friendly ease between them

'Good evening,' Evie murmured, taking a place at the table beside Sebastian. She smiled as she glanced up at him. 'Are you clever with numbers, my lord?'

'I've always thought so,' Sebastian replied ruefully, 'until now. Rohan . . . are the other croupiers adept with probability calculations?'

'Adept enough, my lord. They are well-trained. They all know how to tempt a player to make wagers to the house's advantage, how to identify a good player from a bad one . . .'

'Trained by whom?' Evie asked.

Cam's grin was a flash of startling white in his honey-skinned face. 'By me, of course. No one understands gaming as well as I.'

Smiling, Evie glanced up at her husband. 'All he lacks is confidence,' she remarked dryly.

Sebastian, however, did not react to the jest. Instead he said abruptly to Cam, 'I want a list, in descending order, of all outstanding loans and their due dates. The account book is on the top shelf in the office. Why don't you go start on it now?'

'Yes, my lord.' Giving a shallow bow to Evie, Cam left with his usual loose-limbed grace.

Standing with her husband in the cavernous, semi-darkened hazard room, Evie felt a prickle of nervousness in her stomach. Over the past few days their interactions had been frequent but impersonal, and it was seldom that they ever found themselves alone together. She leaned over the

214

table and reached for the discarded dice, depositing them in a small leather dice box. As she straightened, she felt Sebastian's hand skim gently over her corseted back, and the hairs on her nape lifted in response. 'The hour is late,' he said, his tone far softer than the one he had used with Cam. 'You should go to bed – you must be exhausted after all you've done today.'

'I haven't done all that much.' She shrugged uneasily, and his hand made another slow, unnerving pass along her spine.

'Oh yes, you have. You're pushing yourself a bit too hard, pet. You need to rest.'

She shook her head, finding it difficult to think clearly when he was touching her. 'I've been glad of the chance to work a bit,' she managed to say. 'It keeps me from dwelling on . . . on . . .'

'Yes, I know. That's why I've allowed it.' His long fingers curved around the back of her neck.

Her breath shortened as the warmth of his hand transferred to her skin.

'You need to go to bed,' he continued, his own breathing not quite steady as he eased her closer. His gaze drifted slowly from her face to the round outline of her breasts, and back again, and a low, humorless laugh escaped him. 'And I need to go there with you, damn it. But since I can't . . . Come here.'

'Why?' she asked, even as he secured her against the edge of the table and let his legs intrude amid the folds of her skirts.

'I want to torture you a little.'

Evie stared at him with round eyes, while her heart pumped liquid fire through her veins. 'When you—' She had to clear her throat and try again. 'When you use the word "torture," I'm sure you mean it in a figurative sense.'

He shook his head, his eyes filled with light smoke. 'Literal, I'm afraid.'

'What?'

'My love,' he said gently, 'I hope you didn't assume that the next three months of suffering was to be one-sided? Put your hands on me.'

'Wh-where?'

'Anywhere.' He waited until she had hesitantly placed her hands on his shoulders, over the fine wool weave of his coat. Holding her gaze, he said, 'As high as the fire in me burns, Evie, I will stoke it in you.'

'Sebastian . . .' She strained a little, and he pinned her more firmly against the table.

'It's my right to kiss you,' he reminded her, 'whenever I want, for as long as I want. That was our bargain.'

She threw an agitated glance around the room, and he read her thoughts easily.

'I don't give a damn if anyone sees us. You're my wife.' A smile chased across his lips. 'My better half, to be certain.' Leaning over her, he nuzzled into the fine tendrils that strayed over her forehead. His breath was hot and soft on her skin. 'My prize . . . my pleasure and pain . . . my endless desire.

I've never known anyone like you, Evie.' His lips touched gently at the bridge of her nose and slid down to the tip. 'You dare to make demands of me that no other woman would think of asking. And for now I'll pay your price, love. But later you'll pay mine . . . over and over . . .' He caught her trembling lips with his, his hands cupping the back of her head.

He was a man who loved kissing, nearly as much as he loved the act of intercourse itself. The kiss began as a gentle brush of dry, closed lips . . . the pressure increasing until he had gained the soft opening of her mouth . . . and then she felt the subtle intrusion of his tongue. Her head tippled back helplessly in the cradle of his palms, the sudden hammering of her heart sending the blood rushing through her veins, making her feel weak and hot. He took more of her, kissing her at every possible angle, searching deeply.

One of his hands eased over her front, passing lightly over her breasts, his thumb searching in vain for the point of her nipple through the thick padding of her corset. Craving the feel of her bare skin, he moved his fingers up to her throat, stroking the rapid throb of her pulse. His mouth slid from hers and traveled along her neck until he found the tender pulse point. Evie stiffened her legs, her hands gripping his shoulders to bolster her failing balance. With a low murmur, Sebastian gathered her more firmly against his body and sought her lips again. She could no longer hold back the pleading sounds in her throat, her mouth working frantically to draw in more of his taste, more of the warm male silk of his mouth, more—

The awkward sound of someone clearing his throat caused Evie to break the kiss with a gasp. Realizing that someone had entered the main room, Sebastian pulled her head against his chest, his thumb caressing the flushed curve of her cheek. He spoke to the intruder coolly, while his heart thumped strongly against Evie's cheek.

'What is it, Gully?'

Jim Gully, one of the club's gaming room staff, replied breathlessly. 'Sorry, milord. Trouble downstairs. The carpenters got a bottle o' blue ruin from somewhere, and all three are howling drunk. They started a quarrel into the coffee room. Two ow 'em are at fisticuffs already, whilst another is breaking the dishes at the sideboard.'

Sebastian scowled. 'Tell Rohan to handle it.'

'Mr Rohan says 'e's busy.'

'There's a drunken brawl downstairs and he's too busy to do anything about it?' Sebastian asked incredulously.

'Yes, milord.'

'Then you take care of it.'

'Can't, milord.' He held up a bandaged finger. 'Busted my knuckle during a fight in the alley last evenin'.'

'Where is Hayes?'

'Dunno, milord.'

'Are you telling me,' Sebastian asked with

dangerous softness, 'that of the thirty employees who work here, *not one of them* is available to keep three drunken sods from tearing up the coffee room when they should be restoring it?'

'Yes, milord.'

In the furious pause after Gully's reply, the sounds of shattering porcelain and furniture hitting the walls caused a vibration that elicited a faint tinkling rattle from the overhead chandeliers. Incomprehensible bellowing accompanied the racket as the fight escalated. 'Damn it,' Sebastian said through gritted teeth. 'What the hell are they doing to the club?'

Evie shook her head in confusion, staring from her husband's wrathful countenance to Gully's carefully blank one. 'I don't understand—'

'Call it a rite of passage,' Sebastian snapped, and left her with long strides that quickly broke into a run.

Picking up her skirts, Evie hurried after him. Rite of passage? What did he mean? And why wasn't Cam willing to do something about the brawl? Unable to match Sebastian's reckless pace, she trailed behind, taking care not to trip over her skirts as she descended the flight of stairs. The noise grew louder as she approached a small crowd that had congregated around the coffee room, shouts and exclamations renting the air. She saw Sebastian strip off his coat and thrust it at someone, and then he was shouldering his way into the melee. In a small clearing, three milling figures swung their fists and clumsily attempted to push and shove one another while the onlookers roared with excitement.

Sebastian strategically attacked the man who seemed the most unsteady on his feet, spinning him around, jabbing and hooking with a few deft blows until the dazed fellow tottered forward and collapsed to the carpeted floor. The remaining pair turned in tandem and rushed at Sebastian, one of them attempting to pin his arms while the other came at him with churning fists.

Evie let out a cry of alarm, which somehow reached Sebastian's ears through the thunder of the crowd. Distracted, he glanced in her direction, and he was instantly seized in a mauling clinch, with his neck caught in the vise of his opponent's arm while his head was battered with heavy blows. 'No,' Evie gasped, and started forward, only to be hauled back by a steely arm that clamped around her waist.

'Wait,' came a familiar voice in her ear. 'Give him a chance.'

'Cam!' She twisted around wildly, her panicked gaze finding his exotic but familiar face with its elevated cheekbones and thick-lashed golden eyes. 'They'll hurt him,' she said, clutching at the lapels of his coat. 'Go help him – Cam, you have to—'

'He's already broken free,' Cam observed mildly, turning her around with inexorable hands. 'Watch – he's not doing badly.'

One of Sebastian's opponents let loose with a

mighty swing of his arm. Sebastian ducked and came back with a swift jab. 'Cam, why the d-devil aren't you doing anything to help him?'

'I can't.'

'Yes, you can! You're used to fighting, far more than he—'

'He has to,' Cam said, his voice quiet and firm in her ear. 'He'll have no authority here otherwise. The men who work at the club have a notion of leadership that requires action as well as words. St Vincent can't ask them to do anything that he wouldn't be willing to do himself. And he knows that. Otherwise he wouldn't be doing this right now.'

Evie covered her eyes as one opponent endeavored to close in on her husband from behind while the other engaged him with a flurry of blows. 'They'll be loyal to him only if he is w-willing to use his fists in a pointless display of brute force?'

'Basically, yes. They want to see what he's made of.' Cam pulled at her wrist, to no avail. 'Watch,' he urged, a sudden tremor of laughter in his voice. 'He'll be all right.'

She couldn't watch. She turned into Cam's side, flinching and twitching with each sound of fists connecting with flesh, of every masculine grunt of pain. 'This is i-intolerable,' she moaned. 'Cam, please—'

'No one forced him to dismiss Egan and run the club himself,' he pointed out inexorably. 'This is part of the job, sweetheart.'

She understood that. She knew full well that her

221

own father had broken up brawls, or participated in them, for most of his life. But Sebastian had not been born to this – he did not have the essential brutishness, or the appetite for violence, that had distinguished Ivo Jenner.

As another man was downed, however, and Sebastian circled warily around his last opponent, it became evident that whether or not it was in his nature, he was willing to do what was necessary to prove his mettle. The drunken man rushed toward him, and Sebastian felled him with a quick combination, two lefts and a right. Collapsing to the ground, his opponent subsided with a groan. The crowd of employees sanctioned Sebastian's victory with approving howls and a round of applause. Accepting the acclaim with a grim nod, Sebastian saw Evie standing in the half circle of Cam's protective arm, and his face turned dark.

The vanquished fighters were helped outside by enthusiastic spectators. Brooms and pails were fetched to remove the debris, while some of the staff threw far friendlier glances at Sebastian than they had before. Using his shirtsleeve to blot a small trickle of blood from the corner of his mouth, Sebastian bent to pick up an overturned chair, and set it in its proper place in the corner.

Cam let go of Evie and approached Sebastian as the room emptied. 'You fight like a gentleman, my lord,' he commented.

Sebastian gave him a sardonic glance. 'Why doesn't that sound like a compliment?'

Sliding his hands into his pockets, Cam observed mildly, 'You do well enough against a pair of drunken sots—'

'There were three to start with,' Sebastian growled.

'*Three* drunken sots, then. But the next time you may not be so fortunate.'

'The next time? If you think I'm going to make a habit of this—'

'Jenner did,' Cam countered softly. 'Egan did. Nearly every night there is some to-do in the alley, the stable yard, or the card rooms, after the guests have had hours of stimulation from gaming, spirits, and women. We all take turns dealing with it. And unless you care to get the stuffing knocked out of you on a weekly basis, you'll need to learn a few tricks to put down a fight quickly. It causes less damage to you and the patrons, and keeps the police away.'

'If you're referring to the kind of tactics used in rookery brawls, and quarrels over back-alley bobtails—'

'You're not going for a half hour of light exercise at the pugilistic club,' Cam said acidly.

Sebastian opened his mouth to argue, but as he saw Evie drawing closer something changed in his face. It was a response to the anxiety that she couldn't manage to hide. For some reason her concern gently undermined his hostility, and softened him. Looking from one to the other, Cam observed the subtle interplay with astute interest.

'Have you been hurt?' Evie asked, looking over him closely. To her relief, Sebastian appeared disheveled and riled, but free of significant damage.

He shook his head, holding still as she reached up to push back a few damp amber locks that were nearly hanging in his eyes. 'I'm fine,' he muttered. 'Compared to the drubbing I received from Westcliff, this was nothing.'

Cam interrupted firmly. 'There are more drubbings in store, milord, if you won't take a few pointers on how to fight.' Without waiting for Sebastian's assent, he went to the doorway and called, 'Dawson! Come back here for a minute. No, not for work. We need you to come take a few swings at St Vincent.' He glanced back at Sebastian and remarked innocently, 'Well, that got him. He's hurrying over here.'

Biting back a sudden smile, Evie withdrew to the corner, understanding that Cam's intention was to help her husband. If Sebastian insisted on sparring according to gentlemen's rules, he would be no match against the ruthless attacks he might encounter.

Dawson, a burly young employee, entered the room.

'Dawson is the best fighter we've got,' Cam remarked. 'He's going to show you a few basic maneuvers to down a man quickly. Dawson, give Lord St Vincent a cross buttock. Gently, though – it wouldn't do to break his back.'

Looking more than pleased to practice the

maneuver on Sebastian, Dawson charged him in a few heavy strides, hooked a meaty arm around his neck, grasped his loose arm, and canted him over his shoulder, causing Sebastian to flip over violently. He landed on his back with a pained grunt. Dawson was about to jump onto his abdomen when Cam interceded hastily, diving forward to grab the enthusiastic young man by the shoulder. 'Good, Dawson. Very good. That's enough for now. Back off, please.'

Evie watched the proceedings with a clenched fist pressed against her mouth.

Cam reached down a hand to help Sebastian up. Spurning the offer, Sebastian rolled and rose to his feet, regarding him with a scowl so forbidding that it would have given most men pause, before continuing. Cam, however, spoke in an instructional tone. 'It's a simple move, really. When your sides come together, lock your arm around the other man's neck, seize his arm, and shift your body like so, and then he'll go over quite easily. Depending on how hard you slam him to the ground, he'll be unable to move for several seconds. Here, try it with me.'

It was to Sebastian's credit that he exercised restraint while practicing the procedure on Cam. He learned quickly, flipping the Gypsy to the ground with an odd mixture of efficiency and reluctance. 'I can't fight this way,' he muttered.

Cam ignored the comment. 'Now, if you're seized from behind, you can usually break it with a backward head butt. Start with your head down, chin to the chest. Clench your teeth, keep your mouth shut, and jerk your head back, hard and fast, into his face. No need to take aim. And for the forward head butt . . . have you done this before? No? Well, the trick is to keep your eyes on your opponent while you're doing it. Aim for a soft part of the face – never go for his forehead or skull. Use your body weight, and try to strike with the area about one inch above your brows.'

Sebastian tolerated the lesson with baleful reluctance, while the two younger men demonstrated throat strikes, foot stomps, and other techniques for attacking the vulnerable places of the human body. He participated when called on to do so, displaying a physical aptitude that seemed to please Cam. However, when the boy began on various methods for delivering a groin kick, it appeared that Sebastian had endured enough.

'That's it,' he growled. 'No more, Rohan.'

'But there are still a few things—'

'I don't give a damn.'

Cam exchanged a glance with Evie, who shrugged and shook her head slightly, neither of them understanding the source of his aggravation. After a moment, Cam dismissed Dawson with a few words of praise, and shooed him out of the room.

Turning to Sebastian, who was tugging on his coat with barely suppressed violence, Cam asked calmly, 'What is the problem, milord?'

Sebastian made a scornful sound. 'I've never

pretended to be a model of virtue. And I've done things in the past that would make the devil cringe. But there are certain things that even I can't stoop to. Men of my position don't stomp feet, knee the groin, or butt heads while they're fighting. Nor do they engage in throat punching, tripping, or God help me, hair pulling.'

Though Evie would have thought it impossible for Cam's eyes to look cold, they were suddenly as hard as chunks of frosted amber.

'What exactly is your position, if you don't mind my asking?' the Gypsy inquired in a lightly barbed tone. 'Are you a nobleman? You're not living like one. You're sleeping in a gaming club, in a room recently vacated by a pair of whores. Are you a man of leisure? You've just ended the evening breaking up a fight between a pair of sodden idiots. It's a bit late to turn particular now, isn't it?'

'You fault me for having standards?' Sebastian countered icily.

'Not at all. I fault you for having two sets of them. The Rom have a saying – 'With one behind, you cannot sit on two horses.' If you want to survive here, you'll have to change. You can't pose as an aristocratic idler who's above this sort of thing. Hell . . . you're trying to assume a job that even I couldn't manage. You'll have to deal with gamblers, drunkards, thieves, liars, crime lords, lawyers, police, and more than thirty employees who all believe you're going to fold up the wagon and depart within the month. Now that Jenner's dead, you've taken his place as one of the greatest marks in London. Everyone will want favors, or try to take advantage of you, or prove themselves superior to you. And no one will ever tell you the complete truth. About anything. You have to sharpen your instincts. You have to make people afraid of crossing you. Otherwise, the odds of your success are so low as to be . . .' His voice trailed away. It was clear that Cam would have liked to say more, but one glance at Sebastian's face seemed to indicate that further words were useless. Raking his lean hand roughly through the disordered layers of his jet-black hair, Cam strode from the room.

A long minute passed before Evie dared to approach her husband. He was staring fixedly at the blank wall in brooding contemplation. She noticed that whereas most people tended to look older when they were tired and strained, Sebastian tended to look younger. Staring up into his face, she murmured, 'Why are you doing it? It's not just for money. What are you hoping to find in this place?'

Unexpectedly, the questions kindled a gleam of sardonic amusement in his eyes. 'When I figure it out . . . I'll let you know.'

CHAPTER 15

The following afternoon Sebastian came to the office to find Evie, who was totaling receipts and listing numbers in an account ledger. 'You have a visitor,' Sebastian said without preamble. He met her gaze over the pile of paper slips. 'Mrs Hunt.'

Evie stared at him in astonishment, her heart leaping. She had struggled with the question of whether to write to Annabelle. She had been longing to see her friend, and yet there was a definite question about what her reception would be. Slowly she stood from her chair. 'Are you certain it's not another deception?'

'I'm certain,' Sebastian said sardonically. 'My ears are still ringing with accusations and invectives. Neither Mrs Hunt nor Miss Bowman will accept that you weren't abducted, raped, and married at knifepoint.'

'Miss Bowman?' Evie repeated dumbly, reflecting in an instant that it couldn't be Lillian. She was no longer Miss Bowman, and was still on her honeymoon with Lord Westcliff. 'Daisy is here as well?'

'And as hot-tempered as a hornet,' he confirmed. 'You might reassure them that you've acted of your own free will, as I believe they're of a mind to send for the nearest constable to arrest me.'

Excitement caused Evie's pulse to quicken, and her fingers tightened on his arm. 'I can't believe they've both dared to come here. I'm certain that Mr Hunt can't know what Annabelle is doing.'

'On that point we agree,' Sebastian said. 'Hunt wouldn't allow his wife within a ten-mile radius of me. And the Bowmans would never approve of their youngest daughter setting foot in a gaming club. However, knowing your friends, I have no doubt that they've concocted some elaborate ruse to cover their actions.'

'Where are they? Don't say you've left them standing at the back entrance?'

'They've been shown to the reading room.'

Evie was so eager to see her friends that she had to restrain herself from breaking into a run as soon as she left the office. Hurrying to the reading room, with Sebastian following, she dashed across the threshold and stopped uncertainly.

There was Annabelle, with her honey-streaked hair curled into shining upswept ringlets, her complexion as fresh as that of the idealized dairy-maids who were painted on tins of sweets. Upon first acquaintance, Annabelle's exquisite English-rose beauty had been so intimidating that Evie had been afraid to talk to her, certain that she would receive a crushing snub from such an exquisite creature. However, she had eventually discovered that Annabelle was warm and kind, with a self-deprecating sense of humor.

Daisy Bowman, Lillian's young sister, had an out-sized personality that belied her small, slight frame. Idealistic and possessed of a decidedly whimsical bent, she devoured romantic novels populated with rogues and villains. However, Daisy's elfin facade concealed a shrewd intelligence that most people tended to overlook. She was fair-skinned and dark-haired, with eyes the color of spiced gingerbread . . . mischievous eyes with long, spiky lashes.

Upon seeing Evie, her friends rushed toward her with unladylike squeals, and Evie let out her own laughing shriek as they collided in a circle of tightly hugging arms and exuberant kisses. In their shared excitement, the three young women continued to exclaim and scream, until someone burst into the room.

It was Cam, his eyes wide, his breathing fast, as if he had come at a dead run. His alert gaze flashed across the room, taking in the situation. Slowly his lean frame relaxed. 'Damn,' he muttered. 'I thought something was wrong.'

'Everything is fine, Cam,' Evie said with a smile, while Annabelle kept an arm around her shoulders. 'My friends are here, that's all.'

Glancing at Sebastian, Cam remarked sourly, 'I've heard less noise from the hogs at slaughter time.'

There was a sudden suspicious tension around Sebastian's jaw, as if he were fighting to suppress a grin. 'Mrs Hunt, Miss Bowman, this is Mr Rohan. You must pardon his lack of tact, as he is . . .'

'A ruffian?' Daisy suggested innocently.

This time Sebastian could not prevent a smile. 'I was going to say "unused to the presence of ladies at the club."'

'Is that what they are?' Cam asked, casting a dubious glance at the visitors, his attention lingering for a moment on Daisy's small face.

Pointedly ignoring Cam, Daisy spoke to Annabelle. 'I've always heard that Gypsies are known for their charm. An unfounded myth, it seems.'

Cam's golden eyes narrowed into tigerish slits. 'We're also known for carrying off *gadji* maidens.'

Before the exchange could continue, Evie interceded quickly. 'My lord,' she said to Sebastian, 'if you have no objections, I would like to speak in private to my friends.'

'Certainly,' he said with impeccable courtesy. 'Shall I have a tea tray sent in, my sweet?'

'Yes, thank you.'

As the men departed and the doors closed behind them, Daisy burst out, 'How can you speak to St Vincent cordially after what he's done?'

'Daisy,' Evie began apologetically, 'I'm so s-sorry about what happened to Lillian, and I—'

'No, not just that,' Daisy interrupted hotly, 'I

mean after what he's done to *you!* Taking advantage of you, forcing you to marry him, and then—'

'He didn't force me.' Evie looked from Daisy's indignant face to Annabelle's concerned one. 'Truly, he didn't! I was the one who approached him. Here, let's sit, and I'll t-tell you everything . . . How have you two managed to come to the club?'

'Mr Hunt is away on business,' Annabelle said with a crafty smile. 'And I told the Bowmans that I was taking Daisy shopping with me on St James Street. I'm her chaperone, you see.'

'And we did go shopping,' Daisy interjected slyly. 'It's only that we've taken this one little detour afterward . . .'

In the following minutes, they sat together in a cluster, with Annabelle and Evie on the settee, and Daisy in a nearby chair. Stammering slightly, Evie relayed the events that had transpired after she had left the Maybricks' home. To her relief, her friends did not condemn her for her actions. Instead they were concerned and sympathetic, even though it was clear that they did not agree with the choices she had made.

'I'm sorry,' Evie said at one point, as she saw the frown that pleated the ivory smoothness of Annabelle's forehead. 'I know you don't approve of my marriage to Lord St Vincent.'

'It doesn't matter if I approve,' Annabelle said gently. 'I'll stay your friend no matter what you do. I wouldn't care if you had married the devil himself.'

'Who is undoubtedly close kin of St Vincent,' Daisy remarked grimly.

'The point is,' Annabelle continued, giving Daisy a swift warning glance, 'now that it's a fait accompli, we want to find out how we can best help you.'

Evie smiled gratefully. 'All I need is your friendship. I was so afraid you might withdraw it.'

'Never.' Annabelle glanced over her and reached out to smooth her tumbled red curls. 'Dear, I hope this doesn't seem presumptuous . . . but since you left your family's home in haste, I'm sure you weren't able to take many gowns with you. So I've brought some things for you to wear. I know you're in mourning, and so I've brought only the browns and black and grays, and of course some nightgowns and gloves and other things . . . I'll have them sent in from the carriage, if you are agreeable. We're nearly the same height, and I think with a few alterations—'

'Oh Annabelle,' Evie exclaimed, throwing her arms around her friend, 'how kind you are! But I don't want you to s-sacrifice any part of your wedding trousseau for my sake—'

'It's no sacrifice,' Annabelle informed her, drawing back and smiling. 'Before long, I won't be able to wear them at all.'

Swiftly Evie recalled that the previous month, Annabelle had confided her suspicions that she might be pregnant. 'Of course, I . . . oh, Annabelle, I've been so pr-preoccupied with my own problems that I hadn't even thought to ask how you were feeling! Is it true, then? The doctor confirmed it?'

'Yes,' Daisy interrupted, standing up and doing a little victory dance, as if it were impossible for her to stay still any longer. 'The wallflowers are going to be aunts!'

Evie jumped up as well, and they cavorted in childish glee, while Annabelle remained sitting and watched them with amusement. 'Heavens, look at the pair of you,' she said. 'I wish Lillian were here – no doubt she would have some pithy comment about your savage romping.'

The mention of Lillian was enough to dampen Evie's elation. She dropped back onto the settee, staring at Annabelle with kindling worry. 'Will she forgive me, for m-marrying St Vincent after what he did to her?'

'Of course,' Annabelle said gently. 'You know how loyal she is – she would forgive you anything short of murder. Perhaps not even barring that. But I'm afraid that forgiving St Vincent is another matter entirely.'

Daisy frowned and tugged at her skirts to straighten them. 'It is certain that St Vincent has made an enemy of Lord Westcliff. Which makes things difficult for the rest of us.'

The conversation was interrupted as tea was brought in by a housemaid. Evie poured some of the delicate amber brew for herself and Annabelle. Daisy declined to have tea, preferring to wander about the room and browse among the shelves of books. She peered closely at the titles that had been engraved on the colored vellum spines. 'There's a layer of dust on most of these books,' she exclaimed. 'One would think that they hadn't been read in ages!'

Annabelle looked up from her tea with a droll smile. 'I'll wager that few, if any, have ever been read, dear. It's not likely that the gentlemen who frequent this club would choose to occupy themselves with books when there are so many more stimulating pursuits available.'

'Why have a reading room, if no one ever reads in it?' Daisy said, sounding outraged. 'I can't imagine *any* activity that could be more stimulating than reading. Why, sometimes during a particularly engaging story, I can feel my heart racing!'

'There is one thing . . .' Annabelle murmured with an unladylike grin. The words were lost on Daisy, however, who drifted farther away along the rows of books. Glancing at Evie's face, Annabelle kept her voice low as she said, 'While we're on *that* subject, Evie . . . it troubles me that you had no one to talk to before your wedding night. Was St Vincent considerate of you?'

Evie felt her cheeks burn as she responded with a quick nod. 'As one would expect, he was very accomplished.'

'But was he kind?'

'Yes . . . I think so.'

Annabelle smiled at her. 'It's an awkward subject,

is it not?' she asked softly. 'However, if there are any questions that you might have about such matters, I hope that you will bring yourself to ask me. I feel very much like your older sister, you know.'

'I feel that way too,' Evie returned, reaching out to squeeze her hand. 'I suppose I do have a few things that I would like to ask, but they're so terribly—'

'Zounds!' came Daisy's exclamation from the other side of the room. They both looked up to see her tugging at one of the mahogany bookshelves. 'When I leaned on this bookshelf, I heard a sort of clicking noise, and then the whole thing started to swing out.'

'It's a secret door,' Evie explained. 'There are several hidden doors and passageways in the club, for hiding things if there's a police raid, or if one needs to leave in haste—'

'Where does this one lead to?'

Fearing that to explain any more would encourage the adventurous Daisy to go exploring, Evie murmured vaguely, 'Oh, nowhere that you would wish to go. A storage room, I'm sure. You'd better close it, dear.'

'Hmm.'

While Daisy continued to examine the bookshelves, Evie and Annabelle resumed their whispered conversation. 'The truth is,' Evie said, 'that L-Lord St Vincent has agreed to undergo a period of celibacy, for my sake. And if he succeeds, he and I will then recommence our marital relations.'

'He *what*?' Annabelle whispered, her pretty blue eyes widening. 'Good God. I don't believe St Vincent and the word "celibacy" have ever been mentioned in the same sentence before. How on earth did you manage to persuade him to agree to such a thing?'

'He said . . . he indicated . . . that he desires me enough to try.'

Annabelle shook her head with an odd, bemused smile. 'That doesn't sound like him. Not at all. He'll cheat, of course.'

'Yes. But I do think his intentions are sincere.'

'St Vincent is never sincere,' Annabelle said wryly.

Evie could not help but remember the desperate urgency of St Vincent's embrace, in this very room. The way his breath had shivered in his throat. The consuming tenderness of his mouth on her skin. And the raw passion in his voice as he had murmured *'I want you more than I've ever wanted anything on this earth . . .'*

How could she explain any of that to Annabelle? How could mere words justify her instinct to believe him? It was ludicrous to believe that she, awkward Evie Jennings, had suddenly become the ultimate desire of a man like Sebastian, who had his pick of the most beautiful and accomplished women in England.

And yet Sebastian wasn't precisely the same man

who had sauntered so arrogantly through Westcliff's Hampshire mansion. Something in him had altered, and was altering still. Had the catalyst been his failed attempt to kidnap Lillian? Or had it started later, during the miserable journey to Gretna Green? Perhaps it was something about the club. He had behaved oddly since the moment they had set foot in it. He was striving for something, a nameless thing that he couldn't explain even to himself—

'Oh no,' Annabelle said ruefully, looking over Evie's shoulder.

'What is it?' Evie turned to follow Annabelle's gaze.

There was no need for Annabelle to explain. The room was empty save for the two of them. One of the bookcases had been left out of alignment with the others. Daisy, predictably, had followed the urges of her own insatiable curiosity, and had gone through the secret door.

'Where does it lead?' Annabelle asked with a sigh, reluctantly setting aside her half-finished tea.

'It depends on which way she went,' Evie replied with a frown. 'It's rather like a maze – one passage branches off into two directions, and there are secret stairs that lead to the second floor. Thank heaven the club isn't open – that minimizes the amount of trouble she could get into.'

'Remember, this is Daisy Bowman,' Annabelle said dryly. 'If there is the least chance of trouble to be found, she will discover it.'

★ ★ ★

Creeping along the dark passageway, Daisy experienced the same thrill that she had always felt as a child, when she and Lillian played a game of pirates in their Fifth Avenue mansion. After their daily lessons had concluded, they had run outside in the garden, a pair of imps with long braids and torn frocks, rolling their hoops and digging holes in the flower beds. One day they had taken it in their heads to create a secret pirate cave, and they had proceeded to spend the entire summer hollowing out a tunnel in the hedge that bordered the front and sides of the mansion. They had diligently cut and clipped until they had created a long channel behind the hedge, where they had scurried back and forth like a pair of mice. They held secret meetings in their 'pirate cave,' of course, and had kept a wooden box filled with treasures in a hole they had dug beside the house. When their misdeeds had been discovered by the irate gardener, who was horrified by the desecration of his hedge, Daisy and Lillian had been punished for weeks afterward.

Smiling wistfully at the thought of her beloved older sister, Daisy felt a wave of loneliness sweep over her. She and Lillian had always been together, arguing, laughing, getting each other into scrapes, and rescuing each other whenever possible. Naturally she was happy that Lillian had met her perfect match in the strong-willed Westcliff . . . but that didn't stop Daisy from missing her terribly. And now that the other wallflowers, including

Evie, had found husbands, they were part of the mysterious married world that Daisy was still excluded from. She was going to have to find a husband soon. Some nice, sincere gentleman who would share her love of books. A man who wore spectacles, and liked dogs and children.

Feeling her way along the passageway, Daisy nearly tripped down a small flight of stairs that presented themselves unexpectedly. A faint glimmer of light from the bottom drew her forward. As she neared the light, she saw that it limned the small rectangular shape of a door. Wondering what could be on the other side of the door, Daisy paused and heard an odd, repetitive tapping. A pause, then more tapping.

Curiosity got the better of her. Placing her hands on the door, Daisy gave it a decisive shove and felt it give way. Light spilled into the passageway as she stepped into a room that contained a few empty tables and chairs, and a sideboard with two giant silver urns. Peering around the door, she saw the source of the tapping. A man was repairing a piece of damaged molding on the wall, sitting on his haunches as he expertly sank nails into the thin strip of wood with deft blows of a hammer. As soon as he saw the door open, he rose to his feet in an easy movement, his grip changing on the hammer as if he might use it as a weapon.

It was the Gypsy, the boy with the eyes of a hungry panther. He had removed his coat and waistcoat . . . his necktie as well . . . so that his upper half was covered only in a thin white shirt that had been tucked loosely into the waist of his close-fitting trousers. The sight of him elicited the same reaction Daisy had felt upstairs – a swift sting in her chest followed by the rapid pumping of her heart. Paralyzed by the realization that she was alone in the room with him, Daisy watched with unblinking eyes as he approached her slowly.

She had never seen any living being who had been fashioned with such exotic dark beauty . . . his skin the color of raw clover honey, the light hazel of his eyes framed with heavy black lashes, his thick obsidian hair tumbled over his forehead.

'What are you doing here?' Rohan asked, not stopping until he was so close that she back-stepped instinctively. Her shoulder blades met the wall. No man in Daisy's limited experience had ever approached her with such directness. Clearly he knew nothing about drawing room manners.

'Exploring,' she said breathlessly.

'Did someone show you the passageway?'

Daisy started as Rohan braced his hands on the wall, one on either side of her. He was a bit taller than average but not towering, his tanned throat at a level with her eyes. Trying not to show her nervousness, she took a shallow breath and said, 'No, I found it by myself. Your accent is odd.'

'So is yours. American?'

Daisy nodded, the power of speech abandoning her as she saw the glitter of a small diamond on his ear-lobe. There was a funny little curl of sensation in her stomach, almost like repulsion, but it made her skin feel very hot, and she realized to her dismay that she was turning bright pink. He was so close to her that she could detect a clean, soapy scent, mixed with the hints of horses and leather. It was a nice smell, a masculine fragrance, very different from that of her father, who always smelled like cologne and shoe polish, and fresh-minted paper money.

Her uneasy gaze skittered along the length of his arms, which were exposed by his rolled-up shirt-sleeves . . . and stopped at the astonishing sight of a design that had been inked onto his right forearm. It was a small black horse with wings.

Noticing her mesmerized stare, Rohan lowered his arm to give her a better view. 'An Irish symbol,' he murmured. 'A nightmare horse, called a pooka.'

The absurd-sounding word brought a faint smile to Daisy's lips. 'Does it wash off?' she asked hesitantly.

He shook his head, his lashes half lowering over his remarkable eyes.

'Is a pooka like the Pegasus of the Greek myths?' Daisy asked, flattening herself as close to the wall as possible.

Rohan glanced down her body, taking a kind of

leisurely inventory that no man ever had before. 'No. He's far more dangerous. He has eyes of yellow fire, a stride that clears mountains, and he speaks in a human voice as deep as a cave. At midnight, he may stop in front of your house and call out your name if he wants to take you for a ride. If you go with him, he'll fly you across earth and oceans . . . and if you ever return, your life will never be the same.'

Daisy felt gooseflesh rise all over her body. All her senses warned that she had better put a stop to this unnerving conversation, and flee his presence with all due haste. 'How interesting,' she muttered, and turned blindly in the circle of his arms, hunting for the edge of the hidden door. To her dismay, he had closed it, and the door was now skillfully concealed in the paneled wall. Panicking, she pushed at various places in the wall, trying to discover the mechanism that would open it.

Her moist palms flattened on the paneling as she felt Rohan lean against her from behind, his mouth close to her ear. 'You won't find it. There is only one spot that will release the catch.'

His hot breath touched the side of her throat, while the light pressure of his body warmed her wherever it touched.

'Why don't you show it to me?' Daisy suggested in her best imitation of Lillian's sarcastic drawl, dismayed to hear that she sounded only unsteady and bewildered.

'What favor will you give in return?'

Daisy strove for indignation, even as her heart clattered against her ribs like a wild bird in a cage. She turned around to face him, launching a verbal assault that she hoped would drive him back. 'Mr Rohan, if you are insinuating that I should . . . well, you're the most *ungentlemanly* man I have ever encountered.'

He didn't budge an inch. His animal-white teeth flashed in a grin. 'But I do know where the door is,' he reminded her.

'Do you want money?' she asked scornfully.

'No.'

Daisy swallowed hard. 'A liberty, then?' Seeing his incomprehension, she clarified with reddening cheeks, 'Taking a liberty is . . . an embrace, or a kiss . . .'

Something dangerous flickered in Rohan's golden eyes. 'Yes,' he murmured. 'I'll take a liberty.'

Daisy could hardly believe it. Her first kiss. She had always envisioned it as a romantic moment in an English garden . . . There would be moonlight, of course . . . and a fair-haired gentleman with a boyish face would say something lovely from a poem just before his lips met hers. It was not supposed to happen in one of the basement rooms of a gambling club with a Gypsy card dealer. On the other hand, she was twenty years old, and maybe it was time for her to start accumulating some experience.

Swallowing again, she fought to control the

reckless meter of her breathing, and stared at the part of his throat and upper chest that was revealed by his partly opened shirt. His skin gleamed like tautly stretched amber satin. As he drew closer to her, his scent invaded her nostrils in a drift of luxurious masculine spice. His hand lifted gently to her face, the backs of his knuckles accidentally brushing the tip of her small breast along the way. It had to be accidental, she thought dizzily, while her nipple contracted tightly beneath her velvet bodice. His long fingers slid around the side of her face, tilting it to an upward slant.

Staring into the dark pools of her dilated eyes, he drew his fingertips to her mouth, stroking the plush surface of her lips until they were parted and trembling. His other hand slid behind the back of her neck, caressing at first, then grasping lightly to support the weight of her head . . . which was a good thing, since her entire spine seemed to have dissolved like melted sugar. His mouth came to hers with tender pressure, exploring her lips with repeated brushes. Warm delight seemed to leak into her veins, flowing through her until she could no longer resist the urge to press her body against his. Rising on her toes, she gripped his hard shoulders with her hands, and gasped as she felt his arms slide around her.

When at last his head lifted, Daisy was mortified to discover that she was clinging to him like the victim of a near-drowning. She jerked her hands away from him, and retreated as far as the wall would allow. Confused and ashamed by her response to him, she scowled up into his pagan eyes.

'I didn't feel a thing,' she said coolly. 'Though I suppose you deserve credit for trying. Now show me where the—'

She broke off with a surprised squeak as he reached for her again, and she realized too late that he had taken her dismissive remark as a challenge. This time his mouth was more demanding, his hands cupped around the back of her head. With innocent surprise, she felt the silken touch of his tongue, a sensation that sent writhing sweetness all through her. She shivered as he searched her mouth intimately . . . as if the taste of her was something delicious.

Finishing the kiss with a last coaxing nuzzle of his lips, Rohan pulled back to stare into her eyes, silently daring her to deny her attraction to him.

She mustered the last few shreds of her pride. 'Still nothing,' she said weakly.

This time he hauled her fully against his body, his dark head lowering over hers. Daisy had never thought a kiss could be so deep, his mouth feeding slowly on hers, his hands pulling her up and against him. She felt his feet pushing between hers, his chest hard against her small breasts, his kisses teasing, caressing, until she quivered like a wild creature in the support of his arms. By the time he released her mouth, she was limp and passive, all her consciousness focused on the sensations that drew her toward some unknown end.

Opening her eyes, Daisy looked at him through a haze of sensuality. 'That . . . that was much improved,' she managed to say with dignity. 'I'm glad I was able to teach you something.' She turned away from him, but not before she saw his quick grin. Reaching out, he pressed at the hidden catch on the door, and opened it.

To Daisy's discomfiture, Rohan went with her into the dark passageway and accompanied her up the narrow stairs, guiding her as if he could see like a cat in the dark. When they reached the top, where the outline of the reading room door was visible, they paused in tandem.

Feeling called upon to say something, Daisy muttered, 'Good-bye, Mr Rohan. We shall probably never meet again.' She could only hope so – because it was a certainty that she would never be able to face him.

He leaned over her shoulder, until his mouth was at her tingling ear. 'Perhaps I'll appear at your window one midnight,' he whispered, 'to tempt you for a ride across earth and ocean.'

And with that, he opened the door, pushed Daisy gently into the reading room, and closed it again. Blinking in confusion, she stared at Annabelle and Evie.

Annabelle spoke wryly. 'I should have known

you couldn't resist something like a secret door. Where did you go?'

'Evie was right,' Daisy said, as flags of bright color burned at the tops of her cheeks. 'It led to no place that I wanted to go.'

CHAPTER 16

Although the clothes that Annabelle Hunt had brought were far more appropriate for half mourning than full mourning, Evie decided to wear them. She had already gone against the dictates of propriety by wearing fabrics other than crepe, and there was hardly anyone in the club who would dare to criticize her; so it didn't make much difference whether she wore black, brown, or gray. Moreover, she felt certain that her father would not have minded.

Picking up the note that Annabelle had included with the clothes, Evie read it once more, a smile touching her lips. '*I had these made in Paris,*' Annabelle had written impishly, '*without taking into consideration the consequences of Mr Hunt's virility. By the time I am able to wear them again, they will be out of fashion. My gift to you, dearest friend.*'

Trying on the soft gray wool, which was lined with silk, Evie discovered that it fit nicely. However, her pleasure in the new gown was swamped in a wave of melancholy as she thought of her father. Wandering disconsolately down to the main hazard room, she saw Sebastian speaking to a pair of dust-covered masons. He was much taller than either of them, and inclined his head as they replied. Then he made some quip that drew laughter.

A glint of humor lingered in Sebastian's eyes as he happened to glance in Evie's direction. His gaze softened, and he took leave of the masons, coming toward her with unhurried strides. Evie fought to contain a rush of eagerness, afraid of appearing foolishly infatuated with him. However, no matter how sternly she tamped her feelings down beneath the surface, they seemed to sift out like diamond dust, sparkling visibly in the air around her. The odd thing was, he seemed similarly glad to be in her presence, for once discarding the guise of a jaded rake, and smiling at her with genuine warmth.

'Evie . . .' His golden head bent over her upturned face. 'Are you all right?'

'Yes, I . . . no.' She rubbed her temples fretfully. 'I'm weary. And bored, and hungry.'

His quiet chuckle seemed to cut through her gloom. 'I can do something about that.'

'I have no wish to interrupt your work—' she said diffidently.

'Rohan will manage things for a while. Come, let's see if the billiards room is empty.'

'Billiards?' Evie repeated reluctantly. 'Why should we go there?'

He slid her a provocative glance. 'To play, of course.'

'But women don't play billiards.'

'They do in France.'

'From what Annabelle says,' Evie said, 'women do many things in France that they don't do here.'

'Yes. A very forward-thinking race, the French. Whereas we English tend to view pleasure with deep suspicion.'

The billiards room was indeed unoccupied. Sebastian sent for a luncheon tray from the kitchen, sat with Evie at a small table at the corner, and diverted her with conversation as she ate. She couldn't quite understand why he would take the time to entertain her, when there were many responsibilities that required his attention. And years of seeing the glazed-over boredom on men's faces when she talked to them had reduced Evie's self-confidence to a crumb of what it should have been. However, Sebastian listened closely to everything she said, as if he found her endlessly interesting. He encouraged her to say daring things, and he seemed to delight in her attempts to spar with him.

After Evie had finished her plate, Sebastian tugged her to the billiards table and handed her a cue stick with a leather tip. Ignoring her attempts to refuse him, he proceeded to instruct her in the basics of the game. 'Don't try to claim this is too scandalous for you,' he told her with mock severity. 'After running off with me to Gretna Green, nothing is beyond you. Certainly not one little billiards game. Bend over the table.'

She complied awkwardly, flushing as she felt him lean over her, his body forming an exciting masculine cage as his hands arranged hers on the cue stick. 'Now,' she heard him say, 'curl your index finger around the tip of the shaft. That's right. Don't grip so tightly, sweet . . . let your hand relax. Perfect.' His head was close to hers, the light scent of sandalwood cologne rising from his warm skin. 'Try to imagine a path between the cue ball – that's the white one – and the colored ball. You'll want to strike right about there' – he pointed to a place just above center on the cue ball – 'to send the object ball into the side pocket. It's a straight-on shot, you see? Lower your head a bit. Draw the cue stick back and try to strike in a smooth motion.'

Attempting the shot, Evie felt the tip of the cue stick fail to make proper contact with the white ball, sending it spinning clumsily off to the side of the table.

'A miscue,' Sebastian remarked, deftly catching the cue ball in his hand and repositioning it. 'Whenever that happens, reach for more chalk, and apply it to the tip of the cue stick while looking thoughtful. Always imply that your equipment is to blame, rather than your skills.'

Evie felt a smile rising to her lips, and she leaned over the table once more. Perhaps it was wrong, with her father having passed away so recently, but for the first time in a long while, she was having fun.

Sebastian covered her from behind again, sliding his hands over hers. 'Let me show you the proper motion of the cue stick – keep it level – like this.' Together they concentrated on the steady, even slide of the cue stick through the little circle Evie had made of her fingers. The sexual entendre of the motion could hardly escape her, and she felt a flush rise up from the neck of her gown. 'Shame on you,' she heard him murmur. 'No proper young woman would have such thoughts.'

A helpless giggle escaped Evie's lips, and Sebastian moved to the side, watching her with a lazy smile. 'Try again.'

Focusing on the cue ball, Evie drew back and struck it firmly. This time the colored ball sank neatly into the side pocket. 'I did it!' she cried.

Sebastian grinned at her triumph and proceeded to set up various shots for her, positioning her body and adjusting her hands, and using every possible excuse to put his arms around her. Enjoying herself immensely, Evie pretended not to notice the audacious caress of his hands. However, when he caused her to miss a bank shot for the fourth time, she turned to him accusingly. 'How could *anyone* make a proper shot when you put your hand *there*?'

'I was trying to adjust your posture,' he said helpfully. At her mock-accusing glance, he smiled and half sat on the billiards table. 'It's your fault that I've been reduced to such behavior,' he continued. 'I assure you, I myself find it appalling that the only pleasure I obtain these days is chasing after you like an adolescent lordling with a housemaid.'

'Did you chase after the housemaids when you were a boy?'

'Good God, of course not. How could you ask such a thing?' Sebastian looked indignant. Just as she felt a twinge of guilt and began to apologize, he said smugly, '*They* chased after *me*.'

Evie raised a cue stick as if to crown him with it.

He caught her wrist easily in one hand and pried the stick from her fingers. 'Easy, firebrand. You'll knock out the few wits I have left – and then of what use would I be to you?'

'You would be purely ornamental,' Evie replied, giggling.

'Ah, well, I suppose there's some value in that. God help me if I should ever lose my looks.'

'I wouldn't mind.'

He gave her a quizzical smile. 'What?'

'If . . .' Evie paused, suddenly embarrassed. 'If anything happened to your looks . . . if you became . . . less handsome. Your appearance wouldn't matter to me. I would still . . .' She paused and finished hesitantly, '. . . want you as my husband.'

Sebastian's smile faded slowly. He gave her a long, intent stare, her wrist still clasped in his hand. Something strange crossed his expression . . . an undefinable emotion wrought of heat and vulnerability. When he answered, his voice was strained from the effort to sound cavalier. 'Without a doubt, you're the first one who's ever said that to me. I hope you won't be such a pea goose as to endow me with characteristics that I don't have.'

'No, you're endowed enough as it is,' Evie replied, before the double meaning of the statement occurred to her. She burned a brilliant scarlet. 'Th-that is . . . I didn't mean . . .'

But Sebastian was laughing quietly, the odd tension passing, and he pulled her against him. As she responded to him eagerly, his amusement dissolved like sugar in hot liquid. He kissed her longer, harder, his breath striking her cheek in rapid drives.

'Evie,' he whispered, 'you're so warm, so lovely . . . oh, hell. I've got two months, thirteen days and six hours before I can take you to my bed. Little she-devil. This is going to be the death of me.'

Feeling rather sorry about the bargain she had made with him, Evie tightened her arms and sought his mouth with hers. He groaned low in his throat and kissed her, and reached out to shut the door of the billiards room. Fumbling with the lock, he turned the key and sank to his knees before her. Her shoulder blades pressed hard against the closed door, and she leaned heavily on the paneling, her mind reeling with confusion and excitement. He hiked up her skirts, his hands searching beneath the layers of fabric, tugging at the tapes of her drawers.

'Sebastian, no,' Evie whispered shakily, mindful that they were in one of the public rooms. 'Please, you can't . . .'

Sebastian ignored her protests, delving beneath her skirts and pulling her drawers to her knees. 'I'll go mad if I can't have at least this much of you.'

'No,' she said weakly, but he was beyond hearing.

His hand was on her ankle, and his mouth was at her knee, nibbling and licking through the silk stocking. Evie felt a shocking jolt of desire, her heart drumming violently, her flesh awakening with irresistible hunger. Sebastian pushed the front of her skirts up to her waist and clamped her hands over the mass of fabric. 'Hold them,' he muttered.

She shouldn't have obeyed, but her hands seemed to possess a will of their own, clenching the wads of velvet against her midriff. Her drawers were pushed to her ankles, and his mouth wandered upward, his breath like puffs of steam against the tender skin of her leg. Evie made a low keening sound as he parted the private curls between her thighs. The two fingers he slipped inside her were immediately clasped and caressed, her inner muscles working as if to draw him deeper. Evie's eyes half closed, and a passion-blush swept over her body in uneven drifts of pink. *Sebastian.*

'Shhh . . .' His fingers pushed higher, and his mouth nudged past the swollen folds of her sex. He teased the straining little peak, licking in a sly counter-rhythm to the gentle thrust of his fingers. Evie arched against the door, her throat aching from the effort not to cry out. He did not pause or relent, did not allow her a single moment to catch her breath, only stroked and tormented her hot, twitching flesh, driving the sensation higher and higher until at last she choked back a scream and shuddered with rapture. His mouth stayed on her, drawing out every last ripple of fulfillment until she was finally still, her weary flesh emptied of sensation.

Eventually Sebastian stood, bringing his aroused body against hers, his forehead pressed to the door behind her. Evie linked her arms around his lean waist, her eyes closed as she rested her cheek against his shoulder. 'The bargain . . .' she mumbled.

'You said I could kiss you,' came his gentle, wicked whisper near her ear. 'But, my love . . . you didn't specify where.'

CHAPTER 17

'You sent for me, my lord?' Evie came to stand before the desk in the small office, where Sebastian remained sitting. One of the servants had brought her downstairs at his request, accompanying her through the barely controlled chaos of the overcrowded club.

On this, the first night of Jenner's reopening, it seemed that everyone who was or wished to be a member was determined to gain admittance. A stack of applications was piled on the desk before Sebastian, while at least a dozen men waited impatiently in the entrance hall to be approved. The air was filled with the sounds of chatter and clinking glasses, and the music of an orchestra that played on the second-floor balcony. To honor the memory of Ivo Jenner, champagne was being served in an endless flow, adding to the atmosphere of uninhibited enjoyment. The club was open again, and all was well with the gentlemen of London.

'Yes, I did,' Sebastian said in response to Evie's question. 'Why the hell are you still here? You should have left approximately eight hours ago.'

259

She stared into his expressionless face without flinching. 'I'm still packing.'

'You've been packing for three days. You don't own more than a half-dozen gowns. The few belongings you have would fit into a small valise. You're stalling, Evie.'

'What difference does it make to you?' she shot back. 'For the past two days you've treated me as if I don't even exist. I can scarcely credit that you even noticed I'm still here.'

Sebastian subjected her to a knifelike stare while he struggled to retain control of his writhing temper. Not notice her? Holy hell, he would have given a fortune for that to be true. He had been torturously aware of her every word and gesture, hungering constantly for the briefest glimpse of her. Seeing her now, her beautifully curved body neatly wrapped in the black velvet dress, was enough to drive him mad. The somber darkness of mourning was supposed to render a woman plain and drab, but instead the black made her skin look like fresh cream, and her hair glow like fire. He wanted to take her to bed, and love her until this mysterious bedeviling attraction was consumed in its own heat. He felt invaded by something, some kind of ardent disquiet that felt like a sickness . . . something that made him go from one room to another and then forget what he had wanted. He had never been like this . . . distracted, impatient, agonized with yearning.

He had to get rid of her. Evie had to be protected

from the dangers and depravities of the club, as well as from himself. If he could somehow keep her safe, and see her in some kind of limited manner . . . it was the only solution.

'I want you to go,' he said. 'Everything has been prepared for you at the house. You'll be far more comfortable there. And then I won't have to worry about what kind of trouble you might be getting into.' Standing, he went to the door, taking care to preserve a necessary physical distance between them. 'I'm going to send for a carriage. In a quarter hour, I want you to be in it.'

'I've had no supper. Is it too much to ask that I be allowed a last meal?'

Though Sebastian wasn't looking at her, he could hear the note of childish defiance in her voice, and it caused a wrench in his heart . . . a heart that he had always believed to be nothing more than an efficient muscle.

He never remembered whether he had intended to allow her to stay for supper or not, for at that moment he saw Cam approaching the office . . . accompanied by the unmistakable form of the Earl of Westcliff. Turning to the side, Sebastian dragged his lean fingers through his hair. 'Bloody hell,' he muttered.

Evie came to him instantly. 'What is it?'

Sebastian wiped his face clean of expression. 'You'd better go,' he said grimly. 'Westcliff is here.'

'I'm not going anywhere,' she said at once.

'Westcliff is too much of a gentleman to fight in front of a lady.'

Sebastian let out a derisive laugh. 'I don't need to hide behind your skirts, pet. And I doubt he's here to fight – that was all settled on the night I abducted Miss Bowman.'

'What does he want, then?'

'Either to deliver a warning, or to see if you need rescuing. Or both.'

Evie remained by his side as Westcliff entered the office.

Cam was the first to speak. 'My lord,' he said to Sebastian, 'I bid the earl to wait, but he—'

'No one bids Westcliff to do anything,' Sebastian said dryly. 'It's all right, Cam. Go back to the hazard tables, or it will be mayhem in there. And take Lady St Vincent with you.'

'No,' Evie said instantly, her concerned gaze switching from Sebastian's mocking face to Westcliff's granite-hard one. 'I'm going to stay.' Turning to Lord Westcliff, she gave him her hand. 'My lord, I have thought so often about Lillian . . . she is well, I hope?'

Westcliff bent over her hand and spoke in his distinctive gravelly voice. 'Quite well. It is her wish that you come to stay with us, if you so desire.'

Although Sebastian had been browbeating her into leaving the club only a few minutes earlier, he was filled with sudden fury. The arrogant bastard. If he thought to come in here and snatch Evie away from beneath his nose—

'Thank you, my lord,' Evie replied softly as she stared into Westcliff's bold-featured face. He had black hair, and eyes so dark that it was impossible to distinguish the irises from the pupils. 'You are very kind. And I wish very much to visit soon. But I have no need of your hospitality at this time.'

'Very well. The offer will remain open. Allow me to offer my condolences on your recent loss.'

'Thank you.' She smiled at Westcliff, Sebastian saw with a stab of jealousy.

As the possessor of one of the oldest and most powerful earldoms in England, Marcus, Lord Westcliff, had the aura of a man who was accustomed to having his opinions heard and heeded. Though he was not classically handsome, Westcliff possessed a dark vitality and masculine vigor that caused him to stand out in any gathering. He was a sportsman and a bruising rider, known for pushing himself to the edge of his own physical limits and beyond. In fact, Westcliff approached everything in life that way, allowing himself nothing less than excellence in whatever he chose to do.

Westcliff and Sebastian had been friends since the age of ten, having spent most of their formative years together at boarding school. Even as boys they'd had an unlikely friendship, for Westcliff by nature believed in moral absolutes, and had no difficulty distinguishing right from wrong. Sebastian had loved to take the simplest matters and twist them into something exasperatingly complex, merely as an exercise of his own cleverness. Westcliff always chose the most efficient and straightforward path, whereas Sebastian chose the crooked, poorly mapped route that would get one into all manner of trouble before finally reaching his destination.

However, there was much that the two friends understood about each other, having both grown up under the influence of manipulative and uncaring fathers. They had shared a similarly unromantic view of the world, understanding that they could trust very few people. And now, Sebastian reflected bleakly, he had broken Westcliff's trust beyond any hope of repairing it. For the first time in his life, he was aware of a sickening pang that he could only identify as regret.

Why the hell had he focused his attentions on Lillian Bowman? When he had realized that Westcliff was taken with the girl, why had Sebastian not troubled himself to find some other heiress to wed? He had been a fool to overlook Evie. In retrospect, Lillian had not been worth the sabotage of a friendship. Privately Sebastian was forced to acknowledge that Westcliff's absence in his life was rather like a blister on his foot that frequently chafed and would never quite heal.

Sebastian waited until the door had closed behind Cam. Then he draped a possessive arm over Evie's narrow shoulders and spoke to his former friend. 'How was the honeymoon?' he inquired mockingly.

Westcliff ignored the question. 'In light of the circumstances,' he said to Evie, 'I find it necessary to ask – were you married under duress?'

'*No*,' Evie said earnestly, inching closer to Sebastian's side as if she were trying to shield him. 'Truly, my lord, it was my idea. I went to Lord St Vincent's home to ask for his help, and he gave it.'

Appearing unconvinced, Westcliff said curtly, 'Surely there were other avenues available to you.'

'None that I could see at the time.' Her slender arm slipped around Sebastian's waist, causing his breath to stop in sudden astonishment. 'I do not regret my decision,' he heard Evie tell Westcliff firmly. 'I would do it again without hesitation. Lord St Vincent has been nothing but kind to me.'

'She's lying, of course,' Sebastian said with a callous laugh, while his pulse began to vibrate frantically in his veins. With Evie's soft body tucked against his side, he could feel her warmth, smell her skin. He couldn't understand why she was trying to defend him. 'I've been a bastard to her,' he told Westcliff flatly. 'Fortunately for me, Lady St Vincent was ill-used by her family for so long that she has no conception of what it is to be treated well.'

'That's not true,' Evie said to Westcliff. Neither of them spared a glance at Sebastian, giving him an infuriating sense of being cut out of the conversation. 'This has been a difficult time, as you can imagine. I could not have survived it without my husband's support. He has looked after my health, and sheltered me as much as possible. He has worked very hard to preserve my father's business. He defended me when my uncles tried to compel me to leave with them against my will—'

'You've gone too far, sweet,' Sebastian told her with baleful satisfaction. 'Westcliff knows me well enough to be certain that I would never work. Or defend anyone, for that matter. I only bother with my own interests.' To his annoyance, neither of them seemed to pay attention to his remarks.

'My lord,' Evie said to the earl, 'from what I have learned about my husband, 1 do not believe he would have acted as he did, had he understood that you were in love with Lillian. That is not to excuse his behavior, but to—'

'He doesn't love her,' Sebastian snarled, pushing Evie away from him. Suddenly it felt as if the room was shrinking, the walls drawing closer until they threatened to crush him in a fatal vise. Damn her for trying to apologize for him! And damn her for putting up a sham pretense of affection between them. 'He doesn't believe in love any more than I do.' He glared at Westcliff. 'How many times have you told me that love is a delusion of men who wished to make the necessity of marriage more palatable?'

'I was wrong,' Westcliff said. 'Why are you so irate?'

'I'm not—' Sebastian broke off as he realized that he was unraveling. He glanced at Evie and felt the startling reverse of their positions . . . she, the stammering wallflower, now serene and steady . . . and he, always so cool and self-possessed, now reduced to an impassioned idiot. And all in front of Westcliff, who observed the pair of them with keen scrutiny.

'What does it take to be rid of you?' Sebastian asked Evie abruptly. 'Go with Westcliff, if you won't go to the town house. I don't give a damn so long as you're out of my sight.'

Her eyes widened, and she flinched as if she had been struck by a metal dart. She remained composed, however, taking a deep breath and releasing it in a controlled flow. As Sebastian watched her, he was nearly overcome by the urge to fall to his knees before her and beg for forgiveness. Instead he remained frozen while she went to the door.

'Evie—' he muttered.

She ignored him and left, squaring her shoulders as she walked away from the office.

Sebastian clenched his hands into aching fists while his gaze followed her. After several seconds, he forced himself to glance at Westcliff. His old friend was staring at him not with hatred, but with something like reluctant compassion. 'This isn't what I expected to find,' Westcliff said quietly. 'You're not yourself, Sebastian.'

It had been years since Westcliff had addressed him by his first name. Men, even siblings or the closest of friends, almost always called each other by their family or title names.

'Go to hell,' Sebastian muttered. 'No doubt that was what you came to tell me tonight. If so, you're about a month too late.'

'That was my intention,' Westcliff admitted. 'Now, however, I've decided to stay and have a snifter of brandy while you tell me what in God's name you're doing. To start with, you can explain why you've taken it upon yourself to manage a gaming club.'

It was the worst possible time to sit and talk with the club so crowded – but suddenly Sebastian didn't give a damn. It had been an eternity since he'd conversed with someone who knew him well. Although Sebastian had no illusion that their former friendship was anything but a shambles, the prospect of discussing things with Westcliff, even an unsympathetic Westcliff, seemed an unutterable relief. 'All right,' he muttered. 'Yes, we'll talk. Don't leave. I'll return in a moment – I can't allow my wife to go through the club unescorted.'

He left the office with long strides and went to the entrance hall. Seeing no sign of Evie's black-gowned figure, he deduced that she had gone an alternate route, perhaps through the central room. He paused in one of the arched doorways and glanced across the sea of heads. Evie's brilliant hair made it easy to locate her quickly. She was heading to the corner where Cam sat. As she passed, several club members moved to make way for her.

Sebastian pursued her slowly at first, then with increasing urgency. He was in a peculiar state, struggling to understand himself. He had always been so adept at handling women. Why, then, had it become impossible to remain detached where Evie was concerned? He was separated from what he wanted most, not by real distance but by a past tainted with debauchery. To let himself have a relationship with her . . . no, it was impossible. His own iniquity would saturate her like dark ink spreading over pristine white parchment, until every inch of clean space was obliterated. She would become cynical, bitter . . . and as she came to know him, she would despise him.

Cam, who was seated on a tall stool overlooking the hazard tables, noticed Evie's approach. He turned on the stool to face her, lowering one foot to the ground. His dark head lifted, and he let his gaze whisk quickly across the room, alert as always to the scene around him. Catching sight of Sebastian, Cam gave a short nod to indicate that he would keep her with him until Sebastian could reach them.

Cam surveyed the room once more, a frown tugging between his dark brows. His shoulders hitched slightly, as if the hair on his nape was prickling uncomfortably, and he twisted to glance over his shoulder. Seeing that no one was behind him, he began to settle back onto the stool. However, it seemed that some nagging instinct caused him to scrutinize the crowd, as if his gaze were being drawn by a magnet . . . He happened to glance upward to the second-floor galleries . . . and Sebastian saw the boy focus with sudden knifelike intensity.

Breaking free of the crowd, Sebastian followed Cam's stunned gaze, and saw a dark, stocky man standing at the east balcony that overlooked the main floor. He was disheveled and dirty, his black hair plastered over the distinctive bullet shape of his skull. *Joss Bullard*, Sebastian realized in an instant . . . but how had he entered the club without being noticed? It must have been through a hidden entrance. The club had more openings and passages than a rabbit warren. And no one knew the place better than Bullard or Cam, both of whom had lived here since childhood—

Sebastian's thoughts exploded as he saw the gleam of reflected light off the barrel of a pistol in Bullard's hand. Even at this angle, the object of his aim was clear. The target was Evie, who was still approximately a half-dozen yards away from Cam.

Driven by raw instinct, Sebastian leaped forward with lightning speed, while hideous fear burned through him. Evie's form became so sharp and detailed in his panicked vision that even the velvet nap of her gown was distinct. Every nerve and muscle strained to reach her, every thundering beat of his heart laboring to feed blood to his fast-moving limbs. Seizing her with frantic hands, Sebastian turned his own body to shield her, and used the momentum of his speed to bring them both to the floor.

The report of a pistol echoed through the cavernous room. Sebastian felt an impact in his side, as if someone had punched him with a fist, and a burst of fiery pain as a lead slug tore through muscle and soft tissue, severing a network of arteries in its path. The hard collision of the floor stunned Sebastian momentarily. He lay partly over Evie, trying to cover her head with his arms, while she struggled beneath him. 'Be still,' he gasped, holding her to the floor, fearing that Bullard might shoot again. *'Wait,* Evie.'

She subsided obediently, while the air was filled with a surfeit of noise . . . shouts and cries . . . thundering footsteps . . .

Levering himself over Evie's prone body, Sebastian risked a glance upward at the second-floor balcony. Bullard was gone. With a grunt of pain, Sebastian rolled to his side and searched his wife for injuries, terrified that the bullet might have struck her as well. 'Evie . . . sweetheart . . . are you hurt?'

'Why did you push me like that?' she asked in a muffled voice. 'No, I'm not hurt. What was that noise?'

His shaking hand brushed over her face, pushing back a tumble of hair that had fallen across her eyes.

Bemused, Evie wriggled out from beneath him and sat up. Sebastian remained on his side, panting for breath, while he felt a hot slide of blood over his chest and waist.

People were crowding to flee the building, threatening to trample the couple on the floor. Suddenly a man came to crouch over them, having fought his way through the rushing horde. He used his body as a bulwark to keep them from being overrun. Blinking, Sebastian realized that it was Westcliff. Dizzily Sebastian reached up to clutch at his coat.

'He aimed for Evie,' Sebastian said hoarsely. His lips had gone numb, and he licked at them before continuing. 'Keep her safe . . . keep her . . .'

Evie let out a shaken cry as she saw the bright crimson that spread over Sebastian's shirtfront and realized he had been wounded. She attacked the buttons of his coat and waistcoat, ripping the plackets in her sudden frenzy. Wordlessly Westcliff stripped off his own coat and wadded his waistcoat into a tight bundle. Evie tore open Sebastian's blood-soaked shirt and found the gushing wound in his side. Her face turned very white, and her eyes began to glitter, but she managed to control her alarm as she took the makeshift pad from Westcliff and held it firmly against the wound to slow the bleeding.

The pressure caused such agony that Sebastian could not prevent a low groan. His hand remained suspended in the air, fingers half curled. The scent of fresh blood saturated the air. Westcliff bent over him and examined the exit wound. 'Through and through,' Sebastian heard him say to Evie. 'No major vessel damage, from the looks of it.'

While Westcliff maintained the pressure on the wound, Evie moved to cradle Sebastian's head on her lap, cushioning him in a soft mass of black velvet. Taking his hand, she gripped his fingers firmly. The clasp of her hand seemed to anchor him, providing a counterbalance to the gnawing pain in his lower torso. Sebastian stared into her downbent face, unable to read her expression. There was a strange, deep glow in her eyes, something like tenderness or sorrow . . . something rare and infinite. He didn't know what it was. No one had ever looked at him that way before.

He struggled to say something to banish the disturbing emotion in her gaze. 'This is what comes of tr . . .' He was forced to pause as thrills of pain stole his breath away. '. . . trying to appear heroic,' he finished. 'I think I'll stick with villainy from now on. Much . . . safer.'

Westcliff's black eyes glinted briefly at the attempt at humor. 'The shot originated from the upper gallery,' he said.

'Former employee . . . Bullard . . . dismissed recently.'

'Are you certain that he aimed for Lady St Vincent?'

'Yes.'

'Perhaps he thought that harming her was the best way to revenge himself against you.'

Sebastian's head was swimming, making it difficult to think clearly. 'No . . .' he muttered. 'Could only be true if . . . he thought I cared for her . . . but everyone knows . . . not a love match.'

Westcliff gave him an odd look but refrained from replying. Sebastian had no means of knowing how he and Evie appeared at that moment, as he gripped her hand and let her cradle him as tenderly as a mother with a hurt child. All he knew was that the wound in his side ached unbearably. Relentless tremors ran through him until his teeth began to chatter. He was vaguely aware of Westcliff leaving them for a moment, and barking out orders, and returning with an armload of coats, though it was unclear whether their owners had donated them willingly or not. The coats were settled over him, and Westcliff continued to apply pressure on the wound.

Sebastian lost consciousness for a moment, and when he came back to his senses, he felt Evie's warm hand caressing the cold, sweaty surface of his face. 'The doctor is coming,' she murmured. 'Once the bleeding slows, we'll take you upstairs.'

His breath shivered between his clenched teeth. 'Where's Rohan?'

'I saw him in pursuit of Bullard, right after the shot was fired,' Westcliff replied. 'As a matter of fact, Rohan climbed up a column to the second floor.'

'If he doesn't catch the bastard,' Sebastian muttered, 'I will. And then—'

'Shhh . . .' Evie soothed, her free hand slipping beneath the mound of coats to reach the bare surface of his chest. Her palm rested over the weak throb of his heart, and her fingertips traced over the thread of fine gold chain that hung around his neck. Following the chain, she discovered the Scottish-gold wedding band dangling from the end of it.

Sebastian had not wanted her to find out that he wore the ring beneath his clothes. Agitated, he whispered, 'Means nothing. Just . . . wanted to keep it safe—'

'I understand,' Evie murmured, flattening her hand on his chest once more. He felt the brush of her lips against his forehead, and the soft caress of her breath. She smiled down at him. 'You realize, of course,' she said, 'that you've given me the perfect excuse to stay. I'm going to take care of you until you're well enough to throw me out on your own.'

Sebastian could not return the smile. Anxiety flooded him as he realized that Evie wasn't safe here or anywhere, until Bullard was caught. 'Westcliff,' he rasped, 'Someone has to . . . protect my wife . . .'

'Nothing will happen to her,' Westcliff assured him.

As Sebastian stared at his former friend, the only honorable man that he had ever known, he saw that Westcliff's face was carefully impassive. They both understood what Evie was too inexperienced to gather . . . that although the bullet had not hit a vital organ, the wound was likely to suppurate. Sebastian would not die of blood loss, but it was likely that he could succumb to a fatal fever. And if so, Evie would be alone and undefended in a world filled with predators. Men like himself.

Trembling with cold and shock, Sebastian forced out a few desperate words, finding that it took several thready breaths to get them out. 'Westcliff . . . what I did before . . . sorry. Forgive . . . forgive . . .' He felt his eyes begin to roll back in his head, and he fought to stay conscious. 'Evie . . . keep her safe. Please . . .' He sank into an ocean of bright sparks, deeper and deeper, until the fluttering lights had faded and he was lost in blackness.

'Sebastian,' Evie whispered, bringing his lax hand to her cheek. She kissed the backs of his fingers while tears trickled down her face.

'It's all right,' Westcliff reassured her. 'He's just fainted. He'll come to in a moment.'

She let out a small, gasping sob before regaining control. 'He deliberately put himself in front of me,' she said after a moment. 'He took the shot for me.'

'So it would seem.' Westcliff watched her speculatively, thinking, among other things, that some interesting changes had occurred in both Sebastian and his unlikely bride since their elopement.

When Lillian had learned that St Vincent had married Evangeline Jenner, she had gone into a fury, terrified about what harm might have befallen her friend.

'That monster!' Lillian had cried upon their return to London from Italy. 'For him to do this to Evie, of all people . . . oh, you can't know how fragile she is. He'll have been cruel to her . . . she has no defenses, and she is so innocent . . . My God, I'll kill him!'

'Your sister said that she did not appear to have

been ill-used,' Westcliff pointed out rationally, though he too had been concerned by the idea of someone as helpless as Evangeline Jenner at St Vincent's mercy.

'She was likely too afraid to admit anything,' Lillian had said, her dark eyes snapping as she paced back and forth. 'He probably raped her. Threatened her. Perhaps even beat her—'

'No, no,' Westcliff had soothed, gathering her stiff body into his arms. 'According to Daisy and Annabelle, there was ample opportunity for her to tell them if she had been abused. But she did not. If it will ease your worries, I'll go to the club and offer her refuge. She can stay with us in Hampshire if she desires.'

'For how long?' Lillian had mumbled, nestling deeper into his embrace.

'Indefinitely, of course.'

'Oh, Marcus . . .' Her brown eyes had sparkled with sudden moisture. 'You would do that for me?'

'Anything, love,' he had told her gently. 'Anything at all to make you happy.'

And so Westcliff had come to Jenner's this evening to ascertain if Evangeline was an unwilling captive. Contrary to all expectations, he had found a woman who seemed eager to stay, who bore obvious affection for St Vincent.

As for St Vincent, so eternally aloof and indifferent . . . it was difficult to believe that the man who treated women with such cavalier cruelty could be the same one who had just risked his life. To receive an apology from a man who had never expressed a single regret about anything, and then to hear him practically beg for his wife's protection, led to an inescapable conclusion. St Vincent had, against all odds, learned to care more for someone else than he did for himself.

The situation was extraordinary. How someone like Evangeline Jenner could have wrought such a change in St Vincent, the most worldly of men, was difficult to understand. However, Westcliff had learned that the mysteries of attraction could not always be explained through logic. Sometimes the fractures in two separate souls became the very hinges that held them together.

'My lady—' he said gently.

'Evie,' she said, still cradling her husband's hand against her face.

'Evie. I must ask . . . why did you approach St Vincent, of all men, with an offer of marriage?'

Gently lowering St Vincent's hand, Evie smiled ruefully. 'I needed a way to escape my family, legally and permanently. Marriage was the only answer. And as you were no doubt aware, suitors were hardly queuing up for my favors in Hampshire. When I learned what St Vincent had done to Lillian, I was appalled . . . but it also occurred to me that . . . he was the only person I knew of who seemed as desperate as I was. Desperate enough to agree to anything.'

'Was it also part of your plan that he manage your father's club?'

'No, he decided that, much to my surprise. In fact, he has surprised me at every turn since we married.'

'How so?'

'He has done everything possible to look after me – all the while proclaiming his indifference.' She stared into her husband's unconscious face. 'He's not heartless, much as he tries to pretend otherwise.'

'No,' Westcliff agreed. 'He's not heartless – though I had my doubts until this evening.'

CHAPTER 18

Although Cam and Westcliff were as careful as possible, the process of conveying Sebastian upstairs weakened him severely. Evie followed closely behind, filled with agonized concern as she saw the stark paleness of Sebastian's face. Cam was distraught, though he kept his emotions battened down as he focused on doing what was necessary.

'I don't know how he got in,' the boy muttered. Evie realized that he was referring to Bullard. 'I know all the ways to enter and leave this place. I thought I had taken care of—'

'It's not your fault, Cam,' Evie interrupted quietly.

'Someone must have let him in, even though I told the employees—'

'It's not your fault,' she repeated, and the boy fell silent, though it was clear that he did not agree.

Westcliff was quiet save for a few murmured instructions as they turned a corner. He carried Sebastian's upper half, while Cam held his legs. Although Sebastian was a large man, they were both quite fit, and carried him to the master bedroom without difficulty. The room had just been refurbished, the walls covered with a layer of cream-colored paint. The old bed had been discarded and replaced with a large, handsome one, moved from Sebastian's town house. Little had anyone thought that this would turn into a sickroom once more, so soon after her father's death.

At Evie's direction, a pair of housemaids ran back and forth, fetching towels and water, and tearing linen into wide strips. Sebastian's limp body was eased onto the bed, and Evie tugged his boots off while Cam and Westcliff worked to remove his bloodstained clothes. By tacit agreement, they left on his white linen drawers for the sake of modesty.

Dipping a clean rag into the warm water, Evie washed the bloodstains from her husband's body, the smears turning rust-colored where they had dried amid the light golden fleece on his chest. How powerful yet defenseless he appeared, the elegant lines of his body trimmed to a new leanness, his muscles honed by constant physical activity and more than a few recent back-alley skirmishes.

Westcliff picked up a rag and gently blotted the oozing bullet wound to have a better look at it. 'From the size of the hole, I would assume that Bullard used a fifty-caliber pistol.'

'I have the gun,' Cam said shortly. 'Bullard

dropped it on the second-floor gallery after he fired the shot.'

Westcliff's eyes narrowed in interest. 'Let me see it.'

The boy withdrew the pistol from the pocket of his coat and handed to him, butt first. Westcliff assessed it with the expert glance of a seasoned sportsman. 'A dueling pistol,' he remarked. 'With a nine-inch octagonal, sighted barrel . . . platinum safety vents, engraved breeches and lockplates . . . a costly weapon, and part of a matched set. Made by Manton and Son of Dover Street.' He looked more closely at the weapon. 'Here's a silver escutcheon plate . . . engraved with the owner's name, I believe. Though it's too tarnished to make out the letters.' He glanced at Cam and arched one brow as he slipped it into his pocket. 'With your permission, I will retain this.'

Seeming to understand that his permission wasn't really required, Cam replied dryly, 'By all means, my lord.'

Further conversation was prevented by the arrival of Dr Hammond, a kindly man of sterling reputation, who had attended her father in the past. Cam and Westcliff left the room while Hammond examined the patient, cleaned the wound, and covered it with a light dressing. 'While no major organs have been damaged,' he told Evie, his bearded face wearing a grave expression, 'it is a significant injury. The recovery will depend on the resilience of the individual, the quality of his care . . . and as always, divine grace. It is almost certain there will be fever, which will have to run its course. Most often in these cases I am compelled to bleed the patient to drain as much of the diseased blood as possible. I will visit daily to determine if or when that will be necessary. Meanwhile, keep him clean and rested, feed him water and beef tea, and administer medicine for his discomfort.'

Evie received a bottle of opiated syrup from him with murmured thanks. After the doctor departed, she covered Sebastian with a quilt, seeing that the effects of shock and blood loss were causing him to shiver uncontrollably.

He opened his eyes and focused on her with difficulty. 'If I need divine grace,' he whispered, 'I'm in trouble . . . unless we can find some corrupt angel to bribe.'

A startled laugh escaped her. 'Don't be blasphemous.' She opened the syrup, poured a spoonful, and slipped an arm behind his neck. 'Take this.'

He swallowed the medicine, made a face, and cursed.

Keeping her arm behind him, Evie reached for a cup of water with her free hand, and pressed it to his lips, until his teeth chattered at the edge. 'Drink,' she murmured.

Sebastian obeyed and settled back against the pillows. 'Bullard—'

'Cam couldn't catch him,' Evie replied, reaching

for a tiny pot of salve. She smoothed some on his chapped lips with gentle fingertips. 'He and Lord Westcliff are downstairs, talking to the constable who was dispatched to investigate.'

'Was anyone else hurt?' Sebastian asked, trying to sit up. A bolt of pain caused his face to whiten, and he fell back with a gasp.

'Don't move,' Evie said sharply, 'you'll start bleeding again.' She rested a hand on his chest, and traced the thin, glinting chain that draped across his upper chest, following it to the wedding band. 'No one else was hurt,' she said in answer to his question. 'And as soon as the club members were informed that the assailant had fled, they all came swarming back in, and appeared quite entertained by the evening's events.'

The ghost of a smile touched his lips. 'Bit more entertainment than . . . I had planned on providing.'

'Cam says it won't hurt business in the least.'

'Safety measures,' Sebastian whispered, exhausted by the effort of talking. 'Tell Cam—'

'Yes, he's hiring more men. Don't think about any of that right now. Your only concern is to get well.'

'Evie . . .' His shaking hand fumbled for hers, feebly trapping her fingers on his bare chest. Under their joined hands, the wedding band on the chain pressed against his unsteady heartbeat. 'Go with Westcliff,' he murmured, his eyes closing. 'After.'

After what? Evie stared into his face, his gray complexion, and realized that he was referring to his own death. As she felt his hand slide away from hers, she gripped it firmly. His hand had changed . . . no longer smooth and manicured, but harder, callused, the nails cut ruthlessly short. 'No,' she said with soft intensity, 'there will be no "after." I will stay with you every moment. I will keep you with me. I won't let you go.' Suddenly her breath was coming hard, and she felt the pressure of panic against the inner wall of her chest. Continuing to lean over him, she turned her hand so that their palms matched, their pulses pressed together . . . one weak, one strong. 'If my love can hold you, I'll keep you with me.'

Sebastian awakened in a haze of pain, not only in his wound, but in his head and bones and joints. He was dry and burning, as if fire had been trapped beneath his skin, and he twisted in a useless attempt to escape the heat. Suddenly a pair of gentle hands descended on him and a wet cloth passed over his face. A hiss of relief escaped his lips, and he reached out for the source of coolness, seizing, his fingers digging desperately into softness.

'No . . . Sebastian, *no* . . . lie still. Let me help you.' It was Evie's voice, breaking through the writhing madness. Gasping, he forced himself to release her and fell back against the mattress. The cold cloth moved over him in long strokes, a temporary ease from the torment. Each soothing pass served to calm him until he was able to lie quietly beneath her ministrations. 'Evie,' he said hoarsely.

She paused to slip a few shards of crushed ice between his cracked lips. 'Yes, darling. I'm here.'

His lashes lifted. Puzzled by the endearment, he watched her as she leaned over him. The ice dissolved quickly against his parched inner cheeks. Before he had to ask her for another, she fed him more. Freshening and wringing out the cloth, she wiped his chest and sides and beneath his arms. The room was darkened except for the daylight that came from a partly shrouded window, and a chilling breeze swept through the half-open casement.

Noticing the direction of his gaze, Evie murmured, 'The doctor said I should keep the window closed. But you seem to rest more comfortably when it's open.'

Sebastian lay steeped in gratitude as Evie continued to bathe him with the cool cloth. Her white dressing gown and fair skin gave her the appearance of some pristine, benevolent spirit, weaving a spell over him in the darkness.

'How long?' he whispered.

'This is the third day. Dearest love, if you can turn a little on your good side . . . let me tuck a pillow there . . . yes.' With his back partly exposed, Evie bathed his aching shoulders and down his spine, and he groaned softly. He vaguely recalled the other times she had done this . . . her light hands . . . her serene face in the lamplight. Somewhere amid the nightmare of confusion and pain, he had been aware of her tending him, seeing to his needs with astonishing intimacy. When he shook with fever chills, she covered him with blankets and held his shivering body in her arms. She was always there before he even needed to call for her . . . she comprehended everything as if she could see inside his tangled thoughts. His worst fear had always been to depend on someone this way. And he was growing weaker by the hour, as the wound became more inflamed and the fever raged higher. He sensed death hovering like a impatient specter, ready to claim him when all his defenses were gone. It retreated whenever Evie was with him . . . still waiting, but far less imminent.

He hadn't comprehended her strength before now. Even when he had seen the loving care she had given her father, he hadn't guessed what it would be like to rely on her, to need her. But nothing repelled her, nothing was too much to ask. She was his support, his shield . . . and at the same time she undermined him with a tender affection that he had begun to crave even as he shrank from it.

Evie's slender, strong arms braced him as she eased him slowly back to the mattress. 'A few sips of water,' she coaxed, supporting his head. Sebastian made a negative sound, for although his mouth was dry and sticky, it seemed that even a drop or two of water caused him nausea. 'For me,' she insisted, pressing a cup to his mouth.

Sebastian slitted her a baleful glance and obeyed . . . and resented it when her praise gave him a ripple of pleasure. 'You're an angel,' she murmured, smiling. 'Good, that's it. Now rest, and I'll cool you some more.' Sighing, he relaxed while the damp cloth slid lightly over his throat and face.

He sank into a thick, smothering ocean of darkness, into dreams that allowed him no peace. After what could have been minutes, hours, or days, he awoke in wretched pain, fumbling at his side, which burned and ached as if a poisoned spear had been lodged in it.

Evie's calm voice stilled his frenzy. 'Sebastian, please . . . Lie back. Dr Hammond is here. Let him examine you.'

Sebastian discovered that he was too weak to move. It felt as if his arms and legs had been tied with lead weights. 'Help—' he whispered raspily, unwilling to remain flat on his back. Understanding at once, Evie hastened to lift his head and prop a pillow behind him.

'Good afternoon, my lord,' came a baritone voice. The portly doctor appeared before him, a slight smile splitting his gray-and-silver beard and warming his florid face. 'I had hoped for some improvement,' Hammond remarked to Evie. 'Has the fever abated?'

She shook her head.

'Any sign of appetite or thirst?'

'He will take a little water at times,' Evie murmured, moving to slip her fingers around Sebastian's. 'But he can't keep down any broth.'

'I will have a look at the wound.'

Sebastian felt the bedclothes being drawn down to his hips and the bandage being peeled away. As he tried to protest the indignity of being exposed so cavalierly, Evie rested her hand on his chest. 'It's all right,' she whispered. 'He's trying to help.'

Too feeble to lift his own head, Sebastian focused on Evie's face as she and the doctor stared the exposed wound. There was no change in Evie's expression, but he saw from the quick double blink of her lashes that his condition had not improved.

'As I feared,' Hammond said quietly, 'it is festering. You see those red streaks extending toward the heart? I'll have to remove some of the diseased blood from his body. Hopefully it will reduce some of the inflammation.'

'But he's already lost so much blood . . .' Evie said uncertainly.

'I will take no more than four pints,' Hammond replied in a firm but reassuring manner. 'It will not harm him, my lady, but rather will help release the constriction of vessels caused by an accumulation of poisons.'

Sebastian had always viewed the process of

blood-letting dubiously, but never more so than when it was about to be practiced on him. He felt his pulse escalate to a weak but frantic tapping in his veins, and he tugged at Evie's hand. 'Don't,' he whispered, his breath coming too quickly. A rush of dizziness overcame him and he fought to see through the showers of sparks that scattered across his vision. He was not aware of fainting, but when he opened his eyes again, he discovered that his left arm had been lightly bound to the back of a chair beside the bed, with a shallow bowl poised on the seat. There was no blood in the bowl – yet – but Hammond was approaching him with a small boxlike device.

'What is that?' came Evie's voice. Sebastian summoned all his strength to turn his head on the pillow to look at her.

'It's called a scarificator,' Hammond replied. 'It is by far the most efficient method of bloodletting as opposed to an old-fashioned lancet.'

'Evie,' Sebastian whispered. She did not appear to hear him, her wary gaze fastened on the doctor as he continued to explain.

'. . . the box contains twelve blades attached to a spring-driven rotary. One push of the triggering mechanism, and the blades inflict a series of shallow cuts that induce the blood to flow.'

'*Evie.*'

She glanced at Sebastian. Whatever she saw in his face caused her to walk around the bed to him.

'Yes,' she said with a concerned frown. 'Dearest, this is going to help you—'

'No.' It would kill him. It was difficult enough already to fight the fever and the pain. If he was further weakened by a long bloodletting he wouldn't be able to hold on any longer. Frantically Sebastian tugged at his tautly stretched arm, but the binding held fast and the chair didn't even wobble. *Bloody hell.* He stared up at his wife wretchedly, battling a wave of light-headedness. 'No,' he rasped. 'Don't . . . let him . . .'

'Darling,' Evie whispered, bending over to kiss his shaking mouth. Her eyes were suddenly shiny with unshed tears. 'This may be your best chance – your only chance—'

'I'll die. Evie . . .' Rising fear caused blackness to streak across his vision, but he forced his eyes to stay open. Her face became a blur. 'I'll die,' he whispered again.

'Lady St Vincent,' came Dr Hammond's steady, kind voice, 'your husband's anxiety is quite under-standable. However, his judgment is impaired by illness. At this time, you are the one who is best able to make decisions for his benefit. I would not recommend this procedure if I did not believe in its efficacy. You must allow me to proceed. I doubt Lord St Vincent will even remember this conversation.'

Sebastian closed his eyes and let out a groan of despair. If only Hammond were some obvious lunatic with a maniacal laugh . . . someone Evie would instinctively mistrust. But Hammond was a respectable man, with all the conviction of someone who believed he was doing the right thing. The executioner, it seemed, could come in many guises.

Evie was his only hope, his only champion. Sebastian would never have believed it would come to this . . . his life depending on the decision of an unworldly young woman who would probably allow herself to be persuaded by the Hammond's authority. There was no one else for Sebastian to appeal to.

He felt her gentle fingers at the side of his fevered face, and he stared up at her pleadingly, unable to form a word. *Oh God, Evie, don't let him—*

'All right,' Evie said softly, staring at him. Sebastian's heart stopped as he thought she was speaking to the doctor . . . giving permission to bleed him. But she moved to the chair and deftly untied Sebastian's wrist, and began to massage the reddened skin with her fingertips.

She stammered a little as she spoke. 'Dr H-Hammond . . . Lord St Vincent does not w-want the procedure. I must defer to his wishes.'

To Sebastian's eternal humiliation, his breath caught in a shallow sob of relief.

'My lady,' Hammond countered with grave anxiety, 'I beg you to reconsider. Your deference to the wishes of a man who is *out of his head with fever* may prove to be the death of him. Let me help him. You must trust my judgment, as I have infinitely more experience in such matters.'

Evie sat carefully on the side of the bed and rested Sebastian's hand in her lap. 'I do respect your j-j –' She stopped and shook her head impatiently at the sound of her own stammer. 'My husband has the right to make the decision for himself.'

Sebastian curled his fingers into the folds of her skirts. The stammer was a clear sign of her inner anxiety, but she would not yield. She would stand by him. He sighed unsteadily and relaxed, feeling as if his tarnished soul had been delivered into her keeping.

Hammond shook his head and began collecting his implements. 'If you will not allow me to use my skills,' he said with quiet dignity, 'and you refuse to heed my professional opinion, I'm afraid I cannot do either of you any good. I can predict nothing but an unfortunate outcome for this situation, if proper treatment is not rendered. May God help you both.'

The doctor left the room, an air of heavy disapproval lingering in his wake.

Relieved beyond measure, Sebastian spread his long fingers over the shape of Evie's thigh. 'Riddance,' he managed to mutter, as the door closed behind Hammond.

Evie was obviously torn between laughter and tears as she looked down at him. 'You stubborn ass,' she said, her eyes wet. 'We've just managed to drive off one of the most renowned doctors in London. Anyone else we find is going to want to bleed you as well. Who should I send for now? A white witch? A shaman? A Covent Garden fortune-teller?'

Using the last of his strength, Sebastian managed to drag her hand up to his mouth. 'You,' he whispered, holding her fingers to his lips. 'Just you.'

CHAPTER 19

Evie experienced a multitude of doubts about her decision not to let Dr Hammond care for Sebastian. After the doctor's departure, Sebastian's condition worsened steadily, his wound became more swollen and angry by the hour, and his fever kept climbing. By midnight, he was no longer lucid. His eyes were demon-bright in his flushed face, and he stared at Evie without recognition as he rambled incoherently in words she could not always understand, with dark revelations that wrenched her with pity.

'Hush,' Evie whispered at times, 'Hush. Sebastian, you're not . . .' But he persisted with terrible desperation, his tormented mind dredging up more, and more, until she finally stopped trying to quiet him, and she gripped his clenching hands in hers as she listened patiently to the bitter litany. Never in his conscious moments would he have permitted anyone a glimpse of his unprotected inner self. But Evie knew perhaps better than anyone what it was like to live in desperate solitude . . . yearning for connection, for

295

completeness. And she understood, too, the depths that his loneliness had driven him to.

After a while, when his hoarse voice had faded to broken whispers, Evie gently changed the cold cloth on his forehead and smoothed salve on his cracked lips. She kept her hand at the side of his face, the golden bristle scratching her fingers. In his delirium, Sebastian turned his cheek into the softness of her palm with a wordless murmur. Beautiful, sinful, tormented creature. Some would argue that it was wrong to care for such a man. But as Evie stared at his helpless form, she knew that no man would ever mean to her what he had . . . because in spite of everything, he had been willing to give his life for hers.

Climbing onto the bed beside him, Evie found the chain amid the soft curling hair on his chest, and she covered the wedding ring with her palm, and let herself sleep beside him for a few hours.

When daylight came, she found him utterly still, lost in a stupor. 'Sebastian?' She felt his face and neck. The fever was blazing. It seemed impossible that human skin could burn so hot. Flinging herself out of bed, she stumbled to the bellpull and tugged it violently.

With the help of Cam and the housemaids, Evie covered the bed with a waterproof cloth and packed muslin bags filled with ice around his body. Sebastian remained motionless and silent through it all. Evie's hopes were briefly raised when the fever seemed to abate, but it soon resumed its relentless climb.

Cam, who had assumed Sebastian's duties at the club as well as his own, looked nearly as exhausted as Evie. Still dressed in his evening clothes, a gray necktie hanging loose on either side of his throat, he wandered to the bedside where Evie sat.

She had never felt real despair until now. Even during the worst of times with the Maybricks, she had always had hope. But if Sebastian did not live, she felt that she would never take pleasure in anything again.

Sebastian had been the first man to reach through her prison of shyness. And from the very beginning, he had taken care of her as no one ever had. Thinking of the first hot brick he had tucked against her feet during the hellish carriage ride to Scotland, she smiled bleakly. She spoke to Cam with her gaze fastened on her husband's waxen face. 'I don't know what to do for him,' she whispered. 'Any doctor I send for will want to bleed him, and I promised him that I wouldn't allow it.'

Reaching out a lean hand, Cam smoothed back the wild locks of Evie's unwashed hair. 'My grandmother was a healer,' he said thoughtfully. 'I remember that she used to flood wounds with salt water, and pack them with dried bog moss. And when I had a fever, she would make me chew the tubers of the four o'clock plant.'

'Four o'clock plant,' Evie repeated blankly. 'I've never heard of that.'

He tucked a straggle of her hair behind her ear. 'It grows on the moors.'

Evie moved her head away from his hand, embarrassed by her unwashed state, especially knowing the great importance Gypsies placed on personal cleanliness. Contrary to popular belief, there were any number of Romany rituals connected to washing and cleansing. 'Do you think you could find some?'

'Four o'clock plant?'

'And the moss.'

'I suppose I could, given enough time.'

'I don't think he has much time left,' Evie said, and her voice broke. Terrified that she might lose control of her emotions, she straightened in the chair, and shrugged away Cam's consoling touch. 'No . . . I'm all right. Just . . . find whatever you think will help.'

'I will return soon,' she heard him say softly, and in an instant, he was gone.

Evie continued to sit by the bedside in a state of exhausted indecision, aware that she should probably make some concession to the needs of her own body for sleep, for food, for some marginal care . . . but she was afraid to leave Sebastian even for a few minutes. She didn't want to come back and find that he had slipped away while she was not there.

She tried to clear away the fog of weariness long enough to make a decision, but the mechanics of her brain seemed to have been disabled. Hunched in the chair, she stared at her dying husband. Her spirit and body had become so weighted that no action or thought was possible. She was not aware of anyone entering the room, or of any movement other than the minimal, nearly undetectable rise and fall of Sebastian's chest. But gradually she became aware of a man standing beside her chair, his presence emanating a vitality and contained force that was startling in the somnolent atmosphere of the sickroom. Blearily she looked up into the concerned face of Lord Westcliff.

Without a word Westcliff reached down and pulled her to her feet, steadying her as she wobbled. 'I've brought someone for you,' he said quietly. Evie's gaze careened across the room until she managed to focus on the other visitor.

It was Lillian Bowman – now Lady Westcliff – dashing and radiant in a wine-red gown. Her fair complexion was lightly glazed with color from the southern Italian sun, and her black hair was caught fashionably at the nape of her neck with a beaded silk-cord net. Lillian was tall and slender, the kind of raffish girl one could envision as captaining her own pirate ship . . . a girl clearly made for dangerous and unconventional pursuits. Though not as romantically beautiful as Annabelle Hunt, Lillian possessed a striking, clean-featured appeal that proclaimed her Americanness even before one heard her distinctly New York accent.

Of their circle of friends, Lillian was the one that Evie felt the least close to. Lillian did not possess Annabelle's maternal softness, or Daisy's sparkling optimism . . . she had always intimidated Evie with her sharp tongue and prickly impatience. However, Lillian could always be counted on in times of trouble. And after one glance at Evie's haggard countenance, Lillian came to her without hesitation, and wrapped her long arms around her.

'Evie,' she murmured fondly, '*what* have you gotten yourself into?'

The surprise and relief of being held so securely by a friend she had not expected to see overwhelmed Evie completely. She felt the pain in her eyes and throat sharpen, until she could no longer hold back her sobs. Lillian tightened her embrace. 'You should have seen my reaction when Annabelle and Daisy told me what you had done,' she said, patting Evie's back firmly. 'I nearly dropped to the floor, and then I called down all sorts of curses on St Vincent's head for taking advantage of you. I was tempted to come here and shoot him myself. But it appears that someone else spared me the trouble.'

'I love him,' Evie whispered between sobs.

'You can't,' Lillian said flatly.

'Yes, I love him, and I'm going to lose him just as I did my father. I can't bear it . . . I'll go mad.'

Lillian sighed and muttered, 'Only you could love such a vile, selfish peacock, Evie. Oh, I'll admit, he has his attractions . . . but you would do better to fix your affections on someone who could actually love you back.'

'Lillian,' came Evie's watery protest.

'Oh, all right, I suppose it's not sporting to disparage a man when he's bedridden. I'll hold my tongue for the time being.' She drew back and looked into Evie's splotched face. 'The others wanted to come, of course. But Daisy is unmarried and therefore can't even *sneeze* without a chaperone, and Annabelle tires easily because of her condition. Westcliff and I are here, however, and we're going to make everything all right.'

'You can't,' Evie sniffled. 'His wound . . . he's so ill . . . he's fallen into a c-coma, I think . . .'

Keeping her arm around Evie, Lillian turned to the earl and asked in a strong voice that was entirely inappropriate for a sickroom, 'Is he in a coma, Westcliff?'

The earl, who was bending over Sebastian's prone form, threw her a wry glance. 'I doubt anyone could be, with the noise the pair of you are making. No, if it were a coma, he couldn't be roused. And he definitely stirred just now when you shouted.'

'I didn't shout, I called out,' Lillian corrected. 'There is a difference.'

'Is there?' Westcliff asked mildly, pulling the covers down to Sebastian's hips. 'You raise your voice so often, I can't tell.'

A laugh rustled in Lillian's throat, and she released Evie. 'Being married to you, my lord, any woman would . . . Good God, that's *horrid*.' This last exclamation had come as Westcliff peeled back the wound dressing.

'Yes,' the earl said grimly, staring at the draining, festering flesh, with its rays of red creeping outward.

Instantly Evie went to the bedside, wiping her wet cheeks. Westcliff, capable as always, extracted a clean handkerchief from his coat and gave it to her. She blotted her eyes and blew her nose as she looked down at her husband. 'He's been insensible since yesterday afternoon,' she told Westcliff unsteadily. 'I wouldn't let Dr Hammond bleed him . . . Sebastian didn't want it. But now I wish I had. It might have made him better. It's just . . . I couldn't let anything be done to him against his will. The way he looked at me—'

'I doubt it would have made him better,' Westcliff interrupted. 'It may well have finished him off.'

Lillian drew closer, wincing as she glanced down at the foul wound and then at Sebastian's unnatural pallor. 'What is to be done for him, then?'

'Mr Rohan suggested flooding the wound with a saltwater solution,' Evie said, gently covering the bullet hole and pulling the bedclothes from Sebastian's hips to his chest. 'And he knew of a plant that might help to reduce the fever – he's trying to find some, as we speak.'

'We might swab it with raw garlic juice,' Lillian suggested. 'My nanny used to do that for scrapes and cuts, and it made them heal much faster.'

'My old housekeeper, Mrs Faircloth, used vinegar,' Westcliff murmured. 'It burned like the devil – but it worked. I think we'll try a combination of the three, and add some spirit of turpentine.'

Lillian regarded him doubtfully. 'Pine tree resin?'

'In a distilled form,' Westcliff replied. 'I've seen

it cure gangrene.' Turning Lillian to face him, he pressed a kiss to her forehead. 'I'll procure the necessary items, and work out the proportions,' he said. His expression was sober, but his dark eyes were warm as they gazed into hers. 'In the meanwhile, I will leave the situation in your capable hands.'

Tenderly Lillian traced the edge of his shirt collar, letting her fingertip touch the tanned skin of his throat. 'You'd better hurry. If St Vincent wakes to find himself at my mercy, he'll probably expire on the spot.'

They exchanged a brief grin and Westcliff left the room.

'Arrogant, high-handed creature,' Lillian remarked, her smile lingering as she watched the earl's departure. 'God, I adore him.'

Evie swayed on her feet. 'How did you—'

'There is far too much for us to talk about, dear,' Lillian interrupted briskly. 'Which is why we'll have to leave it all for later. You're half dead with exhaustion. And frankly, you could do with a bath.' Hunting for the bellpull, she located it in the corner, and tugged on it. 'We're going to have a tub filled, and you can wash, and then you're going to have some tea and toast.'

Evie shook her head and opened her mouth to argue, but Lillian overrode her objections firmly. 'I will look after St Vincent.'

Wondering how and why her friend would volunteer to nurse a man who had abducted her, Evie stared at her warily. Lillian was hardly known as a forgiving sort, and although Evie was certain her friend would never harm a helpless man in a sickbed, she did have a few trepidations about abandoning Sebastian to her mercy.

'I can't believe that you would be willing . . . after what he did . . .'

Lillian smiled wryly. 'I'm not doing it for his sake. I'm doing it for yours. And for Westcliff, who for some reason can't seem to give him up as a lost cause.' She rolled her eyes impatiently at Evie's lingering hesitation. 'For heaven's sake, go and bathe. And do something about your hair. You needn't worry about St Vincent. I'll be as kind to him as I would be to my own husband.'

'Thank you,' Evie whispered, feeling the sting of tears in her eyes once more.

'Oh, Evie . . .' Lillian's face softened with an expression of compassion that Evie had never seen on her before. She reached out and hugged Evie once more, and spoke into the wild tangles of her hair. 'He's not going to die, you know. It's only nice, saintly people who suffer untimely deaths.' She gave a quiet laugh. 'Whereas selfish bastards like St Vincent live to torment other people for *decades*.'

With the help of a housemaid, Evie bathed and changed into a loose day gown that required no corset. She braided her clean, damp hair into a long plait that hung down her back, and stuck her feet into a pair of knit slippers., Venturing back into Sebastian's room, she saw that Lillian had straightened the room and drawn the curtains open. A cloth had been tied around her waist as a makeshift apron, and it was splotched and stained, as was her bodice.

'I made him take some broth,' Lillian explained. 'I had the devil of a time getting him to swallow – he wasn't precisely what one would call conscious – but I persisted until I had poured a quarter cup or so down his throat. I think he relented in the hopes that I was a bad dream that might go away if he humored me.'

Evie had been unable to induce Sebastian to drink anything since the previous morning. 'You are the most wonderful—'

'Yes, yes, I know.' Lillian airily waved away the words, uncomfortable as always with praise. 'Your tray was just brought up – it's there on the table by the window. Mulled eggs and toast. Eat every bite, dear. I should hate to have to use force on you too.'

As Evie sat obediently and sank her teeth into a slice of lightly buttered toast, Lillian changed the cloth on Sebastian's forehead. 'I must admit,' Lillian murmured, 'it's hard to despise him when he's been brought so low. And it does count in his favor that *he's* the one lying here wounded, instead of you.' Occupying the bedside chair, she glanced at Evie with frank curiosity. 'Why did he do it, I wonder? He's selfish to the core. Not at all the kind who would sacrifice himself for someone else.'

'He's not completely selfish,' Evie mumbled, and washed down the toast with a swallow of hot tea.

'Westcliff thinks that St Vincent is in love with you.'

Evie choked a little and didn't dare look up from her tea. 'Wh-why does he think that?'

'He's known St Vincent from childhood, and can read him fairly well. And Westcliff sees an odd sort of logic in why *you* would finally be the one to win St Vincent's heart. He says a girl like you would appeal to . . . hmm, how did he put it? . . . I can't remember the exact words, but it was something like . . . you would appeal to St Vincent's deepest, most secret fantasy.'

Evie felt her cheeks flushing while a skirmish of pain and hope took place in the tired confines of her chest. She tried to respond sardonically. 'I should think his fantasy is to consort with as many women as possible.'

A grin crossed Lillian's lips. 'Dear, that is not St Vincent's fantasy, it's his reality. And you're probably the first sweet, decent girl he's ever had anything to do with.'

'He spent quite a lot of time with you and Daisy in Hampshire,' Evie countered.

That seemed to amuse Lillian further. 'I'm not at all sweet, dear. And neither is my sister. Don't say you have been laboring under that misconception all this time?'

Just as Evie finished the plate of eggs and toast, Lord Westcliff and Cam entered the room, bearing armloads of pots, bottles, potions, and assorted strange articles. A pair of housemaids accompanied them with steaming metal ewers and piles of folded toweling. Although Evie wanted to help, they bid her stand back as they arranged the objects at the bedside, and draped towels over Sebastian's sides, legs, and hips, leaving only the wound exposed.

'It would be best if he could take some morphine first,' Westcliff said, using thread to wrap a wad of linen tightly around a wooden dowel to form a long-handled swab. 'This procedure will likely pain him far more than the gunshot itself.'

'He can be made to swallow,' Lillian said decisively. 'Evie, shall I?'

'No, I will.' Evie went to the bedside and measured a dose of morphine syrup into a glass. Cam appeared at her elbow and gave her a folded paper packet filled what appeared to be dark green ash.

'The four o'clock plant,' he said. 'I found it at the first apothecary I visited. The bog moss was a bit more difficult to find . . . but I managed to get some of that too.'

Evie leaned her shoulder against him in wordless thanks. 'How much of the powder should I give him?'

'For a man of St Vincent's size, I would think at least two teaspoons.'

Evie stirred two spoonfuls of the powder into

the glass of amber medicine, turning it black. It undoubtedly tasted even worse than it looked. She only hoped that if Sebastian did consent to swallow it, he could somehow manage to keep the vile mixture down. Climbing beside him on the bed, she stroked the dull locks of his hair and the parched, blazing surface of his face. 'Sebastian,' she whispered, 'wake up. You must take some medicine . . .' He did not rouse even when she slipped her arm behind him and tried to lift his head.

'No, no, no,' came Lillian's voice from behind her, 'you're being far too gentle, Evie. I had to shake him roughly before he awakened sufficiently to take some broth. Let me show you.' She climbed onto the bed beside Evie and jolted the semi-conscious man a few times until he moaned and half opened his eyes, and stared at the pair of them without recognition.

'Sebastian,' Evie said tenderly, 'I have some medicine for you.'

He tried to turn away, but the effort caused pressure against his injured side, and the pain caused a violent reaction. Evie and Lillian both found themselves cleared from the bed with a swipe of his powerful arm. 'Ouch!' Lillian muttered as they were knocked to the floor in a heap, with Evie just barely managing to preserve the contents of the glass.

Panting, groaning in delirium, Sebastian subsided on the bed, his large frame wracked with tremors.

Although Evie was dismayed by his resistance, she was glad of the sign of remaining strength, which was far preferable to the deathlike stillness of before.

Lillian, however, did not seem to share her sentiments. 'We'll have to tie him down,' she said curtly. 'We'll never be able to hold him still while we treat the wound.'

'I don't want—' Evie began, but Cam astonished her by agreeing.

'Lady Westcliff is right.'

Evie was silent as she struggled up from the floor. She reached down to Lillian, helped her to her feet, and stood looking at Sebastian's trembling form. His eyes were closed once more, his fingers twitching convulsively, as if wanting to clench something other than air. It was incredible that such a vital man could have been reduced to this colorless, spare figure, his lips cracked, his eyes black-circled.

She would do whatever was necessary to help him. Resolutely she took up some clean rags and handed them to Cam over Sebastian's half-exposed body.

The boy looked grim as he moved to each corner of the bed, deftly tying both of Sebastian's arms and one leg to the iron bedstead. 'Shall I give him the medicine?' he asked, glancing at Evie.

'I can do it,' she replied, climbing beside Sebastian once more. After wedging a pillow beneath his head to raise it, she clamped her fingers on his nose. As soon as Sebastian gasped for air, she poured the thick febrifuge down his throat. He choked and gagged, but to her satisfaction the medicine was downed with a minimum of fuss. Cam raised his brows as if impressed by her efficiency, while Sebastian cursed and yanked helplessly at his bonds. Bending over him, Evie stroked and soothed him, whispering endearments as his opium-laden breath wafted feebly against her face.

When he had finally subsided, Evie glanced up to find Lillian staring at them oddly. Her brown eyes were narrowed, and she shook her head slightly, as if she were amazed by the situation. Evie supposed that since Lillian had known Sebastian only as the arrogant, sartorially splendid rake who had sauntered about Westcliff's estate, it was no less than astonishing to see him in these circumstances.

In the meanwhile, Westcliff had removed his coat and rolled up his shirtsleeves. He was stirring a concoction that sent a caustic reek throughout the room. Lillian, who was especially sensitive to smell, grimaced and shuddered. 'That is the most beastly combination of odors I've ever encountered.'

'Spirit of turpentine, garlic, vinegar – and some other ingredients that the apothecary suggested, including rose oil,' Cam explained. 'He also said to apply a honey poultice afterward, as it keeps wounds from turning putrid.'

Evie's eyes widened as Cam opened a wooden box and withdrew a brass funnel and a cylindrical object with a handle at one end and a needlelike projection at the other. 'What is th-that?' she asked.

'Also from the apothecary,' Cam said, holding the device up to squint at it critically. 'A syringe. When we described what we were planning, he said that with a wound this deep, the only way to irrigate it thoroughly was to use this.'

He laid out a row of implements, containers of chemicals and a pile of folded rags and towels, then Westcliff paused at the bedside and glanced at the two women. 'This is going to be rather unpleasant,' he said. 'Therefore, if anyone has a weak stomach . . .' His gaze lingered meaningfully on Lillian, who grimaced.

'I do, as you well know,' she admitted. 'But I can overcome it if necessary.'

A sudden smile appeared on the earl's impassive face. 'We'll spare you for now, love. Would you like to go to another room?'

'I'll sit by the window,' Lillian said, and sped gratefully away from the bed.

Westcliff glanced at Evie, a silent question in his eyes.

'Where shall I stand?' she asked.

'On my left. We'll need a great many towels and rags, so if you would be willing to replace the soiled ones when necessary—'

'Yes, of course.' She took her place beside him, while Cam stood on his right. As Evie looked up at Westcliff's bold, purposeful profile, she suddenly found it hard to believe that this powerful man, whom she had always found so intimidating, was willing to go to this extent to help a friend who had betrayed him. A rush of gratitude came over her, and she could not stop herself from tugging lightly at his shirtsleeve. 'My lord . . . before we begin, I must tell you . . .'

Westcliff inclined his dark head. 'Yes?'

Since he wasn't as tall as Sebastian, it was a relatively easy matter for Evie to stand on her toes and kiss his lean cheek. 'Thank you for helping him,' she said, staring into his surprised black eyes. 'You're the most honorable man I've ever known.' Her words caused a flush to rise beneath the sun-bronzed tan of his face, and for the first time in their acquaintance the earl seemed at a loss for words.

Lillian smiled as she watched them from across the room. 'His motives are not completely heroic,' she said to Evie. 'I'm sure he's relishing the opportunity to literally pour salt on St Vincent's wounds.' Despite the facetious remark, Lillian went deadly pale and gripped the chair arms as Westcliff took a thin, gleaming lancet in hand and proceeded to gently open and drain the wound.

Even after a heavy dose of morphine, the pain caused Sebastian to arch and twist, his face contorting, while incoherent protests came from low in his throat. Cam helped to pin him down so that even minimal movement wasn't possible. The real difficulty came, however, when Westcliff began to flush out the wound with salt water.

Sebastian cried out harshly, fighting in earnest while the syringe was deployed repeatedly until the saline solution that soaked the towels beneath him ran pink with fresh, clean blood. Westcliff was steady and precise, working with a brisk efficiency that any surgeon would have admired. Somehow Evie managed to conquer her own anguish, pushing it far down beneath layers of numbness as she worked with the same outward detachment that Westcliff and Cam displayed. Methodically she snatched away the filthy towels and tucked new ones against her husband's side. To her vast relief, Sebastian soon fainted and went slack, now oblivious to the treatment of his injury.

Once the raw flesh was cleaned to Westcliff's satisfaction, he soaked a swab with the turpentine mixture and saturated the wound thoroughly. Moving aside, he watched intently as Cam wrapped some bog moss in a clean square of muslin, soaked the bundle in honey, and carefully packed the area. 'That's it,' the boy said with satisfaction. He untied the rags that had tethered Sebastian's hands and foot as he spoke. 'The healing will start deep within. We'll keep packing it for a few days, and then we'll dispense with the moss and let the skin come together.' It took their combined efforts to wrap a linen bandage completely around Sebastian's lean waist and to change the damp sheets so that the bed was clean and dry.

When it was over, Evie felt the ruthless self-discipline leave her limbs, and she began to shake from head to toe with strain. She saw with surprise that even Westcliff seemed fatigued, letting out a long sigh as he used a clean rag to blot the abundant sweat on his face. Lillian came to him at once, her arms going around him in a quick hug as she murmured an endearment in his ear.

'We should change the packing and dressing about twice a day, I think,' Cam commented to no one in particular, washing his hands with soap and water. 'If the fever doesn't improve by nightfall, we'll double the dose of four o'clock plant.' Gesturing for Evie to come to him, he washed her hands and arms as well. 'He'll be all right, sweetheart,' he said. 'When the earl was draining the wound it didn't look as bad as I thought it would.'

Evie shook her head wearily, standing with childlike passivity as he blotted her wet hands. 'I can't let myself hope for anything. I can't let myself believe . . .' Her voice trailed off as the floor seemed to tilt beneath her feet, and she jerked clumsily in an attempt to correct her balance. Cam caught her swiftly and scooped her up against his hard young chest. 'Bed for you,' he announced, carrying her toward the door.

'Sebastian . . .' she mumbled.

'We'll take care of him while you rest.'

She had little choice, as her sleep-deprived body refused to function any longer. Her last memory was of Cam laying her on her own bed, drawing the covers over her and tucking them at her sides as if she were a little girl. As soon as her body heat began to collect beneath the slick, icy-cold sheets, she plummeted into a dreamless slumber.

Evie awoke to the cheerful glow of a tiny flame. A candle sat on the bedside table. Someone was sitting on the edge of the bed . . . Lillian . . . looking rumpled and tired, with her hair tied at the nape of her neck.

Slowly Evie sat up, rubbing her eyes. 'Is it evening?' she croaked. 'I must have slept all afternoon.'

Lillian smiled wryly. 'You've slept for a day and a half, dear. Westcliff and I have looked after St Vincent, while Mr Rohan has been running the club.'

Evie ran her tongue inside her pasty mouth and sat up straighter. Her heart began to thud with dread as she struggled to ask, 'Sebastian . . . is he . . .'

Lillian took Evie's chapped hand in hers and asked gently, 'Which do you want first – the good news, or the bad news?'

Evie shook her head, unable to speak. She stared at her friend without blinking, her lips trembling.

'The good news,' Lillian said, 'is that his fever has broken, and his wound is no longer putrid.' She grinned as she added, 'The bad news is that you may have to endure being married to him for the rest of your life.'

Evie burst into tears. She put her free hand over

her eyes, while her shoulders shook with sobs. She felt Lillian's fingers wrap more firmly around hers.

'Yes,' came Lillian's dry voice, 'I'd weep too, if he were my husband – though for entirely different reasons.'

That caused a hiccupping giggle to break through Evie's muffled sobs, and she shook her head, still covering her streaming eyes. 'Is he conscious? Is he speaking?'

'Yes, he has asked for you repeatedly and was quite annoyed when I refused to awaken you before now.'

Lowering her hand, Evie stared at her through a film of moisture. 'I'm certain he didn't mean to sound ungr-grateful,' she said hastily. 'After all you've done—'

'There's no need to make excuses for him,' Lillian said sardonically. 'I know him fairly well. Which is why I still don't believe he cares about anyone but himself . . . and perhaps a little – *very* little – bit for you. But if he makes you happy, I suppose he shall have to be tolerated.' Her nose wrinkled, and she appeared to hunt for an unappealing scent before detecting it on the sleeves of her gown. '*Ugh* . . . it's a good thing my family owns a soap company. Because I'll need a hundred bricks of it to remove the smell of that blasted poultice.'

'I will never be able to thank you enough for taking care of him,' Evie said fervently.

Standing from the bed, Lillian stretched and

shrugged. 'Think nothing of it,' came her cheerful reply. 'It was worth it, if only to have St Vincent in my debt. He'll never be able to look at me without the humiliating recollection that I've seen him naked and unconscious in his sickbed.'

'You saw him naked?' Evie asked, feeling her brows rise up to her hairline.

'Oh,' Lillian said airily, going to the door, 'I caught a glimpse now and then. It was impossible not to, considering the location of the wound.' Pausing in the doorway, she gave Evie a sly glance. 'I must admit, regarding that rumor that one occasionally hears . . . it doesn't *begin* to do him justice.'

'What rumor?' Evie asked blankly, and Lillian left the room with a low laugh.

CHAPTER 20

Before a full week had passed, Sebastian had become the worst patient imaginable. He was healing at a remarkable rate, though not quickly enough for his satisfaction, and he frustrated himself, as well as everyone else, by pushing every conceivable limit. He wanted to wear his regular clothes, to have real food . . . he insisted on leaving his bed and hobbling around the apartments and the upper gallery, stubbornly ignoring Evie's exasperated protests. Even knowing that he could not force his strength to return, that it would require time and patience, Sebastian couldn't help himself.

He had never had to rely on anyone . . . and now, to owe his life to Westcliff, Lillian, Cam, and most of all, Evie . . . he was swamped with the unfamiliar feelings of gratitude and shame. He couldn't look any of them in the eyes, and so his only recourse was to take refuge in surly arrogance.

The worst moments were when he was alone with Evie. Every time she entered the room, he experienced a frightening connection, a surge of unfamiliar emotion, and he fought it until the internal battle left him drained. It would have helped if he could have provoked an argument with her, anything to establish a necessary distance. But that was impossible when she countered his every demand with patience and infinite concern. He couldn't accuse her of expecting gratitude when she had never once hinted that it was owed. He couldn't accuse her of hovering over him when she took care of him with gentle efficiency and tactfully left him alone unless he rang for her.

He, who had never feared anything, was terrified of the power she had over him. And he was afraid of his own desire to have her with him every minute of the day, to stare at her, to hear her voice. He craved her touch. His skin seemed to drink in every caress of her fingers, as if the sensation of her could be woven into the human fabric of his body. It was different from mere sexual need . . . it was some kind of pathetic, full-blown addiction for which there seemed to be no remedy.

Sebastian was further tormented by the knowledge that Joss Bullard had tried to kill Evie, and his reaction came from some primitive place in himself that would not be tamed by reason. He wanted Bullard's blood. He wanted to tear the bastard to pieces. The fact that he was helpless in his sickbed while Bullard was roaming freely in London was enough to drive him mad. He was not at all pacified by assurances from the police inspector who had been assigned to the case, that everything possible was being done to find Bullard. Therefore, Sebastian had summoned Cam to his room and had directed him to hire more private investigators, including an ex-Bow Street Runner, to conduct an intensive search. In the meanwhile, there was nothing else that Sebastian could do, and he stewed in his enforced inactivity.

Five days after his fever had broken, Evie sent for a slipper tub to be brought to his room. Relishing the opportunity for a tub bath, Sebastian relaxed in the steaming water while Evie shaved him and helped to wash his hair. When he was clean and dry, he returned to his newly made bed and allowed Evie to bandage his wound. The bullet hole was healing so quickly that they had ceased packing it with moss, and now simply covered it with a light layer of linen for the sake of cleanliness. It was still a source of frequent twinges and mild pain, but Sebastian knew that in another day or two, he would be able to resume most of his normal activities. Except for his favorite one, which, by virtue of his infernal bargain with Evie, was still forbidden.

Since the entire front of Evie's dress had been drenched from the bath, she had gone to change her clothes. Out of sheer perversity, Sebastian rang the silver bell at his bedside approximately two minutes after she had left.

Evie returned quickly to his room in her dressing gown. 'What is it?' she asked with obvious worry. 'Has something happened?'

'No.'

'Is it your wound? Does it hurt?'

'No.'

Her expression changed, concern replaced by relief. Approaching the bed, she gently took the bell from Sebastian's hand and replaced it on the night table. 'You know,' she said conversationally, 'the tang of that bell will be removed unless you learn to use it more judiciously.'

'I rang because I needed you,' Sebastian said testily.

'Yes?' she asked with exquisite patience.

'The curtains. I want them opened wider.'

'You couldn't have waited for that?'

'It's too dark in here. I need more light.'

Evie went to the window, tugged the velvet panels far apart, and stood silhouetted in the wash of pale winter sunlight. With her hair loose, the soft red curls hanging nearly to her waist, she looked like a figure in a Titian painting. 'Anything else?'

'There's a speck in my water.'

Padding barefoot to the bed, Evie picked up his half-full drinking glass and viewed it critically. 'I don't see a speck.'

'It's in there,' Sebastian said grumpily. 'Must we debate the matter, or will you fetch some clean water?'

Biting back a reply with remarkable self-control, Evie went to the washstand, emptied the water into the creamware bowl, and poured a fresh glass for him. She brought it back, set it on the table, and looked at him expectantly. 'Is that all?'

'No. My bandage is too tight. And the loose end is tucked in at the back. I can't reach it.'

It seemed that the more demanding he was, the more annoyingly patient Evie became. Bending over him, she murmured for him to turn a little, and he felt her gently loosening the bandage and retucking the ends. The glance of her fingertips on his back, so cool and delicate, caused his pulse to throb sharply. A stray curl slid silkily over his shoulder. Resting on his back once more, Sebastian fought with the desperate joy he felt at her nearness.

He glanced wretchedly up at her face . . . the beautiful bow-shaped mouth, the cream-satin skin, the irresistible sprinkling of freckles. Her hand settled lightly on his chest, over his thumping heart, and she toyed with the wedding band on the chain.

'Take it off of me,' he muttered. 'The damned thing is annoying. It gets in the way.'

'In the way of what?' Evie whispered, staring at his averted profile.

Sebastian could smell her skin, the scent of warm, clean woman, and he shifted on the mattress, his senses sharpening with awareness. 'Just take it off and put it on the dresser,' he managed to say after a ragged breath.

Ignoring the command, Evie half sat on the mattress, leaning over him until the ends of her unbound hair feathered over his chest. His body was motionless, but he quaked inwardly as he felt her draw a finger along the edge of his jaw. 'I gave you a decent shave,' she observed, sounding pleased with herself. 'I may have missed a spot or two, but at least I didn't cut your face to ribbons. It helped that you were so still.'

'I was too terrified to move,' he replied, and she made a sound of amusement.

Unable to keep his gaze from hers any longer, Sebastian brought himself to look into her smiling eyes . . . so round, so astonishingly blue.

'Why do you ring that bell so often?' Evie whispered. 'Are you lonely? You have only to say so.'

'I'm never lonely.' He said it with cool conviction. To his dismay, she did not draw back, and although her smile turned quizzical, it did not fade.

'Shall I go, then?' she asked gently.

Sebastian felt treacherous heat rising inside him, unfurling, spilling, spreading everywhere. 'Yes, go,' he said, closing his eyes, hungrily absorbing the scent and nearness of her.

Evie stayed, however, the silence spinning out until it seemed that the pounding of his heart must be audible. 'Do you want to know what I think, Sebastian?' she finally asked.

It took every particle of his will to keep his voice controlled. 'Not particularly.'

'I think that if I leave this room, you're going to ring that bell again. But no matter how many times you ring, or how often I come running, you'll never bring yourself to tell me what you really want.'

Sebastian slitted his eyes open . . . a mistake. Her face was very close, her soft mouth only inches from his. 'At the moment, all I want is some peace,' he grumbled. 'So if you don't mind—'

Her lips touched his, warm silk and sweetness, and he felt the dizzying brush of her tongue. A floodgate of desire opened, and he was drowning in undiluted pleasure, more powerful than anything he had known before. He lifted his hands as if to push her head away, but instead his trembling fingers curved around her skull, holding her to him. The fiery curls of her hair were compressed beneath his palms as he kissed her with ravenous urgency, his tongue searching the winsome delight of her mouth.

Sebastian was mortified to discover that he was gasping like an untried boy when Evie ended the kiss. Her lips were rosy and damp, her freckles gleaming like gold dust against the deep pink of her cheeks. 'I also think,' she said unevenly, 'that you're going to lose our bet.'

Recalled to sanity by a flash of indignation, Sebastian scowled. 'Do you think I'm in any condition to pursue other women? Unless you intend to bring someone to my bed, I'm hardly going to—'

'You're not going to lose the bet by sleeping with another woman,' Evie said. There was a glitter of deviltry in her eyes as she reached up to the neck-line of her gown and deliberately began to unfasten the row of buttons. Her hands trembled just a little. 'You're going to lose it with me.'

Sebastian watched incredulously as she stood and shed the dressing gown. She was naked, the tips of her breasts pointed and rosy in the cool air. She had lost weight, but her breasts were still round and lovely, and her hips still flared gener-ously from the neat inward curves of her waist. As his gaze swept to the triangle of red hair between her thighs, a swell of acute lust rolled through him.

He sounded shaken, even to his own ears. 'You can't make me lose the bet. That's cheating.'

'I never promised not to cheat,' Evie said cheer-fully, shivering as she slipped beneath the covers with him.

'Damn it, I'm not going to cooperate. I –' His breath hissed between his teeth as he felt the tender length of her body press against his side, the springy brush of her private curls on his hip as she slid one of her legs between his. He jerked his head away as she tried to kiss him. 'I can't . . . Evie . . .' His mind searched cagily for a way to dissuade her. 'I'm too weak.'

Ardent and determined, Evie grasped his head and turned his face to hers. 'Poor darling,' she murmured, smiling. 'Don't worry. I'll be gentle with you.'

'Evie,' he said hoarsely, aroused and infuriated

and pleading, 'I have to prove that I can last three months without – no, don't do that. Damn you, Evie—'

She had disappeared beneath the covers, stringing kisses along the hard line of his chest down to his abdomen, taking care not to dislodge the bandage. Sebastian struggled to sit up, but a sharp sting in his half-healed wound caused him to fall back with a grunt of pain. And then he grunted for an altogether different reason as she reached the stiff, aching length of his cock, and delicately nuzzled the tip of it.

It was obvious that Evie had never done this before . . . she knew nothing of technique, and very little of male anatomy. But that didn't stop her from proceeding with innocent ardor, pressing tiny kisses along the sensitive shaft and lingering when she heard him groan. Her warm hands played inexpertly with his testicles, while she experimented with her lips, her tongue, progressing all the way back to the throbbing head of his organ and then trying to discover how much of him she could fit into her mouth. Sebastian clutched great handfuls of the bedclothes, his body slightly arched as if he were stretched on a torture rack. Sensual pleasure raced from nerve to nerve, sending frantic messages to his brain, making it impossible to think clearly.

Any memories of other women were banished permanently from his mind . . . there was only Evie, her red hair streaming and curling over his stomach and thighs, her playful fingers and frolicsome mouth causing him an agony of pleasure like nothing he had ever felt before. When he could no longer hold back his groans, she climbed over him carefully, straddling him, crawling up his body slowly like a sun-warmed lioness. He had one glimpse of her flushed face before she sought his mouth with teasing, sucking kisses. The rosy tips of her breasts dragged through the hair on his chest . . . she rubbed herself against him, purring with satisfaction at the hard warmth of the male body beneath her.

His breath snagged in his throat as he felt her hand slip between their hips. He was so aroused that she had to gently pull his sex away from his stomach before she could fit it between her thighs. The crisp red curls of her mound tickled his exquisitely sensitive skin as she guided him between the hot folds of her body.

'No,' Sebastian managed, recalling the bet. 'Not now. Evie, no—'

'Oh, stop protesting. I didn't make nearly this much of a fuss after our wedding, and I was a virgin.'

'But I don't want – oh *God*. Holy Mother of God—' She had pushed the head of his sex into her entrance, the sweet flesh so snug and soft that it took his breath away. Evie writhed a little, her hand still grasping the length of his organ as she tried to guide him deeper. Seeing the difficulty she was having in accommodating him caused him to swell even harder, his entire body flushed with prickling excitement. And then came the slow, miraculous slide, hardness within softness.

Sebastian's head fell back to the pillow, his eyes drowsy with intense desire as he stared up into her face. Evie made a little satisfied hum in her throat, her eyes tightly closed as she concentrated on taking him deeper. She moved carefully, too inexperienced to find or sustain a rhythm. Sebastian had always been relatively quiet in his passion, but as her lush body lifted and settled, deepening his penetration, and his cock was gripped and stroked by her wet depths, he heard himself muttering endearments, pleas, sex words, love words.

Somehow he coaxed her to lean farther over him, resting more of her body against his, adjusting the angle between them. Evie resisted briefly, fearing she would hurt him, but he took her head in his hands. 'Yes,' he whispered shakily. 'Do it this way. Sweetheart. Yes. Move on me . . . yes . . .'

As Evie felt the difference in their position, the increased friction against the tingling peak of her sex, her eyes widened. 'Oh,' she breathed, and then inhaled sharply. 'Oh, that's so—' She broke off as he set a rhythm, nudging deeper, filling her with steady strokes.

The entire world dwindled to the place where he invaded her, their most sensitive flesh joined. Evie's long auburn lashes lowered to her cheeks, concealing her unfocused gaze. Sebastian watched a pink flush creep over her face. He was suspended in wonder, suffused with vehement tenderness as he used his body to pleasure hers. 'Kiss me,' he said in a guttural whisper, and guided her swollen lips to his, slowly ravishing her mouth with his tongue.

She sobbed and shuddered with release, her hips bearing greedily against his as she took his full length. The rim of her sex clamped tightly around him, and Sebastian gave himself up to the squeezing, enticing, pulsing flesh, letting her pull the ecstasy from him in great voluptuous surges. As she relaxed over him, trying to catch her breath, he drew his hands over her damp back, his finger-tips gently inquiring as they traveled to the plump curve of her bottom. To his delight, she squirmed and tightened around him in helpless response. If he had his usual strength . . . oh, the things he would have done to her . . .

Instead, he collapsed back in exhaustion, his head spinning. Awkwardly Evie lifted away from him and snuggled by his side. Using the last of his strength, Sebastian filled his hand with her hair and brought it to his face, rubbing the bright curls against his cheek. 'You're going to kill me,' he muttered, and he felt her lips curve against his shoulder.

'Now that you've lost the bet,' Evie said huskily, 'we'll have to think of another forfeit, since you've already apologized to Lord Westcliff.'

Though Sebastian had nearly choked on the words, he had forced out a repentant speech to both Westcliff and Lillian before they had left the club. He had subsequently discovered that the only thing worse than making an apology for something was being forgiven for it. But he had deliberately apologized at a time when Evie hadn't been present.

'Lillian told me,' Evie said, as if reading his thoughts. She lifted her head with a sleepy grin. 'I wonder what your new forfeit should be?'

'No doubt you'll think of something,' he said darkly, and within seconds of closing his eyes, he fell into a deep, healing sleep.

Westcliff came to the club the next evening, registering surprise when he learned that Sebastian had gone to the main hazard room for the first time since the shooting. 'A bit soon, isn't it?' he asked as Evie walked with him from their private apartments to the second-floor gallery. They were watched carefully by an employee whom Cam had stationed at the gallery, as one of the increased security measures at the club. Until Bullard was caught, all guests were monitored with discreet attention.

'He's pushing himself,' Evie replied with a frown. 'He can't abide the idea of appearing helpless – and he doesn't think anything can be done correctly without his supervision.'

A smile glimmered in Westcliff's dark eyes. 'St Vincent's interest in this place seems quite genuine. I confess, I would not have expected him to undertake such responsibility willingly. For years he has been aimless and idle – a complete waste of his considerable intelligence. But it appears that all he needed was a suitable outlet for his talents.'

Coming to the balcony, they both rested their elbows on the railing and looked down into the main room, which was filled wall-to-wall with patrons. Evie saw the antique-gold gleam of Sebastian's hair as he half sat on the desk in the corner, relaxed and smiling as he conversed with the crowd of men around him. His actions of ten days ago in saving Evie's life had excited a great deal of public admiration and sympathy, especially after an article in the *Times* had portrayed him in a heroic light. That, and the perception that his friendship with the powerful Westcliff had renewed, were all it had taken for Sebastian to gain immediate and profound popularity. Piles of invitations arrived at the club daily, requesting the attendance of Lord and Lady St Vincent at balls, soirees, and other social events, which they declined for reasons of mourning.

There were letters as well, heavily perfumed and written by feminine hands. Evie had not ventured to open any of them, nor had she asked about the senders. The letters had accumulated in a pile in the office, remaining sealed and untouched, until Evie had finally been moved to say something to him earlier that morning. 'You have a large pile of unread correspondence,' she had told him, as they had taken breakfast together in his room. 'It's occupying half the space in the office. What shall we do with all the letters?' An impish smile rose to her lips as she added. 'Shall I read them to you while you rest?'

His eyes narrowed. 'Dispose of them. Or better yet, return them unopened.'

His response had caused a thrill of satisfaction, though Evie had tried to conceal it. 'I wouldn't object if you corresponded with other women,' she said. 'Most men do, with no impropriety attached—'

'I don't.' Sebastian had looked into her eyes with a long, deliberate stare, as if to make certain that she understood him completely. 'Not now.'

Standing elbow to elbow with Westcliff, Evie watched her husband with possessive pleasure. Sebastian was still too lean, though his appetite had returned in full measure, and his elegant evening clothes hung a bit too loosely. But his shoulders were broad and his color was healthy, and the lost weight only served to highlight the spectacular bone structure of his face. Even though he moved with obvious care, he still possessed the predatory grace that women admired and men tried in vain to emulate.

'Thank you for saving him,' Evie heard herself say to Westcliff, still staring at her husband.

The earl slid her a sideways glance. 'You saved him, Evie, on the night you offered to marry him. Which is evidence, I suppose, that moments of lunacy can occasionally lead to positive results. If you don't mind, I want to go downstairs and

332

inform St Vincent about the latest developments regarding the search for Mr Bullard.'

'Has he been found?'

'Not yet. But soon. After I cleaned the escutcheon plates on the pistol that Bullard used, it was still impossible to make out the engraved name on the weapon. Therefore, I brought it to Manton and Son's, and asked them to provide information on the original commission. It turns out that the pistol is ten years old, which entailed a lengthy search through many boxes of old records. They told me today with certainty that the gun had been made for Lord Belworth, who happens to be returning to London this evening, for some parliamentary business. I intend to call on him in the morning and ask into the matter. If we can discover how Mr Bullard came into possession of Belworth's pistol, it may help us to locate him.'

Evie frowned in worry. 'It seems impossible to find one man hiding in a city populated by more than a million people.'

'Nearly two million,' Westcliff said. 'However, I have no doubt that he will be found. We have resources and the will to accomplish it.'

Despite her concern, Evie could not prevent a smile as she reflected that he sounded very much like Lillian, who never accepted defeat. Seeing that Westcliff's brows had quirked slightly at the sight of her smile, she explained, 'I was just thinking what a perfect match you are for a strong-willed woman like Lillian.'

The mention of his adored wife brought a glow to the earl's eyes. 'I would say she is no more determined or strong-willed than you,' he replied, and added with a swift grin, 'She merely happens to be noisier about it.'

CHAPTER 21

While Westcliff went to talk with Sebastian, Evie retreated to her room for a soothing bath, adding a liberal splash of perfumed oil to the water to soften it. After a long soak her skin was moist and fragrant with the scent of roses. She donned one of Sebastian's velvet-lined silk robes, rolling back the sleeves several times. Curling up in a chair before the hearth, she brushed her hair while the housemaids removed the bath. One of the maids, a dark-haired woman named Frannie, remained to tidy the room. She turned down the bedclothes and ran a warming pan between the sheets.

'Shall I . . . shall I prepare your room, milady?' the maid asked cautiously.

Evie ducked her head a little as she considered her reply. It was well-known among the servants that she and Sebastian had maintained separate bedrooms even before the illness. They had yet to share a bed together for a night. Although she was not quite certain how to broach the subject to Sebastian, she knew that after all that had transpired, she did not want to play games with him any longer. Life was too uncertain to waste time. There was no guarantee that Sebastian would be faithful to her. She had nothing but hope – and the instinct that although the man she had initially married was not deserving of such faith, the man he was becoming just might be.

'I don't think so,' she said to the maid, continuing to draw the brush through her hair. 'I will stay in this room tonight, Frannie.'

'Yes, milady. If ye wish I'll—'

Frannie broke off, the thought forever going unfinished, as they both became aware of Sebastian's tall form entering the room. He stopped just inside the doorway, resting his back against the wall as he silently contemplated his wife. Despite the warmth of the fire, gooseflesh rose all over Evie's body, and an erotic shiver chased down her spine.

Sebastian's posture was relaxed, his collar open, his black necktie hanging loose. The hearth light danced over his elegant form and cast a golden glow over features that might have belonged to some ancient god of idolatry. Even though he had not yet regained his full vigor, he radiated a dangerous male potency that made her knees weak. It didn't help that he remained utterly silent, his glinting gaze slipping over her with unnerving slowness. Helplessly recalling the feel of his satiny skin beneath her fingers, and the hard muscles beneath his loosely tailored clothes, Evie colored.

Frannie hastily gathered up Evie's discarded gown and hurried from the room.

Sebastian continued to watch Evie as she set aside the brush and stood with an inarticulate murmur. Pushing away from the wall, he came to her, his fingertips coming to her upper arms and tracing over them through the thickness of the robe. Evie's heart began to pound, and her skin tingled beneath the layers of velvet and silk. She closed her eyes as he eased her closer, and his lips touched her eyebrow, her temple, the crest of her cheek. Such light caresses, while his intense arousal – and her own – seemed to enfold them in a burning mist. They stood together for a long time, barely touching, simply feeling each other's nearness.

'Evie . . .' His whisper stirred the tiny wisps at her hairline. 'I want to make love to you.'

Her blood turned to boiling honey. Eventually she managed a stammering reply. 'I-I thought y-you never called it that.'

His hands lifted to her face, his fingertips exploring delicately. She remained docile beneath his caress while the scent of his skin, fresh and clove-like, drugged her like some narcotic incense.

Reaching to his own throat, Sebastian fumbled beneath his shirt and extracted the wedding band on the fine chain. He tugged it, breaking the fragile links, and let the chain drop to the floor. Evie's breathing hastened as he reached for her left hand and slid the gold band onto her fourth finger. Their hands matched together, palm to palm, wrist to wrist, just as they had been bound during their wedding ceremony. His forehead lowered to hers, and he whispered, 'I want to fill every part of you . . . breathe the air from your lungs . . . leave my handprints on your soul. I want to give you more pleasure than you can bear. I want to make love to you, Evie, as I have never done with anyone before.'

She was now trembling so violently that she could hardly stand. 'Your w-wound – we have to be careful—'

'You let me worry about that.' His mouth took hers in a soft, smoldering kiss. Releasing her hand, he gathered her body closer, applying explicit pressure against her shoulders, back, hips, until she was molded completely against him. Evie wanted him with a desperation that almost frightened her. She tried to catch his gently shifting mouth with her own, and pulled at his clothes with a fumbling urgency that made him laugh softly. 'Slowly,' he murmured. 'The night is just beginning . . . and I'm going to love you for a long time.'

Evie, whose legs were wobbling, tugged harder at his coat. 'I can't st-stand up much longer,' she said plaintively.

She saw the flash of his grin as he shrugged out of his coat, and heard the passion-roughened timbre in his voice as he said, 'Go lie on the bed, love.'

Evie obeyed gratefully, crawling onto the mattress and half reclining as she watched him shed the rest of his clothes. The sight of the white bandage crossing the hard musculature of his stomach reminded her of how close she had come to losing him. She felt her face tighten with emotion. He was so infinitely dear to her . . . the prospect of sharing this night with him filled her with a happiness that felt like anguish. His weight depressed the bed, and she rolled to face him, their bodies separated only by the dressing-gown. She reached up to touch the dark blond fleece on his chest, her fingertips sinking through the coarse curls to the hard flesh beneath.

His mouth stroked over her face, his breath rushing across her skin in hot drifts that made her quiver. 'Evie . . . during the past few days I've had nothing to do but lie in this bed and think about things that I've spent my entire life trying to avoid. I once told you that I wasn't meant for a wife and family. That I wouldn't have any interest in a child, if you . . .' He hesitated for a long moment. 'But . . . the truth is . . . I want you to have my baby. I didn't know how much, until I thought that I would never have the opportunity. I thought—' He broke off, a self-mocking smile touching his lips. 'Damn it. I don't know how to be a husband, or a father. But since your standards in both areas seem to be relatively low, I may have half a chance at pleasing you.' He grinned at her mock frown, then sobered. 'There are many ways I can prevent you from conceiving. But if or when you ever decide that you're ready, I want you to tell me—'

Evie stopped him with her mouth. In the blazing

minutes that followed, no further words were possible. She felt herself slide into a bewilderment of pleasure, reaching an intersection of emotion and lust that seemed to dilate her senses until every sound, touch, taste, became painfully magnified.

Sebastian teased the sides of the robe away from her pale body and caressed her exposed breasts with strokes as light as the wings of a plume moth. Her nipples swelled and tightened, aching for his touch, and when he finally drew a hard peak into the velvety heat of his mouth, she moaned with relief. He used only the tip of his tongue at first, plying her with a delicacy that made her writhe upward with an incoherent plea. Gradually he gave her more, flicking, sucking, until she felt a corresponding throb in her loins with every tug.

The velvet robe suddenly felt oppressive to her oversensitive flesh, and Evie fought to be free of it, tugging at the swaths of clinging fabric with frustration. Murmuring gently, Sebastian reached to help her, pulling the sleeves from her arms, stripping the garment away from her back and hips. A gasp of relief escaped her lips, and she arched against him, wrapping her arms around his bare shoulders. His gentle hands eased over her body, coaxing thrills from her susceptible nerves. She couldn't think or speak, could only respond helplessly as Sebastian stroked and arranged her limbs in ever-more revealing positions, while his mouth coursed slowly over her skin.

Inquisitive masculine fingers slipped between her thighs to find the elixir from her aroused flesh. Evie blushed and moaned as he spread the moisture in erotic circles, his fingertips dipping playfully into the entrance of her body. 'Sebastian . . . please, I can't wait any longer, I—' She broke off as she felt him turning her away, tucking her hips back against him so that they lay curved together on their sides. His arms closed around her, making her feel safe and protected, even as he reached down and parted her thighs with a soothing hand.

Evie stirred in confusion as she felt the pressure of his sex and realized he was entering her from behind. Gasping, she turned her face into the muscular arm that was wedged beneath her neck.

'Easy,' Sebastian whispered, smoothing the locks of hair away from her ear and throat, kissing her exposed skin. 'Let me love you this way, sweetheart.' His caressing fingers cupped her, kneading gently until she relaxed. He teased her with the head of his sex, barely penetrating her, then withdrawing just as she thought he would enter her fully. She began to rock against him, her hips pressing backward. By the time he slid all the way inside her, she was groaning loudly. As their position did not allow for a broad range of motion, he thrust in deep-seated nudges, while she arched in frantic encouragement.

His quiet laughter riffled through her curls. 'You're too impatient, love,' he whispered. 'Don't struggle for it . . . let the pleasure come to you.

341

Here, rest against me . . .' Reaching for her top thigh, he pulled it across his knees so that her legs were spread wide, her hips partially supported by his. Evie whimpered as she felt him slide even deeper, while his fingers stroked in rhythmic counterpoint to the prodding of his shaft.

Driven beyond sanity, Evie drew tight in every muscle, waiting as he built her pleasure at a leisurely pace. He took her to the edge and then retreated, then drove her closer, closer, making her wait, and wait, until at last he let her come in a series of convulsions that made the bed shake.

Sebastian was still hard as he withdrew from her. His tousled hair glittered like pagan gold as he pressed her to her back and dragged his open mouth over her flat stomach Evie shook her head with groggy denial even as he bent her knees and pushed them upward. 'Too tired,' she said thickly, 'I – wait, Sebastian—'

His tongue searched her salty-damp flesh with assuaging licks, persisting until her protests died away. The gentle ministrations of his mouth lulled her into peace, her heartbeat slowing to measured beats. After long, patient minutes, he drew the swollen bud of her clitoris in his mouth and began to suck and nibble. She jerked at the delicate aggression of his mouth. He drove her higher, his tongue flicking and swirling in a deliberate pattern, his arms clamping around her thighs. It seemed her body was no longer her own, that she existed only to receive this torment of pleasure. *Sebastian . . .* she could not voice his name, and yet he seemed to hear her silent plea, and in response he did something with his mouth that launched her into a series of incandescent climaxes. Every time she thought it was over, another ripple of sensation went through her until she was so exhausted that she begged him to stop.

Sebastian rose over her, his eyes glittering in his shadowed face. She moved to welcome him, opening her legs, sliding her arms around the powerful length of his back. He nudged inside her swollen flesh, filling her completely. As his mouth came to her ear, she could hardly hear his whisper over the thumping of her heart.

'Evie,' came his dark voice, 'I want something from you . . . I want you to come one more time.'

'No,' she said weakly.

'Yes. I need to feel you come around me.'

Her head rolled in a slow, negative shake across the pillow. 'I can't . . . I can't . . .'

'Yes, you can. I'll help you.' His hand drifted along her body to the place where they were joined. 'Let me deeper inside you . . . deeper . . .'

She moaned helplessly as she felt his fingertips on her sex, skillfully manipulating her spent nerves. Suddenly she felt him sliding even farther as her excited body opened to accept him. 'Mmm . . .' he crooned. 'Yes, that's it . . . ah, love, you're so sweet . . .'

He settled between her bent knees, into the cradle of her hips, driving hard and sure inside her. She encompassed him with her arms and legs, and buried her face in his hot throat, and cried out one last time, her flesh pulsing and tightening to bring him to shattering fulfillment. He shook in her arms, and clenched his hands into the warm spill of her hair as he gave himself over to her completely, worshipping her with every part of his body and spirit.

When Evie awakened alone in the large bed, the first thing she beheld was a scattering of pale pink splashes over the snowy white linens, as if someone had spilled blush-colored wine in bed. Blinking sleepily, she propped herself up on one elbow and touched one of the pink dabs with a single fingertip. It was a creamy pink rose petal, pulled free of a blossom and gently dropped to the sheet. Gazing around her, she discovered that rose petals had been sprinkled over her in a light rain. A smile curved her lips, and she lay back into the fragrant bed.

The night of heady sensuality seemed to have been part of some prolonged erotic dream. She could hardly believe the things that she had allowed Sebastian to do, the intimacies that she had never imagined were possible. And in the drowsy aftermath of their passion, he had cradled her against his chest and they had talked for what seemed to be hours. She had even told him the story of the night when she and Annabelle and the Bowman sisters had become friends, sitting in a row of chairs at a ball. 'We made up a list of potential suitors and wrote it on our empty dance cards,' Evie had told him. 'Lord Westcliff was at the top of the list, of course. But you were at the bottom, because you were obviously not the marrying kind.'

Sebastian had laughed huskily, tangling his bare legs intimately with hers. 'I was waiting for you to ask me.'

'You never spared me a glance,' Evie had replied wryly. 'You weren't the sort of man to dance with wallflowers.'

Sebastian had smoothed her hair, and was silent for a moment. 'No, I wasn't,' he had admitted. 'I was a fool not to have noticed you. If I had bothered to spend just five minutes in your company, you'd never have escaped me.' He had proceeded to seduce her as if she were still a virginal wallflower, coaxing her to let him make love to her by slow degrees, until he was finally sheathed in her trembling body.

Remembering the hours of searing tenderness, Evie dreamily performed her morning ablutions and dressed in a gown of silk-lined wool. She went downstairs to find Sebastian, who was most likely in the club office, poring over the previous evening's receipts. The club was empty save for the employees who were cleaning it for the coming evening, and the contractors who were busy laying new carpet and painting woodwork.

Entering the office, Evie found Sebastian and

Cam on opposite sides of the desk. They both mulled over account ledgers, scratching out some entries with freshly inked pens, and making notations beside the long columns. Both men looked up as she crossed the threshold. Evie met Sebastian's gaze only briefly; she found it hard to maintain her composure around him after the intimacy of the previous night. He paused in mid-sentence as he stared at her, seeming to forget what he had been saying to Cam. It seemed that neither of them was yet comfortable with feelings that were still too new and powerful. Murmuring good morning to them both, she bid them to remain seated, and she went to stand beside Sebastian's chair.

'Have you breakfasted yet, my lord?' she asked.

Sebastian shook his head, a smile glinting in his eyes. 'Not yet.'

'I'll go to the kitchen and see what is to be had.'

'Stay a moment,' he urged. 'We're almost finished.'

As the two men discussed a few last points of business, which pertained to a potential investment in a proposed shopping bazaar to be constructed on St James Street, Sebastian picked up Evie's hand, which was resting on the desk. Absently he drew the backs of her fingers against the edge of his jaw and his ear while contemplating the written proposal on the desk before him. Although Sebastian was not aware of what the casual familiarity of the gesture revealed, Evie felt her color rise as she met Cam's gaze over her husband's downbent head. The boy sent her a glance of mock reproof, like that of a nursemaid who had caught two children playing a kissing game, and he grinned as her blush heightened further.

Oblivious to the byplay, Sebastian handed the proposal to Cam, who sobered instantly. 'I don't like the looks of this,' Sebastian commented. 'It's doubtful there will be enough business in the area to sustain an entire bazaar, especially at those rents. I suspect within a year it will turn into a white elephant.'

'White elephant?' Evie asked.

A new voice came from the doorway, belonging to Lord Westcliff. 'A white elephant is a rare animal,' the earl replied, smiling, 'that is not only expensive but difficult to maintain. Historically, when an ancient king wished to ruin someone he would gift him with a white elephant.' Stepping into the office, Westcliff bowed over Evie's hand and spoke to Sebastian. 'Your assessment of the proposed bazaar is correct, in my opinion. I was approached with the same investment opportunity not long ago, and I rejected it on the same grounds.'

'No doubt we'll both be proven wrong,' Sebastian said wryly. 'One should never try to predict anything regarding women and their shopping.' He stood to shake the earl's hand. 'My wife and I are just about to partake of some breakfast. I hope you will join us.'

'I'll take some coffee,' Westcliff said with a nod. 'Forgive my unexpected call, but I have some news to share.'

Sebastian, Evie, and Cam all stared at the earl intently as he continued, 'I was finally able to meet with Lord Belworth this morning. He admitted that he was the original owner of the pistol used to shoot St Vincent. He went on to relate in confidence that approximately three years ago, he had given the set of dueling pistols to Mr Clive Egan, along with some family jewelry and other trifles, as a bribe to allow him more time to settle his financial debts to the club.'

Evie blinked in surprise at the mention of the former club manager. 'Then Mr Egan is harboring Mr Bullard?'

'Possibly.'

'But why? Does this mean that Mr Egan may have engaged Mr Bullard to make an attempt on my life?'

'We'll find out,' Sebastian said, his face set. 'I intend to pay a call to Egan today.'

'I'll accompany you,' Westcliff said evenly. 'I have resources who were able to obtain Egan's address. It's not far from here, actually.'

Sebastian shook his head. 'Thank you for your help, but I won't have you inconvenienced by any further involvement. I doubt your wife would appreciate my allowing you to be put at risk. I'll take Rohan with me.'

Evie began to object, knowing that in this

situation, Sebastian would be safer in Westcliff's company. Sebastian had barely begun to recover from his injury. And if he took it in his head to do something foolish, it would not be easy for Cam to restrain him. Cam was, after all, his employee, and he was at least eight years younger. Westcliff knew Sebastian far better, and had infinitely more power to influence him.

Before Evie could say a word, however, Westcliff replied. 'Rohan is indeed a capable lad,' the earl agreed smoothly, 'which is why he should be entrusted with Evie's safety, and remain here with her.'

Sebastian's gaze narrowed as he prepared to argue. The words halted on his lips as Evie curled her hand around his arm, and leaned against him with light, confiding pressure. 'I would prefer that,' she said.

As Sebastian glanced into her upturned face, his expression softened, giving her the heady feeling that he would do whatever was in his power to please her. 'All right,' he murmured reluctantly. 'If Rohan's presence would put you at ease, so be it.'

Part of Sebastian's objection to taking Westcliff with him to see Clive Egan was the residual awkwardness between them. It wasn't exactly comfortable to spend time in the company of a man whose wife you had once kidnapped. The beating Westcliff had given him afterward had cleared the air somewhat, and Sebastian's subsequent apology had also helped. And it seemed as if Sebastian's marriage to Evie, and his willingness to sacrifice himself for her, had inclined the earl to view him with a cautious approval that might, in time, rekindle their friendship. However, their relationship had been cast in a new form that might never fully recapture their previous ease.

For a man who had once dedicated himself to living without regrets, Sebastian was having quite a few unwanted second thoughts about his past behaviors. His actions regarding Lillian Bowman had been a mistake on many levels. What an idiot he had been, willing to sacrifice a friendship for the sake of a woman he had never really wanted in the first place. Had he bothered to consider his alternatives, he might have discovered Evie, who had been there right beneath his nose.

To Sebastian's relief, the conversation with Westcliff was amicable as the carriage traveled through the west side of London to the outskirts where fashionable middle-class developments were being built on greenfield sites. Clive Egan's address was one of a man who possessed solid means. Reflecting sourly on how much money Egan had gained from years of skimming and pinching the club's profits, Sebastian told Westcliff everything he knew about the former manager. The subject led to the current condition of the club's finances, and the necessary restructuring of investments. It was a pleasure to confide in Westcliff, who had one of ablest financial minds in the country, and offered a knowledgeable perspective on business issues. And it did not escape either of them that the discussion was a drastic departure from the past, when Sebastian had prattled about scandals and affairs, which had always resulted in rather patronizing lectures from Westcliff.

The carriage stopped at a new residential square, with tiny paved yards set behind them. All the houses were three stories tall and exceedingly narrow, none being wider than approximately fourteen feet across. An old and worn-looking cook-maid opened the door and stepped aside with a low grumble as they barged inside. The house seemed to be one of the indifferently decorated, ready-furnished variety, often let to middle-class professional men who had not yet married.

Since the entire residence consisted of three rooms and a closet, it was not difficult to locate Egan. The former club manager was settled in a large chair by the hearth of a parlor that smelled strongly of liquor and urine. A collection of bottles lined the sills of both windows, and a few more were set by the heart. Wearing the glassy-eyed expression of a perpetual drunkard, Egan beheld his two visitors without surprise. He looked exactly as he had when Sebastian had dismissed him two months earlier, bloated and unkempt, with carious teeth, a great red bulb of a nose, and a ruddy complexion webbed with spidery veins. Lifting a glass of spirits to his mouth, he drank deeply and grinned as he regarded them with watery gray eyes.

'I heard your guts had been blasted out,' he said to Sebastian. 'But since you don't look to be a ghost, I suppose the story was false.'

'Actually, it's true,' Sebastian replied, his gaze chilling. 'But the devil wouldn't have me.' The thought that Egan might be responsible for the attempted murder of his wife made it difficult for him to keep from attacking the bastard. Only the fact that he had information they needed was sufficient to keep Sebastian in check.

Egan let out a low chuckle and waved toward the row of bottles. 'Pour yourselves a drink, if you like. Not often that I'm visited by such high-kick gentlemen.'

Westcliff spoke calmly. 'No thank you. We've come to ask about a previous visitor of yours. Mr Joss Bullard. Where is he?'

Taking another deep guzzle of the spirits in his glass, Egan regarded him stonily. 'How the devil should I know?'

Withdrawing the custom-made pistol from his pocket, Westcliff displayed it in an open palm.

The drunkard's eyes bulged, and his face was suddenly covered in a wash of purple. 'Where did you get that?' he wheezed.

'Bullard used it the night of the shooting,' Sebastian said, struggling for discipline, when every nerve was singing with rage. 'And although I doubt the misshapen lump that is currently

352

sitting on your shoulders contains anything close to a functioning brain, even you should be able to figure out the implications of your involvement in attempted murder. Care for a nice long stay in a Fleet Ditch jail? That can be arranged in a matter of—'

'St Vincent,' Westcliff murmured in quiet warning, while Egan spluttered and choked.

'He must have stolen it from me!' Egan cried, the liquor splashing from his glass to the floor. 'Thieving little bastard – I didn't know he'd gotten it. It's not my fault, I tell you! I want nothing except to be left in peace. Damn his eyes!'

'When was the last time you saw him?'

'Maybe three weeks ago.' Polishing off his drink, Egan snatched up the bottle from the floor and nursed from it like a starving infant. 'He came to stay every now and again, after he left Jenner's. He had nowhere to go. They wouldn't even let him sleep in a padding ken, once the pox started showing.'

Sebastian and Westcliff exchanged a swift glance. 'Pox?' Sebastian asked suspiciously, for there were many different diseases that were referred to as pox. 'What kind?'

Egan stared at him scornfully. 'Distemper. Pox that led to madness. Even before he left Jenner's, there were signs . . . the slow speech, the tremors of his face . . . the cracks and dents on his nose. You'd have to have been blind not to notice.'

'I'm not usually given to examining my employees'

appearances that closely,' Sebastian said sardonically, while thoughts rushed through his mind.
Distemper pox was a nasty disease transmitted by
sexual contact, leading to what doctors referred
to as 'paresis of the insane.' It resulted in madness,
sometime partial paralysis, and a gruesome wasting
of the fleshy parts of the body, including the soft
tissue of the nose. If Bullard was indeed the victim
of distemper pox, and it had progressed this far,
there was no hope for him. But why, in the grip
of dementia, had he focused on Evie?

'His mind has probably gone by now,' Egan said
bitterly, raising the bottle for another numbing
swig. He closed his eyes briefly against the burn
of the spirits, and let his chin rest on his chest.
'The boy came here the night of the shooting,
ranting about having killed you. Shaking in every
limb, he was, and complaining of noise and pain
in his head. He was full of whims and notions.
Beyond reason. So I paid a man to take him to a
ward for incurables – the one at the turnpike that
leads to Knightsbridge. Bullard is there now, either
dead or in a state that would make death a damned
mercy.'

Sebastian spoke with taut impatience rather than
compassion. 'Why did he try to kill my wife? God
knows she never did him any harm.'

Egan replied morosely. 'He always despised her,
poor little bastard. Even in childhood. After one
of Evangeline's visits to the club, when Bullard
saw the delight Jenner took in her, he would be

sullen and bilious for days. He would make jest of her . . .' Egan paused, a reminiscent smile whisking across his lips. 'Funny little creature, she was. Speckled, shy, and round as a porpoise. I heard that she's a beauty now – though I can't quite picture it—'

'Was Jenner his father?' Westcliff interrupted, his face expressionless.

The abrupt question startled Sebastian. He listened intently as Egan replied.

'Could have been. His mother, Mary, swore up and down that he was.' Carefully Egan tucked the bottle at his side and rested his interlaced fingers on the bulging platform of his stomach. 'She was a bawdyhouse whore. The luckiest night of her life was when she worked the brass for Ivo Jenner. He took a liking to Mary, and paid the madam to keep her for his exclusive use. One day Mary came to him and said she was bellyfull, and the child was his. And Jenner, who was a soft touch, gave her the benefit of the doubt. He supported her for the rest of her life, and let the boy work at the club when he was old enough. Mary passed on many years back. Just before she kicked off, she told Bullard that Jenner was his father. When the boy confronted him with it, Jenner told him that whether it was true or not, it would stay a secret. He didn't want to acknowledge Bullard as his. For one thing, the boy was never what you'd say was a likely sort, and for another . . . Jenner never gave a damn about anyone but his daughter. He wanted Evie to have everything when he finally kicked off. Bullard blamed Evie, of course. He thought that if it wasn't for her, Jenner would have claimed him as a son, and would have done more for him, given him more. He was likely right about that.' Egan frowned sadly. 'By the time she brought you to the club, my lord, Bullard was already ill with the pox . . . and it was then that the madness began. A sad ending to a melancholy life.'

Glancing at the two of them with gloomy satisfaction, Egan added, 'You'll find him at Tottenham's Hospital, if you wish to revenge yourself on a poor bedeviled lunatic. Take what satisfaction you can have, my lords – but if you ask me, Bullard's maker has already contrived the worst punishment a body can endure.'

CHAPTER 22

During the hours that Sebastian was gone, Evie occupied herself with menial tasks around the club; sorting money and receipts, answering correspondence, and finally attending to the pile of unread letters addressed to Sebastian. Naturally she had been unable to resist opening a few. They were filled with flirtatious nonsense and innuendo, two of them even hinting that by now Sebastian must have wearied of his new bride. Their intent was so obvious that Evie actually felt embarrassed for the sake of the letter writers. They also served to remind her of Sebastian's promiscuous past, when his main occupation had been to indulge in games of amorous pursuit and conquest.

It wasn't easy to place her trust in such a man without feeling like a naive fool. Especially in light of the certainty that Sebastian would always be admired and coveted by other women. But Evie felt that Sebastian deserved the chance to prove himself. It was in her power to give him a new beginning – and if her gamble proved successful, the rewards for both of them would be infinite.

She could be strong enough to take the risk of loving him, to make demands of him, to have expectations that he might sometimes find difficult to meet. And Sebastian seemed to want to be treated like an ordinary man – to have someone look beyond the mortal beauty of his facade, and ask more of him than his erotic skills. Not, Evie thought with a private grin, that she wasn't appreciative of his looks and skills.

After watching – with a twinge of satisfaction – the letters burn to ashes in the fireplace, Evie felt sleepy. She went to the master bedroom for a nap. In spite of her weariness, it was difficult to relax while she was worried about Sebastian. Her thoughts chased round and round, until her tired brain put an end to the useless fretting and she dropped off to sleep.

When she awakened an hour or so later, Sebastian was sitting on the bed beside her, a lock of her bright hair clasped loosely between a thumb and forefinger. He was watching her closely, his eyes the color of heaven at daybreak. She sat up and smiled self-consciously.

Gently Sebastian stroked back her tumbled hair. 'You look like a little girl when you sleep,' he murmured. 'It makes me want to guard you every minute.'

'Did you find Mr Bullard?'

'Yes, and no. First tell me what you did while I was gone.'

'I helped Cam to arrange things in the office.

358

And I burned all your letters from lovelorn ladies. The blaze was so large, I'm surprised no one sent for a fire brigade.'

His lips curved in a smile, but his gaze probed hers carefully. 'Did you read any of them?'

Evie lifted a shoulder in a nonchalant half shrug. 'A few. There were inquiries as to whether or not you've yet tired of your wife.'

'No.' Sebastian drew his palm along the line of her thigh. 'I'm tired of countless evenings of repetitive gossip and tepid flirtation. I'm tired of meaningless encounters with women who bore me senseless. They're all the same to me, you know. I've never given a damn about anyone but you.'

'I don't blame them for wanting you,' Evie said, looping her arms around his neck. 'But I'm not willing to share.'

'You won't have to.' He cupped her face in his hands and pressed a swift kiss to her lips.

'Tell me about Mr Bullard,' Evie urged, her hands coming up to caress his wrists.

She was silent as Sebastian described the encounter with Clive Egan, and the revelations about Joss Bullard and his mother. Her eyes became very wide, and she was filled with pity. Poor Joss Bullard could not help his origins, or the indifferent upbringing that had made him so resentful. 'How strange,' she murmured. 'I'd always wished and even hoped that Cam was my brother, but I never gave a thought to the possibility that Joss Bullard might be.'

Bullard had always been so unapproachable and belligerent . . . and yet how much of that might have been the result of Ivo Jenner's repudiation? To feel unwanted, to be kept a shameful secret by the man who might have been his true father . . . surely that would make anyone bitter.

'We went to the Tottenham hospital,' Sebastian continued, 'where he had been admitted to the ward of incurables. It's a foul place, and in dire need of funding. There were women and children who—' He broke off with a slight grimace at the recollection. 'I'd rather not describe it, actually. But an administrator at Tottenham said that Bullard had been admitted in the last stage of distemper.'

'I want to help him,' Evie said resolutely. 'At the very least, we can have him sent to a better hospital—'

'No, sweet.' Sebastian traced his fingertips over the fine bones of her hand. 'He died two days ago. They showed us to the plot where he and two other patients were buried in the same grave.'

Evie looked away, absorbing the information. She was surprised to feel her eyes moisten and her throat tighten. 'The poor boy,' she said huskily. 'I feel sorry for him.'

'I don't,' Sebastian said flatly. 'If he grew up without a parent's affection, he was no different from countless other people who have to make their way in the world alone. He had an easier time of it than Rohan, whose Gypsy blood makes him an object of prejudice. Don't cry, Evie. Bullard isn't worth a single tear.'

Evie let out an unsteady sigh. 'I'm sorry. I don't mean to be so emotional. It's just that it's been a very trying few weeks. My feelings are all a bit too close to the surface and I can't seem to manage them properly.'

She was collected against his warm body, his hard muscles surrounding her, his voice weaving through his hair. 'Evie, love, don't apologize for being emotional. You've been through hell. And only a heartless brute like me could truly appreciate the courage it takes to be honest about your feelings.'

Evie's voice was muffled against his shoulder. 'You're not heartless.' She sighed shakily. 'Perhaps it is wrong of me, but even though I do feel sorry for Mr Bullard, I'm relieved that he is gone. Because of his actions, I almost lost you.'

His mouth searched through the loose curls of her hair until he found the fragile rim of her ear. 'You won't be that fortunate.'

'Don't,' Evie said, unable to smile at the light quip. She drew her head back to look at him, while his arms remained locked around her. 'It's not something to joke about. I . . .' Her voice wobbled sharply as she forced herself to continue. '1 don't think I could live without you now.'

Sebastian's large hand passed gently over the back of her head, pulling her to his shoulder, and he buried his face in her hair for a moment. 'Ah,

Evie,' she heard him say softly, 'I must have a heart, after all . . . because right now it aches like the devil.'

'Only your heart?' she asked ingenuously, making him laugh.

He lowered her to the bed, his eyes sparkling wickedly. 'Also a few other things,' he conceded. 'And as my wife, it's your duty to ease all my aches.'

She lifted her arms and drew him down to her.

Oblivious to the personal issues of Jenner's owners or employees, the club patrons continued to crowd the building nightly, especially as it became known that there were no more available memberships, as the limit had been set at twenty-five hundred. Those who wished to become members were obliged to subscribe to a waiting list in hopes of a vacancy.

The odd pairing of a penniless viscount and a gaming club in decline had resulted in a surprising alchemy. The employees were either swept along in the current of Sebastian's dynamic energy, or they were discarded in his wake. The place was run with a ruthless efficiency that Jenner's had never seen before. Even Ivo Jenner in his heyday had never ruled his small empire with such an iron hand.

In the past, Ivo Jenner's hidden resentment of the aristocracy had caused him to treat many of the club members with a fawning subservience that had made them vaguely uncomfortable. Sebastian, on the other hand, was one of their own. He was relaxed and yet so dashing that his presence seemed to infuse the atmosphere with excitement. Whenever he was near, club members laughed more, spent more, talked more, ate more.

Whereas other clubs served the eternal beefsteak and apple tart, the lavish buffet at Jenner's was constantly replenished with ever-more-artful dishes . . . hot lobster salad, casserole of pheasant, prawns on pillowy beds of puréed celery root, quail stuffed with grapes and goat cheese and served in pools of cream sauce. And Evie's favorite – a sticky flourless almond cake topped with raspberries and a thick layer of meringue. The food and entertainment at Jenner's had improved at such a rapid rate that wives began to complain that their husbands were spending far too many nights at the club.

Sebastian's manipulative nature had found a perfect outlet in Jenner's. He knew how to provide an environment in which men could relax and enjoy themselves, and in the process he divested them of their money with ease. The games were run with scrupulous honesty, since gaming was, in theory, forbidden by law even though it was practiced openly throughout London. Operating a respectable club was the best way to avoid prosecution.

If at first Sebastian had to endure a few mocking comments from his acquaintances, their manner quickly changed as they found themselves in the position of asking him to extend credit, or to forestall the payment of their debts. For a man who had never had much money, Sebastian had a surprising ability to manage it. As Cam had said admiringly, Sebastian demonstrated the ability of a rat terrier to sniff out a risky bank balance, or anything else that might affect a member's ability to pay.

One evening as Evie stood beside Cam's desk in the main room to watch Sebastian presiding over a hazard game of particularly deep play, she became aware of an elderly man beside her. She turned and recognized him as Lord Haldane, a gentleman whom Sebastian had introduced to her the previous week. 'My lord,' Evie murmured as he bowed over her hand. 'How nice it is to see you again.'

He smiled, his brown eyes kind in his jowly face. 'The pleasure is mine, Lady St Vincent.'

They both glanced back at the main hazard table, where Sebastian had just made a quip to ease the tension of the game. A low rumble of laughter went through the crowd. Evie silently marveled at how natural he seemed in his role, as if he had been born to it. Strangely, he seemed more at home in the club than even her father had. Ivo Jenner, with his excitable nature, had always found it difficult to conceal his worry when a club member had followed a run of extraordinary luck that threatened to break the bank. Sebastian, on the other hand, remained cool and unruffled no matter what the circumstances.

Lord Haldane was occupied with similar reflections, for he stared at Sebastian's distant figure and said absently, 'I never thought to see another of his kind again.'

'My lord?' Evie questioned with a half smile, as Sebastian noticed her presence and began to make his way over to her.

Haldane seemed lost in a memory of days long past. 'In all my years, I've seen only one other man who walked through a gaming club that way. As if it was his personal hunting ground, and he the most charming of predators.'

'Are you referring to my father?' Evie asked, confused.

Haldane smiled and shook his head. 'Bless me, no. Not your father.'

'Who—' Evie began, but her question was lost as Sebastian reached them.

'My lady,' Sebastian murmured, resting one hand at the small of her corseted back. Regarding Haldane with a slight smile, he continued to speak to Evie. 'It seems I'll have to warn you, my love . . . this gentleman is a wolf in sheep's clothing.'

Although Evie would have expected the elderly man to take offense at such a remark, Haldane chuckled with pleasure, his vanity flattered. 'If I were twenty years younger, my impudent fellow, I would steal her away from you. Despite your much-vaunted charm, you are no match for what I was then.'

'Age hasn't tamed you a whit,' Sebastian replied with a grin, drawing Evie away from him. 'Pardon us, my lord, while I remove my wife to safer territory.'

'It is obvious that this elusive fellow has been

caught firmly in your snare,' Haldane told Evie. 'Go, then, and pacify his jealous temperament.'

'I . . . I will try,' Evie said uncertainly. For some reason both men laughed, and Sebastian kept his hand on Evie's back as they left the main room.

His head bent to hers as they walked. 'Is everything all right, sweet?'

'Yes. I . . .' She paused, smiled, and said lamely, 'I just wanted to see you.'

Stopping with her behind a column, Sebastian ducked his head to steal a kiss. He looked down at her, his eyes sparkling. 'Shall we go play a game of billiards?' he whispered, and laughed huskily as she blushed.

The popularity of the club increased further when newspapers began to commend it in overblown prose:

> At last Jenner's may assume a place among the elite gentlemen's resorts in London, distinguishing itself as a venerated pavilion in which every sprig and stripling of the aristocracy aspires to be one of the select. The cuisine satisfies the most discerning palates, and the expanded selection of wines appeals to the most fastidious tastes . . .

And in another editorial:

> Too much cannot be said about the quality of the newly refurbished surroundings, which

provide an ornate backdrop to the gatherings of patrons characterized by intellectual and personal superiority. It is no surprise that the number of candidates for membership far exceeds the number of vacancies . . .

In yet another:

Many have suggested, and few disagree, that the renaissance of Jenner's could only have been brought about by one gentleman, who, with devilish charm, manages to be conversant with all the worlds of fashion, politics, literature, and the aristocracy. It is, of course, the infamous Lord St Vincent, now the owner of a beau-ideal club that promises to be an important institution in West End life . . .

Sitting in the office one evening, Evie read the editorials. She had not expected the amount of public attention that Sebastian and the club were receiving. While she was glad that he was making it a success, she could not help but wonder what it would be like when she eventually came out of mourning, and they began to take part in London society. She had no doubt that they would be invited to many places. And the fact was, being a wallflower did not afford one many opportunities to practice social skills. She would have to overcome her awkwardness and shyness. She must learn the art of making repartee . . . She must learn to be charming and confident—

'Why are you frowning, sweet?' Sebastian came to sit on the desk, glancing down at her with a quizzical smile. 'Did you read something unpleasant?'

'Just the opposite,' Evie said glumly. 'Everyone is waxing ecstatic about the club.'

'I see.' A gentle forefinger stroked the edge of her jaw. 'And that gives you concern because . . .'

Her explanation came out in a rush. 'Because you're b-becoming very well-known – that is, for something other than skirt chasing – and therefore you will be sought-after, and someday I'll come out of mourning which means that we'll go to balls and soirees, and I don't think I'll be able to st-stop myself from hiding in the corners. I'm still a wall-flower, you know. I must learn how to be witty and poised and talk to people, or else you'll be vexed with me, or even worse, ashamed, and I—'

'Evie. Hush. Good God . . .' Sebastian hooked a foot around a nearby chair, dragged it against hers, and sat with his knees braced around hers. Taking both her hands, he smiled into her eyes. 'You can't go twenty minutes without finding something to worry about, can you? You won't have to be anything other than what you are.' He bent to kiss her hands, and when he lifted his head, his smile had faded and his eyes smoldered. His thumb came to the surface of her wedding band, rubbing gently over the engraved words.

'How could I be ashamed of you?' he continued. *'I'm* the one who's been an utter villain. You've never done a blameworthy thing in your life. And as far as drawing room airs and graces are concerned . . . I hope you never become like those shallow fools who chatter endlessly without managing to say anything of interest.' Tugging her closer, he nuzzled into her neck, where the corded-silk edge of her gown lay against her pale skin. His mouth tasted her lightly, and then he whispered against the moist spot he had made, causing her to shiver. 'You're not a wallflower. But you have my permission to hide in corners, my sweet – so long as you take me with you. In fact, I'll insist on it. I warn you, I'm very badly behaved at such affairs – I'll probably debauch you in gazebos, on balconies, beneath staircases, and behind assorted potted plants. And if you complain, I'll simply remind you that you should have known better than to marry a conscienceless rake.'

Evie's throat arched slightly at the light stroke of his fingers. 'I wouldn't complain.'

Sebastian smiled and nipped tenderly at the side of her neck. 'Dutiful little wife,' he whispered. 'I'm going to be a terrible influence on you. Why don't you give me a kiss, and go upstairs for your bath? By the time you finish, I'll be there with you.'

The bath was only half-filled when Evie entered the bedroom. Frannie and another housemaid each picked up a set of wood-handled ewers in preparation for one more trip downstairs. Feeling warm and dreamy in the aftermath of Sebastian's kisses, Evie began to unbutton the sleeves of her gown.

'I'll unfasten you when I come back with the last of the water, milady,' Frannie offered.

Evie smiled at her. 'Thank you.' She wandered to the dressing table and picked up a flacon of perfume, a gift that Lillian had recently sent. With her unusually sensitive nose, Lillian loved to occupy herself with scents and perfumes, and had recently taken to experimenting with her own combinations. This fragrance was lush and well-rounded, with roses and pungent wood spices fixed in amber. Evie carefully poured a few golden drops into the bath water, and inhaled in pleasure as the fragrant steam rose into the air.

Returning to the dressing table, she sat in a small chair and bent to remove her shoes and stockings, reaching beneath her skirts to unfasten her garters. With her head angled downward, she could see very little . . . but a sudden icy slither down her spine and a soft tread on the carpeted floor caused all the hairs on her body to stand erect. She saw a shadow slide quickly across the floor. Sitting up, Evie followed the shadow to its origins, and a startled sound escaped her as she saw a ragged figure coming toward her. She sprang from the chair, overturning it in her haste. As she whirled to face the man who had entered the room, he spoke in a grinding voice.

'Not a word. Or I'll slit you open from neck to muff.'

A long, wicked knife was clutched in his hand. He stood very close to her – he could reach her with one lunge, if he chose.

No image wrought from nightmares or childhood fears of monsters, could ever match the sight of the intruder's gruesomely corroded form. Evie inched toward the slipper tub, trying to position it between herself and the madman. He was dressed in clothes that were little more than a heap of rags. He favored his left side oddly, as if he were an off-kilter string puppet. On every inch of exposed skin – his hands, his throat, his face – there were open, oozing sores, as if his flesh were decaying right off his bones. Most horrifying of all, however, were the tattered remnants of what had once been a nose. He looked like a chimera, a collection of flesh and limbs and features that didn't belong together.

Despite filth and sores and the shocking ruin of his face, Evie recognized him. It took great effort for her to remain calm when all her veins were filled with stinging panic. 'Mr Bullard,' she croaked. 'The hospital said you were dead.'

Bullard's head lolled oddly on his shoulders as he continued to stare at her. 'I left that bloody 'ell pit,' he growled. 'I broke a window and 'scaped at night. I 'ad enow o' those demons trying to pour their devil brews down my throat.' He started toward her with arrhythmic steps. Evie circled the

371

tub slowly, while her heart pounded hard in her chest. 'But I wasn't going to kick off in that cursed place wivout sending you to 'ell first.'

'Why?' Evie asked softly, fighting not to glance at the doorway, where she saw movement from the corners of her eyes. It must be Frannie, she thought feverishly. The blurred shape disappeared without a sound, and Evie prayed that the house-maid had run to fetch help. In the meantime, the only recourse was to keep away from Joss Bullard.

'You took ewerything from me,' he snarled, rounding his shoulders like an animal backed against the wall of a cage. ''E gave it all to you, the damned bastard – 'e only wanted an ugly little tangle-tongue, when I was 'is son. 'Is *son,* an' I was 'id away like a filthy chamber pot.' His face contorted. 'I did whotever 'e asked . . . I'd of killed to please 'im . . . but it never mattered. It was allus *you* 'e wanted, you bleedin' parasite!'

'I'm sorry,' Evie said, and the genuine regret in her voice seemed to disorient him momentarily. He paused and stared at her with his head tilted at an odd angle. 'Mr Bullard . . . Joss . . . My father did care about you. His last request was that you should be helped and taken care of.'

'It's too late for that!' He gasped and raised both hands to his head, including the one with the knife, as if there was unbearable pain in his skull. 'Goddamn it . . . ah . . . devil take 'im . . .'

Seeing a chance to flee, Evie broke for the doorway. Bullard caught her at once, slamming her hard against the wall. As her head hit the hard surface, an explosion seemed to go off in her brain, and her vision was fragmented into a sea of glittering gray and black. Struggling to focus, she blinked and moaned. There was an unpleasant pressure high on her chest and a pinching sensation at the side of her throat. Gradually she realized that Bullard's arm was locked around her neck, with the long knife blade completing the circle. The sharp steel pressed against her with every inhalation. Bullard was breathing harshly, the puffs of air from his lungs reeking of foulness and decay. She felt the tremors of his body, and his efforts to stiffen his muscles against them. 'We'll go see 'im together,' he said near her ear.

'Who?' Evie mumbled, her gaze slowly clearing.

'Our father. We'll go see 'im in 'ell . . . you an' me.' A laugh rattled in his throat. ''E'll be running a cribbage game wiv old Scratch 'imself.' He urged the knife against her, seeming to enjoy the way she flinched. 'I'll cut you,' he muttered, 'an' then meself. 'Ow would Jenner like that, to see us arm in arm, strolling into 'ell together?'

As Evie sought for words that might bring him temporarily to reason, a quiet voice came from the doorway.

'Bullard.'

It was Sebastian, looking astonishingly cool and unperturbed. Although the danger to her had not lessened, Evie felt a rush of relief at his presence. He entered the room slowly. 'Apparently the

373

record keeping at Tottenham's leaves something to be desired,' Sebastian commented, not sparing a glance for Evie. His gaze was fixed on Bullard's face, his eyes light and hypnotic.

'I thought I'd put a bullet in you,' Bullard said roughly.

Sebastian shrugged casually. 'A trifling injury. Tell me . . . how did you manage to get into the club? We have men at every door.'

'Coal cellar. There's a bolt 'ole in it what leads to Rogue's Lane. No one knows about it. Not ewen that 'alf-bred Rohan. Go back, or I'll stick 'er like a pigeon on a spit.' This last came as Sebastian came a step closer.

Sebastian's gaze shot to the knife, which Bullard now angled as if he intended to plunge it into Evie's breast.

'All right,' Sebastian said, retreating at once. 'Easy . . . I'll do whatever you ask.' His voice was soft and friendly, his expression calm, though glittering trickles of sweat had begun to course down the sides of his face. 'Bullard . . . Joss . . . listen to me. You have nothing to lose by letting me speak. You're among friends. All your . . . your sister and I want is to honor your father's request to help you. Tell me what you want. I can get you morphine to ease your pain. You can stay here for as long as you wish, with a clean bed to sleep in, and people to take care of you. Whatever you want is yours.'

'You're playing me false,' Bullard said suspiciously.

'I'm not. I swear it. I'll give you anything. Unless you harm Evie – then I can do nothing for you.' As Sebastian spoke, he moved slowly toward the window, forcing Bullard to turn. 'Let her step away from you, and—'

'Stop,' Bullard said crossly, with an impatient shake of his head. A tremor shook him, and he let out an animal grunt. 'Damned noise in my ears . . .'

'I can help you,' Sebastian said patiently. 'You need medicine. And rest. Lower your arm, Joss . . . there's no need to hurt anyone. You're where you belong. Lower your arm, and I can help you.'

Incredulously Evie felt Bullard's arm begin to relax as he was drawn to Sebastian's soothing voice. At the same time, he turned more fully toward Sebastian.

A deafening blast of sound rent the air. Evie was released with a force that sent her reeling backward. Her dazed mind had only a moment to register the sight of Cam in the doorway, lowering a smoking pistol. Sebastian had deliberately moved into the room to position Bullard so that Cam could get a clear shot.

Before Evie could look at the crumpled heap on the floor, she was seized and whirled around, and crushed against Sebastian's chest. All the tension he had kept so tightly constrained for the past minute was released in hard shudders as he gripped her against him, clutching her back, her limbs, great handfuls of her hair as it tumbled from its pins. She had no breath to speak, could only stand against him helplessly while he cursed and groaned into her hair.

It seemed that her pulse would never return to normal. 'Frannie fetched you,' she finally managed to say.

Sebastian nodded, sliding his shaking fingers into her hair until they curved over her skull. 'She told me there was a man in your room. She didn't recognize him.' Dragging her head back, he saw the tiny cut the knife had made on her throat. His face drained of color as he saw how close Bullard had been to the main artery. He bent to kiss the thin mark, and then dragged his mouth feverishly over her face. 'Holy hell,' he whispered. 'Evie. Evie. I can't bear it.'

She twisted in his arms to glance at Cam, who had just draped his own coat over Bullard's head and shoulders to conceal them. 'Cam, you didn't have to shoot him,' she said thickly. 'He was going to let me go. He was lowering his arm—'

'I couldn't be certain,' the boy said in a monotone. 'I had to take the shot when I saw it.' His face was blank, but his golden eyes were brilliant with unshed tears. Evie realized that he had just been forced to kill a man he had known since boyhood.

'Cam—' she began compassionately, but he made a staying gesture and shook his head.

'It was kinder to him,' he said without looking at her. 'No creature should have to suffer that way.'

'Yes, but you—'

'I'm fine,' he said, his jaw hardening.

He wasn't, however. He was pale beneath his golden tan, and he looked so shaken that Evie couldn't stop herself from going to him and putting her arms around him in maternal consolation. He allowed the embrace, though he didn't return it, and gradually his tremors quieted. She felt the briefest pressure of his lips on her hair.

That, it seemed, was all that Sebastian was willing to allow. Coming forward, he retrieved Evie and spoke brusquely to Cam. 'Go send for the mortuary man.'

'Yes,' the boy said almost absently. He hesitated. 'They'll have heard the noise downstairs. We'll have to offer an explanation of some kind.'

'Tell them someone was cleaning a gun, and it went off accidentally,' Sebastian said. 'Tell them no one was hurt. When the mortuary man arrives, bring him up the back way. Pay him for his silence.'

'Yes, my lord. What if a constable should make inquiries—'

'Send him to the office – I'll deal with him there.'

Cam nodded and disappeared.

Pulling Evie from the apartments, Sebastian locked the door, pocketed the key, and took her to another bedroom down the hallway. She accompanied him in a daze, trying to make herself comprehend what had just happened. Sebastian was silent, his profile granite-hard as he tried to marshal his composure. With great care, he brought her into the bedroom. 'Stay here,' he said. 'I'll send a maid to attend you. And a glass of brandy – I want you to drink all of it.'

Evie looked up at him anxiously. 'Will you come to me later?'

He gave her a short nod. 'I have to take care of things first.'

But he didn't return to the room that night. Evie waited for him in vain, finally going to bed alone. Her sleep was broken by frequent awakenings, her hand fumbling to the empty space beside her as she searched in vain for Sebastian's warm body. Morning arrived to find her worried and exhausted, her gaze bleary as she beheld the maid who had come to light the grate.

'Have you seen Lord St Vincent this morning?' Evie asked huskily.

'Yes, milady. His Lordship and Mr Rohan have been up most of the night, talking.'

'Tell him that I wish to see him.'

'Yes, milady.' The maid set a ewer of hot water on the washstand and left the room.

Climbing out of bed, Evie performed her morning ablutions and smoothed her hands over the untamed curls of her hair. Her brush and comb and pins were all in the other bedroom, where—

She shivered with revulsion and pity as she remembered the events of the previous evening. How glad she was that her father had not lived to see what had become of poor Joss Bullard. She wondered what his true feelings for the young man had been, or if he had ever let himself believe that Bullard had been his son. 'Papa . . .' she murmured, staring at her own blue eyes in the looking glass. Ivo Jenner's eyes. He had taken so many secrets to the grave with him, and had left so much unexplained. She would always regret not having known him better. It gave her comfort, however, to think that he would have been pleased to know that Jenner's would finally achieve the heights he had always aspired to . . . and that his own daughter had set in motion the events that would result in the club's salvation.

As her thoughts turned to Sebastian, he entered the room, still wearing the same clothes he had worn the previous evening. His hair was a disordered mass of gold and amber, and his light eyes were heavily shadowed. He looked fatigued but resolute, with the air of a man who had made unpleasant decisions and was determined to stand by them.

His gaze combed over her. 'How are you?'

Evie would have run to him, but something in his expression checked her. She stood by the washstand, staring at him curiously. 'A bit weary. Not so weary as you seem, however. The maid said that you were awake most of the night. What did you and Cam discuss?'

Sebastian reached up to rub the nape of his neck. 'He's having a bit of difficulty coming to terms with what happened last night. But he'll be all right.'

Evie stood before him uncertainly, wondering why he was trying so hard to appear remote. As he glanced over her nightgown-clad form, however, he could not conceal the flare of yearning in his eyes. The sight reassured her. 'Come to me,' she said in a low voice.

Instead of complying, Sebastian walked to the window, away from her. Silently he gazed at the busy street lined with carriages, the pavements crowded with foot traffic.

Perplexed by his behavior, Evie watched the long, sleek line of his back, and the taut set of his shoulders.

Finally Sebastian turned toward her, his face carefully blank. 'I've had enough,' he said. 'You're not safe here – I've said it from the beginning. And I've been proven right one time too many. I've made a decision that will not be altered. You are leaving on the morrow. I'm sending you to the country, to stay at the family estate for a while. My father wants to meet you. He'll be pleasant enough company, and there are a few local families to provide some diversion—'

'And you intend to stay here?' Evie asked with a frown.

'Yes. I will manage the club, and I'll come to visit you from time to time.'

Unable to believe that he was proposing a separation between them, Evie gave him a round-eyed stare. 'Why?' she asked faintly.

His face was grim. 'I can't keep you in a place

like this, worrying constantly about what might happen to you.'

'Things happen to people in the country, too.'

'I'm not going to argue with you,' Sebastian said gruffly. 'You'll go where I want you to go, and that's that.'

The old Evie would have been cowed, and hurt, and would probably have obeyed without further argument. The new Evie, however, was much stronger . . . not to mention desperately in love. 'I don't think I can stay away from you,' she said in a level tone. 'Especially when I don't understand the reason for it.'

There was a crack in Sebastian's composure now, a wash of color that crept up from his collar. He raked both hands through his hair, further disheveling the glittering locks. 'Lately I've become so damned distracted that I can't make a decision about anything. I can't think clearly. I've got knots in my stomach, and constant pains in my chest, and whenever I see you talking to any man, or smiling at anyone, I go insane with jealousy. I can't live this way. I—' He broke off and stared at her incredulously. 'Damn it, Evie, what is there for you to smile about?'

'Nothing,' she said, hastily tucking the sudden smile back into the corners of her mouth. 'It's just . . . it sounds as if you're trying to say that you love me.'

The word seemed to shock Sebastian. 'No,' he said forcefully, his color rising. 'I don't. I can't.

That's not what I'm talking about. I just need to find a way to—' He broke off and inhaled sharply as she came to him. 'Evie, no.' A shiver ran through him as she reached up to the sides of his face, her fingers gentle on his skin. 'It's not what you think,' he said unsteadily. She heard the trace of fear in his voice. The fear that a small boy must have felt when every woman he loved had disappeared from his life, swept away by a merciless fever. She didn't know how to reassure him, or how to console his long-ago grief. Raising on her toes, she sought his mouth with her own. His hands came to her elbows, as if to push her away, but he couldn't seem to make himself do it. His breath was rapid and hot as he turned his face away. Undeterred, she kissed his cheek, his jaw, his throat. A low curse escaped him. 'Damn you,' he said desperately, 'I've got to send you away.'

'You're not trying to protect me. You're trying to protect yourself.' She hugged herself to him tightly. 'But you can force yourself to take the risk of loving someone, can't you?'

'No,' he whispered.

'Yes. You must.' Evie closed her eyes and pressed her face against his. 'Because I love you, Sebastian . . . and I need you to love me back. And not in h-half measures.'

She heard his breath hiss through his teeth. His hands came to her shoulders, then snatched back. 'You'll have to let me set my own limits, or—'

Evie reached his mouth and kissed him slowly,

deliberately, until he succumbed with a groan, his arms clamping around her. He answered her kiss desperately, until every part of her had been set alight with tender fire. He took his mouth from hers, gasping savagely. *'Half measures.* My God. I love you so much that I'm drowning in it. I can't defend against it. I don't know who I am anymore. All I know is that if I give in to it entirely—' He tried to control the anarchy of his breath. 'You mean too much to me,' he said raggedly.

Evie smoothed her palm over his hard chest in a soothing circle. She understood his desperation, the emotions that were so unfamiliar and powerful that they overwhelmed him. It reminded her of something Annabelle had confided to her, that at the beginning of their marriage, Mr Hunt had been quite unnerved by the intensity of his feelings for her, and it had taken time for him to adjust to them. 'Sebastian,' Evie ventured, 'it won't be like this all the time, you know. It . . . it will seem more natural, more comfortable, after a while.'

'No, it won't.'

He sounded so passionate, so certain, that she had to hide a smile against his shoulder. 'I love you,' she said once again, and felt a tremor of longing run through him. 'You can s-send me away, but you can't stop me from running back to you. I want to spend every day with you. I want to watch you shave in the morning. I want to drink champagne and dance with you. I want to mend the holes in your stockings. I want to share a bed with you every night, and to have your children.' She paused. 'Don't you think I have fears as well? Perhaps you'll wake up one morning and say that you've tired of me. Perhaps all the things you tolerate so well now will become too exasperating to bear – my stammer, my freckles—'

'Don't be an idiot,' Sebastian interrupted roughly. 'Your stammer would never bother me. And I love your freckles. I *love*—' His voice cracked. He clutched her tightly. 'Hell,' he muttered. And then, after a moment, with bitter vehemence, 'I wish I were anyone other than me.'

'Why?' she asked, her voice muffled.

'*Why?* My past is a cesspool, Evie.'

'That's hardly news.'

'I can't ever atone for the things I've done. Christ, I wish I had it to do over again! I would try to be a better man for you. I would—'

'You don't have to be anything other than what you are.' Lifting her head, Evie stared at him through the radiant shimmer of her tears. 'Isn't that what you told me earlier? If you can love me without conditions, Sebastian, can't I love you the same way? I know who you are. I think we know each other better than we know ourselves. Don't you dare send me away, you c-coward. Who else would love my freckles? Who else would care that my feet were cold? Who else would ravish me in the billiards room?'

Slowly his resistance ebbed. She felt the change

in his body, the relaxing of tension, his shoulders curving around her as if he could draw her into himself. Murmuring her name, he brought her hand to his face and nuzzled ardently into her palm, his lips brushing the warm circlet of her gold wedding band. 'My love is upon you,' he whispered . . . and she knew then that she had won. This imperfect, extraordinary, passionate man was hers, his heart given over completely to her safekeeping. It was a trust she would never betray. Overwhelmed with relief and tenderness, Evie clung to him while a teardrop slipped from the outside corner of one eye. Sebastian smoothed it away with his fingers, staring into her upturned face. And what she saw in his glittering gaze stole her breath away.

'Well,' Sebastian said unsteadily, 'you may have a point about the billiards room.'

And she smiled as he lifted her in his arms and carried her to bed.

EPILOGUE

It was nearly the end of winter. Since Evie's mourning period coincided with Annabelle's confinement, the two of them had spent a great deal of time together. They were both precluded from attending social events such as balls or large suppers, but that suited the women quite well, as it had been bitterly cold since Christmas, and spring seemed reluctant to arrive. Instead of gadding about town, they huddled next to the great fireplace at the Hunts' luxurious hotel suite, or more often they gathered with Lillian and Daisy in one of the cozy parlors at Westcliff's Marsden Terrace. They read, chatted, and did handiwork while consuming endless cups of tea.

One afternoon Lillian sat at a writing desk in the corner, laboriously composing a letter to one of her sisters-in-law, while Daisy reclined on a settee with a novel, her slight frame bundled in a cashmere lap blanket. Annabelle had occupied a chair by the blazing fire, one of her hands resting on the burgeoning curve of her belly, while Evie sat on a stool before her, rubbing her aching feet. Wincing and sighing, Annabelle murmured, 'Oh, that feels lovely. No one warned me that pregnancy makes one's feet so sore. Though I should have expected it, with all the extra weight I'm obliged to carry. Thank you, Evie. You're the dearest friend in the world.'

Lillian's sardonic voice came from the corner. 'She told me the same thing, Evie, when I last rubbed her feet. Her devotion lasts only until the next massage. Admit it, Annabelle – you're a lightskirt.'

Annabelle grinned lazily. 'Just wait until *you* conceive, dear. You'll be begging for foot rubs from anyone who is willing to give them.'

Lillian opened her mouth to reply, seemed to think better of it, and took a sip of wine from a glass on the desk.

Without looking up from her novel, Daisy said, 'Oh, go on and tell them.'

Both Annabelle and Evie turned to stare at Lillian. 'Tell us what?' they both asked in tandem.

Lillian responded with a quick, embarrassed lift of her shoulders, and sent a bashful grin over her shoulder. 'Come midsummer, Westcliff will finally have his heir.'

'Unless it's a girl,' Daisy added.

'Congratulations,' Evie exclaimed, temporarily abandoning Annabelle. She went to hug Lillian exuberantly. 'That is wonderful news!'

'Westcliff is beside himself with delight, though he tries not to show it,' Lillian said, returning the hug. 'I'm certain he is telling St Vincent and Mr Hunt at this very moment. He seems to believe it is entirely his accomplishment.'

'Well, his contribution was essential, wasn't it?' Annabelle pointed out in amusement.

'Yes,' Lillian replied, 'but the greater part of the undertaking is clearly mine.'

Annabelle grinned at Lillian from across the room. 'You'll do splendidly, dear. Forgive me if I don't leap across the room; just know that I am truly overjoyed. I hope you have the opposite of whatever I'm having and then we can arrange a marriage.' Her tone turned whiny and cajoling. 'Evie . . . come back. You can't leave me with just one foot done.'

Shaking her head with a smile, Evie returned to the stool at the hearth. She glanced at Daisy, noticing the fond, pensive gaze that was directed toward her older sister. Perceiving the girl's wistfulness, Evie said as she resumed her place at Annabelle's feet, 'In the midst of all this talk about husbands and babies, we mustn't forget about finding a gentleman for Daisy.'

The dark-haired girl sent her an affectionate grin. 'You're a dear, Evie. And I don't mind having waited for my turn. After all, *someone* had to be the last wallflower. But I am beginning to wonder if I'll ever find a suitable man to marry.'

'Of course you will,' Annabelle said reasonably. 'I don't foresee any difficulty, Daisy. We've all broadened our circle of acquaintances quite a bit, and we'll do whatever is necessary to find the perfect husband for you.'

'Just keep in mind that I don't want to marry a man like Lord Westcliff,' Daisy said. 'Too over-bearing. And not one like Lord St Vincent either. Too unpredictable.'

'What about one like Mr Hunt?' Annabelle asked.

Daisy shook her head firmly. 'Too tall.'

'You're becoming a bit particular, aren't you?' Annabelle pointed out mildly, her eyes twinkling.

'Not in the least! My expectations are quite reasonable. I want a nice man who likes long walks, and books, and is adored by dogs, children—'

'And all the superior forms of aquatic and plant life,' Lillian said dryly. 'Tell me, dear, where are we to find this paragon?'

'Not at any of the balls I've been to so far,' came Daisy's glum reply. 'I wouldn't have thought it possible, but the selection this year is even worse than last. I am beginning to believe that any man worth marrying is not to be found at such occasions.'

'I think you're right,' Lillian said. 'There's too much competition at those affairs – and the best quarry has already been thinned out. Time to hunt in a new field.'

'The club's office has files on all its patrons,' Evie volunteered. 'Approximately twenty-five hundred gentlemen of means. Of course, a large number of them are married – but I'm certain that I could find the names of many eligible ones.'

'Would Lord St Vincent allow you to have

389

access to such private information?' Daisy asked doubtfully.

Lillian countered in a droll tone, 'Does he ever refuse her *anything*?'

Evie, who endured frequent teasing from them about Sebastian's obvious devotion, smiled and glanced down at her wedding band as it gleamed brightly in the firelight. 'Rarely,' she admitted.

That drew a mocking laugh from Lillian. 'Really, someone should tell St Vincent that he's a living cliché. He has become the embodiment of everything they say about reformed rakes.'

Annabelle settled back into her chair and asked Evie, 'Has he reformed, dear?'

Thinking of the tender, wicked, loving husband who awaited her downstairs, Evie felt her smile broaden into a grin. 'Just enough,' she replied softly, and would say no more.